You know the Bible lessons
and children's stories,
the myths and legends.

Now read the tale's
historical account,
one of war, sacrifice,
treachery, and love.

Book One

The Prophet *and the* Dove

By Kirby Lee Davis

The Prophet and the Dove is a work of fiction
based on books of the Old Testament.
Any perceived references to modern day events,
people, places, or products is purely coincidental.

Book design, covers, maps, and graphics
by Kirby Lee Davis.

Published in the United States
for Fashan Books, Tulsa, OK.

ISBN Number (print): 9781706272052

First Printing

1 2 3 4 5 6 7 8 9 10

Dedicated
to Pat, Becky,
Nancy, and Janet,
whose encouragement
and faith
sustained me
for many years.

Books by Kirby Lee Davis include:

God's Furry Angels

A Year in the Lives of God's Furry Angels

The Road to Renewal

The Prophet and the Dove

Learn more at www.kirbyleedavis.com

The world of Jonah…

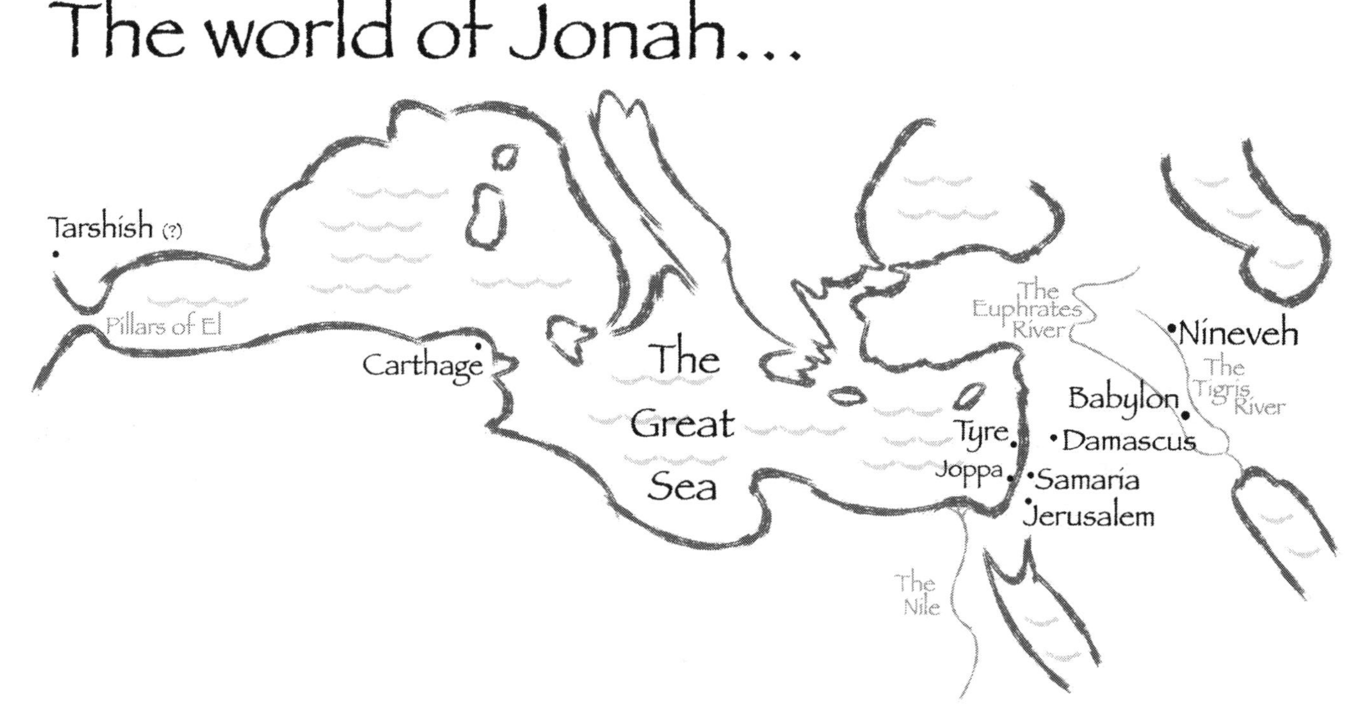

Damascus
ARAM
Mount Hermon
Dan
PHOENICIA
Tyre
Hazor
Acco
Sea of Chinnereth
Aphek
The Great Sea
Mount Carmel
Mount Tabor
Megiddo
Taanach
Jordan River
ISRAEL
Tirzah
Samaria
Shechem
Mount Moriah
Aphek
Joppa
Bethel
PHILISTIA
Mount Pisgah
Jerusalem
JUDAH
Salt Sea

Chapter 1
Betrayed

I think I felt it through my dreams. The deep, desperate strain of bones stretched beyond their capacity. The sway of a leaf whipped by Yahweh's storm blasts. The spray of an angry sea.

That bitter day, my dreams borrowed from my world.

"Awake!" came an urgent call. "Do you wish death? Up! Now!"

Even in such torment, awareness did not come easy. I felt the chaotic pulse of the sea, the fading strength of the timber, drops of saltwater – and yet I slept.

"Come on, boy!" My shoulders shook with near-violent intent. "We need you! Awake!"

My head rattled against one of the ship's massive ribs. It left me writhing, but I guess it was for the best, for it did rouse me. The captain swore a sailor's curse and went to the slumbering Dove.

In a breath or two, I became aware. They had left us to rest at the back of the cargo hold, just above the ship's wide, curved bottom. But for the oil lamp wavering in the grasp of a frightened, soaked sailor, we would have risen to night as black as ash. Then the sea bucked, the bow jumped, and we fell into darkness.

Thank the Lord the spilled lamp went out.

"Bellet!" shouted the captain. From the void came a "Here!" The faint gray outline of a square hole formed above us. Within a burst of light appeared a blue-banded arm thrusting a new lamp down, where a dripping, rattled sailor took it. The captain shook Jonah, even as I heard voices on the deck above. Those men drew stones from a pouch to better understand their fate.

"Lots," growled the captain.

"Been known to work," said the sailor.

"Can't stomach it on my ship." The captain jogged the Dove again, rocking his head against a wooden spur.

"Careful!" I shouted, fearful he might go too far.

"I need him awake!" the Phoenician said. "I'll not harm him!"

"Draw them again," came the words of a sailor above us.

"Wake up!" demanded the captain.

"Again!" said the voice.

The wood groaned all around us, pressed inward by pounding waves. The captain hesitated, listening to his ship's woeful strain, then nodded to the sailor and shouted once more for Jonah. The Dove quivered as in spasm, snorted. His eyes inched open.

"Three times," said a decided voice.

"Yes… it must be true," answered another.

Most times, the use of lots did not bother me. In my more dubious days, Hosea had told me once how the priests drew stones or threw ivory dice when the guidance of the Lord remained unclear. But in this setting, the lots frightened me. I do not know why, but they did.

"Ah," moaned Jonah. His eyes quivered. "Why is it so dark?"

"A storm threatens us," the captain informed him.

Footsteps echoed across the upper floor. The drenched head of a bald, dark-skinned Egyptian appeared in the hole.

"We have found cracks in the base timbers," he said in tones unshaken by our travails. "Spurs have come loose fore and aft."

"Understood," answered the captain. "Return to station." Then he twisted to face us, hard determination molding every facet of his being. "I will not lose my ship. Get up and pray to your god. Pray for our deliverance. Maybe he'll take notice of us, so that we will not perish."

Jonah stretched, listening all the while to the torment of the wood. His eyes twisted about in weary anguish. His brow sagged in defeat.

"We will pray," he allowed, his words low and drawn, "but I doubt it will help."

"Why not?" came a brittle voice. Saln dropped into the shadows among us, spraying seawater from his soggy tunic. His drenched hair hung in thick strands over the stained cloth binding his forehead.

The captain frowned. "Who directs the fight?"

"Brans," the First replied, even as two other sailors jumped down from the hold, one carrying the lots in a small brown bag of wet goatskin. "He prays to Melqart, Asherah, Resheph, even Baal, but the storm rages on. We have cast off as much cargo as possible, secured the oars, dropped sail, sealed our holds. Now we bail."

The newcomers focused on the Dove.

"Tell us," said the blonde-haired one cradling the lots. "Who is responsible for all this trouble?"

That angered me. He asked "who," but his eyes said "you." Still, the others were more direct.

"What did you do?" wondered a burly man, his long brown hair parted to reveal a deep scar across his left cheek.

"Nathan!" scolded the captain.

"Where are you from?" continued the sailor. "From what people are you?"

"Enough!" the captain declared.

"No," said Jonah in submission to this budding catastrophe, "they are due such answers and have sought them from the right man. I am a Hebrew, and I worship the Lord."

The Dove surprised me, treating this hostile group as friends. In my past I suffered sharp rebuke for explaining the Lord to outsiders, much less revealing our Hebrew words before them – and at that time I little cared, doubting His existence as I then did. Yet perhaps Jonah meant to turn aside their anger with honesty. If so, he failed.

"A Jew?" said the First, even as he tightened his girded tunic. The cloth gushed seawater from the strain. "I don't believe it! What god of shepherds could do this?"

Jonah spoke words as hard as iron hammers. "God of heaven. The God. He who made the sea and the land. Sustainer of all that is… and will be."

I would not have guessed it, since these Phoenicians worshipped the family of Baal over all things, but when Jonah proclaimed the realm of the Lord, they looked at each other in sheer terror!

"What have you done?" the First exclaimed.

"Brought his curse upon us, he did!" spat a bronze-skinned man.

"Quiet!" bellowed the captain, rising to his feet. The boat pitched, but he stood firm, twisting his beard between the thumb and fingers of his left hand as he pondered it all. His ship groaned once, then again, and once more, before he said, "Forgive me, but I know nothing else to do. Guess I should have foreseen this. I heard the signs and ignored them."

In sadness our commander looked down to the Dove and said, "What should we do to you to calm the sea?"

"Do to him?" I exclaimed.

Jonah looked the captain square in the eye. A new sense of direction lined his brow.

"Throw me to the waters," he said. "Only then will the sky and sea rest."

The Dove had a way of stumping me – just surprising me so well that little made sense. But nothing he ever did stunned me as much as that.

"No!" I protested. I had not trailed Jonah all this way just to watch him die! Surely Hosea had not foreseen this!

The Dove met my challenge with kindness. "Now, Benjamin, these men are right. It is my fault this peril is upon us. It is as Ansephanti said: to save my people, I have given up the Lord."

"You can't mean that!"

"Do not be surprised. You have argued against me all this way. The vision was indeed of the Lord. You know it, I know it. It was arrogance, I guess. Pure arrogance. To grow up seeing these happenings in my head, all these possible outcomes, with God showing me just what strings to pull… what to do here, what to say there, to shape things just the way He wanted. You live a lifetime doing this and you begin to think some of the control is yours. That's my sin, Benjamin. Believing I mattered in all of this. Believing He needed me to arrange His creation."

Jonah laughed at his folly, yet it rang hollow, with no joy. The ship quaked in desperation, but he was too consumed by his introspection to notice.

Even then, with all the chaos spinning around him, I witnessed the brilliance of his mind at work, seeking a solution in the darkness.

"Not once did I see any images of the sea. Not one! That's why we're here, Benjamin. I guess in my heart, I slipped into heathen blindness, thinking perhaps here I could escape even God."

Water fell across his face from the rafters. Jonah's gaze twisted in his dark judgment.

"I was wrong," he admitted. "I have sinned. But this is still my life! Not His! He may have outwitted me, and stopped me, but He cannot force me to go any further. It is my life, to do with what I choose! To ask me to betray my people… forgive me, I cannot! If our Lord demands my death for this choice, so be it. At least I will not have died a traitor."

Those words so horrified me, so consumed my soul, that for a moment, just drawing a breath caused me pain. In great fear I felt my mind turn, and I listened as the spirit of accusation moved me once more.

"A traitor to the Lord," I whispered.

His eyes sank in the dim light, casting cold, bitter reflections, like those of a corpse. His lips were still.

"Can you live with that?" I put to him.

"Perhaps not long," the Dove said, leaning against the broad timbers as the ship pitched left, then lifted right. "But could I have fulfilled His bidding, knowing what I do of the Assyrians? Never."

Never. Few words are so brutal, so hard… so often misused.

The hand of judgment settled upon me like a brash wind sweeping down the mountain.

"If it is the Lord's will," I declared, "it will be done."

"Perhaps. But not by my hand."

"Oh, yes. This will not stop Him."

Cold, numbing shock claimed the Dove. He stared at me with eyes awakened to new possibilities – and it frightened him, if only for a moment.

A firm hand took my right arm. "Come forward," said the captain. "Help us."

I noticed then that we were alone. The other sailors had departed, bolting the door at our heads.

Looking me in the eyes with a fierce, independent spirit, I knew the captain had no mind to follow Jonah's advice. To the Dove he spat, "Stay here. Bring your curse no closer to us." Then he took the lamp in his left hand and led me to the center of the shadowy cargo deck.

"We should not have hit such a storm this time of year," he told me, as if to answer a question I had asked. "We had a clear sky just an hour ago!"

Passing the thick mast root, its heart groaning in the grasp of the shrieking wind, we came to the central cargo hold, a broad portal that passed through every deck to the sky. Wood doors sealed access to the small cargo bay below and to the top deck, but the portal just above us remained open, bridged by a ladder of twisted reeds. The captain motioned me to the lashed steps, then grabbed my shoulder and whipped me about.

"You fainted this morning, didn't you?" When I nodded, he cursed his fate. "What have you strength to do?"

I had no idea, so I said, "Anything." I was willing to do anything, if it meant stopping Jonah.

Perhaps the captain sensed some indecision on my part, or maybe he thought I was not ready for the challenge. Whatever moved him, he scowled as might the fiercest wind, then motioned me up, mumbling curses all the way.

We emerged in the lower rowing deck, a dark hall filled with seven narrow benches along each side of the ship. A closed square portal looked out to the sea just below each seat; above them hung two rows of dormant oars. Thin streams of dark green seawater rolled across the floor as the vessel pitched in the storm.

Two swaying oil lamps to the stern illuminated a large group of huddled, restless, worried sailors, most stripped down to their dripping white loincloths. Even wearied by the sea, they were the most imposing figures I had seen since King Jeroboam's bodyguard paraded in victory across the Hermon battlefield.

"What are you waiting for?" the captain snapped.

"The First suggested we would row," a balding Phoenician answered. "Here, out of the storm."

The boat lifted at port, twisting so that I fell headfirst to the starboard wall. The crew little moved, each member keeping his place by gripping holes in the wood I had not noticed.

The captain listened to the groans of the overstressed hull, laying his palm against the flat of a rib to better judge its pulse and strain. In exasperation he turned to me and spat, "Is your god so vengeful he would cause all this, just to doom one man?"

The fear in his voice shook me. Stumbling to grasp the hard truth of what he asked, this emergency reminded me just how little I knew of the Lord. In my emptiness, a myriad of words rushed through my mind, but the simplest, most straightforward answer seemed an honest nod. The captain responded with one of his own, a nod of submission.

"Break out the oars," he shouted to his men. "Prepare to get underway. All strength, men! Our lives are in our hands."

The crew separated into two groups, one unlatching the oar tethers, the other unbolting the square portals. The wet breath of the Great Sea soon washed over us, but the crew struggled against it, breaking into teams to secure their long oars against the overwhelming pull of the storm.

"Perhaps by our steadfastness, we can satisfy your god," the captain told me. "I will not commit murder; I can say that right now."

With the fourteen oars in place, the teams secured themselves on the damp benches, the First at their front. Saln called out a loud, monotone cadence as another wave swept over us. The rowers began their fight.

Little in life prepares one for such a struggle. Behind me,

across the central portal, were six teams of men putting every thought, every effort, into the rhythm of their oars. Before me, around the root of the mast, were eight more teams of three, spreading across the deck from one side to the other, their spirits bound in every stroke. As one they lifted, swung their oars forward and pulled against the very grain of the sea. There was power in their unity, their passion. I felt it in the core of my being. Yet the ship rolled and bounced as if their strain meant nothing.

An infantile gesture sprang from my heart. "Lord," I prayed, "if it is within Your plans, please let us live!"

The captain stared at me as if I spoke a garbled tongue.

"Come," he said. Between strokes we slipped to the stern, where a ladder led to closed doors above and below us. As I stood fast, halted by a lurch of the sea just beneath the bow, the captain tied a long rope about his waist. He then handed me one.

"What are we doing?" I called against the storm. But he chose with a sigh to ignore me, taking the other end of my rope and tying it about my stomach.

"When we get topside," he warned, "tie your line to the ship or you will be washed over."

Without another thought he bolted up the ladder. The door flew open in his grasp, and he was gone.

Even as I stood at the base of the entwined steps, I felt the maelstrom strain to lift me. I looked past the ladder to see lightning blaze across a black sky. A keg's hold of angry water poured through the portal, soaking me to my toes.

"Captain!" I shouted. "Captain!"

Thunder rocked the heavens. At once every element within the winds, every fiber in the wood, every bone within me, all trembled with the bellows of the storm. Lightning flooded the world with a blaze of brilliant white. The burst echoed through my mind. The sea washed over me.

"Captain!" I wailed.

Shadows closed around me. I stood in mist at the back of the narrow deck, watching some twenty-eight men I little knew putting every last muscle to their harrowing task. The sight bewildered me.

Oh, Lord, in all my life have I ever endured such isolation? I look back upon all my years in chains, my bound servitude, and recall no time more desperate than I felt then. I know it was wrong! I know You never left me! But Lord, if You Yourself could experience Your wrath, as I did… if You could feel the terror of such utter domination, of total surrender, as I did… perhaps You could understand me. Oh, but even such thoughts are sins! Of course You understand! You made this storm, this sea! You created all this!

Dear Lord, forgive me!

Even now I recall the dread that almost stole my soul. I stared into the darkness of the portal, into the churning heart of the violent storm, and had no idea what to do. My every thought abandoned me as if tossed from my mind by the gales. Then You spurred me as a rider would his paralyzed horse – the bow ripped high, throwing all sorts of loose items my way – and so, to avoid them, I spurted up the wall, into the holocaust.

Before I had even left the ladder, the wind lifted me clear of the portal and sent me rolling across the soaked deck. My back collided against the ledge wall. I screamed, but the howls of the storm drowned my voice. Streams from the sea sloshed over my lips.

A surge of force pummeled me, bending my chin to my knees as if they belonged together. Only when it passed did I realize the force was water. Water! I watched the last ebbs of that wave roll down the deck, then felt the brash wind cast me back hard against the ledge.

Through the bones in my seat I felt something strike the beams of the stern. As lightning crashed near the mast, I bounced through the black sky, past four men bound to the steering oar, past the captain at the steersman's post. My heart surged in seeing him. I reached for him, stretched every muscle in my being. It was not enough.

I feared the sea itself awaited me. The wind took me in its arms, a toy for its amusement, then snapped me back onto a deck straining under pitching waves. The ship rocked starboard, sending me tumbling, then yanking me back. I thought my spine would snap.

Only then did I remember the rope about my waist. I grasped it, praising God, and in a flash of lightning followed its taut strands with my eyes. Thus, once more I found the captain, his face as stern as granite as he hung onto the frayed ends of my tether. Hand over hand he pulled me forward, even as I struggled to reach him. Together we overcame the power of the waves and wind.

He tried speaking, but the force of the storm squelched every phrase. He pointed in the flashing lightning to the twisting clouds above us, the ripples of the torn sail, the wash of sea between the deck benches. In time I understood. The ship was caught in a vortex of power, a ripping hole of wind, rain, and surf that circled the vessel with no remorse. No power of earth could have freed us.

"Oh, Lord, have mercy!" I shouted. "Have mercy!"

The captain tried to shove me left. I knew not why and so held my place, reaching out for support with my left arm. In that way I rediscovered the open portal. The captain did not need to push me again – I dove into the hole!

A wave of the sea followed me, but I did not pay it attention – the spray little mattered against the full fury of the storm. In precious peace I collapsed against the deck, my body aching from more aggravated muscles than I had ever imagined possible.

The captain fell to my side. "We stand no chance against it," he spat, shaking the saltwater from his hair almost to the First's cadence. "Had we a full crew, a fleet of ships, it would be nothing. No chance at all."

"Then are you ready?" came a patient voice.

Coughing for breath, coughing to spew the Great Sea from my lungs and gut, I fought my own body to lift my stinging eyes and see this interloper. There, still somewhat dry, stood the Dove. A gracious understanding warmed his gaze.

"The sea grows even wilder," he told us. "You must do as I say."

"Must?" Though exhausted, the captain struggled to regain his feet, only to rock against the Dove as the ship lurched about. Jonah tried to steady him, but with sharp, angry thrusts, the captain forced himself free. “Must? You dare tell me what to do?”

“It is the Lord who tells you,” implored Jonah. “Will you listen?”

Screams fought through the rushing gales. I heard the cadence stop, the rowing cease, even as the bones of the ship flexed under intolerable strain. The pressures behind the storm seemed to pause, as if awaiting all the terrors of Hell to break around us.

The bow rode a surge of water. Then the wave disappeared. The whole ship fell with a crashing thud we felt from our ankles to our jaws.

Words rang down the deck. “Cast out the broken shafts!” “Close up the shutters!” But their terror did not break my thoughts from the captain. Hunched on his knees, he spat out a mouthful of green fluid and turned to me. For the first time I saw indecision in his gaze, beseeching me for help. But I had none to give. My mind was awash, my soul silent. The Lord withheld His guidance.

A slow moan escaped the Phoenician’s lips. He rolled his forehead to the deck, his waterlogged beard slumping into the slosh of the sea.

The First rejoined us, with four or five others. “That last swell snapped our oars as twigs,” he stammered, winded and defeated. “We have sealed out the water, to what avail?”

“None,” the captain muttered. “Any injured?” When Saln nodded, the captain bid they be cared for, then told him to gather three others and accompany him. “I need witnesses.”

They met at the ladder, the First and his men struggling to catch up. The captain treated the Dove as a forsaken idol not to be touched. Binding themselves with ropes, the sailors took the dangling strands of the captain’s and my tethers, joining them in a chain to theirs. But none touched Jonah.

“Let it be written and remembered,” said the captain, “that by his own admission, this man has brought doom upon us. By his own judgment do we now act.” He twisted to climb the ladder, then with a change of heart he pivoted to face Jonah. "I know not what you have done to earn this. To be truthful, I do not care, though I am surprised. Your faith is honest; I can see that."

The Dove nodded, his eyes contrite. "This is a matter of choice, of deliverance… salvation. I do not expect you to understand."

"Certainly not from that!" the captain grunted. "But it little matters. In respect of your faith, I will not bind you. Now follow."

The ship rocked to starboard, then port, then back to starboard, but we managed the climb without great difficulty. The wind attacked at once, but with the strength of our human chain, I held my place. As did Jonah.

Truly, no feat of strength has ever impressed me more, before or since, than that of the Dove that day. The maelstrom seemed to embrace him, shredding his tunic, his undergarments, even his sandals, yet Jonah came to no harm. Nor did he flinch under the assault. Indeed, it unnerved me to look upon him, standing at peace amid all that chaos, knowing his death drew near. I knew he was stubborn, but I could not have sustained myself under such distress!

The captain did not hesitate. Leading him to the steering oar, the Phoenician shouted above the wind: "Oh Lord, please do not let us die for taking this man's life."

I stiffened. This outlander prayed to our Lord? Spoke to him?

"Do not hold us accountable for killing this man," continued the captain, stumbling at times over what to say, or the storm, "for you, Lord, have done as you pleased. You have proclaimed his guilt."

Before his words could fade in the gale, the Dove was gone. The captain offered his hand to send Jonah forth, and the sailors made threats with their fists, but the Dove stepped of his own accord into the sea. Accepting death and desecration, he turned against the Lord, and yet Jonah gave his life in judgment.

What kind of man can do that – thrive under such conflicting convictions?

I stood there, stunned, waiting for him to emerge from this.

After all, he had seen the vision. The Lord had called him to minister to Nineveh – therefore Jonah had to come back. I firmly believed it!

Even as the storm broke and vanished, I waited. In the expanse of a breath the winds died, the sea turned to glass, and the sky awakened to the soothing light of the setting sun. But the Dove did not return.

The awe-struck sailors gathered at the boat's edge, whispering.

"He just stepped in!" remembered one.

"Sank like an anchor!" replied another.

A dark shape flowed beneath the waves, a shadow that dwarfed their ship, yet the sailors gave it but a passing thought. For in the instant the storm cleared, they were seized by faith little demonstrated even in Solomon's Temple!

"Truly, You are the Lord!" they cried to the heavens. "Praise be! All praise be given the Lord!"

Even in awe of His power, or of Jonah's sacrifice, nothing struck me so hard as to see these heathen Gentiles bowing in divine understanding – yes, even true and honest faith! The captain, the crew, all hovered about me, praising God and asking questions of His grace, His love. Even in full memory of His vengeance, they saw Yahweh as the Lord of love and light, and they sought instructions on how to praise Him.

I provided them.

No, I was and still am not trained for such things. But was Jonah? Was David? When the Lord says to go, you do not cast off His hand for lack of directions – they will come to you. So, though I knew little more of God than they did, in my own stumbling, naïve way I led them in sacrificing a milk goat they had stored below, burning it within an overturned shield of bronze. I shared with them what Hosea had taught me, from the evils of Jeroboam's misguided delving in false gods to the joys of the true faith – many of which I experienced for the first time at that moment, with them and through them. And one by one, they vowed their lives to the Lord.

I embraced these men, accepting their conversions, not realizing I did what the Dove most feared doing. But then, I had not beheld his visions.

Oh, Jonah… if only I could have upheld your heart!

Jonah!

Chapter 2
Faith at twilight

Blood-stained fingers tough as tree roots yanked me up by my beautiful hair. I cried out, angry and sore at this painful disgrace, but all that fled before the murderous gaze of one of your terrible master butchers. With his massive left hand, the soldier held me dangling above the shifting sands. With his right, he turned his blood-red dagger to my whimpering lips.

And that, my young students, was how I first came to know Jonah.

It seems many lifetimes ago… a dreadful age when time bore no life to speak of, and I, ever stalked by death, considered all talk of the Lord nothing but vicious lies. Much has happened since, more than any man should endure, and yet I have, as was my calling. For I was born to witness the dawn of a new age.

But you don't care about that, do you? Thrills, adventure, death! Yes, that's what you came to hear! The knife at my throat!

Oh, I have many such stories to share. Kings I have counseled, and warriors I've led. These hands drove a chariot surrounded by the enemy! These feet strolled the Nile shores! These eyes gazed upon the ruins of Jerusalem!

But all that pales before my witnessing the Jonah Cycle. For who would have dreamt a man could live beyond his death? Certainly not I! But with Jonah, our Lord had a special need, and it changed the world.

Come closer now, as I tell the tale. I have little breath left to speak above these Nineveh winds.

I was barely a man then, scrambling just before daybreak up the rocky slope of Mount Hermon, my hair –

Oh, go ahead and laugh! I heard you before, struggling not to. Believe me; I truly had a full head of magnificent hair back then. Thick, shiny black strands so long, I could tie them about my chin and pretend I had a beard! Oh, but that's another story.

Yes, I clawed my way up Hermon's gravel face, my soft purple tunic girded, my sandals flopping, my heart racing. It had been a long jaunt from the royal tent. My toes stung from scrapping against the dark sands, and the cool morning air burned my lungs. But even so, I felt great! What courier wouldn't, running the battlefield when we yanked the plains of Damascus from those Assyrian dogs! It promised to be a momentous day for all of Israel – King Jeroboam would reclaim the lands of our legendary ancestors – and I, a lowly slave, would play a part!

Yes, my juvenile pride mastered me, making my pittance of a role in that great war seem consequential, but there was more to my jubilance. Dashing from boulder to boulder through the highland twilight, with this historic cause before me, for the first time in my young, wretched life I entertained a promise of freedom, a hint of greatness. It charged my every breath with a passion I'd never dared dream for myself. It intrigued and uplifted me, and for a moment at least, gave me hope I might escape my doom.

Such wonder mastered my every thought… until I topped a crest in the ripped earth and gazed for the first time upon our soldiers taking positions just below me. Working by shielded torchlight, the men struggled against the stubborn rock and their own weariness to carve a line of haphazard pits and ravines in the hardened dirt. Their somber display chilled my heart. These "warriors" numbered not more than three hundred; a pittance to put against the devil's own. They wore not the fine battle dress of the king's infantry, but the odds and ends of a riotous mob. And in their eyes, those cold, uncertain eyes, I beheld none of the grim determination of the palace guard, but the frightened obedience of humbled commoners submitting to the call of death.

Staring into their empty faces, my mind grasped the truth in this approaching horror. These were not soldiers! The hands preparing for battle belonged to simple townspeople, undisciplined souls like those I had served since my youth. A few I recognized – tailors, carpenters, fishermen, and others who usually hawked their wares from ramshackle carts outside the palace at Samaria.

"This can't be," I muttered. These vagabonds had no place on the front lines. "Have we no one else?"

I must admit, my youthful heart stumbled in newfound fear. There was no hope here! The devil hounds would overrun these innocents in a second.

"And me too," I realized in a moment of desperate clarity, my eyes pinned by the dust rising from the approaching Assyrian feet. They must have been giants to raise such a murky cloud of churning grit from Hermon's distant foothills. With each breath the building storm drew nearer. Death rode in its winds.

Despite the heat, an icy sweat crawled down my trembling spine. Oh, how I wanted to flee!

"Calm yourself," came a weary voice. "They might hear."

Chastised, I knelt behind an overshadowing boulder under a brilliant crimson sky and searched the encroaching shadows for my unexpected comrade, whoever he might be. But headstrong as I have always been, I did not regret my outburst.

"Have you no eyes?" I spat. "We are going to die!"

My observer let this pass. "Have faith," he told me. "The Lord has brought you here. Listen, and learn."

The Lord? Those musty words pierced me like a shot of spoiled wine. I'd not heard anyone speak of that myth since my days at the Bethel temples, when as the heathen priests' kitchen boy I'd thrown scraps to the old hermit charged to oversee those dusty treasures seized from the Jerusalem temple. That decrepit dirt rag of a man voiced beliefs similar to the Judean cult, outlandish tales of a mighty spirit working through Moses, David, and Elijah to lift up his "chosen people," we Hebrews. I'd always thought such broken fables best fit a beggar. If there was such a god, why would he hide in shadows while his people suffered so? Why would he allow his treasured temple gold to collect dust in a corner, forgotten, guarded by the filthiest of paupers? Why would this so-called god not rise up and revel in his might before all the world?

I will tell you why. Because he was nothing but a myth, and all those stories of heroes and miracles were just that – stories.

That's how I felt at that time, filled with contempt toward any concept of God. But even then, though I loathe to admit it, I came to admire the earnestness of that hermit's madness. At least he believed in something. It gave him strength, and an enduring spirit. I knew only my misery, but that scabby, disease-pocked man took abuse from everyone, including me, and answered with prayers and a smile. He never relented in his faith.

Now, standing half a world away, I sensed that same honest belief in this interloper's speech. Paralyzed with fear though I was, I couldn't help but respect his faith, even though in all other ways, he seemed quite the same madman.

A sudden blow of dust stung my eyes. Rubbing them clear, I motioned towards our men and stammered, "These people, they can't match Assyrians." Oh, a handful managed to masquerade like soldiers, having somewhere found some haggard leather vests, leggings, even a few iron caps – but did that give them battle experience? A fighting chance?

"Look at them!" I insisted. "They're fat, clumsy halfwits, or half-broken dotards! Why, they stumble about no better than I do!"

"And what is wrong with that?"

Coming from the darkness, the playful innocence of that retort seemed a sarcastic taunt.

"Open your eyes!" I snapped. "They're nothing but cobblers, shepherds, merchants, tailors. They have no business fighting a war."

"You dismiss them so fast," the man countered. "Look again. Look!"

Fuming, I gazed once more down Hermon's torn slope. Wisps of peaty vapor crawled up from the warming earth, sparkling in the rising sun like red hot campfire embers. It cast a strange shadow over the ground, making it look like rivers of mud flowed to the valley beyond.

"Even Hermon bleeds," I mumbled.

Far down the slope, a new line of our soldiers entered the battlefield from the fleeing shadows prowling that mountain pass. To my untrained eye they seemed little different than the others – a tad better equipped perhaps, but no more effective.

My advisor disagreed. "See how they march? Their spears held high, swords ablaze at their hips? Shields swaying, rising and falling almost in unison? And their faces… ah, such serenity. I tell you this: give me a few hundred such believers and I could take Nineveh itself! For such determination only comes from faith in the Lord."

I almost laughed then in my rankled terror, thinking how silly a couple hundred commoners would look assaulting the dreaded capital of our enemy. It was said Nineveh commanded a world unto itself, home to more than a hundred thousand of the worst Gentiles, the blood-hungry Assyrians. Each one trained to fight, taking pleasure inflicting torture and death.

No sane mind would contemplate a foolish attack on the evil one's own citadel! But as Jonah spoke, I was intrigued by his sincerity. As he talked of faith, I recalled the legends of Jericho. And his idea no longer seemed so silly, if you accepted the legend. Which I could not.

You see, I had been born and abandoned in Jericho. I hated the place.

"You're serious?" I wondered aloud.

"Have faith… and believe."

"That's impossible."

"Nothing is impossible."

Muffled echoes penetrated the wind song. Pausing to listen, I heard the steady pounding of a thousand determined footfalls, each round pulsing through hundreds of voices raised in a low, grumbling chant of our pending doom.

My heart shuddered.

It seemed beyond belief. The Assyrian locusts marched upon

Hermon, and this man spouted superstitions?

I almost laughed then. "Are all your plans built on what you choose to believe?"

"On faith, lad. There is nothing else."

"That's crazy. You can't turn these people into soldiers just by wishing it! The Assyrians will slaughter them. They're born killers! It's all they know how to do."

The interloper grunted, as if that alone dismissed my point. This gave me some strange satisfaction, assuring me I had scored a wound in this odd debate. I drove home my argument: "What makes you think these men won't just run away when the fighting starts?"

"Because," came a subdued reply, "they know the Lord will see them through. He has several times already."

That provided my first hint of the Dove's intricate mind as the architect of this battle. I settled on my quivering haunches, pondering his words, and saw a lean figure rise in the shadows of a nearby limestone slab.

Recognition brought a fearful chill at my insolence, and a deep, paralyzing awe.

There, gazing from the fleeing darkness, stood Jonah, whose name means Dove, the temperamental adviser to King Jeroboam the Second.

Chapter 3
Battle

His head hung low, and his shoulders sagged, but exhaustion could not blunt the concentration in Jonah's gaze or the stern lines along his furrowed brow. At first, I feared the volatile Dove might break me with words of retribution, as I'd often heard him deal with our cranky monarch, but I later realized that did not happen without strong cause, for Jonah's was a calculating mind, not a cold one. Indeed, he gave little attention to issues he deemed unimportant in Yahweh's grand strategies, though I was slow to grasp that.

"You were sent to me?" the Dove asked.

I stared at him like a dim, sluggish cow, offering only a nod in reply. How could I not be daunted, standing but an arm's length from a man I'd seen browbeat the king himself? No other advisor held such sway. And now, here he was, the commanding general, speaking to me. Me!

And I argued against him!

"Must say, I am surprised," he continued. His eyes softened. "This is your first time, isn't it? Into the field."

Sudden revulsion left me numb. I stiffened, realizing with shame that Jonah well understood the fodder of my existence.

Confronted with that fate I struggled each day to ignore, something inside me rebelled. In guilt I exclaimed, "It's not my fault the king never…"

My challenge puttered out under my own disgust.

"Of course not," Jonah allowed. "All this is a blessing compared to the blasphemy you endure. It's been, what? Four months since he plucked you from that den of debauchery?"

I nodded. It was not something I wished to remember.

You see, in my short time at the palace, I soon become the favorite attendant of crusty old Jeroboam, the thirteenth king to reign over the northern kingdom of Israel's tribes since the scribes charted the death of that legend Solomon, some 180 would-be years before. Of the six boys Jeroboam's steward kept on hand, many a time the king allowed me, and only me, to wait at his side. The dotard gazed at me with ancient, lusty eyes I tried my best to not see.

Oh, I knew what he had in mind – why he'd lifted this abandoned child from the corrupted temple grounds, washing my soiled limbs with sweet perfumes and dressing me in fine silks, all in patient readiness for that one, perfect time in which to celebrate his sick needs. The other palace attendants made all this clear to me many times over. They too had been nurtured by the so-called priests for this very purpose. But once those first days crept past, miserable but uneventful, I soon found my destiny easy to ignore. That's not hard to understand – just imagine how enchanting it was, at such an age, to observe the king's court from the shadows of the throne itself! Even with all I have endured since, those memories move me.

I had waited on Jeroboam hand and foot as he renewed his pride-fueled bid to reclaim the vast borders of Solomon's storied realm. In battle after battle my swift-footed comrades delivered words to Jonah and his commanders, and each time these couriers returned with romantic tales of deeds that drew my envy. Dreaming of freedom, my jealousy grew with each success, for though the king held off my fate for that final victory, Jeroboam rarely let me leave his sight.

"I feel for you," Jonah whispered. "Both of us taste the bitter herbs of his madness, though my hardships pale before yours. But all is not dark. I see God's hand around you. You have friends you do not know."

He spoke with kindness, and yet his words stirred the hopelessness of my soul. "Friends?"

I, whose birth brought the death of my mother?

I, who being the third son too many, and an infant at that, had been sold by his desperate, overwrought father into the temple slave pits for ten pieces of silver and a full wineskin?

I, who awoke each day fearing that sunrise would be my last?

"Friends? Never have I known one!"

"No?" His eyes sparkled in the bright dawn. "How then do you find yourself here?"

"That's… that's easy," I protested, though in trying to answer him, I found I couldn't. My fate changed this morning without warning.

Unable to sleep, in darkness I had crept to the outer chamber of the royal tent, deciding against my heart's wish to await the king's desire for his morning meal. To my surprise, at my heels entered Nathaniel, Jeroboam's prim steward, still in his sleeping robes! Seeing me there filled him with distress until, at his prodding, I explained that I was there of my own volition and had yet to see the king – words that transformed Nathaniel's fears to great joy. A sudden need had awakened the king, he then told me, filling my sire's heart with a desperate urge to reach the Dove. Pressed for action and finding no other runner available, Nathaniel sent me.

That's how I came to cower near our front lines, wondering just what my fellow couriers found so invigorating doing this. Gazing upon our troops, hearing Jonah's mad strategies even as the enemy approached, I felt nothing but anguish and trepidation.

"You have a message?" the Dove reminded me.

With timid hands I offered him a worn scroll from my belt. Jonah extended the goatskin within the tender shadows of dawn. A chuckle escaped his lips as he read the document. Then he cast it aside as if its words meant nothing.

"Do not fear," he said, smiling at my astonishment. "There is always hope. Have faith."

Have faith. Part of me wanted to scream out just how mindless his faith could be. How only a madman could live so, taking no responsibility for his own destiny. Then I looked anew at this man who asked me to believe in something I couldn't see, touch, or smell, and I felt even worse.

The more I stared at him, the more I wondered how this unkempt man could walk in the king's shadow. His long black hair fell in reckless abandon about his shoulders, neither combed nor oiled, mixing with the curls of his graying beard to give the impression more of a groveling beggar than a stern commander of thousands. Even in that cool spring morning he wore no cloak, and his dull brown tunic, unadorned with sign or symbol of his life, carried many stains from spills and mud. His girdle was of a simple goat-hair cloth, wrapped so loose about his waist that I wondered if it might slip away.

Nathaniel would never allow himself to be seen this way. Yet as I looked upon Jonah, such appearance seemed fitting.

To delve into the Dove's eyes… ah, that was more the mystery. Jonah cast a gaze that pierced your soul as it befriended your heart. In the rising sun he had but looked upon me with those hazelnut eyes when I knew – I knew! – that my innermost secrets were his own.

Strange though it seemed, I felt I could trust him. And that frightened me.

As fresh golden light cast aside most shadows, he spoke with a voice of deepest regards. His words were limited – "Benjamin, is it not?" – and yet I stood before him in fearful confusion, wanting more than anything to just run away.

"Yes, my lord," was all I could manage.

"I am not your lord. But you can help me now. Stay close."

That request left me numb. I stood amazed that Jonah had distracted me through all this talk, but with sudden shock I remembered our looming danger. The stones themselves grumbled from the approaching Assyrian feet!

"But Nathaniel wished me to report back," I said.

The Dove waved his hands through the air to brush away the steward's demands. "I am ordered to tell our king when things are ripe. That would have been difficult, for as you see, I was alone. My commanders are consumed by their tasks, and the rest departed long ago on other errands. So, you see, I need you at my side. Relax, young one! You're where you long wished to be; you might as well stay. I need you."

That stilled some worries, but even so, I feared not obeying the steward. It was not without reason Nathaniel was called the lion of the palace. The king's right hand was so prompt, so efficient, even his meals digested on schedule. He detested anything that might delay him – or anyone who refused him.

But with Jonah's untroubled eyes upon me, his tired brow lifted in sincere warmth, I realized I didn't mind so much risking the steward's wrath. Besides, how could I refuse Jonah, the one man I'd seen stand toe to toe in debate with Nathaniel and Jeroboam, and walk away the victor?

"This is not their first battle," the Dove said with calm patience, gazing once more at our foot soldiers. That made me smile. This was my first conflagration, but Jonah did not bother to remind me.

"These cobblers and shepherds, as you call them, they have routed the Arameans four times," said Jonah. "Now their Assyrian masters have no choice – the dogs have to get involved themselves.

"Today," he whispered, "today it will end."

And so I stayed, watching our would-be soldiers dig in above the main road, in full view of the hills leading to Damascus and the approaching Assyrian horde. In nervous silence I waited, minute by ever-slowing minute, taking some comfort from the Dove's quiet presence, yet wondering when Nathaniel's long arm would swat me away, or even worse, when death would catch up with these vagabond warriors… and me, who hid behind them.

Now understand, I had never seen the devil's soldiers before, but my imagination supplied plenty of fearful images. They paled before the real thing.

Strange though it was, Jonah forewarned me not to expect the armies of lore – "The kings of Ashur have more important battles than to worry about us," he said at least twice – but the two legions I watched were disheartening enough. Five wooden chariots dressed in gold and bronze led the procession, pulled by pairs of straining black chargers. The center war wagon sported a crimson umbrella to shield the governor of Damascus from the sun. Behind them jogged the devil's horde, even as a small band of mounted archers skirted each flank.

To look upon their foot soldiers did much to explain the Assyrian advancements of battle, even to a novice such as I. Each of the long-haired butchers wore an oiled leather cloak and skirt over his hardened limbs, the thick garb emblazoned with layers of bronze plate. Conical iron helmets guarded their sunbaked brows, made to match disks of decorated bronze protecting their hearts. But their art of war went beyond armor. Long swords hung from each waist, their sturdy blades adept at sweep and thrust. Many footmen carried heavy shields of wood and bronze, some strapped to their arms, others across their broad backs. A few of the more resourceful warriors boasted lace-up boots.

Even their approach seemed ordered. Between lines of swordsmen strode a core of unhorsed archers, teamed with stout men brandishing shields wide enough to protect a trio of bowmen. Beside them came rank after rank of soldiers wielding long barbed lances. Together they marched in disciplined formation, pounding the earth behind the rumbling chariots.

To look upon the thousand-some warriors was to see our doom. I no longer doubted that. Our men were nothing against them.

In sudden fear I looked to Jonah. The madman stood as one with the rocks, glaring in defiance at the enemy.

The fury in those eyes gave me hope.

"May your Lord help us," I said without conviction. But the Dove didn't notice my slight.

"Pray louder," he said.

The Assyrians did not provide me the chance. Marching straight toward our crest, the lead soldiers blew shrill rifts from a battery of ram's horns. Before their echoes died, the three-man chariots flew forward, masking their troops in waves of dust.

A great cry arose from the rushing devils. I jumped up, ready to flee. My heart wished to! But the Dove turned to me, a warm smile upon his lips. Trembling, I held my place.

"Watch," he said.

The great Assyrian steeds found the pitted incline difficult, and with the slope covered by uprooted boulders and sharp stones, the chariots could not keep to a straight path or pick up speed, and so they turned back. Yet their mounted troops charged on, throwing spears into our lines before circling to reform, their bows drawn and primed. The devil's foot soldiers took the lead, singing what atrocities they would commit in Ashur's name.

I will never forget the deep, dark terror I felt then. The earth groaned under the crushing hooves. Dust billowed over the battlefield from each footfall, rolling in waves up the slope. One black steed burst through a cloud beneath me, his rider screaming rage. Long braids of black hair danced about his bronze-plated shoulders as he cast his spear into the cowering ranks of our men. I sank to my knees in alarm. I watched the thick-chested warrior draw his sword, looking for new targets, and knew for certain my life would soon end. With a surge of malevolent power, the magnificent steed almost bounded over my perch, so close was his charge! But the rider had other intentions, swinging his sure-footed beast aside.

There I sat, quaking. I could smell the stallion's foul breath!

Jonah peered down the hill, stern and unshaken. "The trap is sprung."

"Trap?"

From disguised holes in the earth sprang Hebrew slingers and archers, assailing the exposed flanks of the Assyrians. Their cavalry turned to meet this new threat when to my – and their – surprise, the proud bodyguard of Jeroboam II emerged from hidden trenches, richly adorned foot soldiers 600 strong. Our mounted troops circled in from the road, cutting off the enemy's escape.

The swiftness of the assault amazed me. "Incredible!" I shouted.

"Patience! It is not over."

To a man our opponents refused to give in. But thanks to the Dove's plans, we now had superior numbers in archers, slingers, and swordsmen, and we held the high ground.

With a vengeance, our bodyguard waded into the penned enemy. A broad bull of a man stormed before them, his silvery sword rolling through opponents as a brash wind through leaves. From his matchless prowess I guessed it might be Jeroboam's battle chief, but I couldn't tell for sure.

Horns sounded from the road below.

"Look!" I jumped to my feet. "Their riders, their chariots – they are fleeing!"

"Yes. Our riders will cut them off. Now, Benjamin! Run swift of foot. Tell Jeroboam to release his reserves. Go!"

Dreading what moved him to urgency, I sped back through the rocky passages. Yet as I drew away, the sound of battle rose behind me. I feared the worst. Even if the mounted troops retreated, I knew their infantry would not surrender, not until the heat and exhaustion left them too weak to stand. No, we had to hurry. Each man we threw into battle now could be a Hebrew life saved!

The king's tents lay secure within a cove of limestone cliffs beyond the ridge, hidden from most approaches. But I had no problems reaching it, knowing a short route. Sliding through sand pits, circling around boulders, I soon pressed myself into the chasm just behind the lavish purple tent of my monarch.

My heart thrilled at the sight. Oh, how glorious went the battle for Israel! At the word of Jonah, Jeroboam was again victorious!

The reality of that burst against my heart like a thunderclap. I saw my long-awaiting fate now looming before me. I wanted to flee!

A call broke the morning. "Benjamin!"

Long ago I'd learned to mind the authority of that voice. I turned to the shout, throwing stinging drops of sweat into my eyes. My vision blurred. My breaths came short and shallow.

"Benjamin!" repeated the call, this time with a hint of frustration.

Blinded, I bit back my tensions.

"Jonah sent me," I struggled to say.

"What took you so long?" asked Nathaniel. "I needed you here."

Even as I wiped my eyes, his form became clear. His laced sandals appeared first through the haze, trailed by the fringe of his beautiful crimson cloak, braided along its cuffs and lined with gold strands up to his neck. As usual, he bound his long black locks with an ashen headband, but his thick beard flowed free.

"Jonah told me to stay, just as he sends me now. He calls for the reserves. It is time."

"Good," Nathaniel said, forgetting whatever anger he held against me. "Good! Now get back there. He may need you!"

The steward raced off without waiting for a response. I just stood there, watching him go, for I had never seen Nathaniel hurry so. Then I realized I was wasting time and started back in a rush. The trail up left me breathless, and I stumbled twice, scraping both knees, but once I regained my former perch, the view was worth it. Below me poured forth what looked like a thousand of Jeroboam's guards, sweeping into the Assyrian lines as hungry lions upon an unguarded flock.

"You were right!" I exclaimed, only to find the Dove gone. Surprised, I searched the limestone that once sheltered him, finding nothing. Then I noticed tracks in the sand leading to the ledge. Following the footfalls, I spied him far below, scampering across the battlefield without regard to the combat around him.

"Jonah!" I shouted. He took no notice; I doubt he even heard me. I breathed deep to call again, but the words stuck in my throat. From my vantage point I could see numerous Assyrians closing on the general from all sides. Bloodlust blazed in their eyes.

Rushing to the precipice, I screamed out a warning. That's when my left foot stumbled on an upturned stone. Cringing with my shrieking toes, I lost my balance and tumbled head over heels over jagged rock and dry, trampled brush. My head drowned in every sort of pain, and then it all gave way to chaos and terror.

Thick, gnarled fingers took hold of my beautiful hair to yank my head high. Crying out, I stared up into the dark, venomous eyes of a mountain of an Assyrian, his growling lips covered with damp gray dust, his bristling beard dripping a rancid mixture of sweat, saliva, and blood. With his left hand he held me dangling in the breeze. With the other he drew a long, chipped dagger to my throat.

Chapter 4
Desperate tasks

It was an old blade, twice the length of my hand, its black iron scarred countless times by battle, bone, and the sharpening stone. I had no doubt the knife could carve out my throat in a second. I breathed deep, gazed down the edge of my nose, and watched the instrument of my death draw near. There seemed little else to do, for it moved so fast.

The sun flashed across a streak of silver. In mid-flight the dagger twisted about, the hand at its hilt spinning away. At the same time my head came free. As I plunged to the earth, I beheld the bloodied edge of a shimmering short sword sailing through the air. The Assyrian screamed.

Never had I been so happy to strike bedrock.

For a while there it seemed someone was juggling my eyes in a thunderstorm. Strange black dots danced about my nose like spooked bees, and my ears pulsed louder than a blacksmith would ever drive his anvil. But through the tirade I heard a call. A hand appeared in the swarm, reaching for me. Grasping it with both my own, I was pulled up from the chaos of stunned bewilderment to one far more sinister.

Gnashing teeth, splitting leather, clashing iron, devout swearing, frantic screaming… the winds seemed bloated with all these horrid sounds and more. Yet far worse proved the scent of decay. The morning was still young, and yet untold wounded and dying soaked the earth with blood and waste. The stench in that listless breeze choked not just my nose, but my eyes. Even my skin recoiled at the smell… or at the sounds, or the sights. Perhaps all three.

I had the complete package at my feet. The Assyrian quivered on his belly, his life draining from a wide gash at his waist to pool within sour rivulets crossing the sand. His blank eyes stared at my toes. His cheeks puffed desperate gasps of breath, broken at times by soft words, defiant yet inaudible. Sounds that in the end made little sense, and yet chilled me to the bone.

Oh, how I wanted to get out of there! To just run and run and never admit I'd ever known Jonah or Jeroboam or anything else to do with this dreadful day! But I couldn't. The agent of death stood at my side, his firm left hand on my throbbing shoulder.

What did I call the Assyrian, a mountain of a man? He had been that, to be sure, but if true, then his conqueror was the all-shattering storm. Though speckled with blood and bathed in dirt and sweat, the warrior stood as one tested and alert, ready for more. His frame may not have towered like that giant, but it declared its solid build, hard and strong. His head stood as a granite monument. His cheeks had been scarred, his nose long ago broken and set. His large green eyes glowed with wild intent, defying all he saw.

He studied me, no doubt making sure I was no threat. Only then did his dusty lips crack a smile.

"Saw you follow Jonah," he explained. Wiping clean his magnificent sword so that it sparkled as crystal, his wary eyes returned to the battlefield. "Brave thing, lad, but stupid."

Even as he tried to be friendly, he spoke with a bear's snarl. That's how I recognized him. Gillian, captain of Jeroboam's honor guard. Commander of a thousand and then some. The king's great chief of battle.

A morning of hard fighting had reduced his armor to a shredded leather vest and leggings, their holes revealing every taut, bruised, and strained muscle in his immense arms, torso, and legs. Three cords tied his long black hair into a rope that snaked across his broad shoulders to circle about that tree trunk of a neck, mixing there with his speckled beard.

His eyes flared in his desire to kill. Hard, desperate calls echoed from right and left. Gillian looked to both, tossing his braided hair from shoulder to shoulder, and made up his mind. Yanking me about, he pointed with his silvery blade back to the high ledge, shouting "Go there!" Then he took the opposite path.

Swords collided about me, but I just stood there. Gillian had seen Jonah's peril, and yet he'd chosen to save me. Why?

That thought made me shudder. Jonah! I'd forgotten about Jonah!

In near panic I twisted about, but I couldn't see the Dove. All the shuffling feet and rolling bodies shrouded the battlefield with an almost impenetrable cloud of dust. In quiet desperation I picked the way I recalled him heading, hoping it was right, and ran.

It was not easy. After about twenty paces I lost my footing and slid into a hole dug from Hermon's sands by Jeroboam's troops. A couple of his would-be soldiers crouched there, covering their heads. They cried out when I fell among them, as did I – though theirs proved louder.

"Augh!" one screamed as dust and filth sprayed over his face. "What are you doing to me? What a stink!"

My left foot slapped the other coward in the head. He swore words I'd never imagined, pushing me into his comrade. That angry one shoved me yet again, to strike hard against the only corner left in their pitiful hole. The impact brought another wave of earth to caress my scalp, which gave my neighbors another reason to scream.

"Clumsy fool!" one wailed, his hands flailing about as if to rid the world of every pesky biter the breeze could harbor. "I've smelled donkeys with more sense than to come around sticking their whifts and sarshes where they weren't wanted."

As I pondered just what that could mean, their fears transformed into disgust. I guess they realized I had tumbled into their hiding spot alone, unpursued... which meant they remained safe after all… though that didn't make them any more welcoming.

"Get out!" one scolded – a merchant, I'd guess, from his soiled tunic, head wrap, belt, and sandals. None of his clothes revealed any history of wear, much like a few other shopkeepers I'd known. "There's no room for three!"

"Yes, out!" agreed the other, too covered in dust and grime to reveal anything of his life. "Out, you scrap eater! Now! And don't let anyone see you!"

With the sun and sky obscured by blowing dirt, I doubted anyone had spied me joining them in the first place. But that did not matter, as I wanted to leave. I could hear the guilt in their words, their anger built upon their shame. Still, I could not blame their acting the way I'd expected them to all along. Indeed, with well-trained killers loose among us, hiding seemed most wise. Any other day I might have joined them if I could, but I had a desperate task before me, and my own shame clawed at my heels.

Scratching my way out of that pit, I took what directions I could and started again into the gritty fog. It seemed I had only just picked up a good speed when I stumbled over the dead carcass of a black steed.

His rider didn't like that.

He must have been a tall man, though it was hard to tell, the way he knelt beside his fallen horse. Bleeding from nasty wounds on his forehead, neck, and left shoulder, he aimed his long sword at my head and hobbled after me, shouting something foul in a twisted Assyrian tongue. I probably could have outrun him, the way he limped, but something stopped me. Hovering under a wild crown of frazzled hair, his eyes burned with a fierce madness almost arcane in its mesmerizing power. As he drew near, spitting what I guessed were curses, I stumbled, almost falling. Yet I couldn't look away.

I rambled backwards, step by step, groping for some defense. The Assyrian matched me. He stabbed with his sword, just missing my left knee. He tried again, cutting my dusty tunic. That made me cringe, wondering what Nathaniel would say about my carelessness. Distracted by that thought, I backed full into a blocking stone. The Assyrian lunged at the chance to skewer me. I yelped as that sword rose. That's when a hand shoved me aside.

It was no rock I'd found, but Gillian! He had turned back for me!

With one exchange of blows, the captain left the fallen rider as dead as his horse. Gillian then turned on me.

"I told you to go back!" he spat. "Why are you out here?"

I did not answer at first. It took time just to catch my breath, which seemed in short supply with all that was going on.

"Why?" Gillian demanded, his patience at its end. The edge cutting his words helped me overcome my anxiety.

"To follow Jonah," I blurted out.

Wiping clean his weapon, the warrior considered my answer but a moment before again asking, "Why?"

That stopped me cold. I had no idea why I felt this need. I just did. But I knew if I said that, Gillian would not listen. While he probably didn't know me, he surely recognized the king's palace garb about my shoulders, weathered though it now was. I stumbled to think of something, anything, that would satisfy him. But that didn't prove necessary. Waiting for me to answer, the commander of a thousand flicked his eyes about, monitoring the battle. Then he stiffened.

"There he is," Gillian whispered.

Surprised, I strained to see what he did. I couldn't, but that didn't matter. Gillian pulled me up by my girded waist and started off. I followed as close as possible, though it was hard, so quick was the war chief. Rounding two crests and a wide hole, we emerged from the battle's edge to reach the well-worn path most caravans used to circle about the mountain. There the breeze had enough strength to master the gritty fog of war, and thus I too spied Jonah. The Dove sprinted to the eastern foothills, toward a knob of golden grass. Atop that hill one of Jeroboam's horsemen circled an overturned Assyrian chariot, its umbrella sticking out of the ground.

Gillian paused, catching his breath. It made me feel good that he too faced such handicaps. I had begun to think him tireless as well as fearless.

From the look on my face, he must have figured out what held my mind. A gentle smile warmed his lips, giving way to bright laughter. I could not help marveling at it. At a simple turn he assumed a playful trait I had not thought possible from the great warrior. He still seemed quite the bear, but perhaps a loveable one.

Pointing toward the hill, Gillian took me by the hand. “Shall we join the great prophet?”

“Oh, yes!”

I drew up my strength for a hard dash, as if I could dare race the great Captain of the Guard. He saw my preparation and made to join me, but then he stopped in abrupt concern. I felt it too, the pulses of rushing thunder through the bones of the peak. It made me pause… and saved my life.

Chapter 5
The hammer of doom

Around a sharp bend of the western road raced two bronze-lined chariots, each pulled by a trio of white stallions. One surged through the spot where I had stood; the other skidded to a stop. That first glance spurred me to bow. Behind the two soldiers driving the first cart stood my king, proud in his purple and white silks, silver belts, and golden rings. Nathaniel rode in the other chariot.

Jeroboam and Gillian saw each other at about the same time. The greatest of soldiers bowed, then rose.

"You have done well," said the king.

"All goes as foretold," the general replied, "until now. Jonah has run ahead."

The king nodded; he must have expected it. "Join me then. Let us see what he has found."

Winded and confused, I watched my savior mount the king's chariot as it drove off. Gillian motioned for me to wait before returning his eyes to his master. The second cart rolled forward as if to follow, only to skid to a halt.

"Get on!" Nathaniel snapped to me. "We must not tarry here!"

Drawn by his urgency, I stumbled onto the floorboard of woven reeds. The driver whipped the horses to speed before I was settled, but it did not matter. It made a short trip, the wheels drawing to a stop before I felt stable. I practically fell off then, coughing from the blowing dirt, and found myself within a circle of arrow-pierced bodies around three broken chariots. One Assyrian remained alive.

Approaching, I looked for the first time at their captive, the governor of Aram and Damascus. He stood stout and secure amid his Israelite guards, the fire in his eyes undiminished. Though someone had uncovered his head, he retained the other trappings of his office: beautiful red and white robes, embroidered with artistic images of his life and gods; a shiny leather belt and sandals adorned with gold, silver, and gems; wristbands of copper, smelt in the form of serpents; jeweled daggers of bronze, iron, and bone; a magnificent sword snug within a scabbard of leather and gold, its wrapped hilt capped by the carved ivory heads of lions.

It stunned me to see such wealth worn in battle, though I don't know if anyone else paid it much attention. Gillian certainly did not. He had already dismounted, running to a cavalry officer standing near the Dove.

A horn bellowed a somewhat flustered note, struggling to be heard over the waving sounds of battle. As black smoke spread across the earth, Jeroboam stepped from his chariot. A band of heavy soldiers appeared from the gritty wind to walk behind him.

"Has he spoken?" the king said, his dark eyes focused on the Assyrian leader standing at ease before them.

A horse soldier, captain of a thousand, answered for his commander. "When his chariots ran aground, his mouthpiece vowed he would address none but you, though he did offer words to Jonah."

A wry smile slipped across Jeroboam's face.

"We had to slay the bodyguard," said Gillian.

"So Jonah forewarned," Jeroboam noted, his words filled with the richness of age, and perhaps wisdom. I couldn't help admiring that, false though I knew it to be. His many years and prolonged illness clawed ever at his strength. But when his unusually soft blue eyes turned to his enemy, his brow twisted with wrath that knew no age. His thinning grey beard flared like a stroked flame.

"You allowed yourself be taken," decided the king.

"This battle is over," the governor admitted, "for now. It hardly matters. We will correct this; you know that full well. The time of my death is my own to choose."

Jeroboam settled upon his heels, a cold snarl on his worn lips. "And now it is mine."

"I think not."

The eyes of the king flared in the sun. "Defiant and direct. Ah, so it is said. The mind of the Assyrian is straight as an arrow, unbending as the desert."

"You honor me."

"Accept it as you will. I would prefer the patience of the earth, the warmth of the sun. But I am an old man. I am allowed such thoughts. Very well; perhaps these things need no subtlety. Hear me, ear of your master. I wish peace."

A sinister smile crept across the prisoner's face.

"For too many years have we skirmished, you and your kind before you," my king continued. "You whittle away our frontiers, exact tribute from our merchants, our cities. It must stop."

"How?" the governor taunted. "This day changes nothing. You have no power."

"The executioner awaits," offered Gillian.

The Assyrian hardened. "I welcome death."

"A cold choice," Jonah stepped in, "when in your hands you hold the wealth of Damascus."

All eyes turned to the Dove in silent recognition of his authority. The governor bent his head, as if calculating his response, or escape.

"You would give it up?" he put forward.

Jonah strode at ease to the king's right. "Gold has no claim on me, Ansephanti Rezin of Aram. I serve the Lord."

"Ansephanti," Gillian whispered. The king also seemed amazed, as if the name had been a well-kept secret. But if the revelation surprised the governor, he did not reveal it. Indeed, his eyes remained on the Dove, flashing in the bright sun as might a cornered tiger seeking any opportunity to tear into his attackers. I found this compelling.

"A brave statement, made at your king's side," said the Assyrian. "Do you not serve him?"

From the slight drift of his brow, I saw Jonah recognized the challenge and would not back down. "When he does the will of God, yes. If not, I walk my own path."

A weak grin passed across the king's shadowed lips. Though I was somewhat familiar with old Jeroboam, I couldn't read what that meant. Yet Ansephanti showed his pleasure.

"A man of honor," he said, little hiding his sarcasm. "Yes, I admit it. Freely! I love the palace, the wine, most certainly the women. Scores of them! But you too covet a treasure. I see it in your eyes! Tell me, oh brave and honest one – if I deliver you this peace you seek, would you abandon your god?"

My fists knotted. I cared nothing for this talk of god, yet even so, the sheer gall of the Assyrian drew my hatred, as it did from others. The soldiers mumbled and hissed, and Gillian spat a curse as he reached for his shiny blade. But Jonah was as stone.

"You have not such power," he stated.

"And you don't want peace!" The Assyrian laughed. "I know your kind. You wish us dead. All dead! Ahh, but in truth, I do not blame you, for I would have no peace with such as you."

"I think you will. We hold the roads between here and Damascus. Look behind us! Your men surrender, Ansephanti. They know no reinforcements will arrive, for you have none. Your empire faces rebellion everywhere – the Chaldeans afoot in Babylon, the tribes of Urartu march south, Mannea west, and all the while your men abandon their legions to tend their homes and save their flocks. Gold slips from your hands with every caravan the marauders snap, and fewer reach Nineveh each year. More and more, your herds fall to disease and hunger, and your allies grow reluctant to replenish them. Your iron mines fall under siege, your timber supplies stand threatened, your precious horses–"

"Enough of this!" the governor snapped.

Jonah straightened to his full height, his head rolling forward as might a bull before a charge. The awesome power summoned into his form cowed me.

"Woe to thee, Assyria, you flock of buzzards! You have grown fat on the work of others, but your enemies shall rise up, and there will be nothing left."

The governor fought to meet Jonah's gaze under the weight of that prophecy. I couldn't help staring, for it was plain I was wrong. Whatever else Jonah was, whatever crazed delusions he held about his god, he was no madman. He spoke not just endowed with might, but with a graceful elegance, and even more, with complete mastery of the situation and all the vast elements that comprised it. Grand were his schemes, and even grander his ambitions.

Never had I met such a man.

The Assyrian cracked under that strain.

"Damnation!" spat Ansephanti.

Gillian twisted him about to slap his dusty cheek. The sound split apart their tension.

By their murmured approval, many around us felt the blow justified, but Jeroboam did not. "Stop!" he commanded, bristling at his soldiers.

The Dove raised his hands, motioning for calm.

"Unbelievers cannot insult us," Jonah said. "Their words mean nothing. But I offer you this, Ansephanti. Listen.

"It's no secret your throne is in chaos. Governors who cannot meet their quotas of gold, iron, horses, or grains do not long survive. And I know the Chaldeans have struck within your territory, stealing valuable supplies, occupying your guards.

"But now we hold the western roads to Tyre and Damascus. They were the lands of David and Solomon, the gift of the God Most High, and we will keep them. You may return to your stronghold, rearm yourself, and die fighting us, or give in to the Lord. Cede these lands to us, and the gold flows unhindered. Lebanon timber, Egyptian spices, Phoenician ores… indeed, all the trades, from Carthage and Tarshish, Tarsus and Athens… all will reach your hands. You may focus on getting them to Assur,

Nineveh, wherever you wish. Your headaches will be lessened, your wealth embellished, your good name restored among the kings of Assyria."

Did I speak before of Jonah's power? I tell you, rarely if ever had I seen anyone command such presence as the Dove showed then!

The hard truth of his words ground against the governor. When he said nothing, the Dove offered his last olive branch.

"These things are within your power, Ansephanti."

"Speak not my name, Jew!"

Gillian trembled with hate at that outburst, as if the dark tone was the greatest of insults, but Jonah remained undeterred. "These are in your power, oh Governor of Damascus. You may accept them and prosper, or retreat upon your pride and die, forgotten among men. It is your choice."

The Assyrian stood resolute, but his eyes quivered in the faint light.

"You," he stammered, pausing to control his voice. "You can grant this?"

"He speaks for me," Jeroboam proclaimed.

"The Lord grants this," stated Jonah. "His will be done."

Though Gillian smiled, the soldiers looked about with restless eyes, and Nathaniel glanced with trepidation at the Dove's mild reproach. The king held his tongue.

A low, grinding moan escaped Ansephanti's lips. Hiding his eyes, he ripped his cloak to leave the designs of his office at his feet.

"I do not bend a knee to you," he whispered. "This I do to preserve our people. But I will watch you."

"As does our Lord," answered Jonah.

"No more!" Ansephanti's eyes burned with rage enough to rekindle his beaten army. "Guard well your steps, prophet. If I see you again, it shall cost you your head."

The king ripped free his sword. Though aged, his countenance remained daunting. "You dare make threats before me?"

"It is nothing," said the Dove, though for a brief moment he too showed some rage. But it passed; how he let it go, I may never know. I couldn't have released mine so quick.

"The will of the Lord be done," he commanded. "Take your court to Hamath."

"Send him on his way," the king ordered, a sentence the captain fulfilled with swift, unceremonious hands and an escort of mounted troops.

A strange, abrasive stillness hung in their absence. The king sheathed his sword, then paused, as if he knew not what to do. His soldiers glanced about for guidance. With a brief nod to Jonah and Nathaniel, Gillian waved the others to leave. Perhaps I should have followed, but my curiosity bid me stay. No one seemed to notice.

The king sank to the earth, taking his head in his hands. "This was not how I wanted it to go."

"We won what we sought," Gillian pointed out. "The Kingdom of Damascus is ours again."

"But he left an enemy."

"He is the enemy," Jonah stated.

Gillian took the king's arm. "Would you rather we ship his head back to Assur, Nineveh, or wherever their king rules now?"

"No," Jeroboam sighed. "I do not wish to battle all of Assyria."

"Bend not your ears from the Lord," Jonah cautioned him.

The king reared like an alarmed viper. "You always urge me to fight these people! Tell me now – do you foresee such a victory?"

Everyone looked then to the prophet, awaiting some revelation. To my surprise, the Dove said nothing, offered nothing. For Jeroboam, who had little patience, that was unacceptable.

"You weary me," he said. "If your god wishes the Assyrians crushed, let Him choose another pawn. I am too old. Leave me."

The king dropped his forehead to his knees. Jonah watched him with genuine pity. At one point he took a step toward Jeroboam as if to comfort him, but then he bowed his head, and whispering "Your will be done," he turned and left.

That's when I heard the hammer of doom.

Watching the Dove walk away, I saw Nathaniel turn toward me with broken eyes, and I realized my fate had caught up with me. Paralyzed, I heard them all again, the harsh taunts and fearful warnings of Jeroboam's stable hands and palace valets, of his many other young attendants and couriers. They came as echoes from the bleeding hills, reminding me of just what lay ahead. Not that I was surprised. Each morning I had awakened wondering if that would be the day the war would end… the day Jeroboam in his sick pleasure would defile me. For I knew I had been saved for just this purpose, for the king's final celebration of victory.

And now, that time had come.

In token reverence to our king, I fell to my knee and bent low my head. Then I scampered after the Dove. I had to get out of there.

Jonah proceeded along the wheel ruts of the path, never looking back. I hurried after him, calling his name. I do not know why; something inside just spurred me to be with him. I sensed security there, even peace.

In a swirl of dust, Jonah crossed over a descending ridgeline and stopped.

"Go back," the frustrated prophet told me. "There is nothing for you here."

I couldn't accept that. Grasping for words, I babbled thoughts I no longer remember. Jonah seemed to ignore me, looking off to some distant horizon. But I could see disgust brewing within him, filling his heart and soul until he could stand it no longer, and so wrapping his cloak about his shoulders he turned away. Only later did I realize he had gazed upon the battlefield, where Jeroboam's troops took their grizzly harvest of the fallen, gathering tokens and trinkets from the battlefield – silver rings, golden teeth, jewels, weapons, clothing. Truly, what they did to claim these valuables… oh, it is too sickening to tell.

Forgive me; I digress.

"I can teach you nothing," Jonah called over his shoulder. "Follow the Lord. He will guide you."

That struck some chord within me. I didn't understand it, for never before had I given the old religious myths any substance, and yet I heard myself spouting, "But He did! You said so yourself!"

Jonah allowed a wry smile at that, as if he recognized my duplicity. Twisting about, he raised his hand to me and questioned, "And what did you discover?"

That stumped me. I stood there, sifting through what I could recall of that long day, and found no ready answers.

The Dove would not bend. "I have no needs or wants of a helper. Go back."

"How can I?" My voice crumbled in fear. "You know what he'll do to me."

That's how I learned the real value he placed on faith. I could see Jonah grieved over my fate, and yet his just heart would not let him bend.

"Go back," he insisted, "and follow our God."

"What?"

"Have faith, Benjamin, and He will provide. Do not lose heart."

That almost broke me. For in lacking beliefs, my mind had no defense against all the poisoned passions erupting in my breast, preying on the knowledge that I would be corrupted, destroyed.

Looking back on all this, I think that is when Jonah proved his mettle to me, and in so doing, planted the seed of my faith. For as I stumbled in my despair, he took me in his arms and lifted me up. That's when I witnessed his pure heart. A sense of justice may have ruled him, but compassion and love laid his foundation.

"Do not be afraid," he told me.

I wavered, trying my best to contain my tears. It was so hard!

"Follow the Lord," he said. "Live your life as best you can, and He will provide. No matter what happens."

I doubt Jonah understood just how little I knew of his god, and how unprepared I was to believe in him. But with these instructions dancing about my head, I saw why I had been led to seek Jonah, both on the battlefield and now. I needed a teacher.

"Please! Please? Can't I stay with you?"

Jonah looked hard into my eyes, then nodded with reluctant admission to both our fates. For we both suffered bitter turns in service to a wicked monarch.

"Go back," he said again, "and have faith. If God wills, we will meet again."

Chapter 6
Cornered

That proved one of the most confusing times in a lifetime of confusing times. Jonah's words seemed the heart of wisdom itself when the Dove first spoke them, but now, as I watched him trudge west along that dry road, the sounds of battle biting at his heels, his echoing advice rang hollow, if not false. His commands challenged me in ways I didn't understand and couldn't accept.

Follow God? I didn't even believe he existed!

Trust God? How? Just because Jonah said to?

What was he to me? He had abandoned me, just like my mother and father!

A hot, gritty gust swept by, obscuring the Dove and everything else. Coughing, I heard a joyous shout from the battlefield, followed by a scuffle. In the heat of the midday sun, three soldiers fought like famished dogs over some golden bauble they'd hacked off a corpse. Many others watched, entertained by the crazed fisticuffs.

Oh, the madness of it all.

A hawk cried out in the wilderness. The sun poured its fury upon the stained earth. The stench of decay crawled like a plague from that place of slaughter.

It all seemed too much. Too much.

I turned and ran, chasing Jonah. He had disappeared around a dip in the road as it traveled west, across the mountain. I propelled myself forward, taking heart at my speed, but when I finally reached the crest, panting, dripping sweat, he was not there. At my feet the slope descended in sharp ripples around splintered tusks and jagged spines of hard, merciless rock, forcing the road to roll in wide curls on its way down Hermon.

Far, far below me strode Jonah, taking his last steps out of Jeroboam's camp.

The sight humbled my mind and soul. Gone was the one man capable of rescuing me from a black fate.

I was alone. Truly alone.

I don't know how long I stood there, aimless, pondering what to do. There seemed no real options. Death stalked the lands I had left. Depravity lay in wait at my feet. There was no hope.

In the simmering breeze I heard the rumble of hard-driven wheels. Feeling a sudden need to conceal myself, I took refuge within a sharp cut in the granite. Just then the king rode by in his grand chariot, his straining horses charging down the worn gravel path.

That was enough for me. I went the other way.

That afternoon I crisscrossed the slopes of Mount Hermon, searching its dark crevasses, pacing with nervous abandon through its musty, sweltering caves, sliding down its sand streams and skirting its plummeting cliffs. With growing desperation, I contemplated every escape path I could think of, perfecting detail after detail, only to scrap each plan when I imagined Jeroboam's guards catching me.

No; there was more to it than that. To be honest, as the sun sparkled across the vast land, there were times it seemed I could see to the ends of the earth. I spied hundreds upon hundreds of towns and villages where the king's arm surely did not reach. I would have been safe in any one of them! But each time I found myself ready to flee for such a haven, I couldn't do it. The thought of striking out on my own proved oh so frightening, even more than the fate I knew.

As night drew close, a cold, piercing darkness settled upon me. It was as if I lay in a sealed tomb, cut off from the world. All was hidden from my sight – the stones at my feet, the tunic on my shoulders and arms, my ash-powdered nose… even the stars in the heavens.

All but Jonah's sage advice. Each breath of wind whispered reminders of the Dove.

I huddled against Hermon's face, paralyzed by indecision and fear, when I saw a blast of fire billow up from the dark far below. It danced against the night, rippling and raging, growing ever higher. Then came another blaze, and another. All at once the silence burst with vibrant songs and shouts of pomp and bluster. With a rush of joy, I recognized these huge bonfires marked the start of Jeroboam's victory celebration. The revelry soon spread so that all our many encampments made merry, in ways I dared not think about.

It was then I realized, to my amazement, that I had no choice but to do as Jonah said.

True, my conscious crafted rationalizations for creeping back toward the camp. Scrambling around Hermon's jagged face had scored my hands and feet with weeping bruises and scars, so I needed the road's gentle, well-worn grade for any chance of managing the long walk ahead. And since the king had secured his camp along the road to guard that passage and supply line, I had to risk approaching its sentries in hopes of getting by. But that also proved beneficial, as the bonfires provided the only light I had to pick my path.

Still, I feared it impossible to draw near the tents and not be found, and I was right. On each path I chose, along every direction I tarried, vigilant guards stood watch. But it was not one of those who caught me – oh, no indeed! In the end, that great feat fell upon a horse trainer floating in his wine.

The wasted man had slipped away to relieve himself, only to lose his steps in the rocks. Quite by accident he came upon me as I cowered from the view of a restless sentry, but even then, this drunken oaf did not find me. As I crouched in the shadows, that mule-headed stablemate just rambled closer and closer until... clunk! He tripped over my stretched back!

Down we went. I should have run then, guard or no guard, but from the way he landed, I feared the mindless fool might have killed himself. But when I checked to make sure he was not injured, I found him not only alive, but quite pleased by his good fortune. Though I begged compassion, I believe he enjoyed forcing me to the king's tent. But then, that collector of flies had always belittled me.

Humiliated and broken, I was shoved before the king, who at that moment regaled over an audience of his champions, patrons, and honored staff. They didn't notice me at first. With their cups full of sweet wine, the air alive with burnt cinnamon and honey spice, they sat on soft cushions around the walls of his largest tent, circling a sandpit where at least a dozen pairs of veil-clad dancers floated as moths about flickering lamps to the playful notes of the lyre, menanaim, and halil. Seductive shadows drifted across their oiled bodies as they joined and parted, man to woman, their movements open flirtation for what their hearts might desire. With each grand revolution they drew ever closer, their hands gliding about each lithe form, their glossy lips brushing ever so near. The audience shared in the rushing passion, awaiting the promised fulfillment.

Standing there, looking upon their indulgences, I felt my life crumbling away. My heart pounded like a battering ram against my aching ribs. My lungs couldn't draw breath.

This was my every nightmare and oh, oh so much more!

Nathaniel was the first to see me, a shock that thrust him from bridled contempt toward the tent's shared ardor to a stiff, frozen panic. Like a lion snatching its meal, he leaped from his post at the rear of the king's throne, slipping behind the onlookers to not draw their attention. It almost worked. But something caught Jeroboam's eye, perhaps the flutter of the steward's shimmering cloak. Whatever it was, as Nathaniel closed on me like a bird of prey, ready to wrap me in his wings and whisk me away, the king raised his hand for silence. The music sputtered to a stop, leaving the dancers adrift in their passion, the audience in sudden anguish and dismay.

"Nathaniel!" called the king. "What have you found?"

The steward held himself still, his eyes rolling up in utter disappointment. When he did not answer, the impatient king thrust himself out of his throne in a rush to Nathaniel's side.

"Ah!" the king exclaimed. "You have him!"

"It was I, sire," chirped my drunken betrayer of a mule nurse, who stumbled forward to offer suitable homage in a most sloppy fashion. I offered nothing, but no one noticed.

It didn't take long for the king's pleasure to sour. His eyes jumped from my dirty face and torn, soiled tunic to the broken blisters on my wrists and fingers, my knees scraped raw, the welts on my ankles, and my bleeding toes. He grazed my left cheek with a fingertip, moving my chin from one side to the other as if to examine every filthy wrinkle. Then his proud, harsh eyes stared into mine. I witnessed there some honest concern, but mostly simmering anger and deep, burning regret.

With a sigh, the king pulled away. Dried blood clung to his finger where he'd touched me. A servant soon swabbed his hand clean.

"You saw battle," he said to me, as one might to a disobedient child. "Were you hurt?"

Having no breath to speak, I shook my head no.

Jeroboam grunted. His gaze twisted to Nathaniel. His brow tightened.

"You knew I was saving him for this! What happened?"

Nathaniel stood his ground. "We needed a messenger," he answered in a calming tone. "No one else was available."

"Do you take me for a fool? You have a camp full of runners! You could have gone yourself, for all I care!"

"You know better than that."

"Curb your tongue!"

"If I displease you, dismiss me. I am certain there are others ready to do your bidding."

"Quiet!"

The tent rippled with shared tension. Only Nathaniel appeared unmoved.

At odds with himself over what to do, the king glanced around, grumbled at that sign of weakness, and threw up his hands in frustration. That's when his eyes fell on me once more. I felt his wrath, and something more, the pain of denied desire. It chilled my heart.

Jeroboam raised his finger toward me, but his angry gaze focused on Nathaniel.

"He's no good to me now," the king snapped. "Get him out of here."

The steward moved before Jeroboam could change his mind, shoving me through several tent folds and crowded lines of the king's servants, their faces open, then hidden. They had listened to the incident and cringed at our approach. For with my future saved, they knew my fate might fall on one of them.

I heard the king clap his hands, shouting for the musicians to start anew. Nathaniel propelled me on. His pace did not slow until he had pushed me out of the tent and the three rings of soldiers guarding it. Only then did we stop in that dry night, breathing deep the musky smoke of many boisterous campfires. Together we sighed with relief.

Oh, has a blacker evening ever looked so bright? I gazed about that dark, uncaring camp and beheld the world in a new light, one full of grace and opportunity!

It seemed everything I had ever known had passed away. At that moment, with that breath, I knew my life had changed.

A gentle hand settled on my shoulder. I looked up to see Nathaniel eyeing me with warmth, as a father to a beloved son.

What was it Jonah had said? "You have friends you do not realize." I recalled those words and felt humbled.

Have faith, he had said. With what I just witnessed, with all that transpired, those words no longer seemed so impossible. And still, it was so difficult to even allow the prospect! As stubborn and downtrodden as I was, how could I possibly learn to believe in anything?

Truly, I needed a teacher. I needed the Dove.

"Go to the stables and wash," Nathaniel told me. "I will speak with the stable master. Do as he says. Cause no trouble. He will give you a bed, clothes, and work to fill your days until we return to the palace."

"And then?"

Nathaniel chuckled at my resilient, impetuous heart.

"I should think that's enough for now. Let us be content with what God has brought about, and be patient with what comes next."

Chapter 7
Solace

It took less than a week for my newfound optimism to wither and die… and Israel's fate with it. In horror I watched disaster after disaster descend upon the land, crushing the life from all those I had known. And I couldn't help wondering, where was the great conqueror when his people needed him? Why did Jonah lead them to such a hollow victory, when he knew it would be their destruction?

And just where was this god Jonah preached of? How could he let this happen?

I can see from your blank stares that I've leaped far ahead of myself. Forgive me.

It is difficult, looking back at those desperate years. To be honest, I think now that we were all guilty. If these evil times have taught us anything, it's that we simply cannot lie dormant in our faith, expecting the Lord to solve all our problems. We must act when what we cherish is assailed. But alas! Under that corrupt reign, we all feared the lash and sword, should anyone lift a voice against the Viper. We did nothing, and our nation was doomed.

Perhaps in our hearts we bore the spreading corruption as our just fate – our punishment for our forefathers' desiring a king. The prophecies of Samuel and Elijah come true, you might say. Or perhaps we were just ignorant. Or even worse, maybe we were simply guilty of rejecting God.

I certainly was.

Oh, I could talk all day and tomorrow too about such things. Forgive me; I promise I will continue the tale, now, for it was in those years of unsettling depression that I received directions from Hosea, and I began to learn the truth.

I remember waking that morning on Hermon to the wondrous smell of horse sweat, dung, and baked straw. Stretching my limbs, I breathed deep under the tent of the king's stable and felt at ease with the world.

Too bad it didn't last.

Uncertainty began to chip away the confidence of Jeroboam's triumphant troops as they shook off their celebratory haze. I heard it spread in whispers that grew more fearful with each retelling… which is easy to understand, once you think about it. For as their general, the Dove had led them from victory to victory. He was the revered conqueror of Judah and the Philistines, punisher of Moab and the Ammonites, the master of Sidon and Damascus. Even Tyre, usually quite defiant behind her unrivaled navy and the unassailable Great Sea, had decided it was better to pay homage to Jeroboam than risk Jonah's military brilliance.

But now, from one astonished lip to another, the Israelites learned that the Dove had left them. For the first time since Jeroboam's lust for power had taken root, his armies no longer moved under Jonah's divine guidance.

It was well for the king that he soon had his soldiers marching again, the mounted troops with Gillian to claim Damascus, the rest to return home. The effort kept their minds occupied, and the promise of home uplifted us all. But despite Nathaniel's forthright leadership, the army returned to Samaria under a cloud of apprehension. For everyone knew Jeroboam would face many rebellious vassals once they learned of the prophet's absence, and no one wanted to confront them without the Dove.

I, too, found myself wondering where Jonah had escaped to, and even more, how I might join him. My heart smoldered with an impatient yearning to sit at his feet and fill my dry, empty soul with a hearty drink from wisdom's depths. But it was not to be.

The stable hands had only just finished settling the weary horses into their pens when word came of Jeroboam's sudden illness. One tale had the king collapsing in pain during some embarrassing diversion, another told of a head-first plunge from his chariot, while a third had him poisoned. Whatever the case, everyone agreed old Jeroboam lay on his death bed.

As an expectant father trembles with anticipation, his very life hanging on his child's birth, so too did everyone in the palace await news of the king's health – not for love of the old fool, but out of fear of what prince Zechariah might do. That hot-headed lad cared nothing for his father's fanciful quests and even less for his servants. Especially those like me, meant for a passion Zechariah didn't share.

Crawling in exhaustion to my bed of hay, sleep came with great reluctance… only to end with a shock. From a restless slumber I awoke to a strong palm clamped over my mouth. I struggled against my assailant, to no avail. By my head, my attacker dragged my writhing body from the stables, where another set of hands took me into custody. Gasping for breath, I tried and failed to determine who these people were.

"Quiet!" a muffled voice snapped. "You'll alarm the horses."

Even in my weariness, I recognized that man. "Nathaniel?"

That's how I found myself returning to where Jeroboam had found me. Well before the sunrise, Nathaniel had me disguised and beholden to a group of cantankerous priests bound for the Israelite temples at Bethel. It was not a thankful reunion, but I give the steward credit for looking out for me, for I doubt anyone else would have taken me in. There are not many callings for a harem boy to a dead king.

Oh, Nathaniel! I will always love your strict nose for saving me!

But I forget my tale. Forgive me.

So, there I was, back among the temple vermin still thriving from Jezebel's ancient patronage. Queen of vileness, she had poured into the many different shrines every kind of depravity you can imagine, and many you hopefully can't. The thought of having to look once again on that hell led me to the brink of despair. More than anything I wanted to spin about on my heels and flee that dreadful place, but linked as I was to the foul-smelling mystics and lechers, I knew better than to run away. Believe me, suffering torture was better than to be a Bethel slave caught leaving his master! So I clung to my hope in Nathaniel and accompanied those men of would-be gods and demons as their caravan journeyed through the day to reach Bethel and the depths of Ahab's temple district. In that shadowy patchwork of broken and rebuilt limestone buildings, makeshift cedar huts and carpeted caves, my hope took root.

The five rotund priests meandered about as drunken fools, to the open amusement of their entourage. But if they minded the jokes, these smelly mystics did not show it. Indeed, my teachers joined in this laughter when one of their own tumbled over his toes or lurched in his numb befuddlement. As a rowdy band of braggarts and brigands we trampled down Bethel's alleys and byways until we ended in twilight at the steps of a large shrine near the center of the district. Beneath rows of blazing torches, the priests gushed over the brass basins brimming over with rainwater and took great delight in the dried blood dabbed again and again over a jagged slab of granite jutting from the entryway.

The blood of infants, no doubt. My stomach churned.

"Ah, gaze long on the blessings of the mazzebah," one instructed the onlookers around me. "The gods favor us this day! Let us praise them!"

That drew hearty shouts of agreement, though I still wonder whether it was due to his encouragement or to the trio of silk-veiled priestesses peeking around the temple doors. Whatever the case, as they rushed up the dark steps to tender embraces, my mind sensed a dangerous opportunity. By instinct I slid backward.

Without a thought they left me behind.

I rested a moment, taking some comfort in the shadows. Not even the rats scrambling over my toes could quell the joy I felt then. But I knew there was much yet to do.

Though bunched together, each temple was the center of its own little world, ringed by merchants offering whatever these particular gods demanded of their worshippers – elixirs and ointments, scrolls of proverbs and incantations, idol carvings, ornamental jewelry and ritual garments, as well as many tools for sacrifices, both living and dead. Ah, it was often a gruesome business. Many carts reeked with the stench of dried entrails, burnt offal, and old blood, but it proved beneficial to me, for with the sun's descent, the shopkeepers retired, and their covered carts and tied-up tents provided many places to hide. I crept from shadow to shadow, making my way around the guards to the shrine's large entryway. To my good fortune, the massive cedar doors remained open. I slid into the blackness behind one of the iron-banded gates and studied the wide avenue for my next escape path.

The view perplexed me. Though I'd walked through this area scant moments before, I recalled very little of how those wine-soaked priests had brought me here. And what I did remember now looked different. Except where torches burned, everything flickered as shifting shades of black, often appearing in recognizable bits and pieces under that fickle light before the darkness again swallowed them whole.

From what I could make out, before me opened a wide intersection of cobblestone roads between four other towering stone gates guarding their own dark temples. Along the ragged brick walls lay uncounted merchant tents and carts, all secured for the night. Even so, a great number of people still milled about, mumbling lifeless chants or kneeling as stones before the many gates, including where I hid.

I waited as group after group crawled by, blocking any chance I had to slip away unseen. My nervous anxiety grew with each pass. I knew I had to be patient, that I couldn't just charge through them and hope to get away. And yet I could feel my options dwindling. It was only a matter of time before the priests noticed my absence, or the temple guards came to secure the gates, or for one of these pilgrims to spy my crouching form in the shadows.

A burst of wind swept around me, rippling at my girded tunic and twisting through my hair. Dust swirled within the tight confines between that hinged door and the stone wall. I couldn't cover my face fast enough.

Coughing, rubbing in desperation to get that grit out from under my eyelids, I backed out of the crevasse.

Someone shouted at me. I'd stepped on a hand, or a foot.

Another gust flew by. From deep within, the door groaned from its misery. Its hinges whined.

The onlookers hesitated, as if taken aback by the wind or my appearance or that ancient tower of wood that sounded ready to collapse at any moment. I used their indecision to stumble into the roadway, mumbling my apologies as I went. Then I fled into the dark.

I didn't get far before the road tilted downward. I tried to follow it, but so black was the way that I soon lost my bearings against the sharp descent and collided face-first with a stubborn brick wall.

You snicker? Well… go ahead, laugh. Yes, it hurt! I feared I had broken my jaw!

Anyway, so there I was. I could barely see, half of my face felt afire, and the only reason I wasn't lying flat on the dirt was because I struck something else first. I guess I kind of staggered backward, numb to everything, right into an anchored cart. One of its handles hit my hip right, well, in that funny spot… yes, that one. Just like that, I doubled over about as far as one can bend and not run his face into the earth. That's when my head collided into what felt like a harvest of sweet melons. My left foot twisted over my right one just about then, and so my own weight yanked me about. I hit the road like a pounding hammer. The cart tipped over beside me, just missing my legs, but each and every one of those tumbling melons managed to find me down there. For days afterward I had bruises from my feet to my neck!

You can imagine how that fruit rolled on down the road, crashing into pots and doors and starting dogs barking from all directions. I was fortunate the merchant guard had stepped away, but still, it wasn't long before someone cried out. I scrambled to my feet and hobbled on.

The dim light of a dying torch reached for me from the muddy corner of some sort of boarding house, its one visible door propped open into a smoky room. I headed as close to the light as I dared, then entered the blackness across the way. Striking a wall, I crept along the ancient stones until I reached a gate. The splintered doors were closed, but not locked. I glanced around, and when I was sure no one could be watching, I pressed the right gate forward and slipped into the realm of darkness on the other side, closing the door behind me.

So, there I was, lost, clinging to that beaten wood. I could feel my heart pulsing through my limbs. My chest hurt so much, it took all my concentration just to draw a breath. Then I heard voices… and the clatter of purposeful footsteps.

I clung to the door as a spider would its web, listening and waiting.

The voices drew closer. There was a spattering of mangled words and rushed exclamations, clouds of frustration broken by fiery outbursts. My muscles tensed at each protest – and formed a knot when the interlopers mentioned the melons. Their anger rose. In near panic I pondered the black engulfing me, wondering with dwindling hope where I might flee to next. But it soon became clear my pursuers had lost my trail, and with that their motivation. After one or two exchanged shouts, they gave in to their disappointment and left.

Listening as the voices faded, a strange thing happened. I heard the winds whistling through hidden trees, and with it the most wondrous music: night birds singing in fluttering harmonies to the hypnotic rhythms of the crickets, locusts, and rustling leaves.

It thrilled me. Honestly. I know that sounds foolish, but I can't remember ever feeling that way before – and not too often since. I closed my eyes, charmed by the resonance of this world, and rested my back against the wood. There was peace in this glade. I could smell it in the air, taste it on my lips. It seemed a perfect place to just forget my troubles and sleep.

Oh, how I wanted to sleep!

"So," came a deep, crumbling voice, "you're finally here."

The dim silhouette of a short, bulky man appeared within a

stone archway not more than four cubits away. At least I assume he was such things. He must have observed me for some time before loosening the fold on his cloaked oil lamp. That move threw light on me while keeping him concealed. But for a flickering sliver escaping the ragged shroud, I doubt I would have seen him at all. My dazzled eyes glimpsed a crusty wart jutting from a sharp nose and bushy beard. Little else.

"Come in, come in," he said. "I've been expecting you."

Confused by all this, my first thought was to brave the street once more. For I knew that weary voice. One does not forget hermits. Especially old, crazed ones who had irritated me to no end with their begging.

He turned about, directing his torchlight onto a small archway of cracking limestone overgrown with leafy lime-green vines. I guess he expected me to follow, but I took comfort in the onrushing shadows and stood my ground.

"You expected me? How?"

His feet shuffled to a stop. His head sagged.

"Come or go, whatever you wish," he said. "But you are welcome here. I doubt you will find that true anywhere else."

With those hard words, the man retreated into a room I hadn't noticed. His light faded with him, leaving me in darkness. But as the cool breeze kissed my cheek, and the night denizens resumed their serenade, I felt little but impatience. Sour memories of an old man could not quell my curiosity over what he was doing within those hidden walls. Pitted against those thoughts, this night lost its enchantment. It wasn't long before I groped my way to where he'd stood. A dim glow in that cold, crumbling entryway outlined a second doorway across a black expanse. Starting across, I stepped on an unseen foot. I backed away from that drowsy complaint to trip over an unforeseen leg. That protest awakened two others, and their surprise raised still more. That rush of anger spurred me to just dart ahead. I do not know how many limbs I bruised then, but by the time I reached the doorway, at least ten exhausted people had condemned my clumsiness – all within that one room! Probably twice that many awaited me in the next one, as I could see within the dimmed lamplight. From the snores echoing through the walls, I guessed even more people drowsed in other secluded spaces. Those I could see slept anywhere they could – on dirty mats and piles of brush and straw, beside a smoldering fire pit, or around several cracked jars.

Visibly fatigued, my greeter rested on a corner bench beside the loose-cowled torch. He stared into my eyes as if searching for something he knew had to be there. Only when I stared back did he offer me a thin, yellow, gap-toothed smile.

"Peace be with you," he whispered. "I, Hosea, greet you in the name of our Lord. Stay. Sleep wherever you can. You'll be safe here. And welcome."

Something in what he said touched my insecure heart. I harbored many worries and concerns, questions about his actions and this place, but I still bore a heavy burden on my soul from my escape, not to mention that great, melon-enhanced weariness from my scalp to my soles. And yet, above all that, I found a strange comfort in this mysterious place. Contentment I could not explain settled within my bones, and it gave me a peace I had never felt before. Within this came a will I could not command, leading me to a vacant spot along a moldy wall, where I tumbled into sleep.

That, my friends, is how I found solace from the descending doom.

Chapter 8
My calling

Two years. Two long, turbulent years. The kind that uproot every hope or dream you believe in, right down to their bedrock foundations, and leave you a broken and empty shell, like a suckled child ripped from its mother. I know now that it was necessary, a disturbing part of God's plan, but it still hurts, speaking of it.

And yet, without these troubles, I would never have learned of truth, or love.

I awoke to the gentle touch of a damp cloth blotting my pummeled face with some kind of oily poultice. It stank as gutted fish left all day in the sun. At first touch I tried to roll away from the revolting mess, but a scab-encrusted hand held my forehead firm.

Not that it took much effort. The way the floor spun, I could not stomach any movement.

"Patience," urged Hosea, soaking the cloth to swab my forehead. "I will be done soon."

"That's disgusting," I grimaced.

The old hermit wiped around my eyes, then my cheeks. I couldn't help squirming; his concoction was like poison to my nose.

"What is that?" I snapped.

"Something to make you better."

"I hope so, or I may get really sick."

I meant that as a joke, silly though it was, but Hosea did not even crack a lazy, patronizing wrinkle of a grin. He seemed content to ignore it, and me. Cradling my head in the folds of his grimy tunic, he dabbed my face with the short, pressing strokes of someone impatient to complete his task.

"There is no time," he told me. With a final touch atop my nose, he tossed aside the soaked cloth and grunted. "Get up."

I choked on the incredulity of that command. My spine ached like a cedar tree whipped about by tempest gales. After that run-in with the limestone and melon cart, my arms reflected about every shade of purple possible. My eyes burned from all the pain and lack of sleep, and my ears pounded like onrushing thunder. Even my lips stung, stretched and swollen as wineskins about to burst.

"I don't think I can," I mumbled.

"Perhaps not," he admitted, "but get up anyway. I need your help."

His hard eyes stared into mine. When I realized he would not relent, I braced my arms to protect my sore neck and tried to sit up. But that only enraged the storm in my skull. Overwhelmed, I gave in to my pain and settled back in his lap.

Hosea sighed.

"Please," I pleaded, "get someone else."

"I wish I could," he muttered. With little care for my comfort, he shifted my throbbing head to a frayed mat before the fire pit. Then, after a deep, steadying breath, he stretched his weary limbs and rose to his feet. "We've run out of time, Benjamin. And there are many, many others here far worse off than you."

That's when my self-pity got the best of me. "Name one," I challenged, trying to hold myself up within my dizziness.

Hosea's head snapped up. Exhaustion dimmed his eyes, but not his anger.

"Your face has a pretty good scrape, that's true, and a nice burn where it's not raw. Looks like you spent a long walk in the sun before hitting a wall or something. You probably could sleep all day, if I let you. In truth, I wish I could, but I need your hands.

Get up!"

"I can't! I'm sick!"

"Yes, I know. But we're out of time, Benjamin."

A half-crazed man stumbled into the room, covered in dust and mud, his lips twitching with whispered, undecipherable fears. Hosea met him with words of comfort, taking the stranger's sagging arm to guide him to a corner where he could rest. As he laid the visitor down, Hosea pointed to the entrance, nodding for me to help. I started to protest, but a hooded lady entered, her wrap wet and soiled, cradling a crying bundle of dank swaddling clothes in her bruised arms. Two tiny girls hid behind her stained tunic, love of their mother overcoming their fear of this place.

It wasn't long before I was on my knees, struggling to wash the feet and cleanse the scrapes and cuts of those around me without vomiting from my queasiness. Those were but the first of the newcomers that long day, some forty in all. Hosea found a quiet spot for each one, always having what they required, meeting their needs with calm, confident authority.

Myself, as I faced the perilous demands of so many others, my own selfish concerns just melted away, like the night before the dawn. How could they not, seeing a new shade of agony on every brow? So tainted I had been by my own lifetime of trouble, I had never spent much time studying what other woes could stalk a defenseless soul. My new knowledge led me to a deep, restless pity, which grew into shame and remorse.

As the last child was laid to sleep and all was at last quiet, I stepped onto the terrace to breathe deep of the chill night air and contemplate the vast scope of all I had seen and done. Hosea was there, resting against that ancient wall of stone and vines, his eyes lost in the stars. I stood beside him, gazing upon his drained face, his shaking hands, and those filthy rags he wore, and I wondered how I could have so misjudged this man. He had fooled me and everyone else, it seems, into thinking he was but a beggar who scoured waste kettles and garbage pits for discarded scrap. How wrong I was.

That day I had watched him clean rancid sores. Set broken bones with but his wits and sure, steady hands. Clear cloudy minds of chaos and insanity with a kind word and welcome heart. I witnessed a mind adept at monitoring room after room of troubled strangers, keeping abreast of individual needs even as he maintained a precise order as to what came next and how it all worked together. And he did it all with a level of patience and compassion I didn't think possible. One I did not have within myself.

"How?" I couldn't help asking. "You knew they were coming. You had everything ready. Even me. How?"

Hosea stood motionless, like a decaying statue, his scarred limbs braced against that dark wall as if part of its aging stone. Sweat glistened about his closed eyes in the lamp's flickering light. His breathing came so slow and shallow, I wondered if he slept. Then a breeze rustled his hair, his nose twitched, and the crumbling statue became a man, one ready to resume his caretaker duties.

"It's getting late, Benjamin," he said, a reluctant admission of his own limitations, "and this, this was but the start. We have a long day ahead of us. Come; let's get some sleep."

"How can I? This question will pester me all night! Please… how did you know?"

A breath of wind whistled through the trees. Hosea paused to listen as if taken by the occasion. Then his curious gaze met mine. The look of those eyes… those honest, authoritative eyes – the eyes of a judge – well, it charged through me like a brush with searing coals. Embarrassment poured through my veins, driven by a humble outpouring of guilt and shame at how I had acted that morning. The onrushing tensions threatened to stifle my will, yet it lasted but a heartbeat. For Hosea smiled with welcome joy, opening a door to my soul that has never closed. He accepted me into his heart as no one had before. Within such grace, my fears and self-doubts faded as wisps of smoke in a breeze.

With a friendly arm, Hosea guided me back into the shelter. "Later, maybe, I will tell you," he allowed. "When you can believe."

That was all I got from him that night, but it was enough. For I knew I had found my calling, and my sanctuary. This was where I wanted to be. This was how I wanted to spend my life – in his example, helping these unfortunate souls. For the first time I had a purpose, so I served in whatever task Hosea asked of me, satisfied to have two meals a day and a corner at night to call my own. Indeed, I thrived in a world where the lessons came at no one's expense, and soft, positive guidance replaced swift retribution. For there was more than enough to do. I was just one among many refugees escaping Israel's sinful passions. Hosea took us all in, granting food and shelter within the most pitiful of Bethel's temples… the original one, as it turned out.

You see, that ramshackle building dated back to the first King Jeroboam, who legends say tore Israel from Judah after the death of Solomon. That Jeroboam apparently built this substitute temple to keep his people from journeying to the true one in Jerusalem – a groundless fear, it turned out, for many in the northern tribes soon turned to other gods. And so this would-be sanctuary fell into disuse and decay – a warehouse for the unwanted and accursed, until Hosea moved in.

The initial wave of bereaved and deprived discovered his charity not long before I arrived. They were an odd assortment, the downtrodden of the second Jeroboam – flogged merchants and olive growers, shriven shepherds and potters, outcast carpenters and tanners – but Hosea welcomed them all, and somehow took care of them. It was difficult, as the second wave came but a week or so on my heels, with the fall of Zechariah.

Oh, that was a sad time. Hardly a month passed after his father's death before the crass, indulgent Zechariah was himself found dead, slain in a conspiracy led by the bitter Shallum, son of Jabesh. I know not what role Nathaniel played in that uprising, but I fear it was profound. One morning I awoke to a stormy sky and learned of his imprisonment. I never heard of Nathaniel again.

A week later Menahem son of Gadi slipped into the palace with a few cutthroats from Tirzah and slew Shallum in his bed. It probably had been quite easy, for no one stomached the evils of Shallum any more than we had Zechariah. But Menahem was of another cut of cloth, a most awful one. The Viper, as we named him in our whispers. He replaced the palace guard with his hooligans, proclaimed himself king, and established a brutal, money-hungry reign far more imposing than any of his predecessors.

So began the years of terror. Menahem ran the palace like a bandit's hideaway, ever seeking new ways to enrich his treasury. Sad though it was, for the most part the people did little more than grumble and obey. Fear mastered them, that and a small army of thugs. Yet our enemies would not suffer blackmail. They knew of Jonah's disappearance and so united around my homeland, forcing the Viper, bit by bit, to give up the conquests of Jeroboam II. Even then, our people tolerated the evils our king forced upon us. Far too many accepted those indecencies as the way of our world.

In that, perhaps, they were right. It was the way of this world. I certainly learned that. But it was not God's way, or so Hosea told me.

From what I saw daily, I was loath to believe it. I was blind, despite all I had seen and endured. So Hosea took it upon himself to educate me. He considered it his calling. For long before my arrival, he had recognized the danger facing our people.

"Our time is ending," he told me. "Judgment draws near."

Chapter 9
Prophesy

This Hosea repeated often. I little understood that and often told him so. Always he would sigh, gazing into the stars for answers.

"You must believe, Benjamin. Nothing will make sense until you do."

I ask you, how can you respond to something like that? When all I saw were the dispossessed and victimized, the downtrodden and broken-hearted, what was there to believe in? The ramblings of a dusty hermit? The relics of a forgotten god?

Oh yes – I had seen the accursed trophies taken by old King Jehoash, a past peacock who, like Jeroboam II, took pleasure in humbling Judah. But unlike my intended tormentor, Jehoash had not settled for tribute. Wishing to punish Jerusalem, he toppled its walls and stole all of the Temple's precious gold and silver, the ornamental lampstands, alters, and tables, even the Ark of the Covenant made to replace the one Shishak carted off to Egypt long ago, or so they said. But plagues stalked Jehoash and his troops on their long march home, and thus that fearful heathen discarded his prizes in Bethel… in the very stronghold we occupied. Hosea showed them to me once – blemished artifacts collecting dust in one of the few rooms he kept locked. I believe the hermit thought I would gain some great insight from seeing them, though why I don't know. The web-smothered antiques didn't stir me.

"I did not mean to impress you!" Hosea barked. "I want you to understand!"

"Understand what? That you're protecting these things?"

"No!"

"Why do you not sell some of that, or melt it down? You would be rich!"

Hosea chuckled long at that. "Yes, I could be wealthy. Live in one of Samaria's great palaces, with servants at my call. Just like those among us once did."

My shock made him smile, though not of pleasure.

"Yes, Benjamin, all those poor wretches we help… they had money once. They had achieved success, as kings and lords would see it. And look at what happened to them. Gold does not bring happiness, Benjamin. It does not give you wisdom or love or faith or peace. No, all that comes from God."

Ah, the heart of the matter.

Long we talked of this, of the ancient tales, of Abraham and Isaac and Jacob and Moses. I little understood a god who could permit such hardship to fall on his people, or a god who needed such strange things as these discarded altars and tarnished candlesticks. And yet I could see that Hosea, like Jonah, did believe in these myths of our forefathers, and this, I found, meant something to me. I had grown to trust his judgment.

So, I opened my mind to all of this, and when he wasn't plagued by that scandalous wife of his, Hosea taught me what he knew of life. And I dwelled upon it. I sifted dirt through my fingers, trying to imagine how, from this dry, dead dust, God created man. I looked upon the stars, wondering just what they were and why I could see their light, and even more, what was light. I bit into leaves of grass and flower petals and the bark of trees, hoping to taste the essence of Eden. I held onto mouthful after mouthful of water, praying I might feel its precious transformation into the blood of my veins. And with my eyes closed, my thoughts still, I would breathe deep of the evening winds and listen as my lungs filled my beating heart with life itself.

It was so hard to make any sense of this. Where in all these experiences was this god Hosea so loved? What was his design for this world? Why were we even here?

Sometimes Hosea would laugh at my naivete. Pointing to those in need around us, he would ask, "What would they do if we were not here?"

Simple as that logic was, I could take heart in it, for the idea mirrored the thanks I often received from the downtrodden. But this reasoning never really satisfied me, and sometimes, I think, it did not work for Hosea, either.

After who knows how many days, I learned why.

Following one stubborn rain, an oh-so-rare outpouring from sunrise to sunset, Hosea called me to join him on the entryway terrace. It took time to find him, for a gray mist hung like a grizzled beard about the trees, making it hard to see anything. I finally came upon him leaning against a wall covered with vines. All that rain and mist, and still the creepers crackled at his back. Streams of water trickled from the thatch roof to his hair and face, but it could not wash away his fatigue.

From his visible agony, I wondered if Gomer had stopped by again. I could not understand how he tolerated such a wife – heavy with her first child, yet embracing a life of prostitution! I suspected her actions tasked his near-limitless compassion, but these troubles Hosea kept locked away. He ever remained a girded man, a soul of great depth, and even greater sorrow.

"Pray, Benjamin," he whispered, opening his aching eyes to the blanketed heavens. "Pray for mercy."

His words filled me with dread. "Why? What has happened?"

"Nothing, yet. But judgment draws near. I can feel the tension building in the breeze, the earth. Ah! The knowledge of it tears my heart."

Now, as I've said, I had often seen him in pain; sometimes from a physical wound of overexertion or mishap, from his wife, or the many sores that plagued his skin. But more often than not, his anguish poured from what he attempted each day. I had seen Hosea rise before the sun – alone, in most cases – and work past sunset, all to help the unfortunate ones. And when he went to sleep, he asked Yahweh's forgiveness for not achieving more.

Such concerns wore daily on his heart. But this night it was something more… a burden plaguing his soul like a raging fever.

"What must we do?" I whispered.

"Do?" His breath wheezed out as his chin fell. "I don't think you understand this darkness that awaits us. We face its vanguard, but it threatens to wage war against generations beyond generations, until the end of time itself."

Terror carried through his words. Until the end of time?

"How can you know this?" I scoffed, not wanting to accept anything so horrible.

"Oh, I have seen much, and foreseen more. The Enemy is not idle in this world, Benjamin. Already he has chosen his champions for the great war to come.

"To the west, spilled blood flows from a splintered hill people. Fierce in their independence, their eyes ever seek the truth, and still their ambition deceives them. With each epoch, the Greek tribes devise new ways to dominate their tiny, insignificant realm. They are toys to the Enemy, playthings striving to annihilate each other, and yet from their many hard-fought battles they will discern great wisdom from the heart of the earth, and great folly, for in it will they place their hopes, ignoring God. But such is their reward for the bold pursuit of earthly desires. Still, they will find illusions of greatness. From their shores, the great conqueror comes to overrun the world, breaking all resistance, molding its will in his own proud fashion, spreading his faith in human virtues, in reason and logic.

"Far-reaching will be his influence, his touch, yet his time is already short. For the Enemy will use the Greek to but set his stage. Farther west, twin heroes forge a bloody throne on a mountainous sword thrust into the heart of the Great Sea. Generations from now, and those well beyond, all will fall under the seed these two now sow. The world will tremble under the boots of its legions. Its fist will crush all who oppose it, and its sword will put the faithful to death. Only when millions have fallen will this empire end, and yet even its passing will echo throughout time. For that is the Enemy's true focus, to weave his darkness of deception, despair, and death. To misshape and steal the hearts of men."

As Hosea revealed his cryptic nightmare, the blurry fog of entangled images burned themselves in my memory. I breathed in every paralyzing word, bound by the vision's dramatic scope. Some of it made no sense to me, and yet I found myself trembling at the world's peril... until Hosea realized my building agony and sought to comfort me.

"But take heart, Benjamin! At the very peak of his evil reign, when all we know falls under the empire, a man unlike any other will break the bonds of this world. Through him, God will rewrite all our notions of goodness and salvation. Through him, we will find grace, and everlasting life."

"Then we should find him!" I blurted out.

What little hope I could see in Hosea's weary eyes faded away.

"Ah, my son, him we will not see in our lifetimes, or in those of our children or their kin. Great evil must precede him for his life to have purpose. Our lands will lie in darkness and doom. That," he admitted with heartfelt reluctance, "that is our fate. So be it."

I squirmed under his dire pronouncement. How could anyone accept this?

"Then what should we do?"

"Do?" That I would raise this again seemed to perturb Hosea, though he girded it well. "We pray that God's will be done, and that we may have the strength to fulfill our part in it."

That's when my inquisitive doubts took charge. "Is that enough?"

"It will have to be."

"But we must do something!"

Hosea chuckled. "So you say," he thought aloud, dismissing my distrust of his faith with a short verbal slap, as he always did. "What more would you have me do? Reject all I know is true?"

"No," I replied, stumbling for words.

"Is not faith enough?"

"Faith in what?"

"In God, of course! That He will triumph over all evil, in His own time."

"Well, I suppose."

"Good, Benjamin. Very good."

"But I wonder, sometimes, if your blind…"

"Obedience?" he said, offering to fill in my broken sentence.

"Servitude," I countered. "I have often wondered if that does not blind you, or limit you."

"And just how would it do that?"

"I don't know! But I can tell you resist something you wish to do. I have worked alongside you now for, what? Two years? You taught me well, Hosea, and I have learned a lot – more than you'd wished, perhaps. I know you well enough to see your hesitation."

Something I said made Hosea wince. I cringed at that, not wanting to ever hurt him. But our eyes met as a wave of mist washed over us. Hosea's face beamed as the morning sun. That tender smile erased the frustration I often felt from these debates he pressed me into.

In truth, as closed as he kept his thoughts, Hosea was the closest I ever came to having a father, and I loved him for it.

"You are right, Benjamin. I have resisted a charge He has placed upon me. In truth, I didn't think you were ready. I didn't know if I was ready, either. But you are right. We cannot just stand by… and the time of my protecting you is over. We must act!"

He stood with sudden determination. "I have an errand for you, or rather, a mission. Your mission."

His changed demeanor mystified and frightened me. I had never seen him act this way before.

"One you are well-suited for," Hosea reassured me. "Indeed, you were born to do this, among other things."

Hosea took a deep breath, gazing long upon me before saying, "Jonah."

I don't know what I did then – a twitch of the eye, a wrinkled brow, or dismayed mumble. I doubt I did anything he could see. But my heart quaked at the Dove's name, at a long-held need yet unfulfilled, and Hosea sensed it.

"You do know him, don't you?" he asked in a voice of confidence.

I nodded, drifting in contemplation. It no longer surprised me what secrets Hosea deciphered.

"From the Damascus campaign," I explained, my voice little more than a murmur.

"Oh, yes, a brilliant triumph. Too bad it could not last."

Thunder rocked the fog-covered trees. Stones quaked under our feet. I took a deep breath, reining in my fear to ponder these events. Their timing seemed more than coincidence.

"Yes," said Hosea, catching his thoughts as well. "I need you to go visit him, check upon him. You can do that."

The last sounded like both a question and command. I nodded, as I did to anything Hosea asked of me, though it left me somewhat conflicted. The desire to learn from Jonah remained within my heart, but the prospect of leaving Bethel troubled me. I was comfortable there. I felt needed.

"He keeps a vineyard, in Aphek," reflected Hosea. There was sadness in his voice, and yet a touch of frustration, perhaps even anger. "You could walk there, I believe. You might even enjoy it."

I had no idea what to think of that. True, it was not far to Aphek, an old city about half the way to Samaria, though more toward the coast. After that day's downpour, I felt sure this month of Ziv had shared the last of its rain, so the trip was not too daunting to contemplate… though so little had I traveled outside of Jeroboam's entourage, I really had no idea what was required. Still, some things about the request made little sense. Pulling together my wits, I asked, "What should I check for?"

Hosea's answer was just as sharp.

"I don't know. Anything, everything. Just watch him. Stay with him."

The vast possibilities of such a vague command stunned me. I sat there, pondering it, and heard myself muttering, "For how long?"

"As long as it takes."

"As what takes?"

Hosea offered a brief, almost painful smile. "Help him, Benjamin, with whatever he's doing."

That undefined answer shook me to the core. "You don't know?"

"Of course not!"

That I had not expected. Hosea always knew what shaped the world!

"Then why send me away?" I blurted out.

Hosea frowned at my open shock. "You were with him, but learned nothing?"

"Well… yes," I defended myself. Pride forced that weak protest, though I doubt it fooled Hosea. He recognized my hollow words.

"I see," he mumbled. "Well then, I will help you. Jonah is a true roeh – a seer. God has spoken to him since childhood. Yes, that itself is rare, but Jonah also sees the future, when he prays. He shares in God's plan."

Like lightning in the darkness, at once I understood the great concealed value Jeroboam had placed in the Dove. Jonah had been told by God how to defeat his enemies! No wonder his armies were always victorious!

Still, I couldn't help questioning how that was even possible. How could anyone talk to a silent, invisible, imaginary being?

I almost asked Hosea about it, until I looked into his eyes and saw no doubts of any kind. And I wondered, was this how Hosea seemed to know so much? Was he in contact with God, too?

"Yet the Lord has a special task remaining for Jonah," Hosea continued, "a dangerous one. True, we face the coming darkness, but we are not forgotten! Quite the contrary, Benjamin! We are blessed to see the Lord's plan begin! For this, the world's great cycle of salvation, will start with a general, a prophet at war with his own heart. Here, in the tiny land of Canaan."

With inquisitive eyes, Hosea watched those words sink into my troubled mind.

"Jonah?"

"Yes! He will bear the brunt of a dark, brutal storm, and to be honest, I don't know if he can weather it. He may suffer, even worse than did Job… and if he falls, all Israel may fall with him. That's why you must go. Jonah must not fail, Benjamin! He needs our help. So, I want him to have a friend nearby. You."

I had no idea what to think of all this. Dizzy with all these ideas, I pondered the stories I had heard of Job, a righteous man tortured by the Evil One, stripped of his family, health, and possessions, and all with God's permission.

That chilled my heart.

Hosea wanted me to join in the torture of Job? To just walk right into it? With the fate of Israel hanging in the balance?

It made no sense! How could anyone possibly sacrifice so much?

I was about to find out.

Chapter 10
Considerations

It's amazing how you can pack food to last days, you can wrap your feet to ward off blisters and jagged rocks, you can even pick just the right oil for guarding your hair and skin against the sun. You can prepare for just about everything a journey may throw at you, except the treachery of man.

My difficulties started about a hundred steps outside the Bethel walls. For my safety Hosea arranged for me to travel with a group of merchants bound for Aphek. But once the gates pulled shut, the caravan betrayed his trust and turned north for Samaria. I protested, to no avail.

It was hard, deciding to go alone. I had never done anything like that before. But the northern path would have taken me far out of my way, and since Hosea feared I should hurry, I didn't want to let him down. And despite the threat of thieves and such, I knew I could do this. You see, without searching for it – perhaps without even really knowing it – in my two years with Hosea, I had found a quiet strength hidden inside me, and a joy for helping others. It awakened within my heart new independence, a sense of initiative, and the budding confidence that I could actually accomplish good things with my own two hands. So I left the caravan behind and started off alone down the western road to Jonah's home – a simple wanderer in my patched tunic and sandals, my few belongings bound within a goatskin sack.

I'll admit I was somewhat scared by the twisting crags and rocky slopes of Ephraim's ancient mountains. I had never traveled there before. For the first hour or so I crept around threatening shadows and hid at every snap and whistle, fearing an ambush by robbers or lions. But as I made my way west, passing scrub hills, cedar groves, rambling brooks, and combed pasture, I drew reassurances from my many travels among Jeroboam's entourage. This walk really did not seem much different; the landscapes certainly weren't. As I convinced myself of that, I pushed ahead with less fear, my eyes wide open. Blue skies lit my way, and fresh springs frequented my path. A few clouds rolled in from the Great Sea, upon winds that sometimes threw dust into my eyes, but these did not discourage me. It was not long before I, the reluctant traveler, found myself blessing Hosea for sending me on this journey.

Ah, how lovely is Canaan in the rising sun! The memories thrill me still! As the uplifting winds invigorated my lungs, so did the rocky gorges thrill my heart, rippling and flaring in poetic design. Between them, I saw all manners of creatures at peace in the pageantry of our grassy fields and wooded slopes. It calmed me, and yet exhilarated me.

Strolling in awe through all these natural wonders, I pondered anew all my questions of God, and why He made us. For here was majestic evidence I had ignored oh so long. Indeed, marveling at the breadth and depth of His world at work, I began to envy the peasant shepherds and tillers I once brushed aside at the palace or Bethel's temple walls. And I had thought them vagabond? Oh, to be a shepherd, living each hour in the center of His glory!

I met two that morning, tending flocks on lands that had been in their families since the twelve tribes first settled Canaan. Both left their sheep to offer me bread and wine in their tents, for the nearby streams were somewhat rank, as the stains of man may sometimes leave them. Though my mission lay before me, I welcomed their company and shared news of Bethel, for tales are always in demand. I left their company refreshed.

It still surprises me how soon that trail passed by. As the hills merged in my memory and the heat of the day rose, I turned northwest curious at just how little commerce there was between Bethel and Aphek. I met only two farmers along my way, both with room in their carts for a young passenger, but one was heading south, and the other was soon to rest. Thus I went on by myself, singing what songs I had learned from Hosea, dwelling all the while on these new feelings moving my heart.

A strange stamina filled me. The time for my afternoon rest came and went, but I did not heed it. With the last rays of the sun, I paused for a meal of wild cucumbers, onions, and a honey-sweet melon, all gathered from along the trail, plus some beans Hosea provided. Under that flaming sunset I washed my hands with cool water from a shaded well and drank my fill. Then I went on, the full moon my guide.

I look back at it now ashamed that I did not see the Lord moving within my every step. Oh, the temptation to sleep moved me, to be sure. I had many opportunities to rest my head. But each time I considered it, I felt an urgent need to hurry on, to not be late… though for what I could not guess.

Early that night I encountered Amorlot, son of Josanah, a pleasant shepherd who had cast his tent along the road to await his brother's arrival from the plains east of Shechem. Amorlot's long tassels and many-colored cloak told of his wealth, blessings of the Most High. I paused to drink wine with him, thanking him for the rest and nourishment. He bid me to stay, and when I refused, he gave me his staff to guard my way.

May the Lord ever bless his witness.

As the night grew old, a weary ache settled into my step. The trail soon led me by the first of two villages that had sprung up like weeds between gruff mountain ribs. Its streets echoed with a vibrant passion for life, though more to the temple harlots than of Hosea's heart. That wasn't for me. But as I reached the second settlement, an angry blister broke where my sandals rubbed against my right big toe. Burdened by pain and the weariness that stalks all untested travelers, I looked with longing at that village for a suitable corner in which to rest. The sleeping inlet appealed to my need for quiet. I gazed down its still, moonlit streets and considered seeking sanctuary, only to hear the call of a brook just over the hill. Stepping soft, I sought out the stream and sank my feet beneath its chilly water. That calming embrace relieved my stiffness, my weary muscles, even my blistered toe. And so, after a welcome time in its care, I walked on.

As day broke along the foothills of Ephraim, my heavy feet approached a worn stone fortress on the distant horizon. Nothing appealed to me more. Straightening my sore, stiff back, I looked past drooping eyelids and almost prayed that dusty town was Aphek, for I needed that. Never in my life had I walked so long or so far. I didn't think I could take much more.

It was in that state of emptiness that the Lord spoke to me for the first time in my life, saying but one word: "Run."

Had anyone else made such an order, even old Jeroboam, I doubt I would have listened. But this was of the Lord, and even if my mind did not recognize His presence at first, my renewed heart surged at His command. Girding my hem, I soon found myself flowing from a stumbling hobble to a ragged skip to a haphazard sprint. Somehow I found energy anew to cross the fields of tall grass providing my straight path to the town. Only as I reached the fortress – slumping to the ground for breath at its walls – did I grasp the significance of what had happened.

Looking back over all these long, heartbreaking years, I wonder if my obstinate mind would have recognized His voice at all had I not been so weary, my thoughts so empty. But after two years of Hosea's instruction, after two days of walking in His creation, there was a growing awareness in my mind and heart. As I leaned against that ancient wall, drawing strength from the stone, I guessed even then that perhaps, just perhaps, the Lord had prodded me on my long, exhausting march just to open my mind to His word. Maybe only in that drained state could I truly recognize His call for what it was. But my analytical self, the side that still listened to Hosea's wisdom, suggested His words would have reached me no matter how I served Him. That argument was simple: The Lord needed me to run, and so it spurred me onward.

Funny, isn't it? How silly it is to try to figure out why the Lord does what He does, as if we could ever understand His ways? And even if we could, would that knowledge truly make any difference? I now tend to think such curiosity does more harm than good. Many a time I've witnessed strong-hearted men put such great effort into debating the intent of God's will, they would actually forget to do God's will. They lose their way in all the interpretations and juxtapositions. But I was too young then to realize that could happen. The very idea that God would actually need me seemed so novel.

Indeed, the concept of God seemed novel. For I still did not truly believe.

My first view of Aphek told a sad truth of our time. Like nearly all cities in Israel, Aphek cowered within a wall of white limestone many times patched and rebuilt. Its southern arms stretched nearly twice my height with its serrated parapet, joining at a gate that looked to be twice again as tall and once again wider around the foundation. Twin doors opened outward, each made of various woods layered with rusted iron.

One sentry stood watch at the gate, armored with little more than an aged leather cloak and iron cap. He had the manner of someone who cared little for his life, slouching in boredom against the rough stone frame.

Only as I approached did I realize I had no idea where the Dove lived. So, I asked the vagabond guard. He sneered at me as if it were beneath him to answer someone a third his age, but when he realized I would not leave without some information, he roused himself from his nest to point a crusty finger not into the city, but towards the eastern slopes. There I spied a small cluster of brick houses and mud-blotched tents cast along a trickling brook. I recognized this place from past travels: grazing land for shepherds traveling to and from Aphek.

"There? Are you sure?" I pressed. The guard nodded, then turned his head aside to spit. Deciding I need not know what he dared chew, I gave my thanks and hobbled upon bruised feet toward the stream.

The brook this day proved wide and shallow, lined with round stones sparkling in the morning light. Beyond it lay a ring of tents encircling seven rectangular, single-room structures within square lots, cradled by mud-brick walls open to the street. No one was about. In the foothills I saw shepherds and farmers, but the village appeared deserted.

At that moment I recalled the Dove's interest in vineyards. That thought led me to the end of the path, where I spied a small grove of olive trees. A woman worked among the thick, gnarled trunks, filling the girded hem of her dark blue robe with trimmed branches. She looked beautiful among the sprouting limbs and white blossoms, with locks of curly scarlet hair hanging loose about the thin blue veil covering her face. The morning sun glowed behind her, casting her image within a fiery blaze that ignited my heart.

The distant barks of a watchdog split the serene silence, but I paid it no mind. She did, however, and looked upon me for the first time, her brown eyes open and unafraid.

I no doubt appeared somewhat foolish, staring at her so, but I had never imagined hair of such color or brilliance. I suspect Jeroboam's wives would have died for so vibrant a treasure.

"May the Lord be with you," she offered. Her voice bounced with melodic joy. It drew my smile from me.

"And with you," I stammered.

"Are you visiting us among the sheep?"

"One in particular. Do you know Jonah, son of Amittai?"

"This is his grove. Though he would not claim it, you know."

She shifted a bit, lifting her hem higher to not spill the toils of her work. Watching, I could not help finding her fascinating in a, well, a womanish way. So I asked, "Would he claim you?"

I know, I know; that was a stupid thing to say. I tend to utter such things when I'm weary or around women. But if it bothered her, she didn't show it. She just laughed, a sound that will ever stand as one of the Lord's most joyous creations.

"Oh, no," she said, stepping toward me. Her eyes danced in the shadows, but as she spoke, their light dimmed. "I am Pelagos, daughter of Matthew, the shipbuilder of Joppa. That explains my name, you see. I was wife to David of Aphek, a fine shepherd, but he was slain by a lion a year ago. Our house was there," she pointed across the street, "facing the sun."

Her frank admission left me tongue-tied. It took what seemed minutes for me to say, "I am sorry."

"You need not pity me, for the Lord has given me shelter. It was hard at first, I will not deny. My love had no family, and neither do I, mostly, and by then my dowry was gone. We had struggled through our short lives, he and I. But with my lamenting's end the elders gave me a small bag of gold from the tabernacle, and Jonah offered me his servant's room, for he had no need of it. Our home they bestowed to a needy family."

"So, then…." I stumbled to sound intelligent before such a beautiful lady. "You serve Jonah?"

"No, he will not allow such things. But I do indeed help him about his grove, for the trees need constant tending, and with his sorrows, he seems less inclined each day to do so. Still, a strong man of God he is. May the Lord bless him always!"

Her tale was warm but confusing. "What bothers the Dove?"

"His heart, I guess. He shares nothing of it with me, or anyone, I believe." She stopped, her brow lifting in recognition. "You might as well ask him, for there he is."

Turning, I saw a crouching man in a dusty tunic step from the cedar door open at the last house, his uncovered hair waving in the breeze. He looked about, kneeling even closer to the earth as he closed the door. Then he slid into the shadows.

This confused me, being not at all what I had expected.

"More the manner of a thief," I thought aloud.

"You don't know him if you think that!" she snapped. "Though I admit, I don't know what he's doing. But go, catch up with him. I am sure he will speak with you."

That struck me strange, for in my soul, I too felt moved to hurry, so I ran, shouting his name. As my voice echoed down the path, the Dove slowed, then dropped to his seat in the dirt.

"Why, Lord?" he shouted. "Why?"

That's how I came upon him, his black hair hanging in the sand, his graying beard brushing his knees.

"Welcome, Jonah," I said, almost stuttering the words, as I found it hard to catch my breath.

"I know why you are here," the Dove spat. "Hosea flexes his muscles."

Another strange twist! "He worries about you!"

"Yes," Jonah countered, dragging the word across the sand as if such stretching enhanced its meaning. "Well, he has his own punishment, as have I."

Exhaling with deep resignation, the Dove rose to his feet, then motioned me forward to his home. "Come on, Benjamin. You might as well share my table."

The very idea awakened my dormant hunger; he couldn't return home quick enough for me. But this did not overcome my curiosity. Before he could step too far ahead, I decided to ask, "What were you doing here?"

"Getting bolder, are you?"

Pausing to consider my question, Jonah tried to shield his eyes from the rising sun, but the effort left him even more frustrated. He bent his brow to the earth and spat, "Or do you accuse me?"

"Why should I accuse you, lord?" I pondered aloud. Or of what? I would have added, had I dared speak it.

For a brief moment his eyes stabbed at me. "Never call me that," he stressed. "I am no one's lord. Not even my own, it seems."

He strode into the yard beside the grove. Following, I sought a last look at Pelagos, but she had turned her gorgeous brown orbs from us to tend the trees, having dumped her trimmings alongside an old stone olive press.

"Where is your vineyard?" I asked, hoping to lighten his mood. It failed.

"Gone, abandoned." He cast his left hand to the western horizon. "I have no heart for it."

Walking into his home, we passed jars of olive oil beneath worn scythes and hoes hanging from wall pegs. Offering a blessing to God at the entryway, Jonah left his sandals on the hardened sod, then beckoned me to follow.

I gazed with sadness upon his quarters, the images dimmed by the faint light creeping through his thatch roof and window lattice. He had ample storage carved into his walls, but outside of a glistening oak kinnor, the shelves held but a small pipe, a ragged blanket, a few loaves of barley bread, and other odds and ends. Tiny jars of seasonings, a knife, three bronze cups... things of that sort. Along the floor sat a few clay bowls and pans beside covered water urns.

Here was a man who had led armies, counseled kings, dictated peace accords… and he lived like a peasant!

The Dove glanced at me with swords in his eyes, but he girded whatever burdened his heart. "Bare your feet and rest," he commanded. "We will eat together."

Happy to slip free of my sandals and traveling sack, I walked across the hard sod to the raised platform across from his door. There I sat with my back to his fire pit. At my left elbow I found a nest of bugs burrowed between the bricks of the wall behind me. I scooted away.

Drawing water from the largest urn, the Dove poured it within the basin and knelt. "May the Lord bless all who give of themselves in this house," he said before washing first my hands, then my bruised feet. My aching toes wallowed in pleasure, and yet it was unnerving, being waited on by such a prophet. I, a simple servant of Hosea! How did I let such a thing happen?

"And may He bless my master," I put forth, reaching for the bowl.

Jonah's snarl stopped me.

"I am no one's master," he growled.

Washing his hands, the Dove emptied the basin out a window. He then handed me his loaf of bread, dipped a cup within an urn, and set it before me. He drew himself another cup of water, gathered the knife and a small jar, and joined me.

"Bow with me please," he asked, in preparation for prayer. When I complied, he lowered his eyes, breathed deep, and in reverence whispered:

Blessed is the Lord!
Blessed is the Flame that lights our path,
Blessed is the Word that thrills our hearts,
Blessed is the Hand that cradles our souls.

Oh Lord, we come together before You
To feed that Flame,
To spread Your Word,
To share Your love,
As You have with the tribes of Israel.
We ask for Your wisdom and blessing
To do what You would have us do,
To go where You would have us go,
To serve You in all things.
To the God of Abraham, Isaac, and Jacob we pray,
Amen.

"Amen," I agreed, touched by his words. They hung in my mind, renewing so many thoughts and feelings I had experienced in my journey to find Jonah. But as I considered these things again, I found the Dove gazing at me with strange, searching eyes, as if he pondered just what moved me. So I whispered, "That was beautiful."

Furious storms spread across his brow. He snorted as one facing a dark affront, only to force it aside, cast out by this host's demanded courtesy.

"All words of the heart are a blessing to the Lord," Jonah muttered, looking away. He broke me off a piece of bread and took one for himself, then poured on a touch of olive oil and ate.

"That," he added between chews, "is but my prayer of gathering."

Even with that dry yet tempting chunk of brown bread in my hands, I just sat there, like a cold, hard rock. I feared to say anything, not knowing what I had done to offend him. To my relief Pelagos entered, her bare feet slipping soft across the floor as she brought first Jonah, then myself a couple of fresh apricots.

"Too bad the grapes are not ripe," she remarked, not noticing Jonah's bridled fury.

"These are fine," I said to thank her. Yet with my words, the Dove must have reached his limit. Looking like some nightmarish dragon, he threw his head back not unlike a snake charmer's pet and snapped, "Confound it, woman, you are not my wife!"

I cringed at his anger, but she was not rattled.

"No, and I doubt I would want to be," she said. "And such talk will never change things. But you have a guest, so you need the fruit."

Challenged, Jonah returned his gaze to the bread. "He can eat what I have."

"That's a cruel insult. You should do better yourself."

"I have what I need." Jonah rolled an apricot between his fingers as if analyzing it for blemishes and finding it wanting. "How did you get this, anyway?"

Her eyes sharpened. "I traded some of your olives to Amorath. How else would I?" She stood over him as if waiting for more, but the Dove never looked up. That seemed to soften her. "Come now. I think you have kept your misery long enough. There is plenty of cropping yet to do, and if you're of no mind to eat, help me."

Jonah mumbled something, but Pelagos paid no attention to it. "It would be good for you to get out," she added.

Too foolish to realize I should have remained a rock, I nodded my agreement. That earned me a stare strong enough to curdle milk, but finding himself cornered, Jonah gave in and followed the lady to the groves. So, I girded my hunger and weariness, spending the morning helping Pelagos and the reluctant Dove. The effort did seem to ease his spirits. Once the last of his anger faded, Jonah went over each tree with expert care, pointing out which branches needed trimming, clearing away worms and locusts, and fertilizing the earth with peat and mulch. In such works his mind displayed its ever-present strength, unbent by the festering frustrations I had witnessed in his home. That gave me hope.

As the midday sun rose, Jonah showed me his storage jars of the last season's harvest, which were kept in shadows beside the shed along his north wall. It was there that Pelagos made her quarters, in a simple brick room not much different from Jonah's. Then he bid me sleep in his home as he rested. I agreed, for working among the trees in the growing heat had renewed my weariness. Thinking little of the consequences, I welcomed the ragged blanket he laid upon the floor and dozed.

When I awoke, he was gone.

I do not know why, but as I gazed around his quarters, I grew fearful. The words of Hosea cornered me, imploring me to act, but I had no idea what to do.

Gathering my sandals, I charged into the street. Dust flew in the breeze. The red sky setting towards the sea suggested a clear night, but the wind spoke of storms.

"Jonah!" I shouted.

The neighbors must have thought I was crazy. A few stood in the roadway shaking rugs, while others gardened or worked on their houses. All gave me puzzled glances.

A growing fear spread over me. I ran to the grove, searching in haste, but he was not there. I went to the shed, where Pelagos was cooking a stew for our supper, no doubt. To my inquiry she replied a surprised "He's not?" and hurried back to his home. There, beside the oil lamp on his one table, lay a piece of goatskin parchment. She picked it up, glanced at the writing, then asked me to read it.

It was good that I could. I read aloud:

Benjamin: Accept my apologies, but I could not stay and let your infantile wisdom twist me around. Go home.

Dear Pelagos. Thank you for all your joy. I have recorded a document in Aphek leaving my family's estate to you. I will not return, so please accept it. You may need to find a mate to keep it, depending on how the elders view this, so hurry it up and get on with your life. But this, at least, is yours. Take care. In the Lord's name, I give you my blessing.

"That sweet old goat," she whispered.

I saw nothing sweet in it. I know I had done many a foolish thing in my life, but did I deserve such an insult? Infantile wisdom indeed!

"That's why he had me sleep," I thought aloud, "so he could escape." Yet for the life of me, I could not see why he needed to. Pelagos also thought that surprising.

"Well," she considered, "what should we do?"

"Do?" I had no idea, although Hosea had left me no options. "I guess I will go after him."

An image returned to me then, of the setting sun and the distant sea.

"Your father was a shipbuilder," I thought aloud. Probably a sailor as well, one who on some distant journey had met this young woman's mother. That would explain the vibrant hair, and her eyes. But I was losing my focus. "Did Jonah know him?"

"I think not. I never knew Jonah before David's death. But I don't know for sure."

She left some room for doubt, though her tone sounded certain. Still, my heart counseled me otherwise. It might explain why Jonah came to her aid.

"Even so, I think that is the way," I decided with sudden conviction. "There is a road west, from Aphek to the sea. I will find him there."

She hesitated. "I don't understand, Benjamin. Why did he leave? And why do you chase him?"

Shadows spread throughout the room. Her innocence glowed in the dim light, a vision of loveliness like few I had ever seen.

"Something dismays him," I stumbled to say, wishing I had a better answer. "I had hoped you might know what that is, for I do not. But I… well, I am instructed to help him. I've been sent to do this, by Hosea."

"Who?"

"Hosea." I started to explain that, but then the whole story seemed complicated and confusing. There appeared no way to talk of this without speaking of faith, and God, and I didn't really feel like doing that. Not yet. But looking into her glorious, waiting eyes, I had to say something, so I sputtered, "I don't know what I am to do, but I must do something."

That probably left her more baffled than before, though I could not help it. Yet her response left me far most puzzled.

"If that must be," she said, "then may the Lord guide you. And may you return to me when you are done, for I have grown fond of you, Benjamin, though I know little more than your name, and not even all of that. Will you consider this?"

As the Lord hears my heart, I swear, a greater temptation I have never faced. Such feelings as I've little known swept over me, swaying me. A portion of my heart longed to forget the Dove and remain at her side. Indeed, I will always wonder what I would have done, had she asked me then and there to stay. But the need to see my mission through was equally strong. My faith, infantile though it might be, allowed no other action.

So, considering everything, I gave her my word. With great joy she slipped out and prepared me a basket of figs, olives, apricots, and bread. "I bet he didn't think to take food," she explained. When that was done, she bid me go with it and the kinnor, which she thought might give the Dove joy. Then she removed her veil and kissed me, which gave me joy.

Thus was I off on my second night journey, one much happier than the first. And much shorter.

Chapter 11
Free will

Making a faceguard of some of Pelagos's spare cloth, I forced my weary frame into a downhill run to Aphek. The light of the moon made picking my footing easier, but my toes still cried out in their misery. The city itself was an unsettling sight. Parapet torches cast daunting shadows about the walls, and while the gates had not yet closed for the night, the dark streets did not look friendly. Thank God, I had no need to see for myself. Circling about the walls, I came to Aphek's western gate, where a rutted trail ran to the horizon. I had not gone far before my lungs ached more than my legs, and so I rested only a stone's throw from the city. Yet that proved enough. Across two hills I saw him shuffling west, to the sea.

Jonah must have heard me, for as I pushed myself forward once more, he cried out, "Why, Lord? Why?"

Seeing him gave me no pleasure. Perhaps I was frustrated, dealing with his simmering anger, or the increasing difficulties of my mission, or by my exhaustion. Perhaps I had just lost faith in the Dove, whom I once honored so. But I guess it little matters now. I moved on, reaching his side, and fell to my knees, my mind muddled by pain. In truth, I waivered then on the brink of physical and mental collapse, though Jonah little cared.

"Why can't you leave me alone?" the Dove snapped.

"I have no choice," I said between gasps.

His eyes flared, as if ready to pronounce some foul judgment. I did nothing, mainly because I was just too weary. But perhaps that was best, for my exhaustion soon tempered his rage. Or maybe it goaded him on.

"Very well then," Jonah said with open reluctance. "Come on. I plan to walk this night, and I will not wait."

Between breaths, I fought to lift myself, but my legs and back rebelled. Worse, the soles of my feet felt damp with more than sweat.

"Where will you go?" I said, hoping to stall him.

"Why tease me? I see through your deception."

I almost asked just what he saw, for I could make out nothing from all this. Instead, I tried something else.

"Are you hungry?"

That made Jonah pause. So I asked again.

"Yes," he allowed. "What of it?"

"I have food. Pelagos sent it."

"Did she?" He looked to the moon, as if debating just what he should do, then took the bait. "That meddling woman probably sent irregular figs," Jonah mumbled, taking a seat in the dirt. "No matter. Let me see it."

Pleased that I had at last succeeded with him, I pushed myself over to his side and unloaded the weights of my burden: her water sack and evening meal, the kinnor, my travel bag, and my rod. When I had it all sorted and settled, Jonah prayed and broke bread, his every act one of aggravated impatience.

"You push yourself too hard," I offered, hoping to unlock his burden.

"Only to keep ahead of trouble, meddlesome one." He took a bite of barley bread softened with honey – the last item Pelagos had tossed into my bag – then allowed a brief, shallow smile. "Life is hard."

That sounded too much like one of Hosea's verbal tests, so I gave an answer that would have made him smile: "Thus we have the Lord to guide us."

This did not work on the Dove.

"Oh, yes," he mocked. "Divine guidance. You know such

words when you hear them?"

"Sometimes," I allowed, thinking back on my morning run. "Sometimes, I am not sure."

"Why not?"

That hit me hard. All at once I felt menaced and harried, wondering just how many of my doubts I dared open before this anguished man of God.

"Well, He is not always so direct."

"Why not?"

"How should I know?"

My defiance broke the night before I could restrain my tongue. I cringed, fearing how the Dove would respond. But Jonah took heart in the answer, seeing in that some shred of honesty he could accept.

"Yes, yes. How should any of us? For that is His way. Even if His messages were written in the sand, they would not always be so clear. Sometimes there are mysteries in His works that man may never understand, mysteries that challenge all we believe in. And then, sometimes, the evil one impersonates our Lord, to deceive us."

His words took a stern tone. The idea of such mysteries reminded me of Jonah's own actions that morning.

"Why do you speak so?" I pressed. "What troubles you?"

He stared at me with eyes shifting from cold accusation to modest inquiry, as if the two sides fought to control him. At its end emerged the compassion I had cherished long ago.

"Do you not know?" he whispered. "Truly?"

"Hosea sent me to help you. He said nothing else."

With those words, a wall broke inside Jonah. He leaned over to hug me, both strengthening and resting upon my shoulder. Unaccustomed to such things, I gave him what warmth I could, pondering how I might console him. Then I remembered the kinnor.

His eyes brightened as I brought it forward. He must have forgotten I carried it.

"A beautiful instrument," I said from experience. Most such harps had seven to ten slivers of sheep gut strings, with a body often little more than a cedar circle with a flat end, where the stretched lines tightened. But the Dove's kinnor offered fourteen strings on a gold-lined frame of oak.

"Do you play?" I said, not realizing then how stupid a question that was.

"So some say," he muttered, taking the instrument. "It was a gift from Jeroboam, when he first campaigned to regain the lands of Solomon and make a name for himself. Oh, the arrogance of kings! He should have spent his time ensuring a good successor to his throne, so that beasts like Menahem could not get their claws on it."

The Dove paused, then lowered his head and examined his gift. Thankful for a break in his melancholy, I prodded him further: "Could you play something?"

With a sly smile, Jonah turned his attention to the strings, making some adjustments I did not understand. "These require great care, especially in this weather. Their tones can go off so easily," he said. Then the Dove lifted the harp's curved back to his shoulder, positioned his left hand at the base of its anchoring rod, and began to play.

The notes etched themselves in the wind… slow, penetrating sounds of joy and sorrow, triumph and defeat. As a melody developed, gushing forth as a river would grow from adjoining brooks, the tale adopted a poignant flavor. Then Jonah added his voice, singing:

Why?
Why should I worry so much
When You are in my life?
Your touch brings me so much joy,
And cleanses all of my strife.
Yet each day I awake with temptations anew,
Creating fears that are hard to subdue.
And sometimes I fall into traps of despair,
Wandering far from Your loving care.

Strange though it was, the Dove sang in a multitude of tones set to very irregular rhythms. His tune flowed like none of the songs I knew, and yet, I rather liked it.

Oh, Lord, I'm so foolish and blind!
Excuses to stray are so easy to find.
I haven't the reason, or I haven't the time,
Or I try, by myself, to make all things mine.
But I fail!
I always fail!
And I run back to Your care,
Only to find You've always been there,
For me! Yes, for me!

Oh, Lord, give me strength to do all things in You,
To keep my heart Holy, my mind ever true.
And should I face the traps of despair,
Remind me that You'll always be there
For me!
Yes, for me!

The music drew a positive response at its end, and yet the words seemed built around a constant, grinding challenge.

"Is that what bothers you?" I inquired. "The traps of despair?"

"So it was when I wrote this, but even then, my pains run deep… deeper than that. Have you heard of Isaiah?"

The name seemed familiar, and yet I could not pin any memory down. "Wait," I urged him. Then it hit me, something Hosea had once said of Jerusalem. "He is at Solomon's Temple, I believe. A young man of great vision."

"Just barely older than you are," said the Dove, "yet draped in the cloak of the Lord. I have seen him in my sight." I must have looked confused at that point, for Jonah grew irritated and said, "My visions. From Yahweh! In that, I saw Isaiah. And heard him. He has foreseen Israel's fall to Assyria."

I waited for more, having heard similar talk at the palace. Jeroboam's staff had dismissed such rants from prophets, calling them pots just a little too broken to mend. But Hosea's teachings gave me a foundation for such dark thoughts.

"Did not Elijah say such things?" I said.

"Indeed," said Jonah, encouraged by that tidbit. "And Amos."

Even so, I scoffed. "But that was a long time ago." Before I was even born!

The Dove seemed somewhat amused, but he went on. "And I have foreseen hints of this. It is inevitable, and ghastly, envisioning such devilry by the Assyrians. A gruesome fate for our people, Benjamin… so evil, truly, that it makes me want to do anything I can to stop it. At least, I mean to try."

I nodded, though such talk unsettled me. Jonah made a heartfelt admission, but it seemed a little too easy. As if something was left out.

"How?" I inquired.

"Yes, how." He glanced first to the glowing moon, then the eastern hills, where a chorus of barking dogs awakened the night. "I have spent most of my life directing our armies against them, clearing our frontiers, rebuilding our land. What else can I do?"

Something prodded me. I gazed into the Dove's dark eyes and asked, "What do you run from?"

He stiffened. "I flee nothing! I go of my own choosing."

"Where?"

"I'm not sure. But I must leave."

"Why?"

"Why?" He seemed dumbfounded. "You look at me and can ask that?"

I looked at him, probing Jonah for faults, excuses, or lies. Outside of his frayed emotions, and a tiny bit more gray in his hair, the Dove looked much the same as he had two-some years before. His beard was longer, of course, but his tunic looked little changed… perhaps a bit dirtier.

"What should I see?" I finally asked.

Jonah gazed at me with eyes spread wider than broken eggs. "You taunt me again! You… a cub of a man! What do you know of the Lord?"

If I had not been so tired, such an attack by such a prophet would have sent me cowering to the depths of the nearest well.

But I was exhausted, and headstrong, a wounded soul comforted by the night. That made me even more stubborn.

"Enough," I stammered. "I know who He is."

That admission shocked me. For the first time, I had declared what Hosea always wanted to hear. And the strangest thing was, I meant it. There would be no more denials, no more backing down.

And yet, my students, I had a long way to go… a lifetime of lessons before me.

Jonah did not pause his attack. "You recognize Him when He speaks?"

Those words shook to me in ways Jonah surely did not intend.

"Twice you have asked me that!" I spat. "What is it that troubles you?"

The Dove stood there, staring at me. I could not tell if it showed anger, frustration, or fear. So I took a different path: "What does He want you to do?"

That hit near the mark.

"I do not know who is behind it," he whispered.

"Behind what?"

"My vision! My damnable destiny!"

Words poured from his lips as wine from a smashed urn.

"How could anyone minister to those devils?" the Dove spat. "Masters of evil – that is what they are! They deserve no grace! Betray my own people? How could anyone make such a choice? With what those, those dogs have done, the evils they have committed…. the evils they will commit! No! It cannot be. He cannot ask it! I cannot do it!"

Caution held my tongue. The Dove collapsed in the sand, sobbing, broken by his torment. I began to lay a comforting hand about his shoulder, but I had no idea how he would take it. His rage seemed chaotic, unpredictable. Yet something had to be done.

"What…." I hesitated, struggling over what to say. "What has He asked of you?"

"Nineveh," Jonah whispered.

It is hard to think of one word more hated by our people.

Nineveh! One of many capitals of Assyria, but the most important, for it was perhaps the largest of all cities, the trading capital of the Gentiles, the bulwark of the Assyrian treasury and butcher's army, all that and more… the center of the unholy.

I was terrified of what this could mean, but I managed to voice, "What of it?"

The Dove rose up, his tears cleaning damp trails in the dust of his cheeks.

"I am to go to Nineveh," he growled. "Warn them the Lord has beheld their evil. That judgment is imminent.

"To Nineveh!" he cried out. "Can you believe it? The Assyrian Empire is collapsing. I have seen it with my own eyes! You saw it in the plains of Damascus! It could disappear in our lifetime! Can you imagine how glorious that would be?

"Yet it is a phantom hope, for I have foreseen its revival. I have beheld the hand of the demon marching across Israel, destroying Samaria, Bethel… a whole tribe of our people displaced, swept across the world to foreign lands for uncounted generations. Ah, such destruction! Evil rises again, Benjamin, snapping at Babylon, Egypt, Jordan! Even Jerusalem! There is no sanctuary against the slayer's army."

Trembling, he fell to his knees. Water flowed from his eyes.

"And how will it be done?" he wept. "By ministering to Nineveh. By my hands."

I sat there, looking at this man of God consumed by guilt over things he had not yet done, and I knew not what to do. Perhaps it was infantile wisdom that moved me, for I sifted through everything I could recall of Hosea and his teachings, the many arguments and debates, and nothing came to mind – nothing but one simple truth.

"It may be as you said," I offered. "There are mysteries in His works, ones we may never understand… mysteries that challenge all we believe in. Yet they are still His."

"So you were listening," Jonah remarked, drying his eyes before sitting up. "But what if they are not His? What if this vision is of Satan?"

My nerves jerked at that name. Hosea had urged me to never

speak it, as if giving breath to that foul word could rain down corruption. But for the first time, I understood the Dove. A whole series of doors opened within my mind, each releasing a monster I had no desire to see, or believe.

"Has your vision ever lied to you before?" I put it to him.

The Dove granted me that, shaking his head negative. "It is the Lord's gift," he admitted. "But could it be tainted by the evil one? Could I be misled? Mistaken? I need only one test for that – would our Lord have any reason to wish Nineveh's survival?"

I knew that answer, at least how Jonah would tell it. Such redemption would give the Lord a tool for punishing Israel, as prophesied.

I witnessed painful remorse settle over him. His eyes turned cold and black as coal. His voice became the tongue of doom itself.

"You may struggle with this, Benjamin. Still, you are young, and have not seen their devilry. I have.

"There is a pillar, a marker outside the ruins of a town east of Golan. I have seen it, written from the time of my father's father. This the pillar says: 'Thus fall the enemies of Ashurnasirpal II. I have destroyed them, torn down their wall, and burned the town with fire; I caught the survivors and impaled them on stakes in front of their homes. Pillars of skulls I placed at their gates, and fed their corpses to dogs, pigs…'"

He stopped to ponder this. I hung on his words, paralyzed by morbid fascination.

"I am sorry," the Dove whispered. "I tried to memorize it, to burn it into my mind so that none would ever forget, yet the very nature of their evil made it impossible. But I recall more: 'I slowly tore off his skin, to another I tore off the hands and limbs, to others the noses, ears, and arms, to many I slit their eyes. The warriors I flayed, and covered their walls with their skins, and placed their heads on poles before the city. Their young men and maidens I burned, and played songs to Ashur as they screamed. The captives I burned with fire; not one was left as a hostage.'"

Jonah wept anew, then shook his head to clear away the terror of that stone.

"And this is how it still is – or would be." He pointed a stern finger right at the tip of my dusty nose. "You heard it from the lips of their troops outside Damascus. Torture is their creed, their ambition."

Yes, I had heard the dark words of their battle songs. Even in defeat. But I could not admit it. I sat there, unmoving, overwhelmed by the carved boastings of a dead Assyrian butcher.

That such people could be allowed to live, much less forgiven….

The Dove gave me a reflective nod, smiling as if he could read my mind and knew I had seen his truth.

"Now, do you understand why I flee? If it is the devil's lure, this dream, then I should step no closer to Nineveh than I am now. I must leave. And if it is the Lord's call…. Well, I will not cause my own people's destruction."

That numbed me. It still does, just thinking about it. I was but an infant in the faith, but Jonah, he was a true prophet. To hear him speak of defying the Lord… I cannot put my thoughts into words.

Strangest of all, I found myself wondering, against all his images of evil, how I could get him to change his mind.

"But if it is the will of the Lord –"

"If it is, then it will be done. But not by my hand."

"But –"

He reared up, towering over me. To my peril, I remembered just how imposing a physical figure the Dove was.

"Those… those devils… are not worthy of grace!" he spat. "Let them burn! That's what I say."

He aimed his hardened gaze at the night sky, its stars fading behind a rising tempest, and made firm his plans. "I'm going on, as far from that place as possible. Do what you will."

His words soon drowned within a whistling wind. At their last echo, I struggled to my feet and changed my life forever.

Chapter 12

Passage

Weary of spirit, my blisters broken and weeping, I forced myself to follow Jonah on a winding trail of wagon ruts and downtrodden weed stocks. He strode west under the moon's silver glow, determined against all things to press on, though in truth I think it was a forced march just to see if I had the heart to keep up. When I didn't falter, he took pity on me and found us shelter under a large knuckle of limestone, or so I thought. In truth, I fell asleep before I fell to the ground. Only as the rising sun awakened me did I see that "boulder" was, in fact, a grim stone obelisk plunged like a dagger into the earth. It marked the border of Philistia, our ancient enemy.

"What are we doing here?" I exclaimed.

A silly thing to say, I know, for I had guessed his destination at Aphek, but my outburst came from a deep-set fear common to my people. Every generation could tell its own war stories of these hated Philistines, each one full of gruesome bloodletting, horrid sacrifices, and idyllic blasphemy. But the Dove gazed with hopeful anticipation to the far horizon, breathing deep the salt sea air.

"Joppa," he announced with no regrets. "Do not worry. You won't be lynched in the streets. Jeroboam's damnable idols won us some friends here. They sell plenty of Joppa's handiwork in Israel. In Judah, too, for that matter."

"You're kidding!"

Jonah laughed. "Where else would Philistine idols come from? But that's only the start of it, Benjamin. You may not know this, but there's growing trade between these people and ours – which always helps those involved forget how much they hate each other."

"That's hard to believe," I whispered. It was even harder to listen to him while my skull throbbed and spasms ripped my spine. The trials of this journey were catching up with me.

"Why? You would have to go to Tyre to find a better port than Joppa. They welcome all travelers here. They need the money, you know. And their plowshares? The best around. Iron's so much better than bronze or bone, and the Joppa metalworkers excel at their craft. That's enough to make you buy from the heathen, isn't it?"

He looked to me with playful eyes, overjoyed to be on his way in this warm morning glow. I stretched and burst a blister on my left heel.

He took my grimace the wrong way.

"Well, you may not think so," allowed Jonah, "but farmers all along these plains would disagree with you. And since we have so few metalworkers of our own – and most of those little worth the effort – we do steady business bringing our goods back to Joppa for sharpening. For all that, they welcome us. What's to fear?"

That may have been true, but it brought me little comfort. Still, the way my body ached, I doubt anything would have soothed my nerves.

"You seem well-versed in Philistia," I mumbled, half-mocking him. The Dove didn't care.

"I have dabbled in these things for years."

That I had not forgotten. All this talk of Joppa only reminded me of Pelagos – her lustrous ruby hair, smooth ivory skin, and earthy eyes, but even more, of her glowing smile and hearty laughter. It's said men on long journeys survived on the dreams of their women, but for me this was new. She was not mine, but I began to fancy her so, and it thrilled me.

Ah, but such dreams were not to be. Indeed, the dream could not thrive within my fears of this foreign land.

Even as the king's aide, my steps beyond Samaria and Bethel proved oh so rare. Now I was leaving my beloved homeland, risking my life, and for what? I had no idea.

No, I take that back. I knew what I was doing. I just had no idea what Jonah was doing.

"You stump me," I said at last. "You vow never to see Nineveh, yet you walk freely into a land just as unholy?"

He turned cold. "The Philistines are nothing like the Assyrians."

"Are they not?" I knew this history. Hosea had taught me well, or so I thought. "Did not our Lord command us to slay all within this land? To not fall prey to their heathen beliefs?"

"That was the Canaanites. The sea peoples came later."

That basic error should have warned me to check my facts, if error it was. But I was tired.

"The Philistines pillage our towns," I persisted. "They burn infants as sacrifices. They have carried off our women, our treasures – even the Ark!"

"It is not the same! They have chosen this land for their home, so you cannot blame them for defending it. Once they took root, we became the invaders, though they tolerate us – now, anyway. Think, Benjamin! These Philistines expand by trade across the sea. They seek a living, a homeland, just as we did when Moses led us from the wilderness. But the Assyrians have all the fields and mountains they've dominated for generations on end, since Nimrod settled them, and still they send their armies across the world, battling for conquest, lusting for gold and blood, all to please themselves and their false gods." He stopped, aiming his pointing finger straight at my heart. "Listen well, upstart. Our faith is founded on peace, bound by love. The Assyrians put their faith in the sword and chariot. That is the difference."

I looked at his firm brow, his harsh, determined eyes, and stumbled into silence. Thus we shared a small meal and headed southwest, growing ever more apart.

As the morning sun warmed our backs, we passed a group of

six farmers working around a pile of fresh-cut barley. With their ragged tunics girded high – those who wore tunics, I mean; a few tanned laborers had but loincloths – these men put their backs to the wind and heaved their harvest high into the air with long-handled forks made of wood. The straw danced away in the sinking breeze, but the grains fell to our earth.

Breaking stride, the Dove gazed at me with enthusiastic eyes.

"They must hurry," he said, "if they are to finish with this wind."

Before I could ask what that meant, the Dove grabbed a spare fork and joined in.

Now I had never seen winnowing before, so I stood there, watching, as these farmers tossed away the straw first with forks, then shovels. The wind soon died, as Jonah had foreseen, but their task was pretty much done. His contribution completed their efforts. Pleased, they hugged the Dove as if he were one of their own, then gathered up our tools and passed around wine to quench our thirst.

I hesitated to take it, giving in only after Jonah frowned at me. To my surprise, the Philistine drink tasted much like our own. Then again, perhaps it was. Our wines get shipped far and wide, I now understand.

Tongues flew then, on topics ranging from the late spring harvests to the rash of lion attacks ("You two walked alone last night?" they asked again and again) to the harsh tribute Menahem squeezed out. Jonah answered them all, speaking in a patient manner I had not expected after the rash anger presented to me. And he had his own questions, though I little understood them. He quizzed these heathens on shipping, on the storms and winds, on the hills and towns ahead of us. They answered all with joyous speech reserved for the best of friends.

As the sun neared its rest, the time came for us to depart. A Philistine named Fenark insisted the Dove take a jar of grain as payment, even though Jonah refused. To account for his gift, the Dove withdrew his kinnor and sang a happy song of spring. So pleased were his friends by the tune, Fenark replaced the jar with a full basket of harvest, about an ephah.

Now that much grain is not easily carried when you are already overburdened, as I felt then. Having endured enough of Jonah's displeasure this day, with carefully chosen words I suggested we leave the gift behind, but Jonah would not think of insulting them. So, with the sun full to the horizon, the Dove kept his instrument on his own back as we struggled forward, the basket held between us.

"The Lord smiles upon us," Jonah said.

With my feet sore, my sandals wet with blood, I could not see it.

"Payment," he explained. "For the voyage."

A thorn chose that moment to lodge between the toes of my left foot. It was a blessing, all things considered, for the pain tore through me, which helped clear my mind. I stopped to yank the spine free and recalled the wounds of a day before, among other things.

"The Lord does not fund defiance," I stated.

The words were out of my mouth before I had considered them, spoken with a voice hardened by my weary frame. I never meant to confront Jonah; indeed, after his rebuke that morning, I chastised myself for getting involved in his dealings. But here I was, a newborn in the faith, telling this roeh how to deal with the Lord.

The Dove hesitated, then ungirded his tunic and tightened the coarse belt about his waist.

"Perhaps," he allowed. "Perhaps."

To the growing swirl of sea winds, we struggled over a grassy crest to gain sight of Joppa. Ringed by two ancient walls, the city offered a narrow strip of white limestone buildings around a broad inlet lined with stone moorings and wooden docks. Three half-circles of mud-brick homes buffered the merchant district – and were themselves ringed by shepherd and merchant tents. At their center rested about seven ships of various sizes, their painted eyes turned toward the sea.

Ah, that last image was a shock. The Great Sea seemed as vast as… as… well, as vast as everything you might imagine. Only the heavens themselves are broader, or more unpredictable. The clear sky swirled a vivid blue against our hot sun, the shore a jumble of tumbling stones, yet the sparkling sea rolled far beyond it all, to what end I could not imagine.

As I looked upon the restless waves for the first time, I decided I had no wish to see any more.

It seemed clear Hosea had never intended me to leave the shore. I could not even swim! What possible use could the Lord have for me out there?

Nothing. I was sure of that.

A wind gust engulfed us atop the knoll, sweeping my face with a cloud of moist dust drawn from the basket. Inhaling the bitter grains, I spun away in frustration toward the eastern horizon. The distant mountains looked so inviting, as golden mounds glowing in the sun's spreading warmth. It swept through me then, the strange need to convince the Dove not to proceed.

"Why must we come here?" I asked, not bothering to turn. But neither did he.

"You already know that."

"But this is wrong."

"Perhaps." For the first time I could hear his misery. A heart torn. "But my mind is decided."

Stubbornness had settled in, I realized. Yet I too could be stubborn, when confronted by a sea I had no intention of riding.

"Think, Jonah. You cannot believe the evil one could twist a gift of the Lord."

Barbed laughter encircled me.

"You seem determined to vex me with your infantile logic," he said, almost like an owl might coax a mouse out from hiding before it struck. "Well then – tell me how to test my fears."

"Test the Lord?" I whispered, pivoting, stiff with hesitation. I had no idea how to answer that!

In his mercy, the Dove took the guise of a teacher. From the gentle patience in his brow, I imagine he must have often played this game with neighboring children.

"There is cause to," he allowed. "The vision told me to preach of Nineveh's impending doom. Yet that is incomplete."

That confused me. "He said more?"

"No! The vision itself was incomplete." Breathing deep, he retraced the foundation of his argument. "Nineveh must repent of its sins… yet those sins are the substance of their lives! To repent, to truly repent, they must take up a new lifestyle – and they would look for me to provide it."

He must have thought this befuddled me. I may have appeared so. In truth, I felt as if I had been cast into a dark, ancient well, my swollen tunic pulling me beneath the black water.

This whole discussion was foolish! I could not debate him!

"Do you not see, Benjamin? Let us say I minister repentance to Nineveh, and they do repent. Then what do I do?" He paused but a moment before adding, "What do I offer them?"

My heart raced, its beat pounding within my head. I listened, but it held no answers.

Neither did I.

The Dove seemed to enjoy the moment. "Surely the Lord could not expect a land of unbelievers to heed prophecies of doom unless they saw a better alternative. Think, Benjamin – they do not know the Lord. They would not respect me, or hear my words, unless I promised a better lifestyle, an incentive for their future. Yet what would that be?" He took a full breath, as if waiting for an answer I did not have, then said, "Salvation? Deliverance?"

I grit my teeth. He was setting me up. I knew that, yet I could see no escape.

"No, of course not," continued Jonah. "We are the children of Abraham, Isaac, and Jacob. To us alone has the Lord promised His kingdom, His everlasting love."

In that, I saw an opening. "There was Ishmael," I sputtered.

"Are all the sands in the sea sons of Abraham?" He smiled. "No, the Assyrians are not even distant cousins of Israel. They have no place in the kingdom of God. That is written. And so, I put it to you again, a different way: what do I offer Nineveh? What could compel them to hear me?"

His smug voice began to irritate me.

"There is our own faith," I pondered aloud. "Our God."

"Oh, Benjamin! You have only now allowed yourself to

believe Him, and still your mind resists! How could you expect Assyrians to do so after all these years of hate?"

That seemed more insult than truth, or so I told myself. To be honest, I think now I knew I could not answer him with substance, and so I stopped trying.

Straightening my jaw, I spat, "Who says you need promise anything?"

"What? Our Lord would have me minister to these people, then abandon them? No, I think not."

Yet in that, I saw an opening. "You said the vision was to warn them. That's all. It is their choice whether to heed your call or not. Indeed, is that not the point?"

His gaze dimmed as he considered it, giving me a much-needed boost. That argument he must have overlooked – or tried to ignore.

"That is incomplete," he declared. "They would expect more!"

"Oh, their lives are incentive enough, I would think. When the will of the Lord became known, it would be enough. Or more would come forth, in God's time."

The Dove turned toward Joppa. "No. I do not agree." He took a step toward the rocky hills, then pivoted. "All that is good in theory, but such vague hopes rarely work in life. People need more."

The teachings of Hosea came to mind. "That is your fear at work, not your faith."

"Faith?"

I felt then a condemning spirit move within me, ignoring the sandy logic I stood upon. "We tested the vision, and it stands."

Jonah smiled. "So you say."

I ignored him.

"Why do you still oppose it?" I snapped.

A twitch of apprehension passed over his face. I saw Jonah's brow quiver, his limbs contract, and felt sorrow in my heart for his trial. Yet he answered me with a step toward Joppa.

Weary, I retrieved the basket of grain and followed his slow descent down that grassy knoll. It was the easiest of our trip, for this was the last crest of our Promised Land, the lip of earth that rolled to the sea. Joppa lay before us.

Passing beyond the one eastern gate, I have no idea how we slipped by the tax collectors. We managed to penetrate several rings of tents and stone homes before my exhaustion struck me. I realize now I must have looked rather ridiculous, with two traveling bags and a water sack upon my back, all balanced against a basket of barley weighing down my arms. But all I thought of then were the spasms that attacked and twisted my spine. In agony I collapsed against the sod road. Jonah was soon at my side, pulling away my baggage, steadying my shoulders.

"Benjamin!" he shouted. "Benjamin!"

I remember lying in the dust, that big, round nose of the Dove bouncing above my forehead, his speckled beard dangling against my eyelashes. The only thing I knew for sure was that my mind had not been detached too long, since Jonah had not used the time to abandon me. In truth, he now seemed more interested in my wellbeing than escape.

"Thank the Lord!" he exclaimed as I came aware. "Ah, you worried me!"

My head ached just above my right eye. I reached up and found a new knob there, and a painful one at that. While it raged, the fibers of my back rebelled yet again from my strain. But these, for once, seemed controllable. As my sight focused once more, and the images of that Joppa street returned, lined by idle people eyeing us, I found myself little harmed by the incident. Except for the grain.

"Oh no," I moaned, staring at the pile of barley scattered across the roadway. My heart sank, wondering how we would pick up all those seeds. Yet the Dove only smiled.

"This is where it ends," he said. Sitting me down, he motioned to a little girl wrapped in dusty blue cloth. She ran into a limestone hut, returning with her mother and another child. Their brash mixture of mismatched rags for clothes revealed their poverty.

"May the Lord be with you," said Jonah.

The lady stopped in the street.

"A Jew," whispered the woman. Hesitating, she glanced at

both of her girls before saying, "Greetings."

I was far too bound by my pain to take exception to her, and Jonah felt no need to. "Accept this grain," he said. "We apologize for spilling it, but my friend has slept little over the last three days. His strength is just about spent."

She looked upon me, frowned, and ran back to her home. But she was gone only a short time before coming back cradling two damp rags. With the first soaked in cool water, she wiped clean my face. The second, sweetened with oil, softened the anger of my bruised forehead.

By the time she was done, her two girls had cleared the road of barley, taking care to brush away the cattle, horse, donkey, and dog waste.

"Most gracious thanks," I said, wincing as I rose. "May… may our Lord bless you."

She showed no hint of gratitude. "Look well upon us, you and your king," she muttered. Gathering her daughters around her, they disappeared into their home. The others watching us turned away, their entertainment over.

"Now do you understand?" Jonah put to me, his words only a bit less harsh than hers. But with that spear of pain bouncing within my skull, I ignored him.

"But what," I mumbled, "what of our payment? For passage?"

"The Lord will provide," Jonah assured me.

A moment later we stood at the docks. I know not how we got there… in truth, I missed something in between, but that little matters now. As my pain lessened, and I gained awareness again, I heard Jonah speaking with a tall, gray-bearded Phoenician, or so I guessed by his girded blue tunic and his skin's dark, oiled tan. Indeed, every crewman I saw was so tinted and adorned.

Oh, that was a proud ship they worked! It stood low in the water, a multi-leveled craft of well-honed Lebanon woods stretching as long as four brick homes strung end to end. At its bow two large painted eyes watched over the sea behind a tall figure of a proud, trident-bearing merman. Oiled leather shields lined its top deck, each emblazoned with the image of a bull, eagle, lion, or serpent. Below that deck ran a bank of oar portals.

A single mast rose from the ship's core, a clustered red sail bound to its high crossbar. Tethered at the ship's broad, upraised back hung a thick steering oar, its base wider than I could spread my arms.

"A ship of Tarshish," I whispered.

"Ah, so you have heard of them," said the Dove, taking notice of me. "This one's the biggest at the dock, by my estimates. It should withstand the worst storm."

I almost reminded him that our sun graced a clear sky, but Jonah's admiration for the ship fueled my own, and so I let it pass. And why not? This vessel was far grander than anything I had dreamed of. Such fanciful thought rarely gripped me, to be sure, but these ambitions sometimes arose when a wounded or worn mariner stumbled into Hosea's care. Usually old and weathered, no longer able to sustain that life, those troubled sailors would boast of their watery past adventures with a passion and vibrancy none of us could ignore.

But did I want to step aboard this ship's brine-encrusted decks? Not for all the gold of Babylon!

"You have no money at all?" I heard the captain ask, his tone an open statement of disbelief.

"I am a servant of the God Most High," said Jonah. "I take no part of man's values."

They stood on the docks, eye to eye, the Phoenician's callused hands curled in distrust or dismay, the Dove's calm at his side.

"You must not understand," said the captain. "This is no pleasure ship. We bear cargo to Thebes, to Carthage."

"Good! I wish to see Tarshish."

The captain stepped back, his brow torn by disbelief.

"That is the end of the world," he exclaimed, "beyond the solid rocks – the Pillars of El himself!" His eyes hardened, reassessing the Dove. "Pirates are a risk outside the rule of Thebes and a vicious hazard beyond Carthage. And the seas are tricky in such faraway places. Dare you such things?"

"I have already given up everything. What I do now… my fate is assured. I have no fears."

The Phoenician stood fuming, his eyes boring into the Dove…

or perhaps he saw nothing at all. I have seen people do that, stare at something, unaware of what they viewed. But soon the captain turned, gazing first at the ship's figurehead, then the clear blue sky. Something he discerned there made him relent.

"Melqart smiles on us, so whatever curse you may bear cannot destroy us. And he has left me without a full hold; I had wondered why." The captain paused, then asked, "Can you rig a spar?"

"A what?"

He took that as a negative. "Cast a harpoon?"

Jonah squinted, saying nothing.

"Read the stars?" the Phoenician continued, grasping for some positive sign.

"I see not by the skies, but by God."

Frustration built within the captain. "There must be something you can do." Then he spied the kinnor. "You play that?"

The Dove allowed a brief smile. "I have some skill."

The captain grunted. "And I suppose you can swab a deck." Then, for the first time, he glanced at me. "And your friend?"

"We will do whatever you ask of us," Jonah stated. "We merely wish passage."

"Passage," the captain muttered. "I hope I do not regret this. You must get your own food, pay your own dock tax – somehow – and arrange your own rests at night. And we go only as far as Carthage. You must find another ship there."

He looked us over again, pondering perhaps the wisdom of all this. But I could tell he was a decisive man, one who would not doubt himself long.

"We will push off soon," he stated. "You both look beaten; you had better go below. Saln the First will show you where you can sleep." Under his breath he added, "And stay out of my beard."

I watched the Dove stride to the ladder and climb aboard. Only then, as three Phoenicians surrounded him, did I understand Hosea did indeed intend for me to ride those dark, desperate seas.

Lord, have mercy!

Chapter 13

Consequences

That brings us to our sea voyage, so let's skip over the storm and press on.

Yes, yes, I know you like hearing that tale, but I am not going to dive into it again.

Why? I do not enjoy discussing suicide. It hurts, and it's wrong. And besides that, you have heard me share this tale three times already. That should be enough.

How could the Dove just walk off the side like that? I answered that, as best as I could. What did I think of it? I was shocked, as you well imagine, and concerned, and a little heartbroken. We talked about that, too. How would you feel if a mentor or friend killed himself before your eyes? It hurts. Bad. But I had so many things to consider then. As those sailors worshipped, as I witnessed their hearts change, I got swept up in my own rattling concerns, and it raised some hard questions for me to juggle. Think about it now – did his death mean Jonah's fears were indeed valid? That his vision to save Nineveh was not from our Lord? Or was this a small sign of what could happen… of what was to come?

I struggled to answer all that as our ship rounded the Isle of Melqarth – the southern twin to Tyre, the island fortress of Phoenicia. We had reversed course from Carthage because the captain – with our newfound familiarity, I learned his name was

Hazorn – said the laws required a death sentence be reported, the loss of cargo recorded, their tales investigated, his name and crew vindicated. But those things did not matter to me. With Jonah truly gone – and I could no longer think otherwise – I had no desire to sail further. Tyre was a bit out of my way, but since I had no money, I figured that did not matter either. At least I could walk home, almost. My sandals would probably wear out, but that I could handle. After all, I had gone barefoot most of my life.

Besides all that, Hazorn wished my advice on building an altar to the Lord near his home. Who was I to stand before such a goal?

Who was I…

Feeling the warmth of His sun on my face, hearing the honesty of their praises, it made me ponder anew just why I was on that bedeviled ship. They looked to me for guidance. Me!

What was I but a misfit, runaway slave? A child abandoned by his family, pledged as fodder to a despised king? A plague to those who had instructed me?

Why had the Lord led me to this place? What purpose did this have in His plan?

Even with Hosea's training and Jonah's guidance, I never thought myself strong enough to guide anyone anywhere, much less to God. Oh, I had learned from these men, but did I have their patience or knowledge, much less their faith?

Confronted with question after question from Hazorn and his men, I faced the sad truth: I was a failure. So often I knew nothing to tell them but to pray for guidance, and I couldn't even explain how to do that.

Why me? Why was I there?

There were times when, amidst this crew's joy and praise, my pride drew its own flattering conclusions. Hosea's command, and Jonah's diversion, marked our Lord's way of getting me on that ship, of awakening my spiritual strength! The Lord must have great things in store for me and my descendants!

For a few long, deep breaths, I reveled in such thoughts… the very notion that I could have a family, that I could build a life beyond my gutter existence… and then someone would humble my "infantile wisdom" with a penetrating thought, revealing an even greater truth. The Dove had ever been the focal point of our Lord's actions, not I.

But that brought more fundamental reasoning to my heart. Living upon that ship those last few days, within the almost continuous rejoicing of the captain and his sailors, I began to ponder whether these events had happened just to convert these men to His service.

You scoff, but there must be some truth to that, no matter how it reflects on the Dove. After the sailors and I spent that first night discussing the Lord, we continued our talks the next day as they set course for Tyre. Even as they worked, we talked. That night, hoping I would have Jonah's forgiveness, I took his kinnor and picked out notes to teach them my favorites from Hosea's psalms. They praised God with all their heart.

What a blessing it was to witness such joy! Oh Lord, how it must thrill You!

Through it all, I couldn't forget that these were Phoenicians. Phoenicians! These sea-faring people had acknowledged His power, acknowledged Him, much faster than did many of the sons and daughters of Abraham!

As the white limestone walls of Tyre emerged on the horizon, I looked upon these outsiders, embraced by the Lord, and wondered if the Dove had not fallen prey to prejudice and hate. These sailors were perfect examples of the Lord's ability to reach Gentiles. Yet Jonah and I had discussed this same thing about Philistia, and the Dove had been right. These people were not like the Assyrians, at least not in their hatreds, their bloodletting. But if the Lord could speak to the hearts of these Phoenicians, could He not open the minds of the Assyrians?

I had no answer to that.

As we sailed into port, two days after Jonah's fall, I came to believe there must have been more in the Dove's visions than he had told me. For he was not that unreasonable, that blinded by hatred, to have acted as he did. But with him gone, such secrets were lost forever.

What was I going to tell Hosea? I prayed each night for an

answer, though my Lord offered none. And that silence only strengthened my guilt. For as I looked back at my own actions, I saw myself as a chief culprit in Jonah's demise. Had I befriended the Dove in earnest, or tried to help him through his troubles? No, in all honesty. Looking back on my actions, from my first step into his home, my comments now seemed wrapped around his guilt before the Lord, whatever that might have been. As if I were any judge of such things.

Had I been wrong, stating my mind so? Often in my childhood I had been told to rest my tongue, to wait for the right time to speak. Such is the role of a slave. Yet should we not correct errors when they are made? I find it hard to think anyone could do otherwise, especially when the error reflects on the Lord. And as I looked back on my days with the Dove, all of our conflicts seemed centered around the Most High. Or most of them.

Still, that gave me no satisfaction, for every argument I might make brought me back to one grievous question: If I had sincerely tried to understand Jonah, to share his heartache, would he have fallen? I suppose I will never know, but I could not help thinking that, had I listened with a more compassionate ear, the Dove and I might still have been together… perhaps even on the road to Nineveh.

Yes, I was wrapped in guilt. It reflects most of my life, I fear.

As these skilled mariners backed their ship into the shore, I knelt at the bow behind its two broad eyes and prayed for forgiveness and guidance. I feared my infantile wisdom had doomed one of the Lord's great warriors.

"Hosea," I whispered, "I failed you. Failed us all."

"Benjamin!" the captain shouted. "All ashore."

Wiping the sea spray from my eyes, I saw we had come to a cove within the northern island's southeastern rim – the Port of Egypt, as Hazorn called it, so named for the direction of traffic it served. Uncounted numbers of ships were tied to the wooden docks or anchored just off the shore. Most were simple harbor cutters, barges, small fishing vessels, or round, short-hop commercial ships. But there were a few other ships of Tarshish among us, most with thick rams before their figureheads.

"Eventful three days," said the First, patting my back. "Would you share wine with my family before you go?"

I hesitated. I knew what I wanted to do, but now that it was time, I had little idea how to do it. A quick return to Joppa – or Joffa, as the Phoenicians called it – would have been ideal, but Hazorn and his crew expected to be bound over for a couple of weeks. They offered to return me to Joppa after that, but I had no desire to wait. I lacked the gall to force my way onto another vessel, as the Dove had, so that left me but one option – walking south, down the coastal plains. Yet that involved great risk, from bandits and animals alike.

The whole idea frightened me. Thus confused, I turned to Saln and said, "I would be honored." As I was.

We disembarked with Hazorn and several members of the crew, the First volunteering to carry my bags while I guarded my kinnor with my shepherd's staff. A large tower of limestone overlooked the single gate, which like the walls were made of cut stones of tremendous proportion.

"Surprising, is it not?" commented the captain. "How thick they must be, with the sea and the world's greatest fleet protecting them?"

"But why not," offered Saln, "with a wealth of limestone across the bay?"

I soon learned why they invested in such protection. If Nineveh was the center of commerce of the eastern lands, then Tyre held that distinction in the west. I tell you the truth, as I stepped through this city's simple gate, I entered the marketplace of the world – a whole menagerie of shops and tents, wagons and baskets, all manned by busy, quick-tongued hagglers. Countless goods abounded: glassware and linen from Egypt, raw silver and tin from Tarshish, golden rods and iron from Tarsus, bronze goods from Ionia, cattle and grains from Assyria, sheep and goats from Arabia. My heart warmed with the sight of wine, figs, and olive oils from my Israel and Judah, all looking superior to those from mainland Phoenicia. Recent arrivals from a merchant's caravan included beautiful forged iron swords from Damascus, emblazoned with gold, ivory, and gems. A southern trader had returned with unequaled picks, hoes, and shovels, all capped with iron crafted in Joppa. From Athens came bottles of herbs and oils designed for medicinal uses. Loaded off barges from the mainland was a grand supply of Lebanese timber – cedar, pine, fir, and terebinth. Tyre itself supplied the finest in royal dyes, reds and purples fit for the wealthiest of the wealthy.

In a way, the marketplace transcended language and custom. Though bigger and busier, it seemed to work much the same as the markets of Samaria and Bethel. True, I heard many different dialects and tongues for the first time as we passed down that center street, but it was not hard to tell what they wanted or that I had no money. That spelled the difference. I soon learned that in Tyre, bartering for something, anything, was as accepted as payment in gold or silver or whatever currency the merchant would take. That was my biggest problem, for the kinnor drew many eyes.

It soon became difficult to escape the traders, and not only for me. Saln stepped in twice to discourage insistent merchants, and the captain once blocked one's approach as the First shoved me to safety. But as the sun passed the midday point, and the heat of the day rose, we reached the inland fields where the shepherds kept watch over herds in transit. To the northwest, the earth rose to a second wall as imposing as the first. Hazorn pointed out that most homes were there, including his own, overlooking the Port Sidon. But Saln kept his family outside the Port of Egypt, in part to keep watch over the ship, in part because his wife liked its gentler climate.

"There," said the captain, indicating a bare knob of earth just outside the inner wall. "I will ask to build an altar to the Lord of Israel there. As a child I loved that crest, for it sees over the sea to the west and the continent east. And so does our Lord."

"God's will be done," I said, embracing him. "Come to Bethel or Jerusalem when you are ready – Bethel if you can. I should get back there sometime." Then I turned to view all those bold sailors who had risked the storm to save Jonah. "Come learn from Hosea. He knows Him best."

"You have taught us well," said Brans.

I couldn't help smiling. "A pittance, compared to what he has mastered."

"If that is your bidding, then I will make it a goal of my life," said Hazorn. "Indeed, I believe we all will."

With that, he embraced me again, followed by most of the crew. I couldn't hold back my tears as they left. The First thought that appropriate.

"They will remember you always," he reminded me. "When you share such peril, you share your heart. Such bonds rarely break."

That has proven true, for I have never forgotten them.

As we turned back, I began to simmer within the burning sun as it passed through the Great Sea's wet winds. God graced us with a short walk. To the back of the marketplace rested an inlet of small homes much like those of Israel. The big difference: limestone. Floors, walls, stairs… just about everything was made from bricks of that sandy white stone.

"With Mount Lebanon so close, we have a wealth of it," said Saln. "And it weathers just about everything. When the storms rise, or the earth about us quakes –"

"Quakes?"

"Indeed. The Lord sometimes shifts the lands themselves, and when He does, sometimes our homes, their walls… well, they just tumble apart. But these bricks do not chip or crack that much when that happens, so we reuse them. Pretty much everything you see here uses them. I dare say we would build a ship of them, if we knew how."

As you may imagine, certain fears flowed through my mind as we stepped into his home, but they soon fled as Saln's hospitality put me at ease. As foretold, his wife had left to join the weavers, as was his oldest daughter. His youngest trained down at the docks.

"Lay the kinnor on a shelf, so that the dog will not get it," he instructed.

I froze. "Dog?"

Saln chuckled. "Be at ease! He is with my woman now."

Their home resembled Jonah's with a few notable exceptions.

Though they had no yard, Saln could claim two more rooms, which I considered a fair trade. And with walls of stone, I saw few bugs.

The entry room seemed the gathering place. Shelves lining each wall displayed items from around the sea, similar to things I had seen that morning within the markets. Pots, clothes, tools… the First had quite a variety. There were shells and stones of many shapes and colors, all somewhat mystical and quite astounding, sorted around jars of wide-ranging size and color. But most of all, Saln seemed to collect writings. There were hardened clay boards from Babylon and Assur, scrolls from Sidon and Athens, skins and parchments of some kind from Egypt. He devoted one wall to them.

"We of Tyre collect the thoughts of others," he explained. "The library here is enormous."

"Admirable," I said, though I felt no need to copy him. With the wisdom of Solomon and the Temple, the words of Yahweh, the laws of Moses, I had enough to learn to fill several lifetimes. Against that, the thoughts of men were of no consequence.

"Surprising, is it not?" he said from the next room. "All the places I have traveled, all the things I have learned, yet only now have I found the truth." He returned with glasses – real glass mugs, filled with sweet wine – setting those down to lay two woven rugs against the limestone floor. "Why do you think that is? Why does not the world share His truth?"

That was a troublesome question. Not knowing what to say, I backed into the issue. As we sat upon the soft wool rugs, drinking his wine, I told him tales Hosea had shared with me concerning evil – of Babel, Sodom, and the flood. I recounted how Joseph had brought God's truth to Egypt, only to be forgotten and my people enslaved. Most of all, I told him of the promise to Abraham, of the test with Isaac. The promise to Israel alone.

After some hesitation, I brought up the command to Joshua to slay unbelievers in the Promised Land, and the evils that had befallen the twelve tribes by their failure… all those things I once ignored as myth. I worried how he would react to such tales of violence, for the Canaanites were offshoots of his people, were they not? But I told him anyway. It did disturb him, though not as I had feared.

"But He has accepted me," Saln stated, striking his chest. "I feel it."

"That is why you must come to the Temple, to learn fully of God's truth. And be circumcised."

That was another issue I underestimated. Not that Saln did not accept it – he did, after I dismissed some of his more tender reservations. But my explanations reminded me once more how much I had to learn of faith and our one God. How little prepared I was for such a task.

Despite my inadequacies, Saln remained quite open to the Lord. "Have there been others, like myself, others outside your Hebrew race, who have come to follow Yahweh?"

That I did not know for sure. Hosea once spoke of travelers with Abraham who accepted the faith, and some in Egypt, Sinai, and Midian. And still other people of Ishmael. But that answer seemed short-sighted.

"Surely He speaks to those around the world," Saln insisted. "He is the Lord of peace, of love. Creator of all! He could not ignore His children across the seas, or beyond Nineveh."

That logic appealed to my heart, yet I had no foundation for it.

"As you said, you have read of many peoples around the Great Sea," I recalled. "And you had never heard of the Lord or found anyone following His truth."

"Quite true," Saln admitted, lying back. "Yet it is puzzling. Sad."

Pondering that, I put my hands behind my head and relaxed. Soon I lost myself in sleep… and a dream.

Chapter 14
An ending

Through my teeth I felt the crippling blow, all before my ears caught that sickening crack of my skull striking sunbaked stone. Yet splintered bone was but one fear among many, and not the worst.

Every heartbeat echoed my pain. My skin smoldered against that simmering brick platform. Tears drowned my eyes in a failed bid to ward off the dazzling sun. And only with purest determination could I force my lungs to draw breath from the greasy cloud of decay cloaking this precipice. Surely millions of others preceded me here in death. I could smell the blood and waste of every life ended upon that ancient, crumbling stone.

Crying out, I hurled myself upward to escape, but it was no use. Yanked off-balance by heavy chains at my wrists and ankles, I fell into a pile of twigs and stubble. Waves of dust billowed up, choking the dry air, even as the limbs snapped and crumbled beneath me. The sounds chilled my soul; I had not heard such horrors since the massacre of Lebonah. My stomach retched, though I tasted but a few drops of bile, having little more than bits of moldy bread in my bowels. Still, the effort sapped my will, and so I collapsed, helpless, as the dust of death settled on my prickly flesh. Through that haze my sight returned, confirming my fears. I lay in brittle piles of fingers, palms, and wrists, their dried flesh crumbling away with each passing wind.

The same fate awaited me.

Uncaring hands hauled me to my feet. My shoulder blades parted for a moment, and I nearly swooned, but these tormentors allowed no escape. Stern fingers grasped my neck like a blacksmith's vise, forcing my throbbing head up. The brilliant sun greeted me again, glaring off the oiled flesh of two eunuchs at my sides, their muscular frames bare above the waist.

Before me waited the bronze stool cradling Banipal's toys. The golden serpent's knife for peeling away skin. The jeweled cleaver, notched by many stubborn wrists. The thick headman's blade. All glowed with devilish intent.

"Unlock him!" came a hard command.

A torrid breeze seared my flesh as my chains fell away. In that moment of liberation and anguish, I discerned for the first time the pulsing screams of the distant crowd. That insight broke upon me like a reproaching slap. Shaken, I struggled to prepare myself for what awaited me. For I now knew where I was. I had stood here before.

Breathing deep, I felt my strength evaporating, but I refused to let my enemies know. For even in that arid breeze I could smell the sweet grasses of faraway hills, untainted by the city stench. I heard the flap of empty human skins rippling like wind-stretched pendants high above the hungry mob. Even as a dark silhouette stepped between me and the unrelenting sun, I knew I stood at the parapet atop the king's tower. The royal stage of torture.

All of Nineveh watched.

The High Priest strode into my hazy sight, a proud, righteous figure bound in black, flowing robes embroidered with his many accomplishments. Curled and oiled, his magnificent beard glowed as a bed of bronze coals, but the fury in his eyes burned hotter still. Lifting a clay tablet for all to see, he bellowed my list of alleged sins, pausing with each count to hear the throng sing for my punishment in an ever-rising chorus of anguish and hate. Only when the stones themselves rumbled with bloodlust did the priest confront me, confident in his power.

"You have heard the judgment of the court," he called out. "But your King is ever lenient. He recalls a time when you served the crown. When you did your duty, not only to him, but to his father. So, before the great god Ashur, he is willing to give you another chance. You may still save yourself. Renounce the false Hebrew god! Recant these desperate prophecies and beg forgiveness for those you led astray!"

In his words I heard my doom. It numbed me to the core, and yet, in all truth, I must admit I felt a twinge of restless hope. For his promise offered to reverse a lifetime of regrets and unfulfilled desires.

Was this not what I had ever sought? To be released from His demands? To live like all those souls I'd envied in silence throughout my days, free to breathe deep of His creation and find my own place in this world? To hold a woman whose only desire was to please me? To raise a multitude of sons, all tall, strong, and proud? To stand at the base of a mountain I myself had tamed, my flocks grazing safe and secure on its slopes, my family at my side? To proclaim to all the world, "I did this! I am my own master!"

Amid that desperate longing, a vision opened in the sky. The lovely Pelagos stood there, her brown eyes shimmering like stars, her scarlet hair drifting in playful joy within the soft breeze, her open arms gesturing a clear invitation to my heart.

This was bitter torture. Had I not prayed for her caress every night?

A tear made it halfway down my cheek before the desert wind devoured its last trace. My tongue licked dry, swollen lips. I swallowed, straining to not cry out.

As I hung there, at that climax of my weakness, the king himself baited the hook before me. Banipal leaned just a bit forward, so that I met his gaze over the priest's shoulder – a grand gesture, that, as the monarch allowed his advisor to represent him and his gods before casting most sentences. I could see the honesty in my one-time friend's softened, imploring eyes. It surprised and humbled me. Despite everything that had happened, Banipal wished for my company once more. He wanted me at his side!

My stomach churned with the tempest of my soul. I could yet

live! I could walk free!

Somehow I found my voice. Mustering all the courage I could spare, I bit back my envy, gazed into the heavens and cried out, “Behold the storm, Nineveh! You have cast yourself against the hand of righteousness!”

Hope faded from Banipal’s weary eyes as he digested that message. With regret he slipped away, perhaps only then realizing that I would never abandon my Lord and God.

The High Priest smiled in vindication. Leather claws raked my back. Terrifying pain! I whipped my shoulders about, but could not loosen the hold of my captors. My jaws snapped on my lower lip, flooding my mouth with hot blood. The crowd roared its delight. And yet my words sputtered forth:

“As I… as I heard… your war machines….”

The flail struck anew, splitting my callused skin. My nerves burned.

“Repent!” demanded the priest.

Crimson flowed between my shoulders, dried under the thirsty wind, tore apart beneath the sun, poured free and dried once more. My knees gave way, but the eunuchs held me up by my wrists. I gasped for breath to go on.

“Crack… crack the bones… of Jerusalem….”

The barbs dug deep, tearing muscle. I knew not how the prophecy continued.

“So… shall… yours… be crushed.”

They yanked my ancient arms tight, even as the lashes bit down. I screamed.

The High Priest laughed. Banipal did not object. Perhaps this was worth delaying his return to Egypt after all.

Ah, Egypt, land of the Nile. Such memories invigorated me! The bleached brick walls of On, molded by my ancestors. Ghost tombs that scrape the sky. The reluctant Esarhaddon.

I tried to stand, to project myself. To let all the crowd hear my prophesy: “As I saw… your warriors… bathe in the… blood of Thebes… so shall the crows… feast… upon your rotting… flesh.”

“Enough!” cried the king of kings. With that frustrated call, the regal Banipal stepped before me, shimmering in robes of gold and silver, the gems of his great helmet bright as a multitude of suns. I watched the king draw his majestic sword, his eyes hot with wrath – and I saw Pulu once more, upon that blistered hillside, his fingers wrapped tight about the withered, white neck of Jonah.

Within me erupted ages-old rage!

"Behold the storm, Nineveh!" I screamed, hindered no longer by the foul winds or my human weakness. "Send forth your last chariots! Whip your last steeds! They are nothing before the Lord! For you have failed the test. Yahweh let loose the Dove in your presence, the olive branch offered in His compassionate words, but you cast it off in bitter arrogance, as you did the hopes of the world. And as it was for Gomorrah, your time is ended."

A flash of light called to my eye. Through my haze, I saw Banipal's long blade dive. My spine quaked. Red life sprayed forth. And so, my prayers were answered. Death brought deliverance.

Oh, Jonah! It is as you wished at long last, though too late, too late.

The skies turn black again. Does it please you? Or has your spirit healed in death what could not mend in life?

Oh, Jonah! To watch this and not cry at your sacrifice! Lord forgive me, the memories tear me still! Help me understand!

Help me understand….

Chapter 15

Many meetings

Dreams…. When they frighten you or distress you, confuse or confound you, when they muddle your prayers or distract your thoughts, when they take you places you would rather not go and show you things you wish you had not seen, when they occupy your nights again and again, all without enlightenment from God, then they are best set aside until discernment comes. Or so Jonah told me.

I wonder now if he knew my fate when he spoke this. How discernment may unveil itself over time, as dreams become reality. In this I learned another truth of his life – just how painful revelation may be.

Oh, let's get back to my tale.

At dawn, Saln and Hazorn took me to the mainland in a little "channel hopper," as they called it. I thought it but a large barge – a strange craft to choose for just three people, but they handled it well. Indeed, in the hands of two such experienced sailors, there was nothing for me to do but enjoy the brisk winds and golden sun.

It all was something to enjoy. Especially Tyre. To gaze upon it now, with the morning mist burning away, was to look fresh upon a jewel of the world. Its walls and buildings towered from the shore as imposing alabaster monoliths, perfect in its elegance, imposing in its supremacy. The sea at its feet sparkled the brightest blue imaginable, while its beaches glowed as fine ivory in a full moon. No wonder Solomon fell in love with its craftsmanship!

"Powerful, is it not?" said Hazorn, his firm hands locked around the steersman's oar.

"Impregnable," declared Saln. "Never taken that I know of."

"Though you have paid tribute," I knew.

"That Hosea taught you well!" the captain chuckled. "Yes, so we have, for long ago we found it more profitable to pay off whoever holds the mainland rather than stay at war and risk our ports closed, even if by our own warships. Trade, after all, is more important than who rules these shores."

"Who does now?"

"The Assyrians have long since pulled back, for whatever reason. I do not know it all, since I am out to sea most of the time, but it is said there are revolts within that empire. Perhaps those dogs will fall at last."

I trembled then with strange irony. "Perhaps," I said, mimicking the Dove.

"We can seek that blessing from the Lord," called the First, tacking down the sail.

"Pray," I whispered. But could we, as Jonah prayed? Would that be proper?

Oh, Lord! Guide my hand!

The shore reared before us as the sun cleared the coastal hills. A small group of huts and tents marked the plains.

"Given any more thought to taking a ship back?" the captain inquired. "I have friends who owe me favors, Benjamin. It is not too late."

Saln had urged this same thing of me last night, in the middle of his wife's excellent stew. But I did not wish for another sea voyage. Ever. I just did not know how to admit that to them.

"The roads are fine," I said.

"Then find a caravan," Saln insisted. To the captain he called, "Caught the tide. Good work."

I felt it in the deck, the sway of the surf pulling us in. With the breeze assaulting the sun, we soon had our feet on the warm sand.

"Caravan, Benjamin," Saln stated. "Believe me, these lands are not safe. This is not Bethel."

"I will be all right."

"Caravan," he repeated.

Under the sun's protective aura, we parted for the last time. At the shore waited two mule trains loaded with cedar logs bound for the Port of Egypt, so Hazorn haggled out a transport price and they were off.

Ah, these were impressive men. I hope they did indeed follow the Lord in their lives, for such strength could be put to good use. But that was in His hands.

Just that quick, I was alone once more, my back burdened with two dusty traveling bags, a full water sack, and the kinnor. Bound for a destination with no notion of how to get there.

Traveling the coast had been my original and only idea. I looked down that rocky shoreline and wondered how I ever imagined I could make such a trip. To walk the water's edge seemed stupid, with all its curls and dips, coves and finger-like peninsulas… surely it would double or triple the length of a dove's flight to Bethel! Yet I had no idea what direction that dove might fly. And Saln was right – the plains were perilous, with bears, lions, bandits, vipers, who knows what else.

"Lord, give me a sign," I whispered. Then I dropped to my knees and prayed for guidance.

The squawk of gulls broke the calming sounds of the surf. Looking about, I saw several in flight to the south, hovering about something on the shore. It was a strange sight for a land-born soul like mine, these lanky white birds flapping their wings against the incoming breeze to hang almost stationary in the air. Giving in to my curiosity, I gathered up my burdens and started toward them.

The beach was not a pleasant thing to see. True, those shells I found were treasures to behold, whether they moved or not, but the sand lay broken by many things, starting with boulders smoothed by the waves yet irritating to walk around. Skeletons and fins of dead fish lay about me, as did countless strands of seaweed. From the tide's sweep remained abandoned pools of water, smelly things that sometimes trapped fish. It seemed tragic and unfair to suffer so, so I threw one back to the sea. Then a defiant crab charged from the sand, its thick pincers snapping the wind as it might my toes, and I abandoned my efforts.

Thus daunted, I rounded a thumb of damp shore and came upon the gulls. Those airborne set upon me. I ducked, shouted at them, but the white knights of the sea circled, squawking as if to ward me off, or to warn me of peril. Then they departed, and I found the cause. A flock of their brethren gathered about something on the beach, throwing out gelatinous pieces of weed, the raw meat of ocean creatures, and other oozing things.

My first thought was to run, lest I get sick. I almost did both, but then a gull moved, revealing a bleached foot.

In that swift moment, my revulsion turned to rage.

Dropping everything, including the delicate kinnor, I took my shepherd's rod and attacked, sweeping its knobby end against the flock. But the gulls gave no resistance. With not even a squawk they departed, leaving upon the sand the chalk-white body of a man, naked, clean. I rose up, gazed full upon him… and dropped my staff.

It was Jonah.

Had I spoken before of his ability to stump me? Well, this was the worst of it. I looked upon him in complete and utter disbelief.

Long before had I fallen in love with his spirit, his determined faith. Now, as he slept his lasting sleep, I gazed upon the fine art of his form – the chiseled tones of his shoulders, his well-honed limbs, his graying hair swept with majesty against the sand, his full beard straight with his commanding jaw.

Oh, Lord, have mercy! It was painful enough before, having to accept that he was dead, that I had failed him so. But to look upon the Dove again, with all the color of life flushed from his limbs… forgive me! I could not bear it!

How long did it take? How long did I stand there, petrified by his still form? No, do not humble me further with such knowledge. Let it be said but once that I did nothing – probably thought of nothing but my own sins, my own loss – until the Dove gasped, rolled his head, his eyes. Broken from my trance, I fell upon him with wretched yet joyful sobs.

"Benjamin?" he stammered, his voice but a distant rasp. "Is that you, Benjamin?"

That moment was worth a lifetime. In truth, hearing those words was beyond hope! Beyond belief!

"Yes," I whispered. Then I cried out for joy. "You live! Forgive me! I had given up hope!"

"What was there to hope for? I gave you no cause for hope. But I was wrong."

"Wrong?"

"Water," he said, waving my question away. "Please, do you have water?"

Running for my water sack, I lifted his upper torso against my knee and brought the bag's mouth to his lips. He took it in his own hands, surprising me with his strength, but allowed only a small sip before he spat it against the sand.

"Got to get that taste from my mouth," he said before taking a long swallow.

"What taste?"

"Bowel." And he drank again, draining the goatskin bag.

I couldn't help wondering if I had heard him right. Hesitant, I admitted, "I don't understand."

"Nor should you. But you shall."

In a mad rush he jumped to his feet and sprinted for the eastern grass. Not knowing what he planned, or how well was his mind, I followed with caution. The Dove leaped within a field of wildflowers, rolling in the sunshine and his newfound joy for life.

"Oh Lord in heaven," he sang, lying flat on his back, "I praise you in humility and gladness! For in the depths of the grave You heard my cries, the cries of a sinner, and You answered them."

"The grave?" His words left me more confused than before. "You… you died?"

"So it was," stated the Dove, gazing upon his arms and hands as if only now he had noticed their dead pallor. "What did you expect when I cast myself into the sea? Death was what I wished for, remember? Well, the Lord provided."

Bewildered by it all, I took a protective step back. This was almost too bizarre to deal with.

"So I thought," I stammered. "I thought you dead. We all did. For three days. But here you are. Here. How? How is this?"

What? was more what I wanted to ask. What are you? Death? Some sort of golem?

I lacked the nerve to say it, but my heart awaited just such an answer.

The Dove stared at me with eyes as wide as the fullest moon.

"A great fish swallowed me whole," he said, "and spewed me up here."

"A fish?" What fish had a size enough to do that? Job's leviathan? "You mean a whale?"

"A fish. Not a whale." Seeing my disbelief, Jonah's brow turned cross. "You think I do not know what captured me? It was a fish, I tell you. The Lord made it Himself for this purpose, to deliver me here, now. The time has come."

"Time? Time for what?"

"Nineveh."

Ah, so that was it… the visions now had all his mind. Part of me rejoiced, for as Hosea had taught me, the directives of our Lord must be fulfilled when received. Yet these statements of faith did not assure me of Jonah's health, or how stable his mind would prove.

I lifted my burdened heart from the sand and found his piercing eyes chronicling my thoughts. A part of me resisted, but most of my soul opened itself to him.

"Benjamin," he began, rising to his knees as if to judge my efforts, "would you join me in prayer?"

That was a pleasant twist. I had expected worse.

As I slipped my hands within his own, the Dove placed them on his shoulders and prayed aloud.

"Oh Lord, God of Abraham, Isaac, and Jacob, I bare myself to You. I commit my heart to You. For You have rescued me as no other could.

"As the depths of the sea engulfed me, I admitted my sins to You, Lord. 'I have been banished from Your sight, deserved as it was. Yet I would look again upon your Holy Temple. Let me serve you once!' Yet Your engulfing waters drew me deeper, until I sank into the pit of death. Such was my own judgment for my sin. Yet as my life drifted away, I remembered You, Lord, and as it was a prayer of my heart, you saved me first with the fish, and now with Benjamin."

My heart leaped at that. Our Lord blessed me? Me!

"Those who cling to lumps of metal, worthless idols, they forfeit the grace that could be theirs," Jonah said. That, I knew, was his heart's opinion of Assyria. That part, at least, remained true to his old desire. "But I, with a song of thanksgiving, will sacrifice to You. What I have vowed I will make good, for salvation comes from You alone, Lord."

His voice lifted in song, notes that matched the fluid sweep of the breeze, the power of the sun's welcome rays, the foundation of the sod beneath us. Try as I might, I remember none of his words, for they were of his heart and as such, captured my own. But in his song, I felt the presence of the Lord… and His forgiveness.

As the Dove finished, his white skin a beacon in that vibrant green field, a gull broke through the wind, squawking as it soared among the hills. Jonah did not respond, but I was curious and leaned up to watch its flight. The white knight broke against the sand just beyond us, snapping at something within the dunes. Then it returned to the skies, a snake writhing in its grasp.

Blessed are the protective hands of the Lord!

"This is not the best place to be," I reminded the Dove. But he had seen the gull as well, and so rose to his bare feet.

"Come," he said.

That surprised me. "Where?" I spoke. He pointed to his answer. There, toward the rising sun, formed a merchant caravan.

"To Nineveh," said the Dove, starting forward. "Our journey begins."

Though barefoot, Jonah strode undeterred across the thorn-pocked hills. I watched him proceed, joyful and proud at his renewed strength, until he stepped atop a ridge. Then I almost collapsed in shock. With the caravan stretched across the horizon, the Dove marched on, naked yet undeterred, in full profile against the morning sun.

"Jonah!" I cried out. "Jonah, stop!"

He didn't.

Oh Lord of Heaven, Creator of all things, Master of the universe, protect us now!

I started to charge after him, chastising myself for not foreseeing this, desperate to save him from this great embarrassment, when I remembered all the things I'd dropped on the sand. By the time I had run back and loaded up my burdens, Jonah was halfway to the forming train of donkeys and camels.

I guess I should not have been surprised that his approach brought things to a halt. Children pointed, speaking with passion among themselves. Women pulled their blue and black veils over the rest of their faces, while the men just stared.

I broke into a run, fearful of what might happen, but soon the kinnor vibrated in a strange chord, so I slowed. Then a man robed in many colors strode with great purpose toward the Dove, and so I sprinted to catch up.

The wind was kind that morning. Though I was yet a while away, I could hear their words.

"May the Lord smile upon you," offered the Dove.

"And yours to you," said the man, a rather large one bound in a beautiful two-piece cloak of rainbow bands, a purple tunic, and a head wrap of crimson linen tied with golden ropes. "Though it appears grace is not with you."

Two younger men ran forward, both also dressed in wealth.

"Send him away!" said one, even as I approached.

"Cover yourself!" swore the other.

I must admit, I was ready to turn back to Tyre, the sea, or anywhere else. Even considering Jonah's zealous indiscretion, these people did not look hospitable. But the Dove stood firm, both forgiving and unashamed.

"I beg your pardon," he said, "but I have been swept up from the sea and have no clothing."

"Or color," the first man spoke. By the prominence of his curled black beard, and the subservience of the others, I felt safe guessing he guided this caravan. "Indeed, as the sun shone upon you, we wondered what curse could taint a man so."

"That of his own making," said the Dove. "I have sinned against God and have been punished. But now I do that which I refused before."

The youngest boy's eyes burned with hatred. "Do not hear them!" he urged. For his part, the older one offered nothing but a wave of three fingers, a sign the pup frowned at. As did I, for I had seen his kind often enough in Bethel, and in the king's court. He was a calculator, a manipulator, ever turning things to his advantage.

I wonder if the Dove realized that.

"Oh?" said the caravan leader, ignoring his sons, yet betraying nothing of his own thoughts. "And what would that be?"

Only then did Jonah acknowledge me with a grasp of his hand. "We are bound for Nineveh. To speak the judgment of God Most High."

That shook the younger men into silence, their tongues drying in the sun. Even the elder could not hide his stunned fascination… or was it amusement? His hands went to his beard, running its curls through his callused fingers. His eyes danced, gazing first to his camels, then to the Dove, then to his women, then the Dove. Twice his lips parted as if to speak, but in the end, they offered only a smile.

At that moment, as even the wind seemed stilled by Jonah's flat statement, every hair of my skin stood. I felt in my core a strong urge to leave. In no way did this man's presence seem right. Yet Jonah shared none of this, from what I could tell.

"If I may ask a pardon of your hospitality," he said with charm, even grace, "may my friend and I walk with you? We have a long trip before us, and neither of us knows these lands."

"A long trip," echoed the man. Looking upon us once more, he erupted in a haughty laugh that sawed against my patience. "My friend, to the edge of the world would you walk? If I were not so sure you had already met death, I would dare say the sands themselves would have judgment on you!"

With a clap of his hands, he commanded one of the young ones to fetch Jonah a tunic, sandals, and cloak. Then he ordered a cover for me as well.

"Forgive me," he asked, pointing with a nod to the Dove, "but I dare not expose my women to such things. Who knows what they might decide they want? But I go beyond myself. Be at ease here! I am Han-Alphinami, sheik of Armanis. Merchant, rancher, ruler of the lands within the southern peaks of western Aram."

"May our Lord bless you, Han-Alphinami, and those of your household. I am Jonah, son of Amittai of Galilee."

The light of recognition illuminated the sheik. "A Jew," he whispered.

"Indeed," Jonah stated, not minding the slant. "And this is Benjamin."

"Son of Gideon," I added with reluctance. But the sheik did not notice.

"I have heard of you," he told the Dove, even as those I guessed were his sons laid clothes at Jonah's feet. The garments were of a durable fabric, by all appearances, but not the garb of royalty. That, at least, proved reassuring.

"You," continued Han-Alphinami, "are the prophet of King Jeroboam II of Israel, he who threw out the Aramaeans and Assyrians from the Damascus plains."

"I am," said Jonah, "though it was the hand of God that fought our battles."

A twinkle of pleasure crossed this herdsman's black eyes. The sheik smiled as one taking pleasure in pain, saying, "And he left you with Jeroboam's death."

"Even before, as the king abandoned Him," Jonah stated. Slipping into the garments, he went on, "Jeroboam fought those battles for his own glory, not the Lord's. I led them for reasons our Lord has not always made clear. But the kings of Israel blaspheme, and bring disgrace on our people and our Lord."

The sheik quaked with those words. As did I, I must admit.

"You do not guard your tongue," Han-Alphinami commented.

Jonah remained hard. "When the Lord leads me, I no longer hesitate."

"Such faith," the sheik marveled. "And so you will speak, to Nineveh?"

That made me realize once more just what Jonah sought to do. And I thought to myself, Do I want to share in this? Do I have any choice? But if the Dove held any second thoughts, he shed them.

"It is the Lord's will," he proclaimed.

"Ah." The smile of Han-Alphinami grew wide. "And how could it not be? For if Israel has earned punishment, then Nineveh draws eternal damnation! Oh, this is worth the company of the dead!"

I almost chastised him then, talking of Jonah as if he were a corpse! But the Dove seemed aware of my thoughts and, with one gentle nod, he defused my anger.

Han-Alphinami moved on without noticing my frustration. "Let us get going!" To his sons he shouted, "Finish the loading! We have customers waiting!" To the women he gave no quarter "What? Have we food enough already? Gather more!" To the children he scowled, and scowled, and scowled some more. But to us he smiled.

"So we travel!" he proclaimed. "To Damascus!"

The Journey

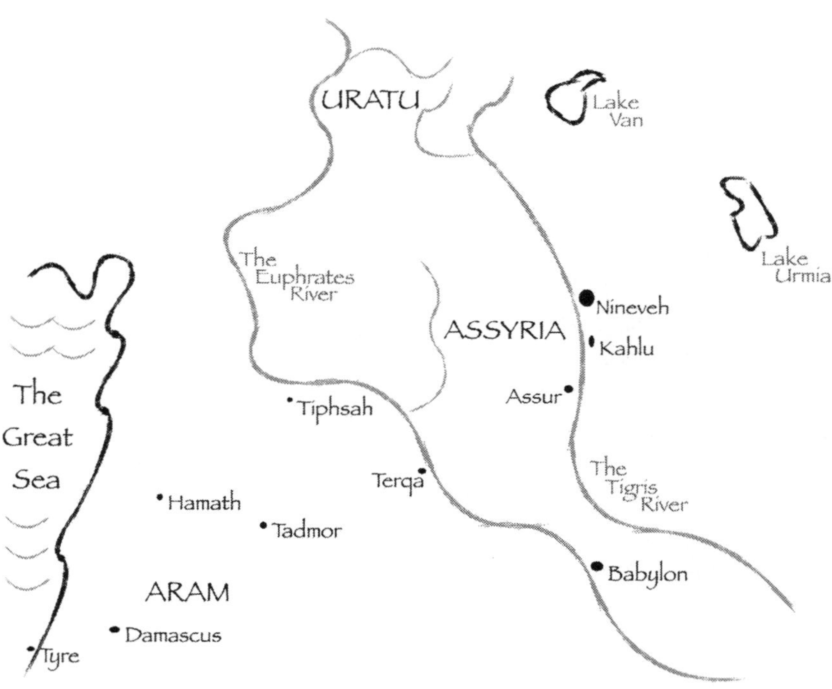
URATU
Lake Van
Lake Urmia
The Euphrates River
ASSYRIA
Nineveh
Kahlu
Assur
The Great Sea
Tiphsah
Terqa
The Tigris River
Hamath
Tadmor
Babylon
ARAM
Damascus
Tyre

Chapter 16
Full circle

The first morning out was the worst. But then, a dog's slurping tongue is a foul way to greet any day.

It struck first against my left eye, then deep within my right ear. I could not wiggle away fast enough.

A girl laughed. As did Han-Alphinami.

"I am sorry," he said as I rubbed my face against my sleeves. "I could not restrain him."

I doubt he tried.

The child chuckled with an uplifting joy that dampened my sourness. "A tongue," I allowed, "is better than teeth."

Only as I finished wiping out my eye did I see just how true that was. The dog was more like a brown wolf, thick-haired and lean despite its impressive bulk. The young child must have been about two and a half cubits tall, and still she had to tiptoe to touch the dog's back. As she tried to hug him, the beast turned its green eyes upon me. Only then did I sense its firm, protective aura.

"Friend, Axe," the sheik told his pet. Then he asked me to speak. "Let him know you."

Now I had never liked dogs. In Bethel they roamed the night in vile packs, sometimes attacking people as the canines raided the streets for refuse. Hosea used to throw them scraps just to keep them at bay. So, as you can see, I had reason to dislike the savage ones. But I knew not to insult the sheik in the tent of his guests, and I could not ignore the beast's finger-length teeth hovering before my face, with breath like the winds of Samaria's dung gate.

"Welcome, Axe," I managed.

"Come, Chani," called Han-Alphinami. The girl answered with a joyous hug about her father's broad chest. His face glowed within her loving display.

"Ah," he cooed as she ran off, "girls are as sweet honey, a true gift of the gods. If only they could be boys."

He laughed as Axe's long tongue lapped my cheeks. "A friend you have found!" the sheik boasted. His laugh made me smile. Lord forgive me, it was but the first of many times I buried my true feelings to placate our host.

Oh, it was a bitter thing to do. Especially when the Dove stepped into view, as he always did. That made me feel even more the hypocrite.

Our first week together I learned of the sheik's three wives, five sons, and seven daughters, most of whom traveled with us. It surprised me, for as rough a person as he seemed to be, Han-Alphinami loved his family and chose to keep them all at his side whenever possible – an impressive chore, since he spent most of his summers trading stock and supplies between Tyre, Damascus, and Sidon.

I soon discovered a travel schedule like that meant careful planning and ample weaponry. To watch his flocks, Han-Alphinami employed about four shepherds and a pack of fourteen dogs. His two older sons played major roles, choosing the caravan's path, overseeing supplies, and negotiating for water rights and low tax rates at villages. And then there were the six mercenaries on horseback, trained by the Assyrians, armored in special bronze plate and skirtings, with the symbol of Han-Alphinami highlighted in gold.

Such are the advantages of wealth.

As you might guess, such a large group required special attention when we traveled. The Dove and I rode on two of the eighteen packed donkeys, while the sheik of Armanis and his sons sat as kings atop their camels, always accompanied by at least one of the warriors. The shepherds walked with the flocks, and the women and children went on foot about the countryside, scrounging for food. In that way the caravan carved a wide swath as it traveled east into the peaks.

To be honest, as we started this venture, I feared bloodshed. With thirty-some travelers and four flocks of sheep in transit, I doubted any farmers and villagers would welcome us at their waterholes. And the sheik, stingy with his wealth, was well-armed and very determined to have his way in things. But I was wrong. From the first day we traveled as might a sick crow, changing directions three times to visit four communities. Such wandering limited our progress towards Nineveh, yet relations with the locals could not have been more pleasant.

"He's a merchant," the Dove later explained. "He must have customers on every hill between here and Damascus."

And so it was. The crow was not so sick after all.

Soon I came to understand their routine. Each morning they woke me before daylight, the women having prepared us a breakfast of bread, butter, and fruit. As Han-Alphinami plotted the day's course with his sons and Scrorant, leader of his war band, the women and children dismantled the tents and, with the shepherds and mercenaries, packed the donkeys. I helped them when I could. Then we were off, our course meandering from friendly cities and towns to needed waterholes. We rested in the heat of the day, then traveled to nightfall, where the men set up camp while the women prepared our second meal, comprised of stew and bread cakes as thin as goatskin parchment.

In such travel, trading was a necessity if you wanted fresh bread, fruit, milk, and butter along your way. To our advantage, or Han-Alphinami's credit, only once in our journey did a morning pass when he chose to press ahead, without stops. But that afternoon we rested at a village, again enjoying buttered bread and figs.

I soon came to treasure those moments. We never had butter at Bethel. Though it was somewhat oily, that taste of sunshine was something I could not forget. Often I lay awake at night savoring the flavor, its essence still fresh on my lips.

Through it all, the Dove remained somewhat distant. Part of that came with the journey – after all, it was hard to sustain a dialogue when suspended atop a burdened donkey in a moving caravan. Yet Jonah often chose to remain silent. Each night he fell more within his prayers, and each day he emerged colder and more anguished than before. And he would not explain why.

Making things even more awkward was the mindset of the sheik and his people. Though we ate together within his tent, with his hospitality ever available, Han-Alphinami never greeted the Dove or offered entertainment, as was the custom. And we held few discussions. Indeed, the sheik seemed to welcome our absence and tried to avoid Jonah whenever possible. His people followed his example, his sons with open disdain.

"Can you blame them?" the Dove said on the fourth day. "The Lord has left a mark upon me none can ignore."

So it was. Every stop we made, every rest we took, our hosts would ever stare and point at the Dove's chalky skin. The spectacle bothered me, but Jonah seemed undeterred.

Our main problem arose with our first Sabbath. While we soon found Han-Alphinami did not follow our customs, his own rules of hospitality would not allow him to simply forget us.

To his credit, the Dove had foreseen the issue. We had camped within the peaks, where the sheik long before had built a set of sheepfolds. As we gathered about the stew kettle, each with a lap of parchment bread, Jonah told Han-Alphinami of our plans to pray together through the next day.

Oh, was the old man ever shrewd!

"Didn't know you could do that atop a donkey," he said, his face a collage of shadows in the dim light of his two oil lamps.

"We cannot," the Dove replied. "We will remain here until that nightfall."

"Remain here," the sheik repeated, his eyes dubious.

"Impossible," stated the oldest son, Harn-Kelnat. "Our schedule allows no rest."

"Neither does ours," Jonah stepped in. "This is worship, not rest."

"Worship?" said the young man.

"The seventh day of each week," I offered as an explanation. But it was clear they were not interested.

"Then we will leave you here," said the other son, Santerith.

"Wait," interrupted Han-Alphinami, offering an enlightened smile. To the Dove he said, "You would give up a day's travel, have me delay a day's business, maybe more, just to worship this god who cursed your life?"

"I cursed myself," Jonah said.

"Oh?" The sheik seemed amused. "How so?"

"By refusing His will," the Dove admitted. "By defying His wisdom."

"Ah, the sins of Nineveh." Han-Alphinami snorted. A wave of dust flew from his beard. "I know you, prophet. You travel now, yet defiance is yet your trade. This trip carves at your heart like maggots on a carcass."

That attack surprised me. "You are wrong," I said in Jonah's defense.

"Am I?" His eyes bore into the stiff Dove. "You find it unbelievable the god of Israel would seek repentance from the Assyrians. For that is what it is, am I right? If he wished the city destroyed, would he not just wipe it clean, as he did Sodom? Or was that a folktale?"

"Your own words accept its truth," Jonah stated, his jaw tight.

It amazed me that this merchant of heathens had seen through the Dove's dismay. But when he laughed, the sheik spoke words that passed beyond my feeble foresight.

"You refuse to think your god could care about us… Gentiles. Is that not what you named us?"

"No!" I interrupted. "I have seen Phoenicians welcome God's truth."

Jonah turned against me, spearing me with his sharp gaze. I found myself reviewing my words, wondering what I had said to earn his fury.

To my fortune, the sheik did not see our division. He was too caught up in his own attack.

"Of course, your god opened himself to the sailors. Was he not with Abraham in Ur? Joseph in Egypt? Moses in the Sinai? He is not just god in your land, but everywhere… if you accept your own faith."

"We are His chosen people," Jonah stated, each syllable stressed as if a piece of profound wisdom. "Outsiders must enter our faith, our people, to join among the saved."

"And that," said Han-Alphinami, "amuses me more than anything."

"Why?" I wanted to know.

"You question my trade, boy," he snapped. "I pass by Dan often enough. I see how your northern temple functions… your people's alleged faith. Why any god would want his followers to be among you is beyond me. Such poor examples."

That made me mad. That it was true did not matter. But the Dove bid me be silent.

"Those upstarts Zechariah, Menahem… they were not the first to install idols in your temples," continued Han-Alphinami. "Your people put more stock in the rituals of Canaan and Philistia, Moab and Ammon. Why, I'll bet I have sold more golden Baals in Israel than Tyre!"

"Nevertheless," stated Jonah. There was a fierceness in his voice that I had not heard there before. "Nevertheless… we will pray tomorrow."

At that, the sons broke their strained silence.

"We will leave you here," repeated Santerith.

"We have no time for such things!" agreed Harn-Kelnat.

"No," said the sheik.

Rarely had such a softly spoken word caused such unrest. Both sons seemed disgusted by the idea. In the dancing shadows of the lamps, their eyes glowed in their hatred of us.

"You cannot do this," protested Harn-Kelnat.

"Father, we would fall behind," agreed Santerith. "Korgathin awaits."

"Is that butcher more worthy of my house?" asked Han-Alphinami. "Can guests be allowed to wander in the den of serpents? These two would not survive a single morning beyond my sight."

"It does not stain our honor to let them choose their fate,"

Santerith fought on, having learned to mimic his father's stubborn heart. But the sheik would not budge.

"To let friends choose disaster is to share in their fate. No, my sons. Once given, our word is our blood."

"And what of your word to Korgathin?" snapped Harn-Kelnat. "To Asperath?"

"They will understand," the sheik said with a sigh. "I will have Scrorant ride ahead. He can tell them." He leaned back, his face cloaked in shadows, then reflected, "I have offered these Jews my house. That is not withdrawn."

These Jews.... To Han-Alphinami, the words were a curse bound by his loyalty. I could not help wondering, if he thought such of us, why he had ever accepted our company.

The meal closed in silence. Feeling awkward among them, I took maybe four more bites, each a struggle, then folded my napkin. The Dove did the same. We asked and received the sheik's blessing to leave, and soon did so.

Even in the night, the moon waning in the east, I felt their lingering hostility. Those who crossed our path turned away in disgust.

"Amazing," reflected the Dove.

"Word passes quickly," I offered.

"Not just any word," Jonah countered, turning toward our shared tent. "His words. Think, Benjamin. They are not unlike those of our Lord, of His promise to me. To everyone."

Lifting the entry flap of goat's hair cloth, the Dove hurried into our tent. One of Han-Alphinami's daughters had already come and gone, arranging our blankets and setting a burning oil lamp to hang from our room's center post.

I rushed after Jonah, admitting, "I don't understand." But he offered nothing else. In time I fell asleep listening to his snores, the call and answer of distant lions, and my growing belief that the Dove was hiding something from me. Irrational, perhaps, yet as the days passed that feeling thrived, for I had many questions of him, many mysteries I wanted explained. And he avoided me.

A dust storm confronted us as we reached Mount Hermon. My thoughts were ablaze with memories of that crucial battle, and my first meeting with the Dove. I often spoke of them, but Jonah maintained his silence. The caravan rounded the peak in a hurry, passing around the mounds of Assyrian dead in the foothills of Aram to reach the plains of Damascus and the Road of Jeroboam, our access lane from Dan to the Great Trunk Road and the King's Highway. But like most accomplishments of its namesake, which were committed outside our Lord, the Road of Jeroboam had almost disappeared beneath fresh weeds and cultivated fields.

The next day we came to the walls of Damascus.

I looked forward to seeing this fortress of our ancient enemy. I had been there only once before, and that just a brief stay, but I had been impressed with its apricot and almond groves, the desert shining east and south, snow-bearded Hermon behind us. Damascus itself seemed rather dirty, its walls scarred from battles beyond number, but what city would not show such scars when it had sheltered men almost since time began?

This day started out of sorts. As the winds circled around and between our tents, shrieking with the demons of that Aramaean earth, a silent Han-Alphinami fed us a meager meal of figs and olive oil on brittle bread. We broke camp and headed straight to the capital city, never once stopping to trade along our way.

By then my seat was well accustomed to the saddle and the knobby walk of the pack-laden donkey. Not that mules or camels would have been better, but not since the last portion of the Jeroboam campaign had I ridden so far on a donkey's back, and, to be honest, I wished no more. So when the well-worn walls of Damascus reared before us, with formidable stone towers as tall as the sea waves that had almost capsized our ship of Tarshish, I was overjoyed to stand on my own two feet – until the gatekeepers came upon us. Looking oh so imposing in their bronze plate armor and conical helmets, their sour faces dry with fine powder from the Syrian breeze, these four men had all the rash appearances of people seeking something to pour their frustrations upon. Han-Alphinami provided it.

"You have a large party, Sheik of Armanis," said one. "Your tax will be high, unless Scrorant spoke true."

"Strange they know one another," I whispered to the Dove.

But Jonah motioned for me to be quiet. His gaze burned in fury.

"Has my word ever failed you?" Han-Alphinami snapped. "They ride behind us."

They?

Wiping my face, I pulled down my wind scarf to see the burly guardsmen walk past the sheik's mercenaries to stop before Jonah. They squinted to view the Dove, their irritated eyes at first suspicious, then fearful, as if by just looking at him, they could be cursed.

"Is he ill?" one asked.

"Pay his lies no mind," said Harn-Kelnat, stepping forward. Taking Jonah's dirt-stained cloak, the young son yanked the Dove from his perch and sent him tumbling across the sand of the road. His head struck a stone, spurring a painful cry. I yelled something and ran to his side, even as the son told them to take us. I had no sooner lifted Jonah's bruised head when the guardsmen's strong hands dragged us to our feet.

"Come along, Jews," said their leader. "Ansephanti awaits."

My heart sank with his words. I well-remembered that name, and his death sentence.

We were betrayed!

Chapter 17
"Burn them!"

Humiliation. Painful, depressing humiliation. Paraded through the southern Damascus gates as a prisoner. I had seen people tortured this way, but never imagined I would suffer so. That sounds strange, considering what I've endured since then – and I always thought myself capable of withstanding most things. But walking with my wrists bound to a thick cedar post weighing upon my neck and shoulders, and that tied to another heavy beam swinging against my hips… oh, it takes a hard soul to not break under such agony.

That's assuming you're strong enough to bear that weight. I don't know how I did, to be honest, but I was young then, and when you are forced to do something, you often find the way. For a while, at least.

Having removed our cloaks, sandals, and headgear, they herded us into the city to the fading taunts of Han-Alphinami and his sons. Only then did I realize the true heart of the merchant.

"Why do you think we were never attacked?" the Dove remarked, laboring to speak. "He traded with bandits."

"Quiet!" a guard snapped.

Jonah gritted his teeth, spitting out dust. "They would not harm their own."

The guard slapped first Jonah's forehead, then his left ear. That sent the Dove tumbling to the hard earth. The sound of his wood beams striking stone within the angled gate, choking him as one fell against his neck… Lord forgive me, I have rarely felt such hatred! Shouting defiance, I earned a blow of my own. My right eye, already aggravated by the blowing grit, began to swell after that painful attack.

"Dogs," I snarled.

"Curb your tongue," a guard warned, "or I will do it for you."

A mad reply came to my lips, but Jonah motioned me to be silent. It was hard.

"They only do their duty," the Dove whispered.

A guard kicked his left hip. Jonah stumbled, but managed not to fall.

"Their duty," I fumed.

Lord help me, I could never forgive them for beating us so! How could he?

Passing through the wide stone entryway, we encountered a marketplace almost abandoned to the dust storm. The merchant tents rippled against their anchoring ties, unmanned, leaving only traders with walls of stone and wood open to buyers. Few braved the streets, Arameans who took one look at the Dove and gaped even in that gritty wind. A few shouted taunts but most crept back, as if wary of catching whatever disease marked him.

Our guards chose a winding path to the governor's palace. Beyond the markets rose hills covered with ramshackle huts of brick and stone, haphazard structures crumbling at their seams, pocked with weeds. Their streets narrowed into dark cobblestone inlets a pack of dogs would have trouble navigating, littered with overflowing waste kettles, piles of fodder, and other decaying filth. The stench tore at my gut, though I had no mind to dwell on it, so hard was our forced march. Twice the posts on our backs proved too wide for the shadowy paths, forcing us into teetering sideways struts. The first time I did not grasp quick enough how to balance the beams, so the impatient guards yanked back the left end of my hip post. That twisted me about as a woman might knead her bread dough. I screamed. The ruffians laughed.

Anger warred with my pain to rule my thoughts. As we entered yet another refuse-ridden passage, its walls so close together we almost had to turn around, I asked why these guards insisted on torturing us.

"You think this bad?" one snapped as another kicked me. "You should be here in the rains. Most everyone wants to leave then."

As I choked on that, we emerged from the stonework crevasses to a broad, wind-swept street leading to a security wall and gatehouse. A crowd formed at the foot of that ancient boundary, merchants and others irritated at having to wait in those dusty gusts before passing beyond the checkpoint, but this blessed us, for it brought our march to a merciful stop. Catching what breath I could in that gritty air, I tried to stomp the muck from between my toes. That's when I spied the silhouette of the governor's citadel atop the next hill. It loomed over the sand-blasted city, dark and imposing, a fortress within a fortress. That image frustrated me, for I knew it was our destination, whether these dogs would admit it or not, and yet they led Jonah and I away from those spires. So I spat this point at our guides, who laughed in their self-ordained superiority and directed us down another narrow path in the wrong direction.

"In a hurry to die?" one asked me.

"Don't worry," said a companion. "The executioner will not leave without you."

I remembered people like this in Jeroboam's service, brutal brigands who took sadistic pleasure when working tasks in their master's absence. These dogs meant to delay our appointments as long as possible. Or they just enjoyed wearing us down. Or both.

Our morning degenerated into a series of endless loops, so that in my weariness, I soon lost track of where I was. My feet cracked and bled worse than they had on the road from Aphek. My back and neck seemed aflame, and I had long since lost all feeling in my arms.

Awakened by a string of torches, I became aware of tight stone walls to either side of that coarse rock scraping my toes. We climbed stairs in a pinched hallway, warmed by smoky air slipping across our ankles and knees. From nowhere came a guard who shoved me left. The wooden slab at my shoulder slapped against one wall, then bounced into another. The echo rippled through my bones. Losing my balance, I started to tumble when hands grabbed my posts and tipped them sideways. My neck felt stretched to the tearing point. I think I screamed, though I do not remember for sure. Then I fell. My skull struck cold stone.

"Lucky," a guard told me with a frown of disappointment, as if he'd lost a bet. "Last time we did that, the bars fell different ways. The man almost got his arms torn off."

Perhaps the ruffian did me good, for his punishing words rekindled anger strong enough to ford the sea of pains numbing my mind. I found myself on my back, my eyes turned toward rows of tall granite columns holding aloft a ceiling of dark cloths stretched over cedar poles. Oil lamps hung from cross timbers, mixing with mounted torches to light a vast chamber. Music flowed everywhere – the whirling ring of the bronze hazora, the sharp, plucked notes of the stringed nebel, the light breeze of the halil pipe, the thumping echoes of many tof drums. The stones echoed the vibrant embrace of the musicians – who by their skills must have been very well cared for indeed.

So enchanting was their play that, for a brief while, I forgot my sorrows. But all things of man come to their end, and so did the song. At its close cymbals crashed, and I heard the call, "Bring the prisoners!" Before its echo died, the guards lifted me to my feet by my posts, then thrust them forward. I somehow kept my balance, shuffling behind the Dove through the soaring columns into a vast chamber of marble walls dotted with etched paintings, flaming torches, and golden engravings accented with a multitude of shimmering jewels.

"The wealth of Urartu," Jonah mumbled, to earn a kick to his left shin.

For the first time since entering the city, I got a good look at the Dove. His left cheek bled from a long, swollen gash, and his tunic was torn in many spots, but otherwise he looked normal – which of course was terrible for anyone but him.

Before us, on a massive throne of marble and oiled oak inlaid with ivory, silver, gold, and jewels, between two large winged bulls cast in bronze, sat proud Ansephanti. The western governor of Assyria seemed none the worse for wear. Though not armed for battle, his silk cloaks boasted multicolored drawings detailing his military victories, and he accented them with what looked like the same glistening, gem-laden leather belt and sandals I saw him wear at Mount Hermon. About his waist danced a ringing symphony of jeweled daggers, and at either side lay magnificent scabbards of gold and ivory, topped by shining hilts in the shape of lions. Around his wrists hung rings of bronze and copper, smelt as serpents. Atop his skull rested a thick bronze helmet with a crest of crimson horsehair.

He sat deep within his chair, his eyes ablaze, his fingers playing with his long black beard. Across his lips spread a foul smile.

I thought I would grow sick.

The guards bid us kneel at the foot of the throne. When the Dove refused, they buckled his knees for him. In silence he tumbled forward, his chin splitting against the stone.

The governor laughed.

"What is this thing you bring me?" he asked his guards. "It looks like something I might cast from my stomach!"

The audience joined in his amusement. I felt like cursing them all but managed to restrain myself.

"Ah, prophet," Ansephanti whispered with a most vile familiarity, "we have traded places, you and I. Your day has swept by in the wind, and I once more sit within my chamber."

"It is God's will," answered Jonah, rising to his knees.

"It is my will!" the governor roared.

"You fool yourself."

At a nod from Ansephanti, the guards struck Jonah's bruised chin with gloved hands. His face slapped from side to side against the unforgiving wood at his neck, but Jonah did not fall.

"No," said the governor, "it is you who's deluded. Where is your god now? Did he not realize the debt Han-Alphinami owes me? Did he not know what deaths I have planned for you?"

"The time of my death," stammered the Dove, "is neither mine nor yours."

"You worm!" Ansephanti spat, lurching forward in his throne. "You dare challenge me?"

At his upraised hand stepped forth a menacing warrior bound in well-oiled leather and bronze. The governor withdrew a golden dagger from his belt and held it before his minion.

"His insolence remains," the governor declared, nodding toward Jonah. "Shave his head."

Snapping upright in salute, the warrior carried the fine blade to the Dove, who was secured on his knees by two of our escorts. The palace guard nodded to them, then lifted the Dove's beard in his hand and pulled his neck taut.

"Twitch and you die," he whispered.

Jonah held his breath, his eyes clamped shut. The warrior scraped the shimmering gold blade against the Dove's alabaster neck. The cut proved clean. Bit by bit, from a few stiff strings to clustered, sticky tufts, I watched Jonah's graying beard float to the floor. Tides of desperation washed over me. Having no idea what to do, I prayed to Yahweh for guidance.

Though I had never seen a man so punished, I had heard of it done. The humiliation of losing that which most represented your life and wisdom was more than most men could bear. For the rest of his days, everyone who looked upon the Dove would see a man humbled before the world. I knew this well. Due to my young age and spotty beard, I was often overlooked and maligned. It was expected and easy to accept. But that did not help the much-older Dove. Even worse, in the eyes of most people, Jonah would be suspect without ever speaking a word, ever placed in league with convicted criminals and rebels. Indeed, I had heard of prisoners accepting death rather than allow themselves to be so defrocked.

The guard finished with a delicate touch, for the white flesh of Jonah's chin still bled from his fall at the gate. But with the last of that beard lying against the stone, the guard wiped the governor's damp blade against his leather knee brace and started on the Dove's scalp.

"You do not gloat now!" Ansephanti crowed.

"This is nothing," Jonah mumbled. "My God branded me far

worse than anything you could do."

The governor's face turned red with fury. Drawing his long knife, he leaped before the Dove and shoved the guard away, his dagger having scraped clean only a third of Jonah's head. Ansephanti placed his long blade at Jonah's forehead, its tip resting atop the Dove's nose.

"It's time to settle things," the governor snarled. "You defaced and belittled me. Now I have you in chains. You sought to wound me. I've now marked you for life. You tried to dictate my future. Now you're mine to command."

Jonah smiled through his bruises. "No one on this earth can stay me," he said.

"No one?" The governor tipped his blade forward. Its point pierced the Dove's white scalp. "You are mine, Jew."

"No."

Ansephanti's eyes turned cold, ruthless. His knife bit deeper.

"Your life is mine. Say it!"

"No," Jonah repeated. Blood flowed between his eyes, yet his voice held steady. "I bear witness to the words of the Lord. None may impede them."

"None? None?"

With his eyes spread wide, his heart enraged, the governor raised his blade high to strike the Dove down with one quick thrust. Jonah breathed deep but did not turn away. I closed my eyes and prayed for relief, not wanting to see the end.

Through the darkness I noted a sly chuckle. Curious, I broke my prayer to find the governor standing in amusement, his blade put away.

"You have lost none of your courage, prophet," he said with reluctant admiration. "I give you that. Speak then your message."

"It is not for you, Ansephanti."

Hearing his name tightened the governor's gaze. "Who then do you seek?"

"I travel with this young man to Nineveh. The Lord Most High has seen its sins and found them unworthy."

"Ah." The governor looked to the ceiling, considering it, then spun about and sank into his throne. "Ah, Jonah, this is sweet indeed! And what judgment does your god proclaim?"

"That is for the Lord to determine, governor. I will learn it when they do. I know only to speak against Nineveh for forty days."

That I had never heard before. Forty days… it seemed a long time to chastise a hostile people for their sins.

Ansephanti settled within his throne, spinning the tip of his beard through his loose fingers. A confident smile accented his cunning gaze.

"I like this, prophet." The governor looked left, nodding to someone behind the support pillars. "Indeed, I think it a grand idea!"

Snapping his fingers to the guards, he commanded, "Release them!" Then he returned his attention to the Dove. "Know you this, Jew. I have aligned myself and my district with Mati-ilu and the Urartu Federation."

"Thus the helmet," Jonah said, his voice little more than a murmur, "and the ironworks, the polished gems."

"Ah, your god told you this?" Ansephanti sounded like he both mocked yet somewhat believed the idea. "Then tell me, was it wise?"

"Wise?" I thought aloud.

"Will the Assyrian bull rise again?" Jonah asked, rephrasing the question for me. "Of course. Will it collapse? That, too, will come to pass. How it will impact Damascus, the Lord has not shared with me."

"As I expected," the governor replied, undisturbed. "I do not mind telling you how the empire has withdrawn. To maintain arms for the swordsmiths, for my troops... to rebuild those things still withering from my father's time… I needed ores from Urartu, Kummuhu, and Kue, and upstart Urartu controls most trade there. Tyre never supplied enough, but then, the mainland routes are our strength. Yet with the collapse...."

He pivoted then, waving his fist in the air.

"The federation promises me endless supplies, and maybe horses for our chariots. And Mati-ilu has delivered, so far, while Assur and Calah babble about problems in Babylon, in Sumer. As for the rest, why, we have had two good harvests, and the trade is good, though Menahem is a boil. Our cattle multiply and the Chaldeans seem intent on settling around Elam, so I am happy with things there.

"Truly, it is good for us, prophet – we are Aram again! And we will fight to stay that way."

Amazing, the transformation that had taken hold of Ansephanti. He now spoke to us as he might to his advisers!

I may never understand the art of intimidation, of trying to subjugate the enemy. It now seems obvious that was Ansephanti's sole purpose for our chains. That realization would have angered me had I paid it much attention, but my thoughts were on other things. With the heavy posts removed from my back, I struggled to stand and stretch, enjoying the rush of lifeblood into my throbbing limbs even as my liberated muscles twisted in spasms. The welts along my back, neck, and arms screamed in their agony.

"You tell me this," Jonah reflected, considering it all, "not fearing excursions by Israel."

The governor laughed. "Menahem? His own people would topple him if they could – would they not?"

That I could agree with, but Jonah gave no indication of what he felt.

"But it would not matter anyway," continued Ansephanti. "What does he have – two hundred good chariots? A hundred? Probably less. But I, with our supplies renewed, I have built nearly ten times that – and I will have more.

"No, Jonah, I tell you this because you forced my hand. To march against Jeroboam with less than fifty chariots… oh, I was so arrogant to think I could have ever won that battle! But those days are ended, and I am past being humbled. Truly, prophet, I bid you well on your journey. I do! Speak judgment on Nineveh. Burn it to the ground!"

When a fool's dream becomes reality, it can numb your mind. At least, that was how it struck me. I stood there like a statue, dumbfounded that the governor of Damascus shared this sentiment with the Dove.

"Burn it," I whispered.

"Indeed," said Ansephanti. "Pronounce your god's judgment. Make it a wasteland none will remember! They deserve nothing less. We are better off without them. Look upon us as you travel – I speak for all those the children of Ashur have trampled and held captive. Have your god destroy Nineveh! Slay them all! I believe your god could do this… and the world will be better for it. Do it, Jonah. Burn them!"

I marveled at his words. Such a statement of misplaced faith.

I waited then, expecting the Dove to say something of how our Lord's judgment was His, and His alone. But Jonah remained still.

Whatever it was – the renewed freedom that flooded my stiff body, the last ebbs of anger with Han-Alphinami and our captivity, my revulsion with the governor, or the sudden diplomacy between that chameleon and the Dove – whatever it was, I found myself filled with apathy toward anything to do with Nineveh and this foul quest. Apathy building itself into hatred.

Could this, this command of death, be as Ansephanti suggested – a passage to secure the annihilation of the Assyrian capital? I saw silent agreement in the Dove's eyes, in hope if not intent. Yet that seemed wrong to me.

No… it did not seem wrong – it was wrong. I did not know what Yahweh's intent was – how could I? – but in my heart, I knew it was not to punish Israel or Assyria. I was sure of that.

"We will see," Jonah whispered. Grimacing as he stood upright, he looked the governor in the eye and sighed. "We shall see."

Chapter 18
Revelations

It took about a month for my welts, my broken skin, even my mind to heal. My restless spirit magnified my suffering, which hurt all the more when I found overcoming these handicaps was not the end, but the beginning of my recovery. For such tests of endurance and pain spur further anguish in ways hard to predict – as I soon discovered.

As we left ancient Damascus in the caravan of Philar-Al'andron – a merchant who called himself Tum for some reason he never explained – I found my arms ached as if they'd been wrenched apart and never knitted back together. Worse still, my spine cried out at any sudden movements. Yet these pains were nothing compared to the trials of my heart.

To be honest, the words of Ansephanti haunted my waking moments, as did Jonah's response, or lack thereof. I prayed for understanding and relief, and yet within me grew an impatience with the Dove… a gnawing frustration bordering on distrust.

But again, I leap ahead of myself. Forgive me.

After twenty lashes, the governor released us without a single guard for escort. Whether that meant he believed in us or not, I didn't know nor care to ask. Jonah's first concern, once we regained our strength from the lash, was to seek out a barber to shave off the rest of his hair and stubble. To my surprise, he seemed content with his bare scalp and jaw.

"People will judge me over the Lord's mark, not Ansephanti's," he said as the barber patched the wounds on his bleached chin. But I wondered.

With that trial behind us, the Dove could focus on our trip. He considered throwing lots over which route to take next – the northern loop passage through the towns Hamath, Harran, and Gozan, which did receive most trade, or the "desert's skirt" passage around Tadmor, Terqa, and Assur. Not knowing what to say, I offered no advice. In the end, the Dove sought help at the northern gate from the merchants who made the journeys, and after the commotion over his bruised white skin died down, Jonah found one trader he trusted – Tum, a rather plump, dark-haired man who loved to wear brushed wolf skins for cloaks. He spoke with a clear voice, though often with a long, bulbous gourd either clutched between his splotched yellow teeth or held at the ready in his left hand, its polished nozzle never far from his lips.

At least, I thought it was a gourd, or perhaps a gnarled wooden rod, hollowed and carved with ornate signs of Assyrian and Babylonian gods. In truth, I do not know what it was; I avoided that thing whenever possible. It stank of the most repugnant ash.

Forgive me; I digress once more.

Tum owned several groomed camels that he offered us to ride. That promised improved speed, until we found others with us riding donkeys, mules, a horse or two, even oxen – a sight I never contemplated before that moment, I can assure you.

I knew not what deal the Dove could make since we had no gold or silver, but it soon worked out. As he spoke with Tum, Jonah lifted a beaten kinnor from the wall of a nearby trader's shack, tuned its strings, and sweetened the dusty wind with his song. At his tale's close, Tum bought him the instrument and promised us transportation.

Thus, we rode well-worn trails toward Tadmor and eventually Nineveh, with Jonah performing at afternoon rests and after each evening meal. Tum was but one of many traders accompanying us, barterers of silks and cattle, wool and weapons, fragrances and jewels, iron and ivory. Our throng was impressive; I had never seen so many people outside stone walls. And from passing among them, I learned several important things.

First, Hebrew was not a common language. That may seem obvious to you, here in the heart of Assyria, but I had grown up in the hills of Israel, and so I knew of few other tongues. As I walked through this throng, I wondered how we could speak to anyone. So confusing were the different sounds, gestures, and symbols, it's no wonder the builders of Babel dispersed in anger!

That thought amused Tum.

"Your land is but a small spot in the world," he said between chuckles. "Why should its tongue be known by other men?"

Why indeed. I had no answer; I just assumed it was, as we were God's chosen people. I guess I had been fortunate this problem had not disrupted my life sooner. But that only brought forth a greater dilemma: Nineveh. How could the Dove preach repentance to a people who did not understand our speech?

Jonah offered no answer to that. Strange, though he learned what he could of the languages spoken around us, the Dove shrugged off this problem as if it did not matter. And soon I discovered why, for as far as our caravan went, he was right. Many of the sheiks and traders seemed well-versed in most tongues, including ours, and they did not mind translating our wishes. But they would not be available in Nineveh.

That quandary haunted my thoughts both times our caravan reached an Assyrian obelisk. Carved images and a serpentine script covered all sides of these stone landmarks. I could make nothing of them, but through translation, I learned these etchings promised an endless stream of Assyrian punishments. That further darkened my fears, for if these people vowed such things to their distant enemies, what would they do to those who brought foul omens to their streets and homes?

To my surprise, the traders and their people paid no attention to these monuments or their tales of atrocities. "Must be what they deserved, defying Ashur," Tum observed, considering that enough of an answer to satisfy anyone.

"What did you expect him to say?" Jonah told me afterward, taking the same attitude. "They are Assyrians."

They both thought their answers sufficient, but I did not. So I watched Tum and his people those early days and saw the subtle fears they warded against in their travels. For protection, they wore carved idols on necklaces and kept protective statues in their travel bags. To ward off danger, they painted foul images on shields, banners, blankets, pillows, and cloaks – those rich enough to wear them. With each drink, Tum and his family whispered prayers to Ashur, and with each camel ride, the merchant gave praise to that god. And they avoided camping near settlements, for fear of any buried dead nearby.

"That is their faith," the Dove explained later, "a mixture of unholy magic, spirit observances, and –" he paused, as if anguished, then said, "respect."

That threw me off. "Respect?"

His gaze grew dim.

"For God," he said, without elaborating. When I pressed, he told me to seek answers from Tum, though I had no strength to do so. And I think Jonah knew that.

My second lesson verified what the captain and Saln had tried to tell me: in the political void of Assyria's collapse, bandits ruled the wilderness. That spurred caravan leaders to unite as many people together as possible to safeguard their long journeys. Tum also was prepared for trouble in other ways, with swordsmen and archers sprinkled throughout our mass. If attacked, this round merchant could wield a small army.

Did I say small? In truth, it was not much less than the largest segment of Jeroboam's troops at Hermon. But Tum did not wish battle, as I learned after a week's passage across the grasslands beyond Tadmor, just after Pentecost.

"Pray to your god it never happens," he told me in the pleasures of his comfortable tent, during a welcome escape from the afternoon heat. Then he did something most strange, though I soon found it commonplace in Assyria. Tum pulled some shredded leaves of some sort from a leather pouch, shoved the crumbled pickings into the hollowed bubble at the end of his rod, and ignited them with flame borrowed from a lamp – all that just to breathe in the dizzying smoke through that stick or gourd he called a pipe.

I almost gagged.

While mystified by his smoldering wand, I was stunned even more by his answer.

"Do you doubt these men?" I inquired.

Since I was with Jonah, I too was a guest of Tum, eating in his tent and sharing of his blessing. But as I contributed little in his eyes, I noticed the round merchant often kept me at a distance, as if I was suspected of something. At that particular moment, the dark-eyed one stared at me from behind his thick brown beard, his brow twisted and cross. Then he turned to the Dove and asked, "Is he dim?"

I suppose I should have been insulted by that. As it was, it took a few breaths for me to realize just what he meant.

Jonah smiled, putting down the kinnor.

"No," said the Dove, "just naive."

"Ah," sighed Tum, his breath a very fog of hot ash. "Still, I am glad it was not overheard." And so, as I finally understood their meaning, Tum pointed his warm pipe towards me. "I tell you, Benjamin, that these are my brothers, my children, my kin by blood. What I do is for them, and what they give, it is for all of us. Death in service to the family is a blessing." He took a deep breath from his gourd, only to add, "I trust them with my heart."

That was what I had thought, of course. "Then –"

"There is no then!" The Assyrian leaned forward, his gaze stern. "We are a long, disjointed train of bumbling old men, women, and children, dependent on our trail for food, water, grazing lands…. When they attack us – when, Benjamin, when – they will have the terrain of their choosing, and if we resist, they can poison the waters we require, run off our herds, even burn the lands around us."

This confused me, sounding like he had given up before anything had happened… as I thought aloud. His stare turned incredulous.

"You silly Jews," he snapped, "sitting within your fine cities, isolated by your hills, complacent, uninvolved with the world!"

That attack angered me, but Jonah motioned for me to say nothing. Lord, it was hard!

"For far more than a thousand years have peoples fought over the plains of Assyria," exclaimed Tum. "A thousand! And through Ashur, we learned long ago that if we did not fight for our homes, our children, then our blood would run until there was none left! So, we have fought, and will again, when the governors and kings stop warring among themselves and face the world once more. Petty squabbling runs us dry, but they will awaken, I promise you that! Until then…."

Shaken by something I could not see, Tum closed his eyes and breathed deep. Then he reclined against a pillow and drained smoke from his pipe.

"Until then," he allowed, "we barter with these scoundrels, scratch out whatever bargain we can, and pray Ashur will soon turn his judgment against them."

Perhaps I was naive. Perhaps I did apply infantile wisdom. But in truth, I had assumed the Assyrians were evil. I had never bothered to guess why else they might do the fearful things they did. The whole idea of some righteous purpose behind their cruelties seemed so stupid, I had never considered it.

"That's irresponsible," the Dove responded that night, as we returned to our tent. And that angered me.

"You think their hurts justify evil?" I asked him.

"They do not consider themselves evil, no more than we consider the punishments of Yahweh evil. We believe different things than they do… it is as simple as that."

"It's still wrong, no matter how anyone looks at it."

"No, Benjamin. What we think is wrong is often accepted by other peoples. Consider the hogs in Shalmanier's party. They might have eaten one tonight. You and I would never do so, but they do not accept our laws."

"That is not the same thing."

"Oh, but it is! Don't you see? This whole journey – the Lord's purpose in Nineveh – all of that circles around what we as people believe. Getting someone to see that what they have always held to be true may, just may, be false. Getting someone to understand a different, a better way of life."

Whether he meant to or not, his statement bound together all the problems I had debated around him.

"Wait," I said, collecting my rambling thoughts. "You mean us as well as them, don't you? Are you saying we might be wrong?"

In truth, I had not realized how far-reaching that question was. Or his answer.

"No," Jonah stressed. "The foundations of our faith – the teachings of the Levites, the word Yahweh speaks to our hearts, the Laws of Moses – these things are the solid foundation of our faith. They are from God, and He is truth. Yet many of our… our 'interpretations,' if you understand me, of what Yahweh would have us do… they may be open to question, or re-evaluation, as our Lord directs."

For some reason that answer bothered me. "By whom?"

"Well, the priesthood, for one. Perhaps the king."

I scoffed at that, having lived within both environments.

"You yourself have belittled the faith of our sovereigns, and for good reason," I said. "And the Levites have not lived spotless lives."

"No one has. We are human. We are all sinners. Yet the Lord does speak to His people. He still provides new direction, new wisdom. And such teachings, such words, could signal changes in our faith. It has happened before."

Perhaps I did not understand him, or just refused to listen. Yet something in his arguments spurred me on.

"Do you not see the unrest such ideas cause?" I pointed out. "Are we to pick and choose what is the Lord's will?"

"That is not what I meant!"

I stood to my full height, even though the Dove still rose above me. "But that is how it sounds. Can you not see it?"

He hesitated, as if he had lost touch with his argument. I watched that, a part of me savoring a sensation of triumph, and I found myself wondering why.

"This is difficult to explain," the Dove began, his words weighed by caution. "It is Nineveh we are discussing, not Israel."

That opened the door to the question I had pondered since leaving Tyre. "Are they not bound together? Didn't you say

Assyria will pillage Israel?"

Tremors of guilt, or brooding melancholy, replaced his harsh stare.

"Perhaps," he allowed. "Yes, I have seen their rampage, and signs of even more. I… I cannot say just yet. But I do know this: we must not judge these Ninevites simply by what we believe. Not without first understanding who they are."

Ah, my days with Jeroboam proved educational after all. "I have heard such logic uphold many an evil deed."

"It need not be evil."

The vagueness of that answer frustrated me, so I cornered him. "You would justify their tortures? Their killings?"

"No!" he spat. Then he reconsidered. "Well, perhaps."

Such words left me blind to his intent, as I told him.

"What would you have me say?" the Dove asked, the light of our oil lamp dancing across his bare face. "The Lord divides me on this. He bids me be patient, to be open to these people. I only now learn who they truly are – victims as well as manipulators. Yet my heart, my heart…."

Torn by his own arguments, he dropped to his bedroll in despair.

"Do I wish Nineveh's destruction? Yes, with all I hold dear! But should I? Probably not, though our people would suffer. Will it impact the Lord's judgment? I… I hope so, but I doubt it."

"You hope so?"

"Indeed!" His grand eyes flared with rare fury. "I admit it, Benjamin. I hate them as no one else. I know it is wrong, wrong to hate… but not for them! It can't be wrong!"

I had laid down, not out of disrespect or to brush away his answer, but because my aching back demanded comfort. It was night, after all, and I was exhausted. But the Dove must have thought I was abandoning him. His face softened, and his brow slumped as if I proclaimed judgment.

"Benjamin, they are evil!" He knelt beside my bedroll, his hands in fists before his face. "I have seen them kill for pleasure – slow, torturous. They made us watch. Forced our eyes open. Oh, the screams!"

As God witnesses my heart, I had never imagined such terrors in his past. Perhaps I should have; I knew an Assyrian warband had rampaged through Israel before my birth, around the time of Amos. At one time Samaria itself had been under siege! But I had never connected that to Jeroboam's great general. Like a sudden revelation, it broke upon me that every question I had asked of him, from our first steps beyond Aphek and perhaps even before, must have pinned his heart – and the Lord's demands – against these memories. For he had directed Israel's armies against those Assyrians.

"Your family?" I asked, my voice a shallow whisper.

His brow writhed in his hurt.

The Dove retreated to his bedroll, slowing his breath, calming his quaking heart. I felt some blame for forcing this upon him and prayed for guidance.

"Why?" I asked. "Why would they do it?"

"I do not know. They suffered great defeat at Aphek's upper wing, and other battles. Yet even as they retreated, stung and hurting, they made time for atrocities. Oh, how hateful I became, trailing them, always in hot pursuit, and still time and time again a day or half-day too late. To come upon," he struggled against tears, "to find their victims, people I knew… it was so humbling! And then, then my own… I still have no idea what they were even doing there. Father had some reason, though I will never know. Never know. But it must have been for some purpose, of that I am sure, just as this is.

"It's so easy to hate, Benjamin. So easy! But to love… that's the difficult thing. To forgive… ah!

"The Lord counsels me through Tum. I think that is why we are with him now. This man speaks the truth. And the Lord bids me accept these things.

"The Assyrians are excellent fighters because for all their lives, and the times of their grandfathers and those before them beyond count, for all those generations they have defended their lands from intruders. Remember, Benjamin, we were a nomadic people before our bondage in Egypt. Thriving in one land is still new to us. But the Assyrians, who had striven only to live in their lands, they have suffered raids and bondage at the hands of Babylon, barbarians, bedouins, and others, almost since time began. It was survival that forced the Assyrians to become somewhat nomadic themselves, assembling their armies each summer to carve out additional lands – first as buffer zones against attack, then as new homelands. I think the logic was to take over the lands of the enemy, to make them Assyrian, in hopes of ending their desire to make war against them. Then their purpose turned to plunder when they could not gain tribute, for war is an expensive thing, after all."

I look back at that night now as the beginning of my education. I was full of questions, some angry, some honestly sympathetic, and some simply ignorant.

"What happened to those who lived there?" I asked.

"Some were assimilated, as was Ansephanti. And it worked, to some degree. Did you not notice how he spoke with pride both of Assyria and Aram? Now he sides with Urartu, yet statues of Assyrian bulls yet stand beside his throne. Still, I'm sure most of those uprooted face uncountable hardships. And as you can see, the way their empire has crumbled back for – what? the third time? – the practice has done little to secure their frontiers."

"Perhaps it is their use of terror that defeats them."

"Perhaps."

A wolf howled in the distance. Our tent covers flapped in the breeze.

I laid in the flickering light, pondering all Jonah said.

"I still say that it is wrong, no matter how they have been treated." Infantile or not, such was my wisdom. "Such things are evil."

The Dove yawned. "Perhaps," he whispered.

"Perhaps?" I was ready to argue further, but his wind turned from words to snores. I wondered then if he faked this, just to get me quiet, but as I pondered this, I too succumbed.

And I dreamed of Pelagos.

I have no idea why. In truth, my thoughts had not turned to her since leaving Tyre. But that night she filled my heart – her curly red hair bouncing from beneath her tranquil blue veil, her patient eyes beaming their welcome, her fine feminine form. We stood together in the olive grove, the trees in full bloom. The transforming horizon soon carried us to harvest, shaking the heavy branches and gathering our fruit. It was a bountiful year, with little remaining for the poor to collect, so she left a basket within the grove. The scene shifted to Jonah's simple home. He sat with us around her pot of stew, sharing parchment bread. Yet it did not matter; her radiant beauty thrilled me and filled me. For the first time, I could imagine the love that must exist between husband and wife, the glorious bonding that Yahweh made possible between two different souls.

Is this what it is like, Lord, to sit in your presence? To feel your everlasting love around us and through us? Oh, to spend a lifetime in such warmth!

"Awake!" came the call. "Rise! Awake!"

My thoughts broke with difficulty. Ah, Pelagos! I did not wish to leave!

"Awake!" resounded the call. In the distance I heard the restless sounds of the caravan, of cattle, sheep and goats, donkeys, people. And camels… always camels. They make little noise, but once you recognize them, the snorts and wallows stand out even in a storm.

"What is it?" I mumbled.

"The source of Tum's irritation," Jonah said, stumbling around despite his fatigue. "We are pursued."

Chapter 19
Confrontation

It was times like this I wished for sandals. These grasslands raised a vast number of thorns and sharp, prickly weeds, and as we joined in the efforts to pack, my feet must have found them all.

Though in a hurry, we left nothing behind. "Let them barter for it later," Tum told us. With everyone joining in, we were geared up and away from the waterhole in just a couple of deep stretches. The shepherds had already started off.

I realized just how serious it was when we did not stop for the morning meal, passing around bags of dried fruit and flesh instead. The meat I ignored, of course. The fruit I wished I had. Jonah offered me some wine, but I doubted it would help my stomach and so passed.

About this time, I began to really hate camels. I had thought riding a packed donkey was uncomfortable, but camels were nauseating. A month atop this foul, single-humped creature had done little to prepare me for that moment when my stomach could take no more. As luck would have it, I was leaning over my left hip when it came up; I doubt the beast would have liked its head so anointed.

The Dove, who had long before mastered his ride, came beside me to ask again if I wanted wine.

Wine! Oh, I should have said yes! I could have shown him

what a mess I could accomplish with wine!

"Good," said Tum, approaching from my other side. "That was well done. We cannot afford to stop for such things."

As the morning passed, and my guts settled down, we overcame the few sheep in our caravan. Tum examined them, decided they were inferior beasts, and told the shepherds to leave them behind.

"Fair bribe," he told the Dove, "though not enough. Still, it's not a difficult choice."

As the midday sun approached on that clear blue sky, Tum faced his trial whether to rest during the hot afternoon or push on, knowing the oxen would slow our procession.

"The donkeys will soon need rest as well," said one trader, a well-dressed man named Meleth-Korat.

"Abandon the oxen and my carts are lost," said another, Delus-Ar'torth.

"I know that," Tum interrupted, though the merchant continued.

"Goods from Carthage, ivory carvings, bountiful rugs –"

"I have seen them," Tum said, showing his impatience. "But they are small compared to the whole."

"But they are mine!"

"You knew the risks," Tum stated. As his tone hardened, the captain of his mercenaries came forward, a stout man named Alport whose every step clattered from his many rattling swords. They spoke as the Dove and I approached. When they ceased, Tum remained hard.

"It seems the sheep were not enough, as we all guessed. And I am reluctant to abandon more, for I doubt they will be satisfied. So, with Ashur at our side, we stand here. With luck, I will bargain our freedom on three pairs of oxen and their carts."

"A long hope," said Delus-Ar'torth. "Pray it works."

As he left, I could not help asking, "He no longer fears for his goods?"

Tum heard me and smiled. "He sees the logic of it, offering them what we would have left behind anyway. And if taken, he will share in our profits once we reach the market, though many of our goods are bound for spots far beyond Nineveh."

"Beyond Nineveh?" I had always thought the city of blood was the edge of the world. But Tum only chuckled.

"Babylon, Indeos, the eastern lands. Nineveh simply controls one edge of the world, not all of it."

Before you laugh, yes, I admit I made a stupid comment. I have already shown how little I knew then. But when you are riding for your life, your fears choking your every breath, it is easy to spout foolish words or make silly snap judgments. I hope you never have to realize that, for I have made more than my share. Perhaps that is a blessing I can give you.

Tum's strategy was a simple one. Sending the livestock forward, he took the caravan back to a waterhole between two tall hills. We had skipped this stone-covered hole due to its coal-marked claim by the Balon'heth tribe, but that little mattered now. Tum centered our tents atop the crests, though most goods he placed along the southern plateau. His mercenaries, accompanied by whatever could not make the heights, manned the waterhole and access to the two hills.

When he was satisfied, Tum rounded up the twelve merchants and families, the Dove and myself. To our backs, in the distant desert plateau, we saw the rising dust of our pursuers.

"Here we shall live or perish, as Ashur decrees," he said. "Alport and I will ride to meet them. Tal-Galerseth shall lead in my absence. Pray for a blessing! Should the Balon'heth find us, make whatever peace you can. Perhaps they will aid us; pray they will. Whatever happens, at nightfall depart once more. Travel light, without pause. But take care in your haste not to pass too close to a tomb."

There was some grumbling at that. I would have added my share, but as soon as it had begun, it ended. I did not understand it until I saw the Dove on his feet.

I suppose I should not have been surprised by the way those around us shuffled away. Though we had been traveling a month, but for our Sabbath stops, these people still did not accept Jonah. I do not know whether it was his white skin or bare head.

Yes, he had shaved his head since Damascus. He seemed to

like baldness.

"I will accompany you," he told Tum.

The proud trader, sheik of the largest family I had ever met, stared at the Dove with eyes that suffered his loss.

"You don't know the risks," he warned.

Jonah laughed. Tum straightened his back as if his will had been challenged.

"We go to negotiate," the trader stressed, "assuming they wish such talk. Our death could lie before us."

The Dove was undeterred. "My God stands with me. I am not afraid."

As Tum discussed it with the plate-armored Alport, I found myself rising. I still have no explanation for it, unless it was Hosea's command.

"I too will go," I decided. "I accompany Jonah."

Tum stared at me as if he saw my death. But the warrior shared not his concerns, and so we were off. Perhaps it was a sign of respect or gratitude, but I left upon a saddled camel, one much smoother in its gait, and cleaner. Our heading was west, toward a fading dust trail.

"They have entered the plains," called Tum. "We must hurry."

If you have never ridden a camel in flight, do so. There is a certain thrill that comes from it, one even the wind-racing Assyrian stallions cannot approach. It is not a matter of speed; the stallions are unchallenged there, at least in short bursts. No, the camel is unique when it begins to shuffle its legs in awkward spurts, almost hopping. You experience it full force, rocking first forward and perhaps left, then backward and right, and still you cover little ground. Indeed, you wonder if indeed you shall ever move at all. But when its speed is accomplished, come hill or valley, desert or rock, the bounding camel shakes one's brain as few things can. To the unprepared, it is at first unnerving, but I think that once I got used to it, I could stand to be so shaken often enough. It was one of the most thrilling things I've ever done. Though I still think camels are just too foul-smelling to have around.

Alport was the first to see them. The desert sands beckoned to our south, the Assyrian horizon shone to our north. Before us, along the Damascus road, came a black-dressed horde on sprinting camels.

"Forty, perhaps fifty," said the warrior, his back stretched high. I noticed then the two scabbards he bore there, crisscrossed over each shoulder. With those he wore at each hip, plus the three knives he carried at his breast, I pondered just how many arms this swordsman possessed.

"Do you recognize them?" Tum asked. But Alport shook his head, his worn iron cap a poor reflector of the sun.

"We must meet them there," he said, pointing to a far hill.

"Then lead us," Tum said.

Our camels bounded away, round hills and over them, aiming for a distant crest. We arrived with our enemies riding hard upon us.

I saw then why the warrior had chosen this spot. We stood upon the heights of the earth's backbone across the horizon. Unless our pursuers stood where we did, the shadows of the ridge could hide a sizeable army.

Tum took the high crest, gazed upon the riding horde, and said, "Now."

With two large slabs of wood from his camel's pack, Alport knelt against the sod and stroked ground pieces of flint over a pile of dry grass stalks. As embers flared into flame, he added the wood, building a smoky fire to signal our enemies.

"The earth is dry," Jonah said to warn Tum, but the trader brushed it aside.

"The winds blow west," he pointed out. "He chose a bare patch. Should the flames spread, so be it."

We waited in silence, hearing the fire grow, watching the smoke billow. Nervous, I looked to the Dove for strength. He was as stone, his eyes locked on the far horizon. Tum paced across the crest, even as Alport examined each shiny blade.

From the hills came the pounding of hooves. The noise rose within me, crushing against my soul. Taken by fear, I knelt in prayer. "Oh Lord, hear my call! In the sea You spared us. In Damascus You protected us. Hear me now! Watch over us!"

A warm hand took my shoulder. The Dove gazed upon me and smiled.

"He hears you. This is not our time."

On the ridge behind him reared black riders against a blue sky. Seeing Alport facing their hill, a silver scimitar unveiled against each shoulder, their leader signaled the mass to halt, then rode to the base of our climb. Three other riders followed, their camels nervous in the wavering smoke.

Alport shouted something I did not understand. The leader of our hooded pursuers answered. That started a short, brittle dialogue.

I edged up to Tum and the Dove, even as Jonah asked the trader what they were saying.

"A contest of titles," said Tum, his voice low and tense. "Alport Den'Quelinar is master of five blades of gold from the eastern provinces, and the Ble'porath champion claims mastery of six of the central plains."

"Mastery?" Jonah inquired.

Tum nodded as he listened. "Alport has won the gold blade of five sword cults; schools where such skills are taught." I must have worn one of my confused expressions, for he looked at me, sighed, and explained further. "Alport defeated in combat every student and instructor the school had, using whatever blade his opponent favored. Only in that way may sword masters gain the honorary blades."

I remember taking a loud, deep breath, awed by the grim man's feats. It is rare to encounter people so specialized.

"Yes," said Tum, "he is to be revered. A true artist. Alport is a rare one, letting his opponents live as often as he does. By reputation alone may we survive here."

The leader of the black horde stepped to Alport's side, drawing a beautiful sword of his own. Its sharp edge shimmered as the sun itself.

"Be not afraid," Tum whispered. "They compare craftsmanship."

So it was. To my surprise the two men traded blades, admiring the artistry of the inscriptions and moldings, the hilt and pommel emblems, the inlaid gold, ivory, silver, and jewels.

"Is it over then?" the Dove asked.

"Oh no," Tum said. "Unless they become friends, this is meaningless. They have accepted each other's claims; nothing more. Now our fates come to my hands."

Our round Assyrian trader strode forward. When Jonah kept by his side, I followed – with reluctance, to be sure, but I followed. The black-garbed raiders did likewise.

Tum said something in a tongue I could not decipher. A tall, lean man answered, his hawkish eyes just visible between the black robes that wrapped him from head to foot. Words soon flew with the wind. Tum gestured with his hands, waving them in dramatic swirls through the breeze. The black one remained still.

"Wonder what they are saying," I mumbled.

"Various claims to land, wrongs, and crimes," Jonah answered.

Alport straightened, his arms growing tense. But my curiosity centered on the Dove. "You understand these people?"

"It is not hard to guess. The Lord opens my ears. Listen to Him, Benjamin, and learn."

Listen to Him? I could count the times Yahweh had spoken to me on one hand, and this was not one of them. Still, it no longer seemed to matter. Tum was angry, his hands going from embracing the hills to firm, imposing fists and stabs at the sky. The black robes watched with eyes afire. The swordsmen were as statues, analyzing each other for weakness.

"The Ble'porath know this is an Assyrian caravan," Jonah explained. "They keep bringing up crimes the Assyrian troops committed against them. Limbs severed, eyes slashed, tongues and ears cut–"

"Enough!" I cried. I suffered under such talk!

My urge was to run, to flee to our camels. Oh, Lord, forgive me! How I wanted to escape! But my heart focused on the Dove. His stern eyes went first to Tum, then our pursuers. As tempers flared, he stepped between them.

"Tell them this," Jonah told Tum. Then he faced our aggressors. "Greetings, Won-Korlash of the Ble'porath! Hold your anger. Who here obeys God?"

Though hesitant, Tum hurried to translate this under the angry stares of these interlopers. The leader of the black robes folded his arms before him, looking with disdain upon the unwanted interloper. He spat a response.

"What god, hairless white-skin?" came Tum's flowing voice. His illuminating words soon flowed as swift and sure as the welcome rain.

Jonah stood firm. "The God of Noah, Nimrod, and Abram, Lord of Lords, Creator of all things."

"The ancient god?" said the Ble'porath chieftain, through Tum. "He departed with the flood before the fathers of my fathers."

"You are wrong, great Won-Korlash. He is here. Now. Behold!"

The Dove pointed across the horizon, but I felt its rush and roar before I saw its terror. The Hand of God surged up from the plain, a wall of swirling wind and soil blasting the earth from one horizon to the next, blotting out the sun.

Awesome is the power of the Lord! All praise Him!

The bedouin's camels snorted and ran, throwing most of the riders. Ours shuffled around the ledge, surrounded by the swirling winds, and settled on their legs, tucking in their heads. Sand flew about us. Most of us – indeed, everyone but Jonah – fell to the earth before the Lord.

"Kor-Tegrith!" cried the man Jonah called Won-Korlash. "Save us! Which of the seven demons is this?"

"The last," said the short one. "It is said the seventh is a whirlwind."

"Fool magician!" Jonah raised his arms about him. "Do you not understand? Repent! Your false gods are nothing before the Lord of Israel!"

It is easy for me to say these worshipped names now, since someone explained them to me some years ago, but neither then, nor now, could I see much sense paying attention to such myths, so I can tell you little of their imaginary deities. In that moment when I first heard their names uttered in prayers for deliverance, the vile words were but icons of evil, brief whispers in the tremendous wind of Yahweh.

Ah, but I digress. The black robes turned from Jonah, shouting among their scattered people. The one called Kor-Tegrith led them in prayer to Shamash, their sun god, yet the wind raged. He called on Namtar, the messenger of the Underworld, to seize Jonah and send him to the Land of No Return. Yet the Dove stood as granite, untouched by the maelstrom.

"Marduk, lord of sun and light, break free of this vile grasp!" shouted the black priest. "Strike down this oppressor!"

"Louder, sorcerer!" answered Jonah. His words were little more than whispers, yet the cyclone echoed them as if they were of the storm itself. "They do not hear you!"

Kor-Tegrith bellowed incantations. He threw potions and ritual bones to the winds. He drained vials of oil to light torches that whimpered and died in the tempest.

"Most powerful Marduk!" he cried. "Hear me! Nabu, aid us! Strike down this blasphemer!"

"Try Tammuz, deceiver!" Jonah's words turned harsh. "Call to Bawa! Call them all, so that the Lord's glory is known!"

The black swordsman raised up, his golden scimitar bared for the Dove's heart. Jonah turned to face him, even as Alport sat stiffly against the sod. The shiny blade lifted, swept forward... and stopped, knocked from his grasp by a sandy gale.

That sword master watched the blade fall, then fled into the churning blackness.

Desperate, Kor-Tegrith retreated to the older sphere of legends. He called to Enlil, the ancient lord of winds and storms, to calm the skies and clear the blasphemy, yet the Hand of God grew ever fierce. He gave chants to the demon Lamashtu and the Evil Thing, whatever that was. He even called to Anu, past king of the gods – Anu the shadow, Anu deposed by Enlil. Yet the wind of God overwhelmed us. Only Jonah withstood it.

"Know you, Ble'porath, the Hand of God embraces your people!" he declared.

"Lies!" cried Kor-Tegrith.

"Enough!" The eyes of Jonah burned for the black-robed

priest. "The Lord God is shown among you! Dare not deny it!"

But Kor-Tegrith would not listen. "Strike them, Marduk!" He forced himself to stand, his sword spearing the sky in defiance, but he could not challenge the winds. A tentacle of swirling sands reached down from the heavens, wrapping about him and through him. He screamed, though we could not see him; the terror blinded us to his presence. Then, with an icy stroke from God, the distressed priest fell silent. When the waves of silt and sand lifted, he was no more. Not even his bones remained.

A bitter breath escaped the Dove's lips. "By his own mouth was he cursed." Yet the storm raged on, and Jonah followed His lead. "Is there anyone who still doubts the Lord?"

The hills trembled before the storm. At last, so did our adversaries.

"You have learned the lessons of defiance," Jonah told those cowering in the grass. "Now rise up! Return to your homes! And live your lives in peace, in love of each other! For your wicked ways are a blasphemy in the eyes of God, and His wrath is quick!"

Without a word the Ble'porath ran for their mounts and departed, never once questioning the raging whirlwind that towered against the clear sky. Yet the storm did not depart. The Dove looked upon it with fearful fascination and whispered, "Now to Nineveh."

Chapter 20

"It begins"

A bright sun followed our Lord's storm, yet our tensions grew with each step toward Nineveh. And it was hard to say why.

At first, the cause was the very means of our salvation. The Hand of God remained with us, as the Dove suggested it would, though the maelstrom sometimes roamed beyond the horizon. The animals of our caravan accepted it with no qualms, as if they recognized and honored God in all His forms, but Tum had a difficult time explaining it to his restless people. Distrust of Jonah led to suspicion of his acts, and Tum's endorsements only emphasized the trader's "unholy" ties to the white-skinned one. Still, once the many merchants realized the storm would not impede them, the caravan proceeded across the tallgrass prairie at a good speed, even as the earth's slope rose towards the highlands of Assyria.

For Jonah, however, the crossing presented a different challenge.

"A year ago, Benjamin, such things would have seemed blasphemous to me," he admitted while shaving his scalp one evening. "The Hand of our Lord at work, saving the lives of these unbelievers. Saving Assyrians, of all things!"

I realized then how much hatred yet remained in him. Still, I sympathized.

"We were saved, too," I pointed out.

"That was nothing. This is nothing."

I stumbled over that and told him so. Jonah sighed.

"What we do now, what we have done since my death, is nothing before what will happen in Nineveh. Were my tale told, I doubt these events would be remembered."

I sometimes forget how important such things can be… to be honored, or remembered. To a person as the Dove, it can dictate a life. Still, in my heart I knew Jonah spoke the truth. What had transpired meant little against what lay ahead.

I do not mean to belittle our passage, for there were things of inspiration at our feet. Terqa, for one, was a fascinating city, the first we saw that took pride in the Assyrian carvings of its walls and the tapestries adorning its public buildings. And the Euphrates, which outlines Terqa's eastern face – that great river flows ever though my dreams and imagination. Nothing compares to it in Israel, or any of the other lands I had crossed up to that point. Indeed, even now, of all the rivers I have endured, only the Nile exceeds it.

The spread of the Euphrates made me gawk and gasp. Without a doubt, it spanned five to six times the length of the ship of Tarshish even at Terqa's narrowest crossing, and from the looks of its smooth brown surface, it must have been deep even then. Square rafts delivered various goods up and down the muddy waters, though they did not seem well-laden.

"It has been a dry spring," noted Tum, during one of his friendlier moments. "But rain is yet to come. And when it does… I tell you, Benjamin, more than once I have seen this whole plain up to my ankles in water! Truly! I mean, talk about your flood! Can you imagine it?

"This," he declared, gazing upon the mighty stream, "this is Assyria. The Tigris is vital, don't get me wrong, but this… this is the lifeblood of my people. It would take you years just to walk its length, but if you did, you would cross the world's greatest fields of wheat and barley, pass hearty flocks of sheep and stout herds of the choicest cattle, pick from a wondrous abundance of fruit of all kinds! You'd see vast forests, extensive iron, copper and tin mines, granite and marble quarries…. Oh, Benjamin, this is a blessed land!"

His outlook dampened as we entered Terqa. A lack of barges meant it took most of a day just to get the caravan across the great river, and that came at great expense. But the tax situation hit the hardest. In Tum's opinion, the city's collectors exceeded their calling and took joy in doing so. They had a reason, of course. Even with the Assyrian troops pulled back, the elders of Terqa chose to remain unaligned from the spreading Urartu Federation – a fact Tum could appreciate and admire. But to compensate for their lost support and revenue, the elders tripled and quadrupled tax rates, and that drew many a curse.

At one point the frustrated Tum put it to the Dove: "Could not your god teach them hospitality?" So Jonah – himself an object of scorn within the small, dusty city, for the locals seemed to think him diseased – raised the concern in prayer, though he doubted anything would come of it.

"It is good to pray about such works of man," he told me in private, "but it is best to act upon them yourself when you can."

That touched upon his and my biggest problem: food. We were now far from the kingdoms of our faith, and so we learned that in the Assyrian heartland, people ate things our Lord had taught us to avoid and they drank things our faith detested. Women roasted and served unclean meats at every table, in just about everything – and to many a cook, there were few insults more offensive than to ask for foods prepared without these obscenities. And you dared not ask for drinkable water. It proved a most guarded commodity, almost like gold, since the rivers and creeks ran rank with waste, and wine was both expensive and rare. What water they spared often went toward a wild concoction called beer, the most common and plentiful drink, though from one whiff Jonah warned me to avoid it.

To our good fortune, the merchants under Tum scrounged up what we required. As with our Sabbath practices, Tum felt the allowance acceptable to retain a musician of the Dove's skill. After seeing the power of our Lord, Tum also developed some respect even for me – a little. At least, he no longer minded answering my questions about his people and culture. Still, I wondered what we would do when we reached Nineveh, and our new friends no longer heard our calls.

"God will provide," the Dove insisted.

So passed the week of travel between the Euphrates and the Tigris, the Lord's spinning sandstorm ever at our backs, the sun and sky clear before us. Along our way scouts brought word of at least three raider groups that picked up our trail, only to think the better of it and depart. The reason was obvious, since tales of our salvation from the Ble'porath had spread far beyond us, discouraging most bandits. Those not deterred soon ran into the wall of wind itself, which seemed to move between our caravan and whatever sought to approach us.

Thus we reached the river Tigris in the first days of Tammuz, a month that never meant much to me before this. Unlike the Euphrates, this vast waterway supported few rafts or ships, at least where we first hit its shores, for the river's current ran fast, and far too shallow, with many dangerous obstructions. But I didn't care to cross anyway, with Assur cresting the hills along the western shore.

Assur, one of three capitals of Assyria, fell somewhere between Samaria and Damascus in size. It spread over three hills, groups of brick villages surrounding several impressive halls and temples, all protected by ancient sandstone barriers. But unlike most cities we reached on our journey, large segments of Assur stared back at us empty of life. Vast battlements with massive gates lined the hills, each capped with great citadels of granite and marble, and yet gaping holes plagued many of the walls. Their once-protective stones lay smashed and scattered, the mortar crumbling.

"It is sad," Tum conceded. With wounded pride, he pointed to one of the great fortresses. "That, my friends, is the supreme temple of Ashur, his home among my people. A magnificent structure! Or at least it once was…. But now, people are reluctant to restore it. You see, Assur was seized in revolt by our past king, Shamshi Adad, and its citizens were punished."

"I can imagine," Jonah whispered.

"Yes, so you may," Tum allowed. "Your people have been

divided for generations. You're constantly battling."

The Dove bristled at that, but Tum didn't notice.

"But it is difficult for us," he continued, "to make war against our own kind. No barbarians did this, nor did Babylon. We crushed Assur ourselves."

"Why?" I had to ask.

Tum eyed me with curiosity. "It is… an involved tale. Shamshi Adad brought division, and some of the people disavowed him. So they fought, and many died. And rather than rebuild, our leaders have left this as a warning. Already a new city rises over the northwestern hill, under the hand of Bel Harran-bel-usur."

His brow clenched at that man's name, so I asked, "What has he done?"

"Done?" the merchant echoed, surprised at the question.

"Yes, that you distrust him so."

"Ah. That I cannot allow myself to think, much less say. I must trade with him, Benjamin. I just… well, the fall of Assur saddens me. Despite what Shamshi Adad did, we should give the supreme god more respect!"

"Your god," Jonah stated.

"Indeed," Tum acknowledged, not taking offense. "For his home to crumble so... that speaks much, does it not?" He pointed beyond the broken gates. "The inner walls were built by Shalmaneser the third, not a hundred years past. Now they are gone. The broad avenues to the gates are but alleys between homes built of their rubble. The temples – oh, these temples once were as grand as Solomon's!"

His voice had risen, as if he could not contain his anger, but in the midst of it he turned away and bowed low, his ear near the earth. I was about to question him when trumpets sounded across distant hills.

"Listen!" the merchant urged us. So we did. As the hot desert winds whistled through the dry grasses, the trumpets sounded once more.

"Miracle of miracles!" Tum cried. "It comes! The fist of Assyria rolls on!"

There are times when you gaze upon something and wish to see more of it… and God fulfills that wish. I looked across the grasslands, wondering once more what the actual armies of Assyria would appear like, when I heard the whirling grind of well-greased axles and the pounding of hundreds of hooves. I scanned the horizons for its source, once and again, and saw the deadly serpent of man appear from across the hills.

Oh Lord God of heaven and earth, it was both beautiful and terrifying to behold! The sun shimmered across thousands of bronze plates shielding chariots, horses, and their riders. The ground quaked from the churning wheels of thunderous war machines riding two abreast beyond the horizon. Dust clouds exploded in their wake like the waves of a firestorm.

"To the sides! To the sides!" Tum shouted. "The sa sheppi ride forth!"

In a well-practiced maneuver, the caravan split along the road, giving the charioteers a wide berth. Yet the mobile troops slowed in their approach to stop before Tum, the Dove, and myself, though not in unity. The horses stomped their hooves and tossed their heads, impatient to begin the race once more. As the dust settled, sunlight blazed on the gold and silver trim of the lead chariot. A massive warrior of leather and bronze held the reins, his arms resting atop a giant shield of gold plate emblazoned with an archer primed to fire. But behind him stood the true leader, a tall, imposing man almost clad from head to foot in bronze scales. Upon his scalp reared the conical helmet of an Assyrian governor, its burgundy crest aflame in the setting sun.

"May Ashur shine upon you, Philar-Al'andron," greeted the governor, though his stern hazel eyes revealed little warmth.

"And on you, Rab Alani Sanscorrab," welcomed Tum, bowing at the waist.

Sanscorrab smiled at this, but then his eyes caught Jonah. He held his grim gaze there long, studying the bald, pale prophet.

"You have prospered, crossing the eye of the rebellion," Sanscorrab allowed.

"I have found an ally," Tum confessed.

"Yes, so I have heard." The hard tone of his voice made me

wonder if he had seen the Lord's wind, but it had retreated across the horizon. I looked back, satisfied the cyclone lay hidden, and found the governor's eye dwelled upon me. Even at that distance, I sensed within him a fury restrained. He gazed upon me as if searching for hidden threats, but when the flames of his anger revealed none of my innermost fears, he abandoned the probe in an impatient huff.

A great sense of relief enveloped me.

Nodding to the trader, Sanscorrab suggested, "In Ashur's wisdom, may it also aid our people." He raised his left hand. The trumpets sounded.

The proud stallions snorted and charged.

In the time it took my nerves to calm, the commander sped away. His vast chain of chariots followed at a rapid pace, though it took several minutes for the line of war machines to pass by. The winds stank of horse sweat for even longer.

"Dwindles every year," remarked Tum at its passing. "Thank Ashur that Kalhu and Nineveh remain strong."

Only then did I understand the ranting of Ansephanti. If this was a sample of an average Assyrian army, truly the band Jeroboam defeated was but a pittance.

"Seems large enough to me," I offered.

"That?" Tum laughed. "The zuk shepi is five times that, and that does not include the cavalry! And when the district sab sharri is raised… oh, you have never seen such a force! Only Kalhu and Nineveh manage mightier hands!"

"No," countered Jonah, "the Lord God is ever supreme."

"I spoke of men," replied Tum, his tongue stern, almost cross, "of Assur's standing infantry and the militia of our district." Then he turned to me once more, his eyes shining. "They fight almost constantly now, chasing these upstart tribes, punishing rebellious cities. Watching Bel Harran-bel-usur, and others. For Sanscorrab to lead his last chariots out, alone, the battle must be fierce. We may see the sab sharri soon, now that the planting season is about over. The peasants can spare a little time to sharpen their swords."

That concept fascinated me… the very idea of everyday

people, the hands and feet of a nation, taking up arms each summer. It worked with Jeroboam – I myself saw that – but that had been a small group of volunteers, not a vast throng of compelled warriors. I could not help wondering whether their frustration with war, growing generation after generation into a cynical weariness, could fuel rebellion across the countryside. It would with me, if our kings had sought constant battle.

"Who was he, anyway?" I put forth.

"The rab alani," answered the trader. Then he saw I did not understand and added, "the governor of the Assur district."

"Equal to Ansephanti," explained Jonah.

A few of the merchants approached, inquiring of something in their native tongue. Tum answered, then told the Dove, "We must decide our next move. With the rab alani gone, the king must also be absent."

"Usually is," interrupted another trader.

"Enough!" Tum snapped. The other cowered, and Tum softened. "It might not be wise to remain here long."

I don't know what spurred me to ask "Why?" but I did. I thank God that the Dove understood, speaking up while Tum fought to control his anger.

"Because most of the troops are now gone," Jonah answered. "The city could be vulnerable."

"More likely we are vulnerable, being outside its walls," Tum corrected him. "Some of the governors are now rather strong, and quite independent. You know that."

"I do not care," the Dove stated. "My mission is to Nineveh."

"That's what I told them," Tum said. "And I, too, will go there, if only to see your god at work. But I need time here to gather supplies. And I must pay tribute."

Staying seemed wise to me. If their army was involved in fierce combat, then the peril of the vast grasslands must have been much higher than I had thought. But the Dove would accept nothing less than a quick departure.

"You forget who walks with us," he told me. "Our challenge is at Nineveh."

"Yet we must eat," I reminded him.

After some debate, Jonah gave in to a brief pause. To our surprise, the caravan remained intact while the twelve merchants accompanied Tum and his helpers into the city, each leading a well-laden wagon. We set up our tents and waited through the sultry afternoon heat, the Dove choosing that moment to shave. At its end the merchants returned, their wagons restocked with grain, dried fruit, water, and oils, and we left.

Little did we know our journey was almost over.

In this, the heart of Assyria, the whole concept of a road took on new meaning. Fording the Tigris across a broad chain of rocks, Tum led us to the Shalmaneser Passage, a grand strip of smoothed stone crossing the hills and valleys of Assyria to Ekallatum, a fair if small community on a hill above the waters, about a day north of Assur. The next day upon the road we spent our afternoon resting outside grand Kalhu, the second capital of the empire. Lying between the junction of the Tigris and the Great Zab, with grayed limestone and black marble citadels on three hilltops overlooking the sparkling waters, beautiful Kalhu thrived on river trade and produce from the surrounding plains – as well as the good graces of the royal household, of course.

"You walk the edge of civilization," said Tum with zeal, pointing to the hilltop citadel that secured his estate. "Your people never understood that north and east of your tiny hills lie the untamed barbarian lands. But for the strength of Ashur, the bite of our blades and the speed of our chariots, your homes would have fallen below the feet of savages long ago."

"How many live here?" I asked, having no idea.

"About the same as Damascus," he said. Seeing that meant nothing to me, he added, "Maybe eighty thousand… or one hundred thousand. Or more."

Impressive numbers, but still little help.

"Three to five times Samaria," Jonah inserted.

"Not close to Nineveh or Babylon," the trader continued, "but mighty besides."

Curious, I prodded further. "Just how big is Nineveh?"

Tum chuckled. "You might as well ask how vast is the Tigris. It is said the arms of Nineveh are as weeds in the plain, but that is stupid. Still, old Shamsi-Adad once counted one hundred and forty-two thousand within the city, and that left out the tent city outside the walls, the farmers and shepherds and merchants and other tenders who inhabit the foothills. It may be double that count, or more. Or less. It is hard to say. They come and go, you know. Like us. But none of this matters. You can make your own guess tomorrow."

"Tomorrow?" The immediacy of it struck me hard. "This finally ends?"

"No," said the Dove, "it begins."

I didn't understand that sort of logic until the moment arose. It came just after the sun struck its midday highs. Weary of the struggle, we crested a sand-blown hill and gazed upon that convergence of humanity that is called Nineveh.

It was not what I expected. Of course, nothing would have been – in Samaria and Bethel, we always considered Nineveh the home of everything vile, a fortress made of bones with fountains that spewed the blood of countless victims. Something like that, anyway. Instead we gazed upon a sea of tents and flocks, broken only by the Tigris and the broad walls – a vast mixture of granite, sandstone, marble, and other rocks, hewed into an impressive structure of sharp corners and circular towers lined with stone teeth about each parapet, protecting the fields of brick homes about several tall hills along the east side of the Tigris.

"Look," said Tum, pointing to a central tower. "Atop the Assur Gate."

I gazed upon the high entrance at the end of our road, just beyond a firm stone bridge across a small stream feeding the Tigris. There were guards aplenty, along with a wall of shiny shields and long, polished bows, but nothing else stood out.

"The flag?" asked the Dove.

I saw it then, a limp sheet of sparkling scarlet silk with gold fringe, hanging atop a pole at the center of the gatehouse.

"The banner of the Council of Ashur-nirari, king of kings of Assyria," revealed Tum. His voice turned grim. "You have picked a dangerous time to come."

"Why?" I asked.

"There is no safe time," the Dove muttered.

"This is the Gathering of Fire," Tum instructed us. "The six arms of Ashur have come together – the stewards of markets, the tenders of herds and produce, the turtans of the army, the Council of Governors, the brotherhoods of the ministries and arts, the lords of the great estates. With their guidance, Ashur-nirari will draw plans for defense."

My first thought was a question, but to this I knew the answer: "Sanscorrab."

"Indeed," Tum reflected. "His force must be the buffer, while the king plots a stronger response. But against whom?"

"It little matters," Jonah declared. "Benjamin, it is time."

With that, he started to jog down the hill towards the bridge and the tent outskirts of Nineveh. At once a strange sort of guilt pierced my heart, quelling my urge to follow. I stood there with my soles firm against the trampled road, watching the thin clouds of dust rise from each determined stride of his bare feet, Jonah's bald albino scalp bobbing in the sun. In newfound fear I wondered what kind of reception these vile people would give him. When I realized just how bad it could get – which did not take long – I sprinted after him. The Dove had already crossed the sandstone bridge and penetrated the first section of tents. With his arms held aloft, the kinnor swinging at his back, he raised his voice in praise.

"Oh Lord of Abraham, Isaac, and Jacob," he shouted, "Lord God of Israel, fill me with Your spirit that I may do Your will!"

The poor merchants gawked at the Dove as if they had never seen a chalk man before. Of course, they probably had not, but for lepers. As you might expect, that realization brought life within the street to a sudden and complete halt. In that air of total stillness, Jonah made his first proclamation. I had just crossed the bridge, yet I heard it as clear as if he were alive now.

"Forty more days," the Dove stated, "and Nineveh will be destroyed."

A rooster crowed. From down the broad road a bull snorted, and a mule declared its stubborn mind. The wind lifted the silt from atop the tents, encircling Jonah with wave after wave of dust. But the people of Nineveh stood stiff in the streets, as if stricken then and there by his claim. The Dove turned his gaze upon each of them, eyes that told the depths of the Lord's anguish.

"Repent!" he commanded. "Repent! For in forty days, Nineveh will be destroyed."

You have to believe none of them ever heard such a proclamation before – even if they understand Hebrew, which I doubt. I ran past many who could but stare, while others surely whispered of his skin disease or his baldness. I still remember many of their exclamations in all those foreign tongues, most of which I have learned over time. It's interesting, how that changes the way I recall things. I try my best to sort it all out and keep these memories clear, but it can so… ahh, I digress. Forgive me.

The elders regained their senses first. Several sent children to gather the guards, while others pointed fingers and issued warnings against Jonah. Soon an uprising brewed within the passageway as young and old alike rushed the Dove, some curious, others insulted or offended. None I heard spoke our language. Yet from their faces and inflection, some must have posed honest questions of who he was and what he was doing.

"Hear me!" Jonah shouted. "Hear me!"

"Why?" came a string of replies, or so Tum muttered afterwards. But the Dove did not cower.

"The Lord God of Israel watches you, Nineveh. He witnessed your sins, your cruelty, and found you lacking. Repent! Repent, or in forty days you will suffer His everlasting judgment!"

His audience understood the threats in that speech. A restless aggravation swept around me like fire across a dry hay mound. This anger spread with their spoken thoughts, yes, and fear as well. But hatred mastered both moods, hatred toward someone who looked so different from them, hatred toward such black warnings, hatred for threatening their lives and homes, hatred for old losses at the hands of their enemies, hatred of commands toward introspection, subjugation, denial. As the waves of the sea might overwhelm a floundering shell, so the people flowed against the Dove, carrying me forward with the leading crest. In horror I watched stones fly. None struck Jonah, though a few fell near him. I fought my way through the crowd, struggling to protect him, even as the Dove called for a re-examination of their lives, their values.

"Blood flows from your hands!" he shouted. "You bear the scars of thousands dead, tortured, defaced."

"Quiet him!" came some shouts, in words I had come to understand, in bits and pieces, during our journey.

"Stand aside!" said others.

Stone flurries soared past me. Reaching Jonah, I put my back to his, thinking beyond reason that I could shield him in some way. But there was no time or escape. Everywhere stretched grasping and punching hands, angry faces, loud screams. I tried to knock them back – I wanted to! – but how could I alone fight off a street full of hostile people? When I gave in to their efforts, binding me with biting ropes, I found the Dove lifted not one eyebrow in his defense.

"Listen," he spoke with a calm, clear voice, hoping to breach their hostility. "Hear me!"

It was a futile gesture, but soon the roar of a ram's horn pierced the chaos. The mob turned to face the newcomer, readying their anger for a new target.

"Release them!" demanded a bitter Tum. He forced his way through the crowd to where they held us, but our captors defied him. Then Alport appeared at his right side, a shining sword in each hand, and everyone turned cautious.

"We hold them for the guards," bellowed a thick-shouldered man, his fingers embedded in an oiled beard of scarlet curls that hung to his waist.

"Your word means nothing here, Philar-Al'andron," spat another of our captors, taller than the first man but less muscular, and with gray locks far less endowed. "Neither you nor your thug are welcome."

"Do not worry about us," Jonah told the merchant.

"Be quiet!" Tum snapped. His eyes scalded the Dove. "That was stupid, running into a busy market like that. Interrupting their sales. What did you expect them to do?"

"What I want or expect means nothing," Jonah answered. But the rotund merchant was not finished.

"You did not even discuss this with me! Why, Jonah?"

"Enough, Philar-Al'andron." Through the parting crowd came a tall man with authority, if his multicolored cloak, golden tassels, and bronze headgear gave any indication. Behind him followed men who needed no riches to get their way. Their bared swords and black, quilted leather armor did that for them.

The leader gazed upon Jonah as if he'd never seen anything like him before. Circling the Dove twice, he examined Jonah from his pale feet cloaked with dust to his sweaty neck and bare white ears.

"What are you?" he said.

Surprising, in our month of travels since leaving Damascus, no one had bothered to ask that.

"I bear the curse of my Lord," Jonah said, once Tum translated for us, "as your people will endure the curse of their lives."

The man bristled. Others shouted their defiance.

"Be happy the king has heard you," the official warned. Sweeping his hood back from his dark, oiled hair, he fixed his deep green eyes upon the Dove and scowled. "If he had not summoned you now, I would gladly claim your accursed scalp. But our king reserves that pleasure for himself. Now, follow me!"

With a nod, Jonah turned to Tum.

"Now you know."

Chapter 21
Trial

I soon found Nineveh fit none of my expectations.

From our treatment at Damascus and our latest reception, I had girded myself for hideous torture. After all, this was the city of blood! The center of the unholy! And yet, though we were prisoners, these Assyrians seemed in no rush to punish us. Indeed, to Tum's gratitude, the captain of the palace guard ordered our bindings removed despite the rumblings of the crowd.

"I trust your friends, Philar-Al'andron," the captain decided, though his voice remained cautious. "Pray they do not disappoint me."

In that way we penetrated the tent city, the Dove and myself ringed by four spear-carrying soldiers wrapped in many layers of leather tunic and breeches, the stout captain in the lead, Tum and Alport to the rear. The crowd spat and cursed us but gave ground under the wrathful eye of the guard.

For a nation of warriors, the looming fortress surprised me, for it showed none of the defensive complexity I'd seen at Tyre and Damascus. Though anchored by tall towers and three-story guardhouses, Nineveh's wide gates featured short, straight passageways into the city. Even Aphek's small guardhouses employed angled tunnels with many traps and hidden barriers, all the better to thwart a determined attacker. Nineveh's curtain walls seemed rather plain in comparison, with a foundation spanning little more than twenty cubits and no outer ditch or slope.

The simplicity of the designs confused me, but then I realized why: these defenses were decorative, for the most part, built more to glorify the city than defend it. Each block in those stone walls bore elaborate carvings and colorful mosaics touting Assyria's rich history. I gazed upon them with wonder – not for their craftsmanship, though that was undeniable, nor for the tales they told, some of which made me shudder and cringe at their bloody results. No, what opened my eyes was the blind arrogance that stood revealed in that stronghold. With the cutter's skilled strokes still visible in the ancient etchings, their countless images of Nineveh's heritage blemished only by age, this fortress showed few if any scars from battle. Unlike every generation raised in Damascus, Samaria, Aphek, or every other city I knew, the Ninevites apparently never faced rebuilding their bludgeoned walls after some enemy's rabid assault. They had no idea what it meant to cringe in their homes, hungry, frightened, their loved ones threatened, their city strangled and burning. They couldn't comprehend enduring a siege, much less losing one.

I noticed one of our guards eyeing me with dark suspicion. His distrust stirred my apprehension.

"Impressive," I commented as I pointed to the artwork, all in hopes of clearing myself.

The man just stared at me as a leopard might its prey, so I sought help by pointing others to the stonework. Jonah shrugged, not interested in the least, but Tum welcomed my praise.

"There is talk of a new foundation expanding north and east," he told me with great pride. As we passed under the wall, Tum brushed his fingertips along the tunnel's huge cut stones, illustrating how smooth their chiseled faces remained after all these generations, and how well the seams meshed without the use of mortar. I nodded with honest appreciation, to which he sighed with grateful acknowledgment.

"Our forefathers had impressive skill, cutting all this, laying it out so perfectly," he said, "but now these walls really are inadequate for our city. We have outgrown them."

As striking as the outer fortress was, the city within proved far more captivating. Passing the inner gatehouse and its eight sentries – each as imposing as our palace guard, with black leather shields, vests, and leggings that shimmered from fragrant oils – we entered into a second marketplace, block after block of crowded streets lined with overloaded wagons and brick storefronts. All were manned by pushy peddlers screaming about their abundant must-have goods… far more than the city enjoys now. Ah, I remember them so well! Shiny glass goblets with sharp facets that flared in the sun like hungry flames. Polished furniture of rare woods and immaculate stoneware, each piece engraved with tales from Assyria's fabled past or images from its enchanting countryside. Elaborate swords, spears, knives, hammers, cooking utensils, and other metalwork, all of a luster and elegance to challenge the master iron weavers of Damascus or Joppa. Glowing gemstones and vibrant jewels to match the wealthiest tastes. Embroidered silks of brilliant hues. Bottles and urns of precious balms, potions, and incense. Scrolls of mighty deeds told not just with words but etched images, shoes and hats and cloaks in colors and shapes that seemed just so silly… oh, I could go on and on about all these things. But to be honest, what moved me most were the temptations to my tongue. Mounds of fruit of every kind imaginable, all ripe and luscious, and that warm smell of baking bread, and savory roasting meats on spits turning above flames right there on the street! My mouth waters at the memory, and the agony of walking past those delicacies without even one bite. And I can't leave out the multitude of services. The winds sparkled from the rainbow-hued banners advertising barbers and physicians, blacksmiths and carpenters, weavers and seamstresses, stonecutters and potters, scribes and intercessors. Musicians played at most street corners, while in the many courtyards stood storytellers entertaining one and all beneath lofty green shade trees. Teachers held class at the edge of large, bubbling fountains or spreading flower gardens, instructing not just boys but girls as well.

My lingering shock surprises you, does it? Well, that is why I instruct you now, to share how different our peoples are. You see, in my homeland you would not find women working side by side with men, sharing in all things, and with their heads uncovered, their hair blowing in the breeze. When I walked the streets of Nineveh and witnessed how they had granted their women such freedom, it was… well, disgusting at first, even disturbing, and yet it stirred things in me….

But God works through all things, even women.

Forgive me; I have steered off course again. About Nineveh… in truth, I had not expected such a rich, active culture. It numbed me. Throughout my life, I considered Ninevites as little more than snarling killers. No, actually, as nothing more than hungry, stalking beasts. Yet these streets flowed with pulsing, inventive, joyous lives. Everywhere I looked, there were long-bearded men in thoughtful discussions. Mothers in elegant gowns chasing playful children. Neighbors sharing good times and laughing at each other's jokes. Friends helping one another. Strangers working together with integrity and respect.

"Is this not wondrous?" I could not help exclaiming.

Tum laughed, tickled by my enthusiasm, but the Dove remained cold.

"Open your eyes!" he snapped. "Look about you!"

That struck me as a plunge into freezing waters. So I did as he said, when I realized he would not relent, and I searched for things that might offend our Lord. And I found them, so embedded in the framework of their lives that I had overlooked them. Emblems of false gods lay in the cornerstones of each wall and the entryways of every home. Small idols and demonic images stood on the counters and windows. Many people wore them on chains about their necks, or had images sewn into their clothing! And sprinkled throughout the markets were busy inns and taverns, usually with the red sash of prostitutes hung about the outer posts. Soothsayers and mystics worked alongside the professionals, proclaiming who and what they were with no fear of reprisal.

Jonah studied me, waiting as might a teacher before a shallow, naive student – which is how I felt.

"A deceptive place," I admitted, humbled by his hard gaze.

"Vile," the Dove spat.

"That's unfair," Tum countered. "What do you know of things? Listen to me now! I travel throughout the world, so I know this better than you. My people are no different from any others you'll find; indeed, we are better than most I can think of. Damascus is a filthier place, with its dry reservoirs and clogged sewers. Oh, how I hate trading there! The stench kills my nose. Each time I visit, I wonder if I will ever savor a rose again! And Tyre! Believe me – that city's far more wanton. The nights when the fleets come in… ah! You lock your doors and don't dare sleep, so wild it gets. And the Philistines! Oh, could I tell you things about them that would spill your guts all over this street!"

I had no idea how to answer his building tirade. No one would deny the disgusting practices of the Phoenician cults, from burning children to sacrificing women and much more. And Tum was right about the widespread evils; many Gentiles practiced similar customs. Still, no one could claim that as a defense, as I expected the Dove to note. But Jonah kept his silence, impatient to reach our goal, whatever that was.

We entered into a hilly area of squeezed brick homes stacked two to three high. The captain guided us in a climb along narrow cobblestone passages crumbling with age. The still air stank of hot sweat and waste pots fermenting in the deep shadows. Sometimes a brick or tile would plunge past our heads, smashing against the beaten paths to throw jagged shards in all directions. That spooked me, to be sure. By about the fourth or fifth alley, I began to fret and mutter, recalling how our guards had led us through such decaying streets at Damascus, but Jonah held his tongue. I saw why when we reached the crest of a ridge, and there before us rose the pitted limestone walls of a vast citadel.

Towering granite titans stood guard at its wide gate, two identical creatures with the feet and legs of a monstrous bull, the hearty frame of a kingly lion, the broad wings of a soaring eagle and the imposing head of their greatest king of legend, Tiglath-Pileser – or so Tum said it was. Each was twice as tall as the Dove, built with three faces so that they could keep watch of every approach to the entrance.

"Is it not impressive?" Tum marveled.

"Wonderful craftsmanship," I agreed, though the Dove scoffed at the notion.

Behind the watchers rose tall cedar doors banded with black iron ribs linked by thick round bolts of glittering gold. In the center of each portal hung the bronze skull of a bull. The captain tapped a dagger against them in sequence, first the left forehead, then the right, then the left. A grinding sound soon followed.

Tum used the brief pause to ask the captain why we were here.

"The king summoned you," came his brief answer.

That struck me odd. "But how did he hear Jonah this far away?"

The wooden doors parted inward, revealing a dark, narrow tunnel of worn mud bricks. The captain strode in, impatient to go on, though a thick slab of limestone blocked the passage. I heard echoes of stretched ropes and grinding rock, then the limestone block lurched forward. I froze, wondering if the wall might collapse upon us, but the captain pressed on, unafraid, and so I followed, realizing the giant stone was retreating into the ceiling, as was another one beyond it. Behind them stood two more doors, adorned with more bronze heads and golden bolts. As we approached, these doorways opened outward to reveal a broad courtyard tiled with marble and granite.

The captain motioned us into the bright light, but his eyes centered on me.

"He did not," he said, deciding to answer my question once Tum shared my words.

"He did not what?"

"Hear you. He did not hear you."

"Then how did you reach us so soon?"

"The High Priest of Ashur foretold your arrival."

The Dove's eyes flared as we entered the light – an act not due to the blazing sun. But he maintained his silence.

Three majestic structures rose above the vast courtyard, each one like the palace of Samaria, their roofs suspended atop tall stone pillars. The scene drew my breath, but so did the ranks of well-adorned men and women milling about this gathering area. I had seen their kind of wealth before, among the interest seekers, judges, and regulators that plagued King Jeroboam's court, but even so, the elegance of these Assyrians drew my respect. They moved with grace and noble bearing until they saw the Dove. Then they just stood and stared, like befuddled cows.

Unperturbed, the captain led us across the gathering area to the largest of the buildings, which sat atop a tapered foundation of chiseled limestone. Reaching the top, we passed within a forest of granite pillars. It terrified me at first, making me feel like an ant among the legs of giants, fearing that at any moment the ground would quake and these tumbling titans would crush my bones to dust. But then the forest thinned, and we entered a series of chambers connected by torch-lit passages that reminded me of the queen's maze outside Samaria. The sick odor of damp mold tainted the air, but I appreciated the walk. All sorts of statues lined our way, many of fine craftsmanship, while the walls displayed fabulous jeweled weapons, painted tapestries, and polished glassware. We passed three libraries of fired clay tablets, and two rooms offered tumbling waterfalls and steamy baths. The guards cautioned us to step with care across the damp floors, which could get slippery on days like that one. But the warning meant little, for with another turn we emerged once more into the web of pillars. As we crossed the sixth row of these stone supports, at our left opened a broad stairway descending to another courtyard and a series of temples. To my joy, we passed it by for a short stair to a walled balcony over the central parkway of Nineveh.

I could not help pausing there to enjoy the splendor of that view. Before me spread all that was Assyria! Even thinking of it now speeds my heart!

With the sky a blaze of light and heat, I gazed across the vast audience of stone roofs and tents that made up the city, the grassy foothills beyond and the mountains beyond that, and everywhere I looked, I saw people. Children playing with toys while their mothers drew water from hillside wells. Blacksmiths hammering hot metal before coal fires. Shepherds guiding their sheep or cattle to still ponds and rolling streams. Peasants harvesting fields of grains. Traders dickering over goods.

These people were of all sizes, dressed in uncountable ways, and as the Lord is my witness, they seemed no different from any I had ever met.

For some reason that confused me. I looked upon them, the likenesses of friends and family I had known all my life, and found myself wondering what these people did that earned our Lord's wrath. Or not done, for that matter.

Hesitant, I turned to find another man speaking with the captain. He stood above us all, wrapped in a shimmering purple cloak trimmed in silver and gold, with silver serpent rings upon each finger and glossy white sashes about his neck and waist. Beneath his conical helmet banded with bronze and gold hung at least a cubit of snowy hair as smooth as spider's silk, flowing about his wizened face to meet a long white beard pressed into waxy curls.

Finding my eyes upon him, he smiled and nodded as a salute. That caught me off-guard. Not knowing what to do, I did nothing. Tum frowned at that, but it did not seem to matter, for without a word the official pivoted and left.

The angry trader leaned to my ear to whisper, "That was the secretary!" But the captain started off in the man's wake, expecting us to follow, and so I soon forgot Tum's words. As we passed a central corridor, I heard the thunder of echoing drums. A brilliant white light loomed before us. Without hesitation, the secretary disappeared within that blinding curtain. The rumbling accelerated. The captain entered the light. Jonah stepped in. The drums ceased.

It was my turn.

With the guards at my side, I strode through the dazzling screen – to find myself in a sunlit courtyard within a chamber of thick marble pillars. Across the way, the secretary stood at the entrance of a spacious hall. At either side awaited twenty sentries wrapped head to foot with tiny, overlapping plates of gold. In their gloved hands rested huge double-headed axes of gold.

The secretary motioned for us to stand before him, then sent the palace captain and our escorts away. "Welcome to the presence of the King of kings," he told those of us who remained, which Tum relayed to Jonah and me. "He bids you enter."

"Thank you," offered Tum, but the Dove decided to wait no longer. With a huff of impatience, he made to stride into the hall. A swift ax fell to block his way.

The secretary stepped into the fray. "None precede me!" he proclaimed.

"Then get on with it!" Jonah replied, undeterred. "The Lord has a message for your king."

The sentry's hard stare met the Dove's molten eyes Neither gave way as Tum shared what Jonah said. Finally, with an exasperated wave of the secretary's finger, the guard lifted his ax and we proceeded into the grand hall, the Assyrian official hurrying forward with Jonah at his heels. I fell in behind him, my curiosity a flame within me. My eyes danced about the place hall, first at the towering pillars and partial ceiling, then to the steady back of the Dove, then to the broad rectangular hole above us and the bright blue sky, and back to the Dove, then to the couple of hundred or so other golden sentries lining the walls, then to the Dove. Over his shoulder I saw a platform of peerless black marble as reflective as the most crystalline pool. There, within a throne of gold between granite pedestals cradling searing hot coals, awaited the king.

I think back upon it now as yet another part of my education. The man who held aloft that ornate silver crown – that man adorned with those fabulous silver and crimson robes, the golden bracelets, the dancing tassels, and embroidered collars – he was such a common-looking fellow that I almost laughed. There was no majesty to his frame, such as Ansephanti enjoyed, nor the countenance of wisdom that marked the face of Jeroboam… though that old man rarely put that asset to use. No, this king displayed no outstanding qualities of any kind. His dim green eyes seemed distant and fearful, his skin blotched pink and yellow, his thin frame wrinkled and weak, his brown beard wiry and dull. And when he spoke, his voice grated my ears as a sharpening stone across a blade scored with many chips.

A cymbal sounded. The secretary bowed before the throne. I

followed his example, though the Dove refused.

"Hail, Ashur-nirari, King of Assyria!" proclaimed the secretary, as Tum translated it to us. "The prophet of Israel arrives."

The king frowned. "He bears the disrespect of his people."

"I bear the message of the Lord Most High," Jonah said. "In His presence, I bow to no earthly king."

"This is the house of Ashur, Jew!" stormed the king. "In this house, his will be done."

"In all houses rules the Lord of Abraham, Isaac, and Jacob," answered the Dove. "Indeed, to this house was I sent."

Four guards stepped from the shadows, garbed in rainbow-hued cloaks, their shoulders and chest plated with gold, their helmets banded with gold and silver. With them came seven elders in black robes, their heads shrouded down to their white beards.

Jonah ignored them. "Hear me, Ashur-nirari. The Lord God of Israel will no longer accept the wicked ways of you and your people. Repent, Assyria! Repent! Or in forty days, Nineveh will be no more."

The strength of his words almost stifled Tum, though he soon overcame that. They filled me with doom. Jonah was a rock, to speak so to the king, even one such as this. But I underestimated this king, as was my folly. He rose before the Dove, the glory and terror of his office spread about him, and laughed. Just laughed!

That earned my respect. Though he might not look the part, this man showed the courage and confidence of a monarch.

"Jonah, your coming was foretold," he informed us, reclining into his throne. "Oh, yes, we did hear the tale of your crossing our heartland. An amusing series of twists. But the priests of the Brotherhoods recognized the signs. And we are ready."

Tum seemed to enjoy sharing that message.

The cries of a goat echoed around the pillars. A black-robed priest led the stubborn beast before us, a beautiful three-year-old weed chewer with curled horns that glowed of fresh oil and a gray and brown wool coat washed and brushed. The priest knelt at the nervous goat's head and spoke aloud prayers to Ashur,

Marduk, and other false names, then withdrew a long knife and sliced the beast's throat, cradling the head and body while the hot blood poured into a bronze basin. The goat made but one jerk and died.

"The water of life is warm and rich, my Lord," declared the priest. Laying the carcass down, he dipped his hand into the basin and lifted out a small portion of the crimson liquid, only to let it run through his fingers. "Dagan proclaims it! There is no sickness here."

I watched with a sick fascination as the elder turned the lifeless body onto its back to part its skin and muscle. Probing the vital organs with his fingers, the man spoke of omens, which Tum explained.

"The middle finger of the lungs has sided with the left," the priest noted. "It signals fame, my Lord. The heart responds to the touch. Truly the strength of Marduk thrives in your house, oh King! And the liver rests full and heavy, its color bright and welcoming. The land will be strong at your service, my lord King!"

Ashur-nirari smiled. "Remove the gift; burn it now as our offering. And fifty more. Let the gods feast!"

"False hopes," Jonah warned as the rainbow-cloaked ones carried away the bloody remains. "Repent, Ashur-nirari. Refuse, and your world dies!"

"Jonah!" Tum snapped in surprised reproach. Alport stepped to my side, his hands near his sword hilts, even as the trader threw himself prostrate before his lord. "Forgive me, my King! I had no idea he would speak this way to you."

I must admit, I only half-heard what Tum said, and even less when the trader recognized his mistake and reverted to his Assyrian tongue. Most of my attention was on Alport, wondering for whom he primed his weapons. But the king revealed no concern. With gentle speech he reassured Tum, then rose to help the merchant back to his feet. Visibly touched and relieved, Tum offered what might have been some parting praise. He then turned, gathered his bodyguard behind him, and fled the room, all without giving Jonah a last glance.

The king returned to his throne, a confident smile upon his lips. "Now, Jonah, you and your friend are alone."

I almost fell to the ground. This Assyrian king spoke Hebrew?

"Never do I walk alone," the Dove replied, unshaken.

"Ah, but this is my palace," countered Ashur-nirari. His voice turned hard. "My palace. Should I deem it, you will not leave."

Jonah did not buckle. "The Lord is my guide. No door stands before Him, no chain can bind Him. His will is supreme."

"Hah!" The king threw his robes back and strode down from his throne, even as the priests of his Brotherhood came forward. "You saw the signs! Long life and strength are bestowed me!"

"Believe not the ruse of false teachings. Repent, Ashur-nirari! Repent!"

"Repent?" The king spoke the word as if it burned his tongue. "Repent?"

"Slay him now, my Lord," urged a black-robed priest, or so I learned later. Others added their agreement. "Let the dust of our sandals taint his blood!"

"Hold!" the king told them. "Are we of his level, to respond so? I will not let the words of such a deformed man influence me." Yet when he turned his gaze back to us, those eyes held nothing but hostility. "What are you that your skin is as chalk? A diseased beggar?"

"I am but a messenger," Jonah answered.

"A messenger?" The king roared to the bright sun. "An undead, more like it!"

"Close," the Dove granted. "But nothing is beyond use to the Lord."

"Even a reject such as yourself." Chuckling, the king leaned around the Dove and patted the kinnor on Jonah's back. The wood rang a hollow, uninspired sound. "Play for me, dead one. Sing of your blight!"

The Dove allowed a confident smile, one that turned sly in its promise. Lifting the instrument from his back, he offered a simple acknowledgment, "As you wish, Ashur-nirari," before launching into a series of cold, introspective chords and note flurries that had me wondering just what devilry he would wish on the king.

His sweet voice soon joined the fray, but his heart whispered his sorrow.

You asked of me things I felt should not be done.
Yet You offered no choice, so I chose to run.
To the oceans I fled on a ship of stout heart.
But in Your tight grip, its strength fell apart.
Your storm of dark judgment bottled us tight;
My sins were proclaimed the source of our plight.
Cornered anew, I gave up my life –
Endless pain and dismay, but dodging Your strife.

Oh, Lord! How more foolish can a man be,
To forsake Your guidance, Your revelry?
And how great is Your love for one such as me
To offer forgiveness so passionately?

For humbled in Sheol I abandoned my will
And prayed to You humbly for salvation still.
From the bowels of a fish, You cast me free
To bring forth Your claims for all humanity.
Thus, I carry Your sign to all of the world;
Bearing Your flag of compassion unfurled.
Proclaim Your will, Lord, and make it mine!
Prepare us to see Your judgment's sign!

The song left a dark cloud on my heart. I pondered the words, confused by a tale I had endured and still didn't understand. And I was not alone. As the notes dwindled and died, the king took his time pondering it, gathering himself within his throne. Anguish weighed upon his brow. For solace, he looked first to his priests, then the Dove. Jonah chose that moment to advance.

"The Hand of God is made known," he declared. "Repent, Nineveh!"

The brash wind enveloped him before his echoes could fade within that cold stone chamber. A dark shadow embraced us. The king's banners took life in the stiff breeze and extended full, even as the bronze shields rang from flying sand. Our torches flickered and died. The clear sky gave way to the Lord's turbulent gray squall, its winds circling about the citadel like a herd of angry bees.

"Draw the storm shields!" the king commanded, though from the rush of the guards, it looked like the secretary had already given that order. "Seal the building!"

A black-robed one strode toward us from the platform. "How dare you threaten the king?" he spat in words I somewhat understood. "How dare –"

"I am but a messenger," the Dove shouted above the wind. "The Lord warns of judgment for Nineveh's wicked ways. Your lives must be turned right again!"

Their priests spouted all sorts of angry comments I little understood. But they quailed before the king, who had no patience for such things.

"This is your doing?" he sought from Jonah.

"The Lord of Abraham, Isaac –"

Ashur-nirari brushed that aside. "Cast it away!"

"It is not in my power or my will."

"My Lord, feel the air," urged a third member of the Assyrian Brotherhood, in words I learned later on in life. "Do you hear the heart of that breeze? The will? It is a god most high who summons it."

"Call on Marduk!" the king demanded. "Cast it aside!"

"Such things require great sacrifice, my Lord," the priest responded. "Or blood."

"Yes," the king said, savoring the word. "Blood. Take these Jews! We will shed their blood and burn their flesh. Marduk should find that amusing."

The guards seized Jonah and myself as the king gloated. High above us, bare-chested palace workers fought against the storm to stretch thick sheets of mended goatskin across the open roof, even as guards brought forth new flame to re-light the torches and lamps.

"You see?" the king gloated in our tongue. "Your timid demonstration accomplished little. Now we will burn your blood, and our gods will disperse your bit of wind."

I waited for the Dove to answer, but he said nothing. His face remained defiant, even aloof, yet he said nothing! I started to ask why, then stopped. From the corner of the room came another priest, black-robed as the others, but girded with a chain of thick gold links.

"No, Ashur-nirari," he stated, speaking first in the language of the court, and then in Hebrew. "You must not slay this one."

The king twisted at his presence. "What, you offer counsel twice in a day? When for years you said nothing?"

This newcomer strode to the throne, unperturbed by his ruler's animosity.

"It was your choice to bring these other priests before you when Ashur alone deserves your ear. Thus the high god speaks not of you – and I offer nothing when Ashur speaks not to me. Yet the god of our people foretold this man's coming, as I warned you. Now he commands I tell you this: release the prophet, Ashur-nirari!"

The king squirmed in irritation.

"Forget not my presence, priest."

"And forget not my title," the man countered, "for I am Ashur-minal, the high priest of our land. In this you will do as I say."

Ashur-nirari stiffened. "And if I refuse?"

"Then you will fall. I am the high priest." He stroked his thin black beard, letting his words rest upon the dry wind. Only when he had met every rebellious eye in the room did he declare, "The prophet must be allowed to proclaim his judgment. This Ashur has spoken."

Jonah allowed a thin smile. I wish I could have managed it. Still, in my heart, I lifted praise to the Lord, though his ways grew ever more mysterious!

The king's eyes burned at the priest, but Ashur-minal would not bend. And so, the monarch softened.

"Perhaps I have overstepped myself," he allowed. "Perhaps I have overlooked my god." Then his tone turned harsh. "Though I know not what value this man of Israel has in Ashur's eyes. But I am not all-knowing."

With a shrug and a sigh of release, Ashur-nirari drew himself into his throne and went about the rituals for reclaiming his tarnished sovereignty. I had seen Jeroboam do such things when contrite, so this didn't surprise me. When the king was comfortable, the secretary brought forward a basin of water, a beautiful cloth for washing, and a small glass bottle of fragrant oil. Another priest approached. The king rinsed his hands and wiped his brow, then settled back as the dark-robed one rubbed oil into his sovereign's hair, cheeks, and neck. The remainder he poured atop the coals, filling the air with a pleasant freshness.

Through this purifying ceremony, the king regained the authority of his crown. It seemed to satisfy everyone in the room; I saw no uncertainty in the monarch's eye, nor a hint of disrespect in the others. But I did witness a vast wellspring of hostility toward what this Ashur-minal had demanded of their sovereign.

The king of Assyria leaned back in his throne, his fingers rolling cadence on the arm of that chair as he evaluated what to do with this pair of Hebrew thorns. My limbs stiffened in nervous agony as I awaited his judgment.

"Very well," he decided, or so Ashur-minal translated. Turning toward his secretary, Ashur-nirari reaffirmed his faith in his god. "Release the prophet and his lad. They are to be wards of the king, under the protection of the Royal Guard. Let all hear them and obey!"

Only our deliverance at sea topped the sense of elation that swept over me then. "Praise the Lord!" I could not help shouting. We had survived!

Jonah gave me a gentle smile before returning his hard gaze to the king. "I will return, Ashur-nirari, for you must also repent your evil deeds."

The king bristled at that, but as the secretary ushered us toward the entrance, the king gave but one response: "May Ashur's will be done."

We walked down dark passages, through halls of gold and jewels, their luster faded beneath the Hand of God. Even so, I felt new life flow into me with each step – though the Dove seemed cold and distant.

"This is but the beginning, Benjamin," he mumbled to cloud my newfound exuberance.

The secretary scowled something I could not understand – and I made the mistake of saying so. That made him even more angry.

"You should fear for your lives, speaking so to the king!" he spat in Hebrew.

I almost stumbled at that, though I should have marked this far deeper in my conscious: Never underestimate these people.

"He is but a man," the Dove countered.

As we neared the passage to the courtyard, now blanketed by thick tent cloth, we came upon the priest of Ashur. He stood beside two golden guards, a blazing torch held aloft in his right hand.

"I will guide them now," he declared in our tongue, speaking it better than most people I know.

The secretary hesitated. "My Lord told me –"

"I will do it," stressed Ashur-minal, waving his left hand to dispatch the secretary, who grumbled as he left. Once the guards parted the goatskins, we stepped into the abandoned courtyard. About us the air lay dry and still, impatient and tense, as if awaiting the maelstrom that churned far above us.

"A unique sirocco," commented the priest, with just a touch of admiration.

Jonah offered no friendship. "You too must repent."

The tall man stopped in surprise. "I? I worship Ashur."

"A mistaken faith. Oh, I admit your kind once knew the truth. The sons of Noah settled Nineveh, Assur… most of Assyria. Theirs was indeed the God of Abraham, Isaac, and Jacob. The one true God. But you have distorted Him, you and your people before you. You have given Him a false name, pouring blood over His hands of love."

"Such is Ashur's way," the priest challenged. "Your belief is no different. Did God not tell your people to slay all within Canaan?"

"Yes, but to keep our faith pure, not our people! You have turned the love of God into a sword for political conquest!"

"As did David, Solomon –"

"Even Jeroboam," I blurted out. Then I realized whom I was agreeing with and held my tongue.

"No," responded the Dove. "Theirs were wars of law. Unrest in the outer lands threatened our lives. They extended our boundaries only to extend our law."

"How are we different?" pressed Ashur-minal.

"You would bring order through terror!" The Dove reached his full height in a failed bid to meet the priest's eye. "You have committed atrocities in your god's name, and glorified in the bloodshed! There is no love in that. Our Lord is not in that."

The priest retreated, his gaze fuming. "You treat me as the enemy!"

"As you are," the Dove agreed.

"But we have sought only to defend ourselves! To beat off the barbarians who would cut us down at a whim!"

"Once that was true. To the east, the north, it may still be. But long ago your kings turned the embrace of God into a sword for their own aims. Why else have you turned west, to lands as developed as your own? To people who need not your butchery?"

The Assyrian reeled at that thought. "We have fought," stumbled Ashur-minal, "to save holy Babylon. To fund our armies, to protect our commerce. We came to you –"

"Exacting tribute," the Dove interrupted. "Or conquest."

"No, no! We seek support for our people!" The priest grew hot. "Do you think it easy, protecting our vast frontiers?"

"Why do you not seek alliances? Forge friendships?"

"Why? Many in the west prey on us as much as from the east or north. But what do you know about all that? You live in a small corner of the world. A developed corner, so you say, but insignificant. We hold the central lands, the focus of countless roaming tribes from all sides. Little disciplined, bound ever for war. And when we found ourselves and Babylon besieged, we went west, to end the bloodshed."

"To grow rich," Jonah said.

"Indeed!" The priest seemed outraged, but that soon gave way to reason. "Indeed. Your hatred shows, Jew. You would have us dead – and we would now be dead, but for the steps we took."

"You stopped relying on God," Jonah stated. "You abandoned the Lord, choosing your own means for survival. We did not. Your path made you vile, vile and cruel."

"And generations of your people died as slaves!"

For once I felt moved to speak. "That was our punishment, for disobeying Him."

"But now we are free," the Dove added.

"Free!" spat Ashur-minal.

Looking upon his darkened eyes and cold brow, I felt my heart under attack.

"Yes," he said, "but for how long?"

Chapter 22
Ministry

Forty days. Forgive me, Lord, but at first, the whole idea frightened me. Tum was gone for good, I felt sure, and we had relied on him for everything. Food. Shelter. Clothing. Transportation. Translations. Even companionship. As we left the citadel, stumbling through that still, arid air into a crowded street, I realized that, but for Jonah, I knew no one here. I had no friends. We were alone.

I look back upon it now and attribute such fears to foolishness. With the Lord at your side, in your heart, you are never alone. You will never hunger – at least, not spiritually, and that is far more important than one's stomach. Even in bondage, those points hold true. But in that, my first time in Nineveh, I was terrified.

It ever surprised me how quick news may travel in such a situation. The Dove wasted no time beginning his witness. Lifting his hands before the grand statues of the winged bull, he shouted "Repent!" into a street crowded with people fleeing their tents for the protection of the walls. And he was recognized.

You see, when the Hand of God had risen from the earth, the tent dwellers all about Nineveh thought it an assault, and so they rushed into the city! But then word spread through the streets that visiting the king was the white-skinned prophet in that tale of the plains, the man who raised the whirlwind of the ancient god! Do not ask me how that happened – rumors have lives of their own. But in this case it helped, for when Jonah walked through the city, demanding repentance, people could look up, see the Hand of God swirling around the vast city walls, and accept him for what he was. Thus, we no longer feared another beating, or at least I did not… I don't know what the Dove thought of it. We found the people curious, and more than a little interested. They listened, even those who understood not a word Jonah said. Their questions reached bystanders who spoke our tongue, and palace guards with similar knowledge. Soon I heard people sharing back and forth what they heard or discerned, which seemed to fuel even more interest. Followers formed in our wake. Debates sprang up like wildfires.

"What sins?" one man asked in the center of a spreading street. Jonah answered by lifting the idol of the Babylonian god Nabu from the man's pocket.

"Why us?" demanded a shopkeeper at the northwest gate, a well-dressed woman who baked the best-smelling bread I could remember (of course, in my hunger even mold-riddled food smelled better than frankincense). To answer, the Dove pointed to the citadel towers, where flew the skins of men who had opposed Ashur-nirari in battle.

Not everyone was so easily satisfied.

"How?" asked a battle-hardened guard, who followed us one day for many hours. Pointing a finger at Jonah's nose, the guard continued, "Just how could this god of hills and shepherds destroy a city as old as time itself? The gods would not allow it."

With a kind smile, the Dove led us through the Assur Gate. Beyond that thick stone, we heard the winds striking against each other, howling as angry wolves restrained from ready meals. We saw the depths of the blackness. A portion of the crowd refused then to follow. I almost stayed with them, but the Dove urged us forward, and where he went, the guard trailed behind. We walked to the forefront of the deserted tent district, the thunder of the storm almost crushing us. There, at the crossing of the stream, little remained of the stone bridge that we had used just days before.

It took us three days to cross Nineveh the first time, ever proclaiming the warning of the Lord. And each day we heard those questions and many, many more. But there was one point that came up far more often than any other – and it was usually put in a most enlightening way.

My favorite? Oh, it was this one:

"What happened to you?" asked a six-year-old girl, her eyes as wide as the sky.

Jonah displayed the broadest smile I ever witnessed upon his lips. Lifting his kinnor, he answered with the tale of his journey through the fish.

Through our first week, Jonah preferred speaking in certain areas. The markets placed high on his list, for there he could confront the face of Nineveh's structured prostitution system. And that, at first, brought chaos… as we should have expected. Tum, after all, had warned us against drawing crowds there. But in some ways, the disturbance was the merchants' own fault. It seems these argumentative traders treasured verbal bartering so much – when they weren't doing business with the crown, they rarely kept anything in writing, whether on goatskin parchment or clay – that when these sellers faced a disturbance such as the Dove caused, they lost not only the business that might have followed his speech, but the transactions in progress… and there were always many of those. So, they often combated us with disturbances of their own. To our good fortune, the Royal Guard about the gates followed the orders of their king and stopped such theatrics before violence erupted. And soon it did not matter, for the Hand of God cut most traffic off from the world's largest city, and that brought merchant trade to a standstill. That may explain why venders were among the first to voice belief in Jonah, for they saw the impact of his words as quick as anyone could. Also, the prostitution outlets – at least those shows and beddings supported by the inns – soon dried up.

Funny, with the influx of people from the tent cities, I doubt the inns and stables long missed that indecent business. Nor did the eateries and taverns, I would think.

Jonah enjoyed speaking in the courtyards and schools, where

translations proved no problem, and both students and teachers loved to debate his message. As I had seen, the Dove was not one to back down from any verbal challenge, and he never lost. How could he, with the Lord's Spirit within him and His Hand darkening the sky? Each day that whirlwind raged, further defying the extent of a typical storm, was a day in witness to our Lord.

Yet the debates illustrated one surprising fact: the Ninevites accepted the complaints against their society, sometimes before Jonah ever said a word. But they knew not our Lord, and so they wondered what interest this distant god had in them, and if he was indeed of such power, why he chose only now to reveal himself. Jonah answered them much as he had Ashur-minal, explaining the roots of the Assyrian god and how their forefathers had abandoned His ways. And the reason for our Lord's interest? Love.

I remember the first time I heard that. It seemed so radical then, that God would offer his love to Gentiles! I know it should not have surprised me so, for I had seen His hand at work on the Great Sea, within the crew of Hazorn, and even with Tum, to some degree. But to hear the Dove speak it when he had so opposed this concept before... oh, that was enlightening. It did not surprise me when Jonah hesitated or evaded answering questions that sought more on the subject, but that became more difficult each day.

Debates grew hottest at the temples. I suspect in normal times this would not have been so, for Assur was the home of Ashur and thus claimed the largest temples of the realm. But Nineveh had its fair share, and perhaps more for the Babylonian gods. And with the Gathering of Fire upon us, there were plenty of priests and governors and scribes who contested Jonah to the fullest. It started that first week, when he ran into the militant Nari-Speltum, governor of Arbil, who was meeting with Ashur-minal. And there were a couple of debates with Marduk-handorali, the high priest of the sun god. And then there was Tenpul-Kidorin, secretary of the citadel, the right hand to the king. Memories of that one will last beyond this lifetime, I am sure.

The storm that evening raged as loud as a prairie fire. The Dove sat against the central fountain beside two wells, their covers lifted for the women of Nineveh's southeastern side to fill their water sacks. At least two hundred adults sat around him, cooling themselves in the mist of the natural spring as Jonah talked of repentance.

"Forgiveness is the greatest of gifts," he explained. "Compassion, the greatest of resources. That the Lord God of Noah and Abraham makes such a pledge is therefore a wonder, a miracle of love, for your sins are great. Open your eyes, my friends! Look at the rash of idols overtaking your people. Look at the indecency of your land, the degrading of your women, the brutality towards your enemies. Such things are wrong in the sight of the Lord."

In that light did the secretary join the fray.

"You attack a sacred blessing," offered Tenpul-Kidorin, taking a seat across the fountain. "Our women offer their fertility to improve our crops, lessen our hunger. Is that not a worthy gift to the gods? Offering that which you most treasure?"

The Dove hardened. "Taking tens to hundreds of men without producing a child… truly that is fertility! But no, it is no gift of the Lord, but slavery. The bond between a man and a woman is a blessing of marriage, not a commodity to be bartered away or a device to praise some false idol. And in truth, the sacrifices are gifts not to their false gods but to the men who abuse them."

"Blindness, Jonah – it unseats you," the secretary countered. "I have seen our production tallies rise from this."

"You have seen well-watered crops flourish while harvests without rainfall yield little."

"You speak insurrection! You attack what our law permits and claim it immoral. Does your god teach us to ignore the law?"

"That law is not of God. Therefore it is wrong and should be changed."

"Be direct, where all can hear you. Do you tell us to defy our king?"

Jonah smiled. "I tell you to petition your king and change the law. Even more, you can ignore not the law but the prostitutes themselves."

"And of the temples, those in praise of the gods?"

"Ah, yes, your structures of worship, where beds and mats outnumber altars." The Dove stood and stretched, the spray of the fountain flowing high at his back to glitter against the fiery sky. "There are but a handful in this town, are there not? When the inns and houses offering corruption overflow on every street? But that does not lessen the sin, especially upon men who urge or force this upon their women and children. Oh, Lord, to have seen seven- and eight-year-olds among the given servants! That is a sin most heinous, as you should know – for did I not see you among the practitioners? Indeed, with many of those about you?"

The secretary hesitated, looking at his companions. It was later that I discovered many members of the Gathering sat there, including such feared men as Pulu, the militant governor of Kalhu, and Tilith-Feyn, his turtan, head of his armies. Not one held kind feelings toward the Dove. But if Jonah was aware of it, the knowledge did not restrain him.

"But truly Tenpul-Kidorin, your acceptance of sin knows no bounds," continued the Dove, "for was not your daughter among the offerings?"

Usually in these types of settings, the crowd listened, asking questions, taking no sides. But at that moment, I heard whispers of such intensity that they overcame the grinding of the cyclone.

"If she was," Tenpul-Kidorin spat, "it is a matter for my heart. Mine, not yours."

"And for the Lord, who gave you the child."

"Yes, she and the three who passed away within their first years," the secretary snapped, mocking his fate. "I am most appreciative."

"You leave out the one miscarried," Jonah added, his voice softened by compassion. "I grieve for you. Such losses are hard to understand. But the messages of our God are sometimes difficult, never taking shape until we stand in their heart."

By now, I was used to these revelations from the Dove. The crowd murmured its astonishment, but I simply logged it as another mark on target. After all, when the Spirit opens your heart, as it did Jonah's, such secrets as miscarriages may become common knowledge.

"Yes," whispered Tenpul-Kidorin, walking to an oil lamp. The orange flame cast hollow shadows about his thin face, even as his eyes shifted in uncertainty, as if grasping for an escape. "Mystery… that is ever the root of your message. It is so easy to attack our lives, our hearts. We are open to you, unashamed. Yet when we ask details of yours, you fall back on the mysteries of your god, expecting us to accept such things."

"Love is no mystery. The power that seals off great and mighty Nineveh is no mystery."

"No?" The secretary laughed at that. "Why then can you not lift it, if not just to let some of our visitors escape undue judgment?"

"That is the Lord's will. Not my own."

"So you say. But I know you, Jonah, advisor to the dead King Jeroboam II and an enemy of our people. You led the troops –"

"Makeshift all."

"– who cast our token force from Israel, then stole away Damascus for a brief two years." Tenpul-Kidorin let that sift through the crowd, playing to their patriotism. The mood crept through me as a parasite might feel crossing your bare skin. "You directed those troops, even when your king placed Canaanite idols in your temples. And his successors have ignored you, taxing the followers of your god of hills and filling his temples with other deities."

There, for once, was a moment when my tongue failed to outpace my mind. I wished to speak, to explain how Hosea had refused to allow such blasphemies in his corner of Bethel, but the mood did not seem right. At the time, I scored that as a victory over my brash mind, for I felt the Dove had to take that debate head-on, to not appear in need of help. But since then, I have learned better.

"False gods all," Jonah said for me.

"You admit that your own people betray your teachings, in worse ways than we do?"

Jonah retook his seat. "I admit they have sinned."

"And," continued the secretary, his voice now reflecting a spirit of triumph, "you admit you led battles against us – that you have sought to thwart our people for decades?"

"Yes, yes, I did – when they invaded our land."

"Was not your push into Aram an invasion? Was not your taking of Damascus an aggression?"

"Those were the rightful lands of David and Solomon," said the Dove, a hint of weariness invading his speech. "The king chose those forays."

"The king?" Tenpul-Kidorin leaped upon that as a beggar might an abandoned coin. "So, you have applied your talents to the work of others, to work you did not believe in?"

A sly smile crept across Jonah's lips. "I often have no choice."

"But we do." The king's secretary turned away from the Dove, casting his eyes upon the people listening at the fountain, the visitors to the temples, those in the streets. "Hear me, people of Nineveh! Hear me! This man admits his intent to disarm us, to turn us from ways that have made us strong! We are a threat to his puny nation. How honest can he be when he harbors hatreds against us? How strong can his god be when his own people abandon him?"

"For the blind, truth is often what you wish it to be," answered Jonah. "If you wish to believe exploitation is wise, then wallow in your sins. I come to you now against my own will, that is true, but it is what my Lord directed me to do. And that, friends, is the issue. You have sinned not against me, though I find these things repugnant. You have sinned against the Lord, the creator of all things. It is He who warns you to repent. And it is He who guides the hand of punishment about us. Your leaders may try to distract you all they wish, to make you see what they wish. But the Hand of God is there, before you. Gaze upon it – dwell upon what you have heard – and decide what is truth."

The next day was the first of five seventh-day Sabbaths during his Nineveh ministry. Our ministry, I guess, would be more appropriate, since I found myself unable to stiffen my tongue. But enough of that. Though we had lost track of our calendar, we kept the Sabbath as best we could and remained that day in prayer in the corner of a stable where we had slept the night before. Imagine our surprise when we found a crowd of people outside, wanting to meet the Dove!

Jonah voiced reluctance, but something pushed him to go out and explain the essence of the Sabbath. Only as he spoke did I realize that, for the first time, he revealed to them a facet of our faith. Oh, I must have been blind to it, not to have seen their thirst before, but the Ninevites responded to the principle of the Sabbath as the hungry before a feast! Several asked how they should pray, and to whom. The Dove stiffened, so I explained it in my own brief way. He then embellished my words, though it burdened him to do so.

From then on, we never wanted for food to eat or clothing to wear or a place to sleep. Having accepted us, many Ninevites opened their hearts to us in more touching ways than one could ever hope for.

From that Sabbath exchange, we slept the next several nights with people who sought to ensure our protection. Enemies had been made, or so they suspected. In truth, I did not care; I was happy to have a corner mat to sleep on instead of hay or dust. But it did show a curious change, for Jonah himself was developing a following among the people. We went about the community, preaching repentance and destruction, yet the questions often turned not to the omens, but to lifestyles. They wondered what was acceptable in the sight of God.

It's strange how events turn full circle. You recall the Dove and I spoke about such things long before, he with dread, myself curious. Alternatives, he had said – they would seek alternatives. And now we found he was right – about their demands, I mean. I still feel he was wrong in his response.

For his part, Jonah sought ever more to evade such points. As the storm grew faster, louder, he discussed the Lord God only after direct badgering. I never hesitated to share the lessons of Hazorn and his crew, for their conversion seemed pertinent. Yet Jonah scowled at that.

As the days passed, we noticed a stiffening in the attitudes of the guards. Officials often came to ridicule or attack Jonah on various things, only to fall before the wisdom of the Lord. The chief problem seemed to be a growing respect for the Sabbath. The Dove brushed it off as an excuse for laziness, but I had seen the hard work of the Ninevites, and their budding faith. The government, however, agreed at once with Jonah. Some leaders said so on our third Sabbath.

Their group came upon us as we prayed in the grazing fields within Nineveh's northeastern district. Jonah led us with about two hundred of his followers. Surrounded by a group of five guards came three officials in colorful robes. They strode straight to the Dove, who sat bowed to God.

"Prophet!" called the first one, a massive beast of a man named Nari-Speltum.

"Call an end to this!" said Ashur-minal, who must have discarded his black robe for the rainbow-hued garment.

I sat up then, checking my eyes against the light filtering through the Lord's storm, but the Dove remained in reverence, his forehead against his knees.

"What would you end?" I asked. It was a stupid question; I admit that. But as they came forward, the defiant Pulu positioning himself almost atop the Dove… well, I was worried.

"We speak not to servants," said Ashur-minal. "Rise, Jonah! Hear the words of the King!"

The Dove did not move.

"I said the King!" snapped the high priest of Ashur. "Hear me!"

In a sharp, hot blast of wind, I felt the spirit of the Lord come over me, and I spoke: "He cannot hear you, false priest. His heart rests with his God. But why attempt to stop them? Your people have water aplenty, meat, and grain enough to feed themselves… and the thousands of cattle here will last for weeks. Should one day of rest each week displease you?"

What those words meant I did not know at that time; at least, not in their full application. But my audience did.

"Yes!" the priest said. Then he muttered, "Damn the King for allowing you –"

"Do not speak that!" Pulu cut him off.

That was truly interesting. Everyone among them froze, the priest most stricken of all.

"I meant no disrespect," he apologized.

"Our king is King!" Pulu stated in his monarch's fierce defense. "King of kings! Misguided, yes. Perhaps terribly so. But he is King!"

"Yes, yes, I understand," the priest responded. "But there remains work to be done."

In that one step, Ashur-minal defused the issue and turned Pulu's anger towards me… I thought it well done.

"Unlike your people," the high priest stated, "we have responsibilities."

"None more important than to the Lord God," I countered.

My words must have broken something in the governor of Kalhu. Twisting once more upon the Dove, Pulu hit him with his staff while shouting, "Get up!"

Strange, that did not rattle me. The Spirit doused my anger, reassuring me that all would be well, and indeed, Jonah showed no response of any kind. But that, of course, angered Pulu more.

He struck Jonah's ribs again, then again, his temper so savage that even his comrades urged him to patience. Yet the quick, calculating governor had already moved ahead in his thoughts, plotting against the Dove.

Oh Lord, why did I not see it then?

"Remember the warning," I urged, rising to my feet.

At once I felt as impervious as the storm, as unassailable as the gates of heaven themselves!

"Remember your sins!" I said. "For those who observe this day do so in remembrance of their folly, offering repentance and seeking forgiveness. You should follow their example."

At that, I thought the red-bearded one – Nari-Speltum, governor of Arbil – meant to kill me. "I will have your tongue for that!" he declared, drawing a long bronze knife with a pommel cast in the head of an eagle. But the high priest stopped him with a stern gaze, and they left.

From that point on, the Sabbath was not an issue raised before the Dove. I do not know how or if observance of it grew, or how it impacted the king's court. I know only that the fight to stop it ended there, to my relief.

The more significant battle raged on, of course. The Dove led me throughout the city those last days, from contest to contest, from hated foes to devout believers and all the skeptics in between. It was never easy. Stifling heat settled upon Nineveh, whether from the storm or the city's tension. Relations grew brittle, even within the Dove. Especially with the Dove. For the more people turned to him, the more repentance seemed likely, the more anguished he became.

One night, as we sought refuge in the grazing fields from the rumbling stones that are men, I could bear it no more and asked of his heart. But he spurned me. Me!

Ah, my Lord, forgive me. It was my arrogance that pushed me to doubt him. But in truth, I sought only to defuse his hatred. Is that not a noble aim?

But enough of me. With the dawn of the thirty-seventh day, on the eve of our last seventh-day Sabbath before the Day of Reckoning, the Dove's true test came. As usual, its disguise was complete.

Jonah ministered to a group of boys and girls outside the temples, which in itself was a chore, as I have said before. But that was one of the strange sides of this ministry – we also had to adjust to God's calling, though I am no longer sure it is such a bad thing. But I digress. Jonah found himself confronted by an insightful crowd, these young ones. And the questions turned to visions… things the Dove had ever refused to tell me. Oh, how his face knotted up! He wanted to resist – he wished to! But these were children, as much his as any could be. Long had he talked with them, giving of himself. Under their pure gaze, he broke.

"You foresaw these things… what? Years ago?" asked a young boy.

"Some of them," the Dove admitted, his eyes turned down. Oh, he wore his heart as an open wound!

"Not all?" continued the boy, probably half my age and five times my intellect. "You mean you put off coming, and so we suffer more?"

Jonah recoiled. "Your people were at war with ours. Indeed, they are at war still. I could not just leave, abandon my king –"

"You said he was evil," interrupted another boy.

"Not… well, not exactly. In some ways…" His voice fumbled to end that sentence, until Jonah was left to admit, "Yes, he was evil."

"Didn't your Lord send you?"

"Indeed. But I could not just leave."

"Or you did not wish to," offered a different lad. "You hated us, didn't you?"

The proud eyes of the Dove tried not to look upon the dark-skinned boy. When they could avoid it no longer, the orbs spoke of his shame.

"Do you still?" asked an innocent child.

Jonah bore the face of someone stricken.

"I hate some things," he admitted. The Dove drew himself up but gained no strength from it. "There was, is, much that is wrong here. And I… I have been wrong about some things. People are people, and the Lord is God. That much is true, whether here or Tarshish, now or later."

"Or tomorrow," offered a young lady.

"Yes," the Dove whispered, "for tomorrow the Lord has new plans. Which elude me."

"And us?" asked a young lad.

"That is a challenge," Jonah said with a sigh.

"No," entered a new voice, full of menace, "the challenge awaits. Come along."

I don't know what you think of such things, but being caught off-guard is one of my chief fears. Though the Dove did nothing, I spun about to stare into the confident eyes of Tenpul-Kidorin, secretary of the citadel. Behind his silver-haired head stood a double handful of the Royal Guard, their golden shields well-oiled, their plate armor a shimmering sea in the storm-filtered sun. Still, nothing glowed brighter than secretary's hateful eyes.

"The King awaits," he commanded. "Come!"

Seeing little else to do, we followed, and entered the trap.

Chapter 23
Pleas and schemes

We followed the secretary with heavy hearts, recognizing what lay before us. Were it not for the Ninevites gathering along our trail, I doubt I could have made that hard walk to our doom.

The newcomers knew nothing of our pending fate. Seeing us shuffle by, they fell in line with the Dove just to remain in his presence. Such things became quite common in his ministry, though from the anguish framing the face of Tenpul-Kidorin, the secretary had no idea how to handle it. For a brief moment I clung to a faint hope that this growing throng would spoil his plans, but at the broad crosswalk before the hilltop refuge of the king, a group of twenty or more well-armed, beardless men converged on us. I guess they were guards, for leading them were Pulu and his turtan of Kalhu. Before that formidable group, the gawkers grumbled but gave way. From that point on, they led us as prisoners.

Through the gate of the citadel we strode, crossing the broad corridor that led to the courtyard. The air was stiff, the stones cold and heartless, though not as much as the eyes that gazed upon us. To them we were as boils to be lanced, burdens to be locked up, buried, and forgotten.

Upon sight of the spiked portcullis, I began to pray. I cannot now remember the words, though I have struggled to do so, for the song that flew from my lips was soon my one source of light.

As the iron gate recoiled and we stepped into the malevolent darkness of Nineveh's dungeons, I threw my spirit into my words, lifting my fears to the Lord as the damp rocks oppressed my heart. Responses came forth – faint echoes and weak comments from other, invisible prisoners – but the moldy stonework swallowed up most sounds within its dank halls and slimy pits. Including mine. That was the most corrupting power of the prison, for I had raised my voice to the Lord and felt little relief.

Through it all Jonah said nothing. At first, I considered it his anger, defiance, or hatred. I had witnessed such things in him from time to time. But when we shuffled down those cold, dim steps, the torches aglow with the sadistic pleasure of Pulu and his eunuchs, I sensed nothing within the Dove but resignation.

After a few twists through narrow rock passages, the air heavy with decay, these warriors thrust us into a small cubicle of rough stone lit by the faint red glow of hot coals. Separating me from the Dove, the guards took turns spinning and striking us before shackling our arms. They confused and locked us so just in case we found an opportunity to escape, as if there were any chance of that.

I wonder now how I even understood what they told us. My ringing ears bled from their assault, and my hands, feet, and loins burned so hot from my punishments, I feared they lay severed and discarded upon the stone. When finished, our torturers dropped us against the sticky wastes of the floor. I tried to rise but could not manage it. My mind lay numb to the world, too exhausted to recognize even who I was. But every fiber of my soul revived when the Assyrians tried to pound burning iron rings about my wrists. Never have I felt such pure, overwhelming panic! I fought against it, scratching, writhing, screaming against all that was unholy, until the ironsmith's hammer smashed the narrows of my neck. With one blow I collapsed into a gagging heap, vanquished. As hands grasped my scalp, the kiss of smelt ore blazed a hole in my left cheek. I did not resist further, but only wept for it to end.

Oh Lord, how true are your lessons of humility! But need I

bear their scars all my life?

Tears drowned my sight as that hammer smote my simmering iron bands for the last time. I looked upon the chain that bound me, black links that let my blistered wrists reach no more than a forearm's distance apart, and heard the Dove cry out in agony.

That erased my hopes.

I do not remember when they abandoned us. After drowning the coals and scattering the ashes, the rogues left me like a fresh, cleaned carcass, dangling upon the wall from the chain locking my wrists. Thus did I face my doom, my arms but sleeping stubs, my legs too beaten to try anything my mind might concoct.

Isolated in time and space, my desperation soon gave way to bitter defeat. Darkness surrounded me… a chill, nauseating blackness that gnawed at my soul as it deceived my eyes with faint glows or imaginary specters. I stared into the empty depths and saw my despair take shape in my past, my loves. Had I been too blind to recognize these evils of my heart? Distant memories replayed themselves… thoughts choked by heinous deviations, callous mutations. All things appeared vile, all motives flocked with deception.

With my last independent thought, I rejected them.

Thus did Satan attempt to break me. But in the depths of my despair was my Lord, a foundation the rages of Lucifer will never crumble. And this last time, there was also Jonah.

"Benjamin," he whispered.

I do not know how long it had been since I had last heard him. But to have such reassurances now... oh, Lord! Such was my joy, it was as if I had found the Dove once more upon the shore!

"Yes, master," I struggled to say. The effort to draw breath sent my mind spinning.

"Join me," came his voice, sounding as beaten as I felt. "It is time."

In blessed honor of the Sabbath, he began David's beloved song:

The Lord is my shepherd;
I shall not want....

As the Dove reminded me of what is truly essential in this world, the worship of our Lord, I felt a renewal, or actually, a rebirth. I knew I was not only forgiven, but beloved. And that, my friends, exceeds the grandest gift this world will ever offer.

We sang together, praising God. How long did it last? It did not matter, for we were one with the Lord. Indeed, it was somewhat of a disappointment when the flicker of a torch shocked my blinded eyes. So comforted was I in the Lord's presence, I did not wish to be disturbed!

Ah, but that was a selfish thought. His mission remained.

The light came full upon us with the outward swing of a thick wood door bound together with many iron bolts. Tilith-Feyn stood there, along with a handful of his armored eunuchs and a filth-covered metalsmith. With little kindness, the guards tossed us to the grime of the floor, where our shackles were cut away. To my lasting surprise, my limbs felt small adverse effects until the turtan of Kalhu put his dagger to my throat.

"Spread any word of this," Tilith-Feyn warned, "and you will die."

It shows my weak heart that even then, warm in the wings of the Lord, I trembled at that simple threat. But the Dove remained firm.

"Fear not," he reassured me. "The Lord can make use of even these foul deeds."

"Quiet, Jew!" The field marshal of the Kalhu armies waved his blade through the faint light, thinking it a menacing show, then strode with impatience through the passages. We followed behind him, the Dove just a step at my back. I dared ask him what he meant.

"Quiet!" snapped Tilith-Feyn.

"The test of repentance," answered Jonah, ignoring the gruff man. "The king has been petitioned."

That meant little to me, but with the guards even more quick-tempered than before, I dared not seek an explanation. Soon it left my mind, replaced by joyous revelations from our Lord. Though tortured, I found I had no trouble climbing the steep stairs or breathing the poisoned air. With each step I felt my wounds healing. Indeed, in the flickering light of the turtan's torch, I could see my bruises fade. With each breath, I was invigorated.

My eyes needed but a simple adjustment as we entered the sun, which was dimmed only a bit by the storm. Overjoyed to be free, to live once more in His world, I tried to prepare my heart for a return meeting with the king. But we had yet to face one more plot against Jonah.

With the winds singing the protests of Ninevites, we traveled across the empty courtyard to the temples. There, deep in the recesses of a restricted pathway, lay the secret chamber of Ashur-minal. With him in that small cellar cubicle waited Pulu.

The bold light of a clay oil lamp provided my first good look at the scheming governor of Kalhu. He impressed me, I must admit. Though he possessed no outstanding qualities, his face did have a touch of elegance, and when his brow tightened, his anger daunted the most determined eye. Dark brown hair hung about his firm shoulders, mixing well with the amber curls of his full beard – which was surprisingly long, considering he wasn't much older than I. That made me wonder just how someone like me could come to wear the fabulous robes of a governor.

He turned his green eyes upon me. They burned, evidence of his fury.

With our last steps, a thick oak door shut off the chorus of protests. The high priest rose from behind a bare wood table, his back stiff with apprehension. Passing by the governor, Ashur-minal's brown eyes remained passive – but his brow twitched, and his hands waved back and forth as if impatient to act. I had just come to a rest when he snapped, "You must stop this."

Not knowing what he meant, I said nothing. I intended to keep quiet anyway, deferring to the Dove.

Jonah stood as impervious as granite.

"The people," the priest continued, "they have protested your arrest about the city. They go about in sackcloth, chanting defiance to the king and repentance to your god. And they fast!"

That blazed a smile across my lips, but Jonah remained as still as a stone.

The priest glared at the Dove, then me. His eyes begged for an escape from a problem I did not understand.

"Oh, enough!" snapped Pulu in our tongue, though with a heavy slur on certain words. "I tell you we do not need them."

"Have you heard the wind?" the priest replied, not bothering to look back. "It carries his name. The people believe in this… this…"

"God," said the Dove.

"Yes," Ashur-minal admitted.

"I care not what the people believe," Pulu declared, stepping from the light. "I have two armies waiting outside the walls and two units of the bodyguard within the citadel. That is enough."

"Perhaps not," Jonah said, entering their discussion as might a close friend. "You seek power, young Adad-nirari, when you should seek wisdom."

"They are the same," Pulu replied, his brow showing but a hint of admiration for the Dove's insight.

"In the Lord God, yes. But not in the hands of man."

The impatient priest drew Jonah's eye. "Listen, white skin. You must help us calm the people."

"No."

"You must! Should the disturbances spread further, the king will act. Many will die!"

"The people cry out to the Lord," Jonah said. "If indeed the king grows angry, it will be with those who imprisoned us without his knowledge."

Pulu chuckled. "You think he cares about you?"

"No. The king cares about his people. The people care about us."

"He should care more about the empire," Pulu retorted.

"Yes, as you intend to." The Dove leaned against a whitewashed brick wall, his skin only a bit lighter in hue. "Great plans you have, for expansion, for commerce and conquest. Grand schemes."

Pulu hardened as the stone at his feet. "Quite achievable," he allowed, "when one's rule is firm."

"You go in the wrong direction. Listen to the people, Adad-nirari. Listen to the Lord!"

Pulu scoffed at that, even as the priest interrupted them.

"We will reveal you to them," he said, his hands motioning toward the wooden door. "They will see you are all right."

"That little matters," Jonah told him. "They fear the Lord, not my loss."

"They fear both!" exclaimed Ashur-minal. He spun about, angry in the face of Jonah's defiance, but a sharp knock at his door surprised him. Stopped in his tracks, the priest struggled to compose himself before the newcomer appeared. But he lacked enough time. The door swung open, at the hands of the secretary to the king.

"He wishes to see them," the cold soul said.

The priest of Ashur seemed a bit shaken by that, but Pulu only laughed. "Then by all means, let him have them! We will adapt."

Palace guards led the Dove and myself away. I was overjoyed as we entered the dry, barren courtyard, but Jonah remained pensive.

"In all his plans he writes death," the Dove whispered. "Yet he sees not the death of his own people."

"Strange prophecy from you," I thought aloud. After all, here was a man of God who hated his captors, these Assyrians, and yet outside the citadel, a crowd of those the Dove hated called for his release. Through it all, Jonah spoke in almost sorrowful terms of Assyria's passing!

"We walk now the last steps of our ministry, Benjamin. The people are repentant, the government not." The Dove took a shallow, broken breath. "Before the king, we shall see which side will triumph."

Chapter 24 Change

Perhaps it was never in question. I may never know. But in my heart, that was the day of reckoning, one that shaped the lives of generations to follow.

With little fanfare and no announcement, we were led into the king's chamber. The covers had been removed from the sky view, allowing the power and rage of the Hand of God to echo among the tall pillars and mighty walls. The Dove walked as if defeated, but I took one look at the concern written upon the king's brow and felt overjoyed.

He wasted no time on ceremony. Rising from his grand throne, aglow from beds of hot coals at either side, the king strode out to greet us – to the indignation of his guards and priests. Indeed, so great was his concern that Ashur-minal hurried past us, motioning his king to stop.

"No! No! This does not become you!" he said over and over, in some form like that. He slipped into our Hebrew language when the king failed to respond to the rest. But Ashur-nirari brushed off those comments as well, along with the high priest of Ashur.

"You look well," this monarch told Jonah with a warm smile. But the Dove, to my regret, remained calm and direct.

"The Lord provides for our needs," he answered. "Even in bondage."

"Bondage?" The king seemed surprised, though his eyes soon turned bitter. "Yes, I see your instrument is gone. So, it was true, all the whispers." He stepped back, glanced at the polished throne of Assyria, then pivoted. "I did not wish to believe it."

"It matters little," the Dove told him. "The future is in our grasp, not the past."

"Ah, that is a kind view of the world," said Ashur-nirari. "Unfortunately, I cannot forget such things."

"But you must. Forgiveness is vital to life. It is God's way."

The Dove paused, dwelling on deep breaths released with a slow, hesitant will, as if he himself wished not to do this. I looked past his worn face to his distant, removed gaze, trying to learn what churned his reluctance.

If the king saw such things in Jonah, he did not dwell upon it. He turned his eyes upon the winds of condemnation raging above us, then strode toward his throne. With each step he cast off a symbol of his power – his golden bracelets, purple and crimson tassels, even the silver crown and collar, all discarded and left upon the floor, to his guard's dismay. At the foot of his royal chair, he threw off his jewel-encrusted daggers and embroidered robes.

"Bring me sackcloth!" he shouted.

A shaken priest crept forward, his black robes quivering in sympathy with his fear. "You cannot mean –"

"Sackcloth!" the king roared, kicking off his sandals. Then he twisted to his left and called, "Tenpul-Kidorin! Read the proclamation!"

I must admit, none of this made any more sense to me than it did Assyria's heathen priests. I looked to Jonah, hoping to ask him what went on, but the Dove seemed consumed with the king, or perhaps, with his own tensions.

The secretary hesitated, pausing first at an oil lamp beside the pillars, then at the platform's step.

"You cannot mean this," he stammered.

"Read it!"

Pulu took bold steps forward, his long brown hair flowing about his bronze vest and armbands. A short sword of iron bounced at his side within a shiny leather jacket.

"Listen not to the rabble," he urged.

The king straightened. Even when reduced to his undergarments, I saw his underlying confidence. It reminded me how I had misjudged him earlier.

"I listen to the people," he corrected Pulu, his words cushioned as if spoken to a loved one. "They are Assyria."

But Pulu was not distracted. "A king must lead his people, father."

Father? That stunned me, for I saw little or no resemblance between them. Pulu had the eyes, the countenance, the imposing build of a king, while Ashur-nirari bore the look of a shepherd or stable hand… though he wore the crown well.

Pulu cast an accusing finger toward the Dove while confronting the king. "You cannot give in to this man's influence!"

"I bow before no man!" declared Ashur-nirari. "But I vow to serve God. The God. Here and now do I make that claim!"

Striding to his throne, the king grasped a bowl of coals and scattered its ashes across the floor.

"Read!" he commanded Tenpul-Kidorin, who stood as one stricken. "In both tongues – theirs and ours, mind you. Now!"

The secretary glanced at Pulu before turning his eyes to a stone tablet.

"Do not... do not let any man or beast, herd or flock, taste food or drink," began the secretary, even as the king lifted ash from the floor to toss about his shoulders and face. "But let man and beast…"

"Animals too?" I could not help whispering. The sudden thought – the very idea of dressing their cattle and donkeys in mourning cloth – well, it amused me, to be honest.

Jonah ignored me, as did most everyone else.

"Let man and beast be covered with sackcloth," the secretary read on. "Let everyone call urgently on God. Let them give up their evil ways and their violence –"

"You cannot do this!" Ashur-minal exclaimed, leaping forward. The other priests followed but did not match the high priest's speed… nor did they really try, I think.

"For who knows?" finished the secretary. "God may yet relent, and with compassion, turn from his fierce anger, that we may not perish."

Ashur-nirari rose up as if attacked.

"You contest me?" he bellowed at his high priest.

But Ashur-minal did not back down. Indeed, his argument took greater weight as Pulu joined him.

"You would surrender the sovereignty of Ashur?" The priest did not hide his outrage. "Never! In this, you must listen!"

"No," the king countered. "In this, you will listen to God."

"Are you serious?" spat Pulu. "Pay heed to the whim of shepherds?" In his rage he picked up the scepter of Ashur-nirari and sent it tumbling across the floor. "Is this how you care for Assyria?"

"Mind your tongue, Pul! Blood will not save you!"

"Nor you, if you disgrace our crown!"

A cymbal crashed. Servants ran into the palace, their arms filled with goat's hair tunics and tent sheets.

"This is all we could find," one stammered, I think.

"It is enough," said the king, who seemed to prefer our tongue now. He seized a wadded sheet of coarse sackcloth, rolled it in the spilled ash, and threw it about his shoulders. "Change, my people! We must seek the grace of God so that we do not perish!"

In wonder I watched many reluctant guards and priests cast off their clothes for the garb of shepherds and slaves. Some chose to shroud themselves in the sooty fabric, while others stomped off, unbending and unrepentant. At their head walked Ashur's high priest and… Pulu, Adad-nirari, Pul, or whatever he was called; I began to lose count of his names by that time. But most onlookers took up their king's command.

We were led to the grand balcony, where Ashur-nirari himself read his proclamation to the vast throng gathered below. I had not imagined so many could live within such a small setting. I looked across Nineveh from the balcony of the citadel and saw little else but attentive people!

At the king's swift close, the throng murmured approval,

though it seemed to withhold sincere support, much less grace. Then Jonah went forward, displayed before the throng, earning shouts of praise that overshadowed even the Hand of God!

"I have never seen such favor," remarked the king, his words both humbled and admiring. "With the deadline upon us, such a chorus must thrill you."

Jonah bound his arms about his chest, refusing comment. Indeed, his pale form seemed as still as limestone. But I was not so moved – or unmoved, as was this case.

"Deadline?" I could not help asking.

Ashur-nirari gazed upon me with humble eyes. "The forty days. They run out tomorrow."

I almost stumbled then, amid the pounding shouts of the crowd and the pressures of the Hand above us. Forty days. That meant the Dove and I had spent a day within the catacombs. More than a day!

"Praise the Lord," I whispered, praying thanks for our deliverance. Yet as I looked upon Jonah, I realized he stood in far greater pain now than before. Though he tried to avoid me, I found his bloodshot eyes sunk within their sockets, and his brow drawn tight about his skull. His hands shook.

"Go to them," Ashur-nirari told us, not noticing my fears or the Dove's torn state. "Their diligence should be rewarded."

The ash-covered secretary, his allegiances now quite brittle, led us in silence out of the citadel. At once the people set upon the Dove, hugging and praising him throughout the streets.

They treated me much the same, I am reluctant to admit. For I… Lord, forgive me! I did enjoy it. The words I little knew, but the enthusiasm, the devotion, was unmistakable.

I would never experience such favor again.

The Dove was not so compromised. Jonah did not respond to the crowd at first – how could he, cast within such an uncontrollable mob? They thrust the Dove where they liked, no matter what he wanted, treating him more like a possession than a person. But as the motion of the throng began to carry us away, Jonah exerted what influence he could. Even so, it took most of the day, accepting thanks, receiving hugs, embracing friends and, more often than not, people we did not know, before Jonah managed to deliver us to a stable just inside the East Gate.

In many ways this adulation was a weighty burden, yet the spirit of the people overshadowed those hardships. For it was such a festive sight to behold! In the streets and on the rooftops, people of all kinds danced together, singing and sharing good cheer. I had not seen revelry so free and open, the name of the Lord lifted in such joy, since the armies of Jeroboam triumphed at Mount Hermon.

But the Dove did not share my view.

"Ask me no questions," he snapped. "I am in no mood to answer."

I stopped, confused by his agony. He stumbled into the stables, a fine cedar structure filled with choice horses, and cradled his head in his hands. The sounds of camels snorting, chewing, and belching filtered through the walls, as did the storm's muffled winds, but no such sounds overshadowed the praise within the streets.

"Is this not good?" I asked the Dove.

"Are you blind? Can you not see what goes on?"

"I see repentance."

"Benjamin!" came a call. A young lad entered; I am sorry, but I do not recall his name. He ran to me and embraced me, then spied the Dove and hurried to him.

"Come, Jonah!" he said, taking the Dove's sleeve. "We have found a kinnor, as you call it. Come and play!"

The Dove tried to pull his arm away. I had never seen him retreat from children before.

"I am in no mood," he grumbled.

"Are you ill?" the lad asked.

"No… it is not that."

"Ah, I understand. You are weary. But our celebration will renew you. Come! Sing away your pains!"

"Renew?" With that doubtful word, Jonah climbed to his feet. "You believe this over?"

The youth shuffled backward, confused by the question.

"I feel your God – the Lord of Nimrod, Noah, and Abraham

that you taught us about – He will spare us. I know it. Yes, He will!"

"And then what?" the Dove prodded.

"We will follow Him," the lad proclaimed, his knowledge of our language near flawless. "We will serve the God who has come among us."

"Indeed." Jonah wiped his face against his tunic, but the scars of his anguish remained. "Indeed. A new world is prepared for us, and I have no part in it. I cannot change so."

"Why need you change?" the child said, a spark of joy lighting his words. His words mirrored my thoughts.

"We are but children," the Dove murmured.

That spurred me. Taking the boy in my arms, I actually scolded Jonah. But he was of another mind.

"Children in the spirit," he continued, "children in the faith, our every concern guided by the Lord. But the day comes when we as a people will reach adulthood, when the Lord offers a new covenant to all people, and we become accountable for our own lives." He hesitated, whispering, "to all people," and erupted in anger. "There is no place for me in such a world, where old bonds are broken, our people cast aside! There is no place for me now." And just that quick, his anguish faded. "I have sinned against God."

I saw then the spirit of the Lord upon him, though I knew not what to make of his words. But the boy slipped from my grasp to clutch the Dove's hand within his own.

"Come," he urged. "Be at peace."

Muted by that simple act of faith, the Dove followed the child into the jubilant street. Jonah's appearance brought the celebration to a respectful halt, as the people – elders and children, warriors and beggars, merchants and scholars – all waited for the Dove to act. All but one. A small girl, her bright smile a beacon to the world, stepped forward with a golden kinnor in her hands.

"The king has sent me to you," a guard said as this girl held the instrument aloft.

Tears ran from his cheeks as Jonah took the gift.

"Oh, Lord," he wept, "must you mock me with kindness?"

With that broke forth an abrupt, total silence. I never witnessed such a thing, before or since. Even the winds stilled. The stable animals paused to listen as the people watched in shock.

"Is this not what I said long ago?" the Dove bemoaned, dropping to his knees. His eyes turned to the sky. "Why else did I flee to Tarshish, but that I knew You were a gracious and compassionate God? A God who relents from sending calamity?"

"Jonah," I began, taking a cautious step towards him.

The Dove did not heed me. His words dropped to a whisper.

"Oh, Lord, take my life. I should die."

Thunder rocked Nineveh. People cried out as the bones of the city quaked at our feet. Sudden, overwhelming hysteria escaped their lips… and that I could not allow, not when they had come so far.

"Hold!" I shouted. The spirit of Yahweh came upon me, lifting my voice through their hearts and minds. "Hold! Do you not believe the words of the Lord? Have faith!"

In that window of uncertainty, the boy of the stables came forward. Ringing his arms about the Dove's neck, he held Jonah as tight as he might his most prized toy.

"God loves you," the child reminded us. "Play for us, and you will find peace. Play!"

The world waited as Jonah gazed with guilty eyes upon that young, smiling face.

"I know not what… what I can do now," he almost wept.

"Play a song of enlightenment," I advised. "A song of joy."

Looking into my soul, the Dove allowed himself a brief smile.

"A song of the new covenant," he allowed, "a tale of what the Lord prepares for us."

I saw then the wound in his heart, his resistance to God. Yet it did not emerge in his works. His fingers stroked the kinnor to release vibrant notes, a flowing melody of patience, grace, and unbending love. He sang with a light voice that overcame his heavy heart.

Tears of joy poured down my face
At the touch of God's redeeming grace.
I've finally found a true resting place
In the depths of His sustaining grace.
Grace! Grace!
Humbled by Christ's loving grace!
Grace! Yes, grace!
Born anew with His gift of grace!

How does one begin to tell
How cherished dreams just go to hell?
It's hard to maintain life support
When destiny works to cut you short.
Torn by anger, broken and alone,
I watched each effort sink like a stone.
Only then did I realize
How sin had left me compromised.
Then tears of joy rolled off my face
In the love of God's embracing grace.
My pain was gone, without a trace,
Washed away by overflowing grace.
Grace! Oh, grace!
Exulting in Christ's loving grace!
Grace! Yes, grace!
Born anew with His gift of grace!

There were times I knew for sure
That I would never find a cure
For the arrogance and pride
That muddled everything I tried.
But to even suggest some ancient creed
Could save my soul if I just believed
Seemed ludicrous beyond compare,
'Til despair had me kneeling in prayer.
That's when tears of joy fell down my face
In the arms of God's forgiving grace,
Freed of all my shame and disgrace

By the power of His cleansing grace.
Grace! Oh, grace!
Comforted by Christ's loving grace!
Grace! Yes, grace!
Born anew with His gift of grace!

To those intent to do life on their own,
I wish you well with the seeds you've sown.
Remember to keep an open mind,
So the lies of this world don't leave you blind.
Sometimes answers may seem far away,
And time will grow shorter every day,
Just know salvation is ever near,
As I learned as His truth became oh so clear.
That's when tears of joy poured down my face
In the heart of Christ's saving grace,
Rest assured, through all time and space,
I will find my peace in eternal grace.
Grace! Oh, grace!
Humbled by God's loving grace!
Grace! Yes, grace!
Born anew with His gift of grace!
Born anew in His gift, His gift, of grace, of grace!
His gift, His gift, of grace!
Yes, *His gift, His gift, of grace, of grace!*
His gift, His gift, of grace!

The strings of the kinnor drew to a gentle stop, their last echoes heard in every corner of the street. I gazed across the many faces, stunned by their attention… and from the light in their eyes, the smiles upon their lips, they understood the tune far more than I.

Perhaps, in this new world God prepared, an untainted mind was more ready to accept such revolutionary teachings than one raised or trained as I had been. For in only forty days, these Ninevites learned to recognize the love and forgiveness foretold by Jonah's song, while I struggled to understand it… I, who had lived what seemed my whole life under Yahweh's covenant, though in fact, it had been but a few years. I may never know the truth of that… unless I use the Dove as my example. The instant the echoes of his song died, his melancholy returned, its strength renewed by his own distractions.

The Hand of God cracked above us. Jonah gazed upon the sky and warned, "Best retire to your beds, to await the Lord's judgment."

"But we know what that will be," burst a joyful young man. "You have delivered us."

"The Lord is our one deliverer! I am nothing."

With that, the Dove turned his back to us and passed through the darkness of the East Gate. I let him go, for at that moment, perhaps for the first time, I realized the choice he had been forced to make. Or refused to make.

Trying my best to put his agony from my thoughts, I looked upon the gathering of faces, some confused, some torn, and brought them together.

"Come," I urged. "Let us join in the courtyard, praising God for our forgiveness."

"And let us pray for Jonah," said the boy.

"We will indeed," I assured him. Who could not, in the presence of such newfound faith?

Chapter 25
Prophesy

I awoke to a new world, but not one foretold by the Dove. Shaking off the stable hay, I stumbled into the midday sun, still weary from our late-night celebration in praise, to find the sky clear, the hot winds faded to wisps. Everywhere you looked stood soldiers, both the gold-plated zuku sa sheppe, their palace colors flying tall and proud, and the oiled leather of the sab sharri, infantry of the people. Along the street, fearful eyes glanced out of windows, through shutters and past curtains. I looked down the deserted passage and saw, hanging from the towers of the citadel, uncounted fresh skins. Severed heads stared motionless from poles about the gate.

A member of the palace guard called my name. As I turned, his gloved hands seized my shoulders.

"I was right!" he said with pride, his dialect stiff and choppy, but understandable. "You are the young Jew. Where is the prophet?"

Where indeed, I wondered.

"Answer me! The king demands to see you."

"Very well," I snapped, just a little angered by this treatment. "Tell Ashur-nirari –"

"No," the stiff man smiled through his dusty gray beard, "not that dog. We made a change. Tiglath-Pileser III rules now."

Perhaps it was my weary mind, but that name proved difficult to swallow. "Tilgath, Tigat... what did you say?"

"Tiglath-Pileser III," he pronounced.

Realization came to me as other warriors joined us before the East Gate. Ashur-nirari had fallen in an uprising.

Though I just learned of it, this news did not surprise me. After all, I had lived through two such overthrows at Samaria. The words of Jonah returned to me: The people are repentant, the government not. When Ashur-nirari accepted the message of the Dove, I had not thought to fear reprisals by his subordinates. How short-sighted I remained!

I looked anew to my guards, only to find they discussed something that consumed them.

"Where?" several asked, or so I thought.

"Atop the crest," came the answer. One guard pointed the way, helping me understand.

A captain of the palace guard instructed the soldier holding me to go tell the king. He then gathered his men from about the street, ordered me not to resist, and led us all out of the city.

About the walls remained a thick ring of tents, little changed from when they had been abandoned the prior month. A little dustier, perhaps, but undamaged. But beyond these tents, the twisting winds had scorched everything around the city across a span two hills wide. Stone markers, trees, brush… all lay shriven, crumbled, or lost altogether.

Atop the second hill waved an excited guard. The captain led us to the ruins of a shredded goatskin tent, where lay Jonah.

The guard stood beside the Dove's bare scalp. There, as everywhere else where his flesh remained uncovered, Jonah suffered a severe red burn. His skin sank against his bones as if drained of life, and his lips and ears dripped thick black blood from several wide cracks. But his eyes spoke most of his pain, bulging within their sockets, staring into the red sun.

"Oh, Jonah," I whispered, running to him. A warrior tried to stop me, but the captain not only gave me leave but offered me his water sack. Blessing him, I shoved aside a withered vine the width of my arm and sat, taking the Dove's head in my lap. Truly, it felt as light as a pillow! His eyes noticed me then, though I know not if he recognized me. Praying for guidance, I wiped layers of dust from his dry face, then cradled the lip of the water sack to his bloodied chin. Only then did Jonah respond, gulping down the brown liquid.

A murmur spread through the breeze. In the gulf between the hills, I saw a growing crowd of Ninevites dared emerge to investigate scars left by the Hand of God. As the Dove lifted his eyes to me, the people saw us.

"Benjamin," Jonah's dry lips whispered. "Benjamin, I had the… the strangest dream."

The soldiers sought to dissuade the people, but in their curiosity, the throng no longer cowered.

"Jonah!" I heard several say. "It is Jonah!"

Beyond them, at the city gates emerged a large contingent of polished palace guards. At their center strode a powerful man in vibrant robes.

The Dove did not appear to notice anyone. I wonder if he even knew others stood about.

"Drink," I urged him. But his mind clung to the dream.

"A shelter," he stammered, "yes, I… I built a shelter. A tent. To watch the, the destruction. But it, it was torn… ripped away. And a vine, a thick vine grew. At my feet. It just grew, Benjamin… a gourd, right up around me. Shielding me! I praised God for it. But at dawn I found a worm, a small worm, among the branches. Eating them. I tried – oh, how I tried to get it off – but I couldn't. That worm ate through my vine, Benjamin. Killed it. Right as the storm blazed upon me.

"I screamed. Had to. I wanted to die. Cried for it. But Elohim admonished me. Me!"

I would have done the same, at one time. After Jonah walked out that night, leaving the Ninevites when they had needed him most, I harbored my own deep anger. The Dove had reverted to the Jonah of Aphek, not the Jonah of the fish, and that burned me. But here… well, my love proved stronger.

"What did He say?" I said, hoping to comfort him.

"Where is he?" a brash voice – a familiar one – demanded of someone behind me.

"This," Jonah whispered, oblivious to the interruption. "He said this: Do you… do you have a right to be angry? I said yes. Yes! I was mad enough to die."

That, of everything, did not surprise me. This marked the third time the Dove had sought death in this mission. He had already succeeded once, if you accept his tale of the fish. And I do.

"And He… He told me this: 'You have loved this vine, though you did nothing to care for it. It sprang up of its own and died of its own. But Nineveh' – always He takes me back to Nineveh! – 'But Nineveh has 120,000 children who know not My ways, and cattle and horses and other things as well. Should I not love that great city?'"

A hand gripped my shoulder. I ignored it.

Life fled Jonah's gaze. His words came as the faintest of murmurs: "Do you understand it, Benjamin? Does it make sense?"

"It is of the Lord," I answered. That, at least, was clear. But the rest of it… well, I knew I would ponder it forever.

As I held him close, seeing both why I loved and anguished over this man of God, a hand at my shoulder lifted me to my feet. One hand, alone! In my astonishment I dropped the Dove, who fell to the earth like a corpse.

"Jonah!" I cried out.

"Enough of him."

Hot with anger, I twisted to see this strong interloper, only to find a bare-chested eunuch. The voice came from Pulu, who stood proud and tall between his stout guards.

Sudden recognition surged through me.

"Tilgit," I whispered, even as the servant dropped me to the earth.

"Tiglath-Pileser III," proclaimed Pulu, proud to wear the regal fashions his father had cast off but a day before.

"Usurper," I chastised him. "Slew your own father!"

"He killed himself, insulting the crown!" Furious at my charge, the king wrapped his hand under my chin and tossed me aside.

"That one is nothing," Pulu told his lieutenants with a

dismissive nod to me. "Slavery for him. The prophet is my true foe."

Into the commotion the Dove screamed: "Benjamin! Benjamin!" A hairless eunuch tried to grab me, but I slipped past his thick fingers to reach Jonah's side. In his blindness, the Dove strove to clasp my hand. Once he did, my friend prayed, his every word a gale upon my soul.

"In the work of the Lord God of Israel and Judah, Yahweh, Elohim, wisest of the wise, I name you Nahum," said Jonah. "May the spirit of the Lord enter you and fill you, lead you and shield you, counsel you and cradle you, from now until your soul is one with Him. Go now and do His work."

With the passing of Jonah's breath upon my face, the power of the Lord settled within me. Visions fell into orbit about my heart, images I realized had haunted the Dove throughout his life. Now they were mine. Paintings in full movement, statues come alive, they were at first a blur… the walls of Samaria broken and lost; my people in bondage, scattered across the world; the Temple of Solomon falling, rising, and falling again; generations and generations in exile; a cauldron of burning bodies; a triumphant return. Even as I tried to sort through them, to understand these visions, the moving paintings remained beyond me, like scattered pieces of a child's toy, useless by themselves. Yet one image seemed at the heart of it all. A structure of wood – two slabs running counter to each other, stained with blood. It had a name: a cross. A cross of blood.

My mind centered on that.

I am told I collapsed, overcome by the weight of Jonah's burden. I know they dragged me to my feet, bound me in ropes, offered me then and there as a slave to be bought – but I recall little of it. My mind was too confused digesting Jonah's revelations. Yet I did hear the last words of the Dove.

A eunuch dressed in a palace cloak held Jonah aloft by the neck, a limp victim hanging before the new king. Yet Pulu was anything but victorious against the prophet.

"You sought to destroy us?" The king spat into Jonah's bloody face. "Puny Jew! We will sweep against your land as vultures upon carrion! Your capital I will smash. Its people I will scatter. So vows Tiglath-Pileser III, King of Assyria, King of kings!"

From somewhere in his heart, Jonah found strength enough to contest the former governor of Kalhu.

"Your pride will undo you, Pulu worm. Eaten the fruit of my efforts? The Lord has tested you, Nineveh, and you have failed. Your people will crush Israel, but your achievements will be soon forgotten. In a few hundred years the grand armies of the world will march past the rubble of Nineveh and wonder what once stood there. For in the eyes of God, you are nothing."

That breath was his last.

"I will enjoy seeing you burn," the king scowled.

At Pulu's delight, the powerful eunuch threw Jonah far through the air, but before his frail frame could tumble down the hillside, the Dove's spirit left on its journey, one far more glorious than that we had just completed. I prayed to the Lord to welcome him, even as Ninevites gathered about his body.

"Away!" shouted a eunuch, striding forward to frighten them from the fallen prophet. But showing their reverence of the Dove, the people clustered together. A few managed to wrap his form in ash-stained sackcloth and slip it away.

In that, at least, Jonah triumphed. For though Pulu spent years searching for those remains, the king went to his death without a last insult to the Dove.

Chapter 26

Perspective

It took another fifty-some years for the body of the Dove to find its rest, in a tomb built upon the abandoned armory of an Assyrian king. The fact that burial came after such a vast span of time illustrates one overlooked truth – that some in Nineveh did indeed follow and grow in the Lord. But I saw little of it. Over those years I was taken in bondage to Babylon, Damascus, Tyre, Turushpa, Til Barsip, Arpad, even to the Nile. And Samaria.

That was my greatest nightmare, seeing that vision of death come to pass. It was Pulu's last vow, to avenge on Samaria the insults he associated with the Dove, and though he took his time to fulfill it, the wait made the city's fall no less heart-rending. That wretched Menahem bought time – and the heart of Tiglath-Pileser III – with a tax bribe, but the Israeli king's passing lifted that block. And so, as a slave to a heathen priest – how much more humiliating could it get? – I watched the siege of Samaria, and as a flesh-burner of Assyrian victims, I witnessed that capital's collapse. My heart bled as the proud citizens of Israel fell captive, a whole tribe scattered and lost to make room for vagrant Assyrian peasants and nobility. I almost buckled under that burden the Dove had feared, the guilt of ministering to Nineveh. I have carried that guilt all my life.

But such was my chief calling, to be God's witness of Jonah's tale to both Israel and Judah. And with both audiences, the telling spurred more ire than insight.

Why should it not, with all the suffering we have endured?

Ancient in years beyond my right, I often sit now upon a grassy knoll overseeing decaying Nineveh, which doubled in size since the time of the Dove. I can see its people engaged with the army as young Ashurbanipal – King of kings, as he likes to prove – prepares to strike out on still another conquest, this time against Egypt. It will be an epic journey, a feat worthy of a great people. Yet if anything, Nineveh is more decadent now than in Jonah's time. It will perish, as the Dove foretold. The Lord shows me such signs each day.

Why then was the journey of the Dove necessary at all? Are there limits to the Lord's forgiveness?

Ah, that is the issue.

With Tiglath-Pileser's death, I was sold to masters who made me minister at a small Ninevite temple to Yahweh. Its following soon dwindled, perhaps justifying Jonah's initial doubts in me. My stingy masters took me ever west, and so, in time, I was made to collect taxes under Hezekiah's settlement with Assyria. I spent more than ten years doing this in northern and southern Judah, ever a target of hatred toward my masters, even though I knew little of what those devils did. I could not bear to watch the arms of Sennacherib.

Oh, a sympathetic few still seek to ease my guilt. Jonah could do no less than what he did, since the Lord forced the mission upon him… or so they say. For Jonah's mission was meant to Nineveh alone, not the empire.

Such people are blind.

To not equate saving the heads of Nineveh with saving the empire is foolhardy. Does anyone believe the Assyrian bull could function long without Nineveh? Indeed not! The city claimed a third or more of all who lived in Assyria! And at the time of Jonah, the empire had fallen to little more than Nineveh, Assur, and Kalhu. A hard, desperate battle had been fought less than a day from Nineveh's northern wall!

No, the empire had been ripe for plunder. Had Nineveh collapsed, as its own people feared, so would the empire have disappeared. And to think that the Lord, with Nineveh destroyed, could have resurrected the Assyrian bull is to expect a miracle of the most distant possibility. Having seen such things happen, I try not to limit our Lord, but in truth, Jonah was right. The prophecies of Amos and Elijah hinged on Nineveh's survival. The Lord meant all along to save the city of blood. That was the point of it. Mercy and forgiveness, even salvation, to the worst offenders, if they would but repent, and believe.

Listen to me now! That is what everyone misses in my sharing this tale – minimizing my own meaningless involvement, of course. The Jonah ministry was to Israel, not just Nineveh. Indeed, to all the world.

The Assyrian people built an empire around everything not of the Lord. Such was their existence. Still, in a simple forty-day period, faced with but the reluctant ministry of the Dove and the Hand of God, these Gentiles repented! Truly repented! Yet when Amos spoke against Bethel and Samaria, we Hebrews laughed. When Elijah confronted our heathen priests, when God made water burn before our eyes and drew rain from dry air, we looked away. Why? Why did we turn from the One who had led us out of bondage? Why do we ignore the many, many miracles in our lives?

Indeed, Jonah was the perfect practitioner of our disjointed Hebrew faith, devoted not to daily communion with the Lord, although he practiced that, but to our own misguided creed of how we thought God wanted us to live. Our beliefs refuse to bend even under the whips of our worst enemies, yet our enemies bent to the Lord's will with but a short word and brief wind.

That must explain the visions of the cross. For only with such great sacrifice can our Lord God topple these walls we have built between Him and us. And even that will human philosophy fight, as I saw in Jonah.

More than anything, I fear the Dove resisted the new world, as he called it, far more than he had the Nineveh ministry. For I now know the offering to Nineveh was to prime the theological well the coming Messiah must draw from – and Jonah the nationalist, Jonah the supremacist, wanted nothing to do with offering salvation to Gentiles.

After living a lifetime under the Assyrian whip, after seeing their wicked indulgences take root from Babylon to Egypt, I understand his reluctance. Yet I witnessed Phoenician sailors and Assyrian scholars, artisans, cooks, herders, even soldiers, take up the Lord's yoke. I know people may change. Even mine.

Thus, the new covenant. Nineveh illustrates that acceptance of the Lord is not enough. The Assyrians failed to act on their faith, to live in His spirit. They will be punished. But the central truth remains, that God, in His love, granted even these evilest of souls a chance to change. They had a choice.

Soon so shall we all.

Afterward and Glossary

The Prophet and the Dove presents a historical tale of legendary power, mystery, and grace, all from a time little remembered, yet vital to the breadth and scope of our lives. We receive this epic from an elderly witness, a teacher who endured these events while a young fugitive slave.

Observing life with his eyes wide open, our viewpoint character (named Benjamin, as you may know by now) admits his naïve ignorance with almost every breath. He can't help weaving this tale without adding his personal reflections, ambitions, and kernels of wisdom. He takes us on this ride hinting all the while of more to come.

Such a wandering message calls for a glossary, a helpful tool for modern audiences unfamiliar with his and our ancient world. In researching these novels in The Jonah Cycle, my amateur historian eyes ranged from translated Assyrian tablets and obelisks to historical books, papers, cookbooks, maps, and other sources. This glossary reprises and synthesizes this mashed knowledge, mixing brief explanations with extracts and quotes from the novel itself. Hopefully this will help readers understand how these names, places, cultures, and other elements fit together in this tale. My Christian perspective also provides a guiding influence, as demonstrated here in my use of faith-oriented terms like BC (Before Christ, for those who have forgotten its original purpose) and Old Testament. My friends of other beliefs kindly grant me such leeway.

With nearly four decades of research marred by some sloppy household moves and transitions through stubborn, disagreeable computer systems, I failed to maintain an exhaustive list of source books and papers. But some general tomes proved quite useful and remain in my library, like *The Assyrians* by H.W.F. Saggs, *The New Manners and Customs of Bible Times* by Ralph Gower, *Eerdmans Handbook to the Bible*, and the *Zondervan NIV Atlas of the Bible* by Carl G. Rasmussen. Insights came from unexpected places, such as *The Ancient Assyrians* by Mark Healy and Angus McBride, and *Everyday Life Through the Ages* from Reader's Digest. I also found valuable resources online. That's a great starting place for readers seeking more than this glossary provides.

Abraham – the starting point of the Hebrew people and heritage, as told in the Old Testament book of Genesis. Abraham became a spiritual patriarch in several world religions.

Adad-nirari – governor of the ancient city of Kalhu at the time of Jonah's mission. This son of the Assyrian king Ashur-nirari also went by the name of Pulu or Pul.

Ahab, King – the seventh king of Israel's northern kingdom following the division of Solomon's realm, and husband of Jezebel of Sidon. Both are reviled in the Old Testament for their disregard of the Hebrew faith.

Ammon – an ancient kingdom that lay just east of Israel and Judah, across the Jordan River. Its people were known as the Ammonites.

Ansephanti – short for Ansephanti Rezin, governor of Aram, a conquered providence of the Assyrian Empire during the time of Jonah. From his palace in Damascus, Ansephanti would lead a revolt as Assyrian power weakened, entering his territory into an alliance with its northern neighbor, the Urartu Federation.

Aphek – this name refers to at least two ancient towns in the Hebrew's northern kingdom, known as Israel. The one we're concerned about lays along the traveling route between the Israeli capital Samaria and the Philistine port of Joppa. Benjamin offered this limited description of Aphek from traveling there to find Jonah: "Like nearly all cities in Israel, Aphek cowered within a wall of white limestone many times patched and rebuilt. Its southern arms stretched nearly twice my height with its serrated parapet, joining at a gate that looked to be twice again as tall and once again wider around the foundation. Twin doors opened outward, each made of various woods layered with rusted iron." Benjamin later describes how that search kept him outside the city walls. "I spied a small cluster of brick houses and mud-blotched tents cast along a trickling brook. I recognized this place from past travels: grazing land for shepherds traveling to and from Aphek."

Aram – an ancient kingdom east of Canaan, in lands now part of Syria. Damascus was its primary capital. Its people were known as Arameans.

Ark of the Covenant – a sacred artifact of the Hebrew faith described in the Old Testament book of Exodus. Israeli craftsmen made the ark to hold the stone tablets of the Ten Commandments and other relics from the Exodus. Benjamin mentions the ark when he tells of his time with Hosea: "Oh yes – I had seen the accursed trophies taken by old King Jehoash, a past peacock who, like Jeroboam II, took pleasure in humbling Judah. But unlike my intended tormentor, Jehoash had not settled for tribute. Wishing to punish Jerusalem, he toppled its walls and stole all of the Temple's precious gold and silver, the ornamental lampstands, alters, and tables, even the Ark of the Covenant made to replace the one Shishak carted off to Egypt long ago, or so they said. But plagues stalked Jehoash and his troops on their long march home, and thus that fearful heathen discarded his trophies in Bethel… in the very stronghold we occupied."

Arpad – an ancient city of Aram that would fall to Assyrian soldiers during Benjamin's lifetime.

Asherah – one of many mythical gods worshiped by people in Canaan and neighboring lands. Asherah was said to be the queen consort of El and Anu, older supreme gods of several Mesopotamian faiths leading up to Jonah's lifetime.

Ashur – the primary god worshipped in Assyria; one that also went by the names of Assur and Asshur. The Old Testament book of Genesis also names Ashur as the second son of Shem, the son of Noah. Ashur and other sons of Noah settled the lands that became Assyria. Note to book readers: for clarity, *The Prophet and the Dove* uses Assur to refer to the city, and Ashur to reference the deity. Asshur gets left out in the cold.

Ashurbanipal – an ambitious king of Assyria within The Jonah Cycle, one Benjamin sometimes refers to as Banipal.

Ashurnasirpal II – king of Assyria about a century before the events in *The Prophet and the Dove.*

Ashur-minal – the high priest of the god Ashur under King Ashur-nirari at the time of Jonah's journey.

Ashur-nirari – the king of Assyria at the time of Jonah. Benjamin described his first views of Ashur-nirari this way: "I think back upon it now as yet another part of my education. The man who held aloft that ornate silver crown – that man adorned with those fabulous silver and crimson robes, the golden bracelets, the dancing tassels and embroidered collars – he was such a common-looking fellow that I almost laughed. There was no majesty to his frame, such as Ansephanti enjoyed, nor the countenance of wisdom that marked the face of Jeroboam… though that old man rarely put that asset to use. No, this man displayed no outstanding qualities of any kind. His dim green eyes seemed distant and fearful, his skin blotched pink and yellow, his thin frame wrinkled and weak, his brown beard wiry and dull. And when he spoke, his voice grated my ears as a sharpening stone across a chipped blade." Benjamin's view of Ashur-nirari changed as they spent more time together.

Assur – one of the ancient capitals of Assyria, home to the nation's largest temple for the god Ashur. As with the deity, the city also was known through antiquity as Ashur and Asshur. For clarity's sake, *The Prophet and the Dove* refers to the city as Assur, the worshipped one as Ashur. Benjamin described the city this way: "Assur, one of three capitals of Assyria, fell somewhere between Samaria and Damascus in size. It spread over three hills, groups of brick villages surrounding several impressive halls and temples, all protected by ancient sandstone barriers. But unlike most cities we reached on our journey, large segments of Assur stared back at us empty of life. Vast battlements with massive gates lined the hills, each capped with great citadels of granite and marble, and yet gaping holes plagued many of the walls. Their once-protective stones lay smashed and scattered, the mortar crumbling." As the travelers looked over the ruins, Tum pointed out a landmark: "That, my friends, is the supreme temple of Ashur, his home among my people. A magnificent structure! Or at least it once was.... But now, people are reluctant to restore it. You see, Assur was seized in revolt by our past king, Shamshi Adad, and its citizens were punished."

Assyria – an ancient culture that rose along the Tigris and Euphrates rivers in upper Mesopotamia, its lands ranging on today's map from northern Iraq to southeastern Turkey. Its people were known as Assyrians. That fertile area supported a cyclical empire-building culture that would reinforce or threaten regional stability (depending on your point of view) for two millennia. During Jonah's lifetime, Assyria's military influence experienced one of its lowest ebbs.

Athens – one of the legendary cities of both ancient and modern Greece.

Baal – a mythical weather god worshipped in Canaan, Aram, and other areas of ancient Mesopotamia.

Babylon – one of the great cities of the ancient world, the head of a critical Mesopotamian kingdom that influenced regional life for more than a millennium. From its southern presence on the Euphrates River, Babylon played an influential role in the history of Assyria. Though it rivaled the Assyrian cities for prestige and power, the people of that northern kingdom came to revere and honor the competitor, its culture, and its religions. Many Assyrians considered Babylon a holy city.

Banipal – short for Ashurbanipal – a king of Assyria who would play a significant role in Benjamin's life.

Beam – in terms of ship construction in ancient times, a beam is a central piece of wood, curved or straight, used as a primary support for the body or deck. A curved half-beam used to support the deck would be called a "spur."

Benjamin – son of Gideon, though not the hero of the Old Testament. In this book, Benjamin is the given name for our viewpoint character. You must read the book to learn more.

Bethel – a city in the splintered kingdom of Israel where the northern kings established one of two temples intended to replace the sacred center in Jerusalem. These kings hoped this would stop Hebrew pilgrimages from Israel to Solomon's Temple in the southern kingdom.

Canaan – in ancient times, this name represented the general area where Moses and Joshua guided the Hebrew people to live in the Exodus. It owes that name in part to a grandson of Noah, also named Canaan, who settled that region long before the Hebrew people existed. These lands spread from the eastern coast of the Great Sea to the Jordan River, rising north from the Sinai Peninsula to the hills of Lebanon. Today this area would include parts of Israel, Syria, and Lebanon. Some definitions of Canaan may feature lands east of the Jordan River. By the time of the Roman Empire, this general area was known as Palestine.

Carthage – one of the great cities of the ancient world, a shipping hub settled and supported by the Sea Peoples and Phoenicians on the Great Sea coast of what is now Tunisia. By Jonah's time, Carthage had established a regional trading empire at the edge of the Hebrew's known world.

Chaldea – an ancient world culture that formed in southeastern Mesopotamia around 1000 BC, possibly paralleling the time Saul became the first king of Israel. The Chaldean people would contest Babylonian and Assyrian power for several generations before falling under their control.

Chariot – a two-wheeled cart led by one to three horses. Its primary use ranged from a lightweight weapon/soldier platform to small cargo/personnel transportation needs and racing. Individually or in fleets, the chariot served as the tank of the ancient world when used on supporting terrain, its carrying capacity and influence evolving with the user's ability to armor, stabilize, and empower this wheeled platform. Its value encouraged the development of road paving and maintenance.

Calah – one of the three capitals of Assyria at the time of Jonah. Also known as Kalhu, Caleh, and Nimrud, this beautiful hilltop community sat along the Tigris and Great Zab rivers.

Cubit – an ancient unit of measurement, its actual length depending on the user's culture. Various sources today have estimated a cubit extended about 18 inches or 44 centimeters. To present a biblical reference, in Genesis 6:14-15, God tells Noah to build an ark 300 cubits long, 50 cubits wide, and 30 cubits high.

Curtain wall – in ancient times, this usually refers to a wall of stone or brick built for defensive purposes. It did not support a roof.

Damascus – one of the ancient world's great cities, capital of the land of Aram, now part of Syria. Benjamin described his approach to Damascus this way: "I looked forward to seeing this fortress of our ancient enemy. I had been there only once before, and that just a brief stay, but I had been impressed with its apricot and almond groves, the desert shining east and south, snow-bearded Hermon behind us. Damascus itself seemed rather dirty, its walls scarred from battles beyond number, but what city would not show such scars when it had sheltered men almost since time began?"

David – the third king of Israel's united monarchy; one of the great heroes of the Bible and our ancient world.

El – the name for a god worshipped among many Canaanite and other Mesopotamian cultures. Definitions of this powerful, and sometimes supreme, figure varied among these societies, some of which used the term generically in their faith for "god." Noting how El is sometimes referred to as the Lord, some researchers link El to the Lord of the Old Testament.

Elam – an ancient culture that arose southeast of Babylon along what is now the Iranian coastline.

Elijah – one of the great Old Testament prophets, his ministry a thorn in the side of King Ahab of Israel's northern kingdom roughly two centuries before the works of Jonah.

Elohim – a Hebrew name for God at the time of Jonah. It gained greater use among later generations.

Ephah – an ancient Hebrew measurement of volume.

Benjamin provides this rough description: "As the sun neared its rest, the time came for us to depart. A Philistine named Fenark insisted the Dove take a jar of grain as payment, even though Jonah refused. To account for his gift, the Dove withdrew his kinnor and sang a happy song of spring. So pleased were his friends by the tune, Fenark replaced the jar with a full basket of harvest, about an ephah."

Ephraim – the second son of Joseph and Asenath of the Old Testament book of Genesis. Ephraim's name lived on as the name of a recognized Hebrew tribe. After the Hebrew nation split in two, the land of the tribe of Ephraim drew cultural importance for hosting the northern kingdom's worship centers.

Esarhaddon – a king of Assyria during the life of Benjamin, and the father of Ashurbanipal.

Euphrates – one of the great rivers of the ancient and modern world, it played a major role in Assyria's development. At the city of Terqa, Benjamin described the Euphrates as the waterway that "flows ever though my dreams and imagination. Nothing compares to it in Israel, or any of the other lands I had crossed up to that point. Indeed, even now, of all the rivers I have endured, only the Nile exceeds it. The spread of the Euphrates made me gawk and gasp. Without a doubt it spanned five to six times the length of the ship of Tarshish even at Terqa's narrowest crossing, and from the looks of its smooth brown surface, it must have been deep even then. Square rafts delivered various goods up and down the muddy waters, though they did not seem well-laden." The trader Tum went on to describe the Euphrates this way: "I tell you, Benjamin, more than once I have seen this whole plain up to my ankles in water! Truly! I mean, talk about your flood! Can you imagine it? This, this is Assyria. The Tigris is vital, don't get me wrong, but this… this is the lifeblood of my people. It would take you years just to walk its length, but if you did, you would cross the world's greatest fields of wheat and barley, pass hearty flocks of sheep and stout herds of the choicest cattle, pick from a wondrous abundance of fruit of all kinds! You'd see vast forests, extensive iron, copper and tin mines, granite and marble quarries…. Oh, Benjamin, this is a blessed land!"

Fertile Crescent – a unifying name for the watered basins of the Nile, Jordan, Euphrates, and Tigris rivers, along with their connecting Great Sea shores, where a large number of early human civilizations began. These lands stretch today from Egypt and Israel to western Turkey, Syria, Iraq, and Iran.

Gentiles – anyone who is not a member of the Hebrew faith.

God – in general terms, this word may refer to anyone or anything with supernatural abilities or ambitions. When capitalized, this word refers to the God of the Hebrew and Christian faiths, the creator of all that is, the first in existence, the alpha and omega, the supreme being, also known as I Am, the Lord, our Father in Heaven.

Golan – a plateau in northern Canaan, east of a body of water known in ancient times as the Sea of Chinnereth (later the Sea of Galilee).

Golem – a creature of Hebrew mythology, its body animated by unnatural means.

Gomer – the wife of Hosea.

Gomorrah – with Sodom, one of two Canaanite cities destroyed by God to end their sinful ways, as told in the book of Genesis.

Great Sea, the – a large body of water today known as the Mediterranean Sea. Benjamin first viewed the Great Sea from the hills above Joppa. He described it thus: "The Great Sea seemed as vast as… as… well, as vast as everything you might imagine. Only the heavens themselves are broader, or more unpredictable. The clear sky swirled a vivid blue against our hot sun, the shore a jumble of tumbling stones, yet the sparkling sea rolled far beyond it all, to what end I could not imagine."

Great Trunk Road, the – one of the ancient world's major roads and trade routes through Asia. It also was known as the Grand Trunk Road.

Halil – a type of flute used by many cultures of the ancient world, a pipe made from reeds, wood, bone, shed animal horns, or ivory.

Hamath – a secondary capital of the ancient kingdom of Aram.

Han-Alphinami – a traveling merchant who befriended Jonah and Benjamin. He was known as the sheik of Armanis, merchant, rancher, ruler of the lands within the southern peaks of western Aram, father of Harn-Kelnat, Santerith, and other children. Benjamin described him thus at their first meeting: "a rather large one (merchant) bound in a fine two-piece cloak of rainbow bands, a head wrap of crimson linen tied with golden ropes, and a tunic of purple."

Harn-Kelnat – the elder son of Han-Alphinami.

Hazorn – captain of the ship of Tarshish taken by Jonah and Benjamin.

Hazora – a type of trumpet forged of bronze, silver, or some other handy metal.

Hebrew – descendants by blood or faith of Abraham, Isaac, and Jacob, central figures of the Old Testament book of Genesis. All three patriarchs came from a family chosen by God to father the people of Israel. They are known as Hebrews, or Jews, an ancient slang word adapted from the name Judah.

Hermon, Mount – one of the tallest points in the ancient land of Canaan, a mountain with two peaks that anchors the region's northeastern horizon. The twin peaks now lie in Syria.

Hosea – a prophet of the Old Testament whose marriage to the adulterous Gomer symbolized God's relationship with the Hebrew people. When Benjamin (in our novel) first met Hosea, our narrator dismissed this prophet as a beggar. Later, Benjamin came to admire Hosea, loving him as a father: "A breath of wind whistled through the trees. Hosea paused to listen as if taken by the occasion. Then his curious gaze met mine. The look of those eyes… those honest, authoritative eyes – the eyes of a judge – well, it charged through me like a brush with searing coals. Embarrassment poured through my veins, driven by a humble outpouring of guilt and shame at how I had acted that morning. The onrushing tensions threatened to stifle my will, yet it lasted but a heartbeat. For Hosea smiled with welcome joy, opening a door to my soul that has never closed. He accepted me into his heart as no one had before. Within such grace, my fears and self-doubts faded as wisps of smoke in a breeze."

Indeos – the lands today known as India.

Isaac – father of Jacob, son of Abraham. A historic father figure and patriarch of the Old Testament and Hebrew people.

Israel – a name with many meanings. It refers to the Old Testament patriarch Jacob, who God renamed Israel, his sons fathering the twelve tribes of Israel. This name also applies to the northern kingdom formed after the death of Solomon. In modern times, this noun is the name of the Hebrew nation.

Jacob – the son of Isaac whose children formed the branches of the Hebrew people. To complete this transition, God would give this Old Testament patriarch a new name: Israel.

Jehoash, King – the twelfth king of the northern kingdom of Israel, reigning for 16 years. The actions of this king would impact Benjamin's life through Hosea and his choice to care for the needy in a former temple: "Oh yes – I had seen the accursed trophies taken by old King Jehoash, a past peacock who, like Jeroboam II, took pleasure in humbling Judah. But unlike my intended tormentor, Jehoash had not settled for tribute. Wishing to punish Jerusalem, he toppled its walls and stole all of the Temple's precious gold and silver, the ornamental lampstands, alters, and tables, even the Ark of the Covenant made to replace the one Shishak carted off to Egypt long ago, or so they said. But plagues stalked Jehoash and his troops on their long march home, and thus that fearful heathen discarded his trophies in Bethel… in the very stronghold we occupied."

Jeroboam II, King – the thirteenth king of the northern kingdom of Israel, holding that throne for forty-one years, according to Old Testament texts. He played a central role in Benjamin's early life, though not with good intent.

Jew – an ancient slang name for the Hebrew people, drawn from the root name Judah, that over time gained widespread acceptance and usage.

Jezebel – wife of Israel's King Ahab, believer of many ancient faiths not of the Lord. Though she lived roughly a century before Benjamin, he faced her legacy: "So there I was, back among the temple vermin still thriving from Jezebel's ancient patronage. Queen of vileness, she had poured into the many different shrines every kind of depravity you can imagine, and many you hopefully can't. The thought of having to look once again on that hell led me to the brink of despair."

Job – a righteous Hebrew patriarch who, under a challenge by Satan to God, fell from riches to poverty, losing his family, home, and most friends. Through this experience, the Old Testament book by the same name provides morality tales of suffering, submission, advice, justice, and God's supremacy.

Jonah – also known as the Dove – an Old Testament prophet who sought to escape God's mission for his life, but through a series of miracle feats, gave in to deliver God's warnings to Nineveh. While Benjamin experiences these biblical events first-hand, he also witnesses Jonah's role as a defender of the northern kingdom, an often-overlooked task mentioned once in the Old Testament.

Joppa or **Joffa** – a primary port for Philistia and Canaan. Jonah said this of the city: "You would have to go to Tyre to find a better port than Joppa. They welcome all travelers here. They need the money, you know. And their plowshares? The best around. Iron's so much better than bronze or bone, and the Joppa metalworkers excel at their craft. That's enough to make you buy from the heathen, isn't it?" Upon approaching the town, Benjamin observed Joppa this way: "Ringed by two ancient walls, the city offered a narrow strip of white limestone buildings around a wide inlet lined with stone moorings and wooden docks. Three half-circles of mud-brick homes buffered the merchant district, and were themselves ringed by shepherd and merchant tents. At their center rested about seven ships of various sizes, their painted eyes turned toward the sea."

Judah – a name with many applications. Judah was the fourth son of Jacob; his descendants became one of the twelve tribes of Israel. After the death of Solomon, the southern kingdom took the name of Judah. As the land of Jerusalem and the Temple, over time, the Hebrew faith became known as Judaism. A shortened form of that – Jew – became a slang name for the Hebrew people.

Kalhu – one of the three capitals of Assyria at the time of Jonah. Also known over time as Caleh, Calah, and Nimrud, the city stood in what today is northern Iraq. Benjamin described Kalhu thus: “Lying between the junction of the Tigris and the Great Zab, with grayed limestone and black marble citadels on three hilltops overlooking the sparkling waters, beautiful Kalhu thrived on river trade and produce from the surrounding plains – as well as the good graces of the royal household, of course.” Tum estimated its population from 80,000 to 100,000. “Not close to Nineveh or Babylon,” the trader continued, “but mighty besides.”

King’s Highway, the – an important Fertile Crescent trade route connecting Egypt to Aram and the Euphrates River.

Kinnor – a type of harp used by the Hebrew people and others in the ancient world; a favorite stringed instrument of King David. Jonah had a beautiful kinnor, as explained by Benjamin: “Most such harps had seven to ten slivers of sheep gut strings, with a body often little more than a cedar circle with a flat end, where the stretched lines tightened. But the Dove’s kinnor offered fourteen strings on a gold-lined frame of oak.”

Kue – a region in the northern lands beyond Urartu, which would place it at the edge of the Hebrew’s known world in Jonah’s time. Today, these Asian lands might include parts of Georgia, Turkey, Armenia, and Iran.

Kummuhu – an Assyrian word for lands north and west of its homeland. In later times this culture became known as the Kingdom of Commagene. Its areas now lay within western Turkey.

Lebonah – a city in ancient Israel where Benjamin endured multiple deaths within events foreshadowed in *The Prophet and the Dove.*

Lord, The – a term that, over time, became accepted as a basic name for God.

Lots – this refers to a method of drawing marked stones named lots (or dice) to make a decision, find answers to posed questions, determine the will of God, or see into fate. Some traditions hold that any lots drawn must produce the same result three times before users should accept their outcome.

Lyre – a stringed instrument used in many ancient cultures, most prominently with the Greeks. The lyre's yoked strings stretch between two arms from a sound box to a crossbar, which allows for strumming or plucked notes.

Mannea – an ancient kingdom that rose around a sizeable lake in what is now northwestern Iran. Its people would prove both allies and enemies of Assyria during the life of Benjamin.

Marduk – a prominent mythical deity worshipped under many names by numerous peoples of Mesopotamia, his aspects changing over time and among cultures. He became the chief god of Babylon and was highly regarded in Assyria. In some cultures, Marduk was known as Lord.

Marduk-handorali – Nineveh's high priest of the sun god Marduk at the time of Jonah.

Mati-ilu – head of the Urartu Federation at the time Jonah traveled to Nineveh.

Mazzebah – the Hebrew word for a standing stone, a marker set in place to honor a covenant with God. This practice of using stones to mark agreements or events was common in such times, employed by many ancient cultures in the Mesopotamian area. Benjamin and Jonah would encounter many such landmark stones left by Assyrian kings to proclaim warnings to the region's inhabitants.

Melqart – a mythical water god worshipped around the Great Sea in ancient times. Also known as Melqarth, Melkarth, or Melicarthus, this was the patron deity of the city of Tyre – and the primary god of the Phoenicians and other Sea Peoples. An island neighboring the isle of Tyre was named for this perceived god.

Menahem – a reviled king of Israel who rose to power during the life of Jonah, wearing the crown for a decade. Benjamin described his coming thus: "A week later Menahem son of Gadi slipped into the palace with a few cutthroats from Tirzah and slew Shallum in his bed. It probably had been quite easy, for no one stomached the evils of Shallum any more than we had Zechariah. But Menahem was of another cut of cloth, a most awful one. The Viper, as we named him in our whispers. He replaced the palace guard with his hooligans, proclaimed himself king, and imposed a brutal, money-hungry reign far more imposing than any of his predecessors. So began the years of terror."

Mesopotamia – a Greek name for regions of the Euphrates and Tigris rivers, a key section of the Fertile Crescent where many early human cultures rose. These lands fall today within Turkey, Syria, Iraq, Kuwait, and Iran.

Moab – an ancient Canaanite culture that rose east of the kingdom of Judah, across the Jordan River.

Moses – one of the great figures not just of the ancient world, but all human existence. If you don't already know this, read the Old Testament book of Genesis (to prime the well) and Exodus (to grasp the significance of it all). Wrap it all up with Leviticus, Deuteronomy, and Numbers. Ideally you may read these through Dennis Prager's *The Rational Bible* series, though that will take time, as he's only published two books to date. But they're the most important ones.

Nari-Speltum – the red-bearded governor of Arbil, who just happened to visit Nineveh as Jonah arrived.

Nebel – a stringed instrument of ancient times, a type of lyre with up to ten strings.

Nimrod – the grandson of Noah through his son Ham. Known as a great hunter, Nimrod settled the lands of Assyria after the great flood. He fathered that culture, as told in the Old Testament books of Genesis and Chronicles.

Nineveh – the legendary capital of Assyria that, from Israel's perspective, anchored one end of the known world with one of its most dangerous societies. Here's one description of this great city, made by Benjamin, tainted by his long-held prejudices: "Nineveh! One of many capitals of Assyria, but surely the most important, for it was perhaps the largest of all cities, the trading capital of the Gentiles, bulwark of the Assyrian treasury and butcher's army, all that and more… the center of the unholy." The trader Tum described its population thus: "You might as well ask how vast is the Tigris. It is said the arms of Nineveh are as weeds in the plain, but that is stupid. Still, old Shamsi-Adad once counted one hundred and forty-two thousand within the city, and that left out the tent city outside the walls, the farmers and shepherds and merchants and other tenders who inhabit the foothills. It may be double that count, or more. Or less. It is hard to say. They come and go, you know. Like us." That sets up how Benjamin observed the city when he first saw it on the horizon: "It was not what I expected. Of course, nothing would have been – in Samaria and Bethel, we always considered Nineveh the home of everything vile, a fortress made of bones with fountains that spewed the blood of countless victims. Something like that, anyway. Instead we gazed upon a sea of tents and flocks, broken only by the Tigris and the broad walls – a vast mixture of granite, sandstone, marble, and other rocks, hewed into an impressive structure of sharp corners and circular towers lined with stone teeth about each parapet, protecting the fields of brick homes about several tall hills along the east side of the Tigris." Benjamin's long-held views of the great city evolved as he stepped within its walls and encountered its markets and culture: "I had not expected such a rich, active culture. It numbed me. Throughout my life, I considered Ninevites as little more than snarling killers. No, actually, as nothing more than hungry, stalking beasts. Yet these streets flowed with pulsing, inventive, joyous lives. Everywhere I looked, there were long-bearded men in thoughtful discussions. Mothers in elegant gowns chasing playful children. Neighbors sharing good times and laughing at each other's jokes. Friends helping one another. Strangers working together with integrity and respect. 'Is this not wondrous?' I could not help exclaiming." That, too, became a point of contention, as the book best explains.

Parchment bread – a term Benjamin uses for large, thin pieces of unleavened bread.

Pelagos – a young woman who befriended Jonah and fell in love with Benjamin. He shared this passion from first sight, which came as he searched for the prophet outside Aphek: "At that moment I recalled the Dove's interest in vineyards. That thought led me to the end of the path, where I spied a small grove of olive trees. A woman worked among the thick, gnarled trunks, filling the girded hem of her dark blue robe with trimmed branches. She looked beautiful among the sprouting limbs and white blossoms, with locks of curly scarlet hair hanging loose about the thin blue veil covering her face. The morning sun glowed behind her, casting her image within a fiery blaze that ignited my heart." Benjamin later described a vision of her this way: "The lovely Pelagos stood there, her brown eyes shimmering like stars, her scarlet hair drifting in playful joy within the soft breeze, her open arms gesturing a clear invitation to my heart."

Philar-Al'andron – a merchant of Assyria who also went by the unlikely name of Tum. Benjamin described him thus: "a rather plump, dark-haired man who loved to wear brushed wolf skins for cloaks. He spoke with a clear voice, though often with a long, bulbous gourd either clutched between his splotched yellow teeth or held at the ready in his left hand, its polished nozzle never far from his lips. At least, I thought it was a gourd, or perhaps a gnarled wooden rod, hollowed and carved with ornate signs of Assyrian and Babylonian gods. In truth, I do not know what it was; I avoided that thing whenever possible. It stank of the most repugnant ash."

Philistia – a culture created as groups of the Sea Peoples settled on the southwestern coast of Canaan. These settlers became known as the Philistines. As the Israelites attempted to possess the Promised Land under the leadership of Joshua and his successors, they failed to oust these coastal settlers, who could escape to the seas when threatened, a skill and defense the Hebrews never mastered. Here's how Benjamin, still early in his journey, described their resulting history: "Every generation could tell its own war stories of these hated Philistines, each one full of gruesome bloodletting, horrid sacrifices, and idolic blasphemy."

Phoenicians – the people of the ancient kingdom Phoenicia, a coastal land of Lebanon and northern Canaan settled by the Sea Peoples, migratory tribes that took root in many natural harbors around the Great Sea. The Phoenicians continued and advanced that seafaring tradition, becoming leading mariners of their age, known for navigating not just the waters of the Great Sea (which we know as the Mediterranean), but also many rivers and coasts of Africa and Europe. To accomplish this, the Phoenicians advanced the art of shipbuilding, creating multi-leveled vessels able to carry sizeable amounts of cargo. Their traders established commercial and social ties among many divergent peoples, which helped to forge regional languages, cultures, economies, and governments. The Phoenician settlements of Tyre, Sidon, and Carthage emerged among the dominant cities of ancient times.

Pillars of El – the impressive stony hills where the Great Sea pours into the outer expanse we now call the Atlantic Ocean. These mounds of rock were considered the edge of the known world by most people in Jonah's time, though mariners knew of coastlands and civilizations beyond those points. These may have included the city of Tarshish (possibly along the coast of what is now Portugal or Morocco). That's why the captain Hazorn reacted this way when Jonah mentioned his desire to reach Tarshish: "That is the end of the world, beyond the solid rocks – the Pillars of El himself!" Today we consider the meeting place of the Atlantic and Mediterranean further west in what we call the Strait of Gibraltar. That tower of stone known as the rock of Gibraltar is itself one of the Pillars of El, or as better known in Greek history, the Pillars of Hercules.

Pul or **Pulu** – informal names for Adad-nirari, the governor of Kalhu at the time of Jonah's mission, and the son of the Assyrian king Ashur-nirari.

Rab alani – the Assyrian equivalent of a governor, a head of local or regional government.

Ram's horn – a literal term that refers to the use of a hollowed horn of a ram as a signal device or musical instrument. Horns from other animals might also see use, depending on their ability to turn channeled air into amplified sound. Modifiers came in the shape and length of the horn, its composition, holes cut into its passage, or the way air was forced through it. Their frequent use helps explain why the cornet, trumpet, and other manmade devices are known today as horns.

Resheph – a mythical deity honored in Canaanite and other Mesopotamian cultures, one often associated with sickness and plagues.

Roeh – a person gifted with not just foresight or visions, but insights to understand and interpret these messages. As Hosea explained to Benjamin: "Jonah is a true roeh – a seer. God has spoken to him since childhood. Yes, that itself is rare, but Jonah also sees the future, when he prays. He shares in God's plan."

Sab sharri – an Assyrian term for infantry units composed of drafted citizens. Raised by governor levies or an order of the king, these units were used to support the "kisir sharruti," the main Assyrian army comprised of professional Assyrian soldiers and absorbed troops from conquered territories or vassal states.

Saln – the first officer on the ship chosen by Jonah and Benjamin.

Samaria – the capital of the northern kingdom of Israel at the time of Jonah and Benjamin.

Sanscorrab – the governor (or in Assyrian terms, "rab alani") of Assur, one of the three capitals of Assyria at the time of Jonah.

Santerith – son of the merchant Han-Alphinami.

Sa sheppi – the Assyrian name for that nation's mobile army wing, fairly new at Jonah's time, comprised of cavalry and chariots. Benjamin described his encounter with the sa sheppi this way: "I looked across the grasslands, wondering once more what the true armies of Assyria would appear like, when I heard the whirling grind of well-greased axles and the pounding of hundreds of hooves. I scanned the horizons for its source, once and again, and saw the deadly serpent of man appear from across the hills. Oh Lord God of heaven and earth, it was both beautiful and terrifying to behold! The sun shimmered across thousands of bronze plates shielding chariots, horses, and their riders. The ground quaked from the churning wheels of thunderous war machines that rode two abreast beyond the horizon. Dust clouds exploded in their wake like the waves of a firestorm."

Satan – the reviled name of the Lord's chief opposer, said by some to be a fallen angel. While not all Israelis in Jonah's time accepted the existence of Satan, speaking his title was frowned upon. Benjamin responded thus when Jonah said it: "My nerves jerked at that name. Hosea had urged me to never speak it, as if giving breath to that foul word could rain down corruption."

Sea Peoples, the – a collective name for mariner tribes that migrated around the Great Sea in ancient times. Like the Vikings of later years, many of these mariners harried commerce and raided settlements. Many of these tribes settled along the Lebanon and Canaan coasts, developing over time into the Phoenician and Philistine cultures.

Sennacherib – the son of Tiglath-Pileser III who assumed the Assyrian throne after his father's death. Sennacherib would continue his father's expansion plans, as would his son, extending Assyrian rule to its highest reaches.

Shechem – a Canaanite city that fell to the Hebrew tribes settling the Promised Land, as told in the Old Testament book of Joshua. Claimed by the tribe of Manasseh, Shechem served for a time as the northern kingdom's first capital. That seat of government would then move to the town of Tirzah before ending in the city of Samaria.

Ship of Tarshish – a classification for large sailing vessels developed by the Phoenician people. Here's how Benjamin described such a craft at the port of Joppa: "Oh, that was a proud ship they worked! It stood low in the water, a multi-leveled craft of well-honed Lebanon woods stretching as long as four brick homes strung end to end. At its bow two large painted eyes watched over the sea behind a tall figure of a proud, trident-bearing merman. Oiled leather shields lined its top deck, each emblazoned with the image of a bull, eagle, lion, or serpent. Below that deck ran a bank of oar portals. A single mast rose from the ship's core, a clustered red sail bound to its high crossbar. Tethered at the ship's broad, upraised back hung a thick steering oar, its base wider than I could spread my arms."

Shishak – an Egyptian pharaoh named in the Bible; modern historians associate Shishak with the pharaoh Shoshenq I. Shishak sacked Jerusalem during the reign of the Judean King Rehoboam, the son of Solomon, according to the Old Testament books of 1st Kings and 2nd Chronicles. Some modern historians, along with popular culture followers (often lovers of the film *Raiders of the Lost Ark*), suspect Shishak may have taken the Ark of the Covenant when his troops plundered Solomon's Temple. Benjamin apparently heard of this event.

Sodom – with Gomorrah, one of two Canaanite cities renowned for suffering God's destruction to end their sinful ways, as told in the Old Testament book of Genesis.

Solomon – the last king of the united Hebrew kingdoms, as told in the Bible. This son of King David and Bathsheba made his mark as a legendary dispenser of wisdom, an accumulator of inestimable wealth, the builder of the first Hebrew Temple in Jerusalem, and the author of the Old Testament book Ecclesiastes, among other highlights.

Sidon – a Phoenician community known in the ancient world for glass artisans. A major facilitator of trade and commerce, Sidon thrives to this day as one of Lebanon's largest cities.

Spar – in ship construction, this refers to a wood pole used to support a sail.

Spur – in ship construction, a spur is a thick, curved piece of wood used to support the deck in places where a full beam may not fit. The term "spur" may also refer to a piece of wood that extends out of the boat's main structure.

Sumer – the earliest known civilization to form in Mesopotamia, rising within the fertile coastal headwaters of the Tigris and Euphrates rivers. The Sumerian culture had a dynamic influence on Assyrian and Babylonian development, as well as other societies.

Tadmor – an ancient city northeast of Damascus that assumed many names over time: Palmyra. Palmyra, Tadmur, Tudmur, and probably others. Tadmor served as an important staging area for trade during Jonah's time, which made it a prime target for Assyrian conquest.

Tammuz – the first month of summer in the ancient Hebrew and Assyrian calendars.

Tarshish – an ancient city during Jonah's ministry, its location lost over time. Benjamin's narration suggests Tarshish lay somewhere along the Atlantic coast of what is now northwestern Africa or Portugal. Modern historians often link its location to Spain, Portugal, or England. Jonah's desire to reach that city shocked sailors in Joppa. "Tarshish?" said Hazorn, captain of the ship Jonah would choose. "That is the end of the world, beyond the solid rocks – the Pillars of El himself!"

Tarsus – an ancient Hittite community that became an important Great Sea trade and mining center. It thrived through Roman times along what is now the southern coast of Turkey.

Tenpul-Kidorin – the secretary of the citadel at Nineveh during Jonah's ministry.

Terqa – a city on the Euphrates River, the western stronghold of Assyria at the time of Jonah's mission. Benjamin described this city thus: "Terqa, for one, was a fascinating city, the first we saw that took pride in the Assyrian carvings of its walls and the tapestries adorning its public buildings. And the Euphrates, which outlines Terqa's eastern face – that great river flows ever though my dreams and imagination. Nothing compares to it in Israel, or any of the other lands I had crossed up to that point. Indeed, even now, of all the rivers I have endured, only the Nile exceeds it."

Thebes – an ancient Egyptian city, also known as No-amon or P-armen, that rose on both sides of the Nile River. Thebes often served as the capital and spiritual center of that historic nation, rising and falling with the culture's fortunes. During the time of Jonah, Thebes lay in a rebuilding stage under the growing influence of the Kushites, also known as the Nubians.

Tiglath-Pileser III – one of the most noted kings in Assyrian history, launcher of this ancient nation's last significant expansion period. In this tale, he assumed this title at the end of Jonah's ministry.

Tigris – one of the major waterways of ancient times and an important asset of the Assyrian culture. Benjamin described the Tigris as Tum's caravan reached Assur: "Unlike the Euphrates, this vast waterway supported few rafts or ships, at least where we first hit its shores, for the river's current ran fast, and far too shallow, with many dangerous obstructions."

Til Barsip – a capital city of the Aramean region known as Bit Adini. Benjamin would live to see the Assyrians conquer this city and area.

Tilith-Feyn – the Assyrian army leader ("turtan") of Kalhu at the time of Jonah's mission.

Tirzah – a small community in ancient Israel, located northeast of the town of Shechem.

Tof – a type of percussion instrument made with a skin membrane drumhead, its beat delivered either with hand pats or stick impacts.

Tunic – a body garment, usually austere, extending from the shoulders to the hips or knees.

Turtan – the Assyrian name for a district army commander or army field marshal.

Turushpa – a capital of the Urartu Federation during the age of Jonah.

Tyre – one of the ancient world's great cities, a Phoenician community formed on an island just off the Lebanese coast that survived all challenges until long after Benjamin's time. Engineering leaders among the troops of Alexander the Great would succeed in building a causeway to reach and conquer the city; subsequent sediment buildup would make that island part of the Lebanon mainland. Benjamin described Tyre thus from the mainland shore: "To gaze upon it now, with the morning mist burning away, was to look fresh upon a jewel of the world. Its walls and buildings towered from the shore as imposing alabaster monoliths, perfect in its elegance, imposing in its supremacy. The sea at its feet sparkled the brightest blue imaginable, while its beaches glowed as fine ivory in a full moon. No wonder Solomon fell in love with its craftsmanship!"

Urartu – this ancient civilization, also known as the Urartu Federation or the Kingdom of Urartu, developed as a competitor to Assyria in what is now Armenia, eastern Turkey, and northwestern Iran.

Yahweh – one of many Hebrew titles referring to God. In later centuries after Jonah, the word would become too sacred for Hebrews to speak aloud.

Zuk shepi – the Assyrian name for that nation's primary infantry force, a professional soldier body also known as the Zuk. It, like the rest of Assyria's military complex, would go through a dynamic makeover at the time of Jonah and the rise of Tiglath-

Pileser III.

Zechariah – heir to Jeroboam II.

Ziv – the second month in the ancient Hebrew calendar.

Zuku sa sheppe – the Assyrian name for the elite units of that nation's main army (the "kisir sharruti") responsible for guarding the king and palace. These were separate from the "qurubti sha shepe," the king's personal bodyguard, which contained its own cavalry, chariotry, and infantry units.